MAXIMUM VELOCITY

MAXIMUM VELOCITY

BRUCE JONES

A DUTTON BOOK

DUTTON
Published by the Penguin Group
Penguin Books USA Inc., 375 Hudson Street,
New York, New York 10014, U.S.A.
Penguin Books Ltd, 27 Wrights Lane,
London W8 5TZ, England
Penguin Books Australia Ltd, Ringwood,
Victoria, Australia
Penguin Books Canada Ltd, 10 Alcorn Avenue,
Toronto, Ontario, Canada M4V 3B2
Penguin Books (N.Z.) Ltd, 182–190 Wairau Road,
Auckland 10, New Zealand

Penguin Books Ltd, Registered Offices:
Harmondsworth, Middlesex, England

First published by Dutton, an imprint of Dutton Signet, a division of Penguin Books USA Inc.
Distributed in Canada by McClelland & Stewart Inc.

First Printing, December, 1996
10 9 8 7 6 5 4 3 2 1

 REGISTERED TRADEMARK—MARCA REGISTRADA

LIBRARY OF CONGRESS CATALOGING-IN-PUBLICATION DATA:
Jones, Bruce
    Maximum velocity / Bruce Jones.
        p.   cm.
    ISBN 0-525-94231-9 (acid-free paper)
    I. Title
    PS3560.04585M38   1996
    819'.54—dc20   96-18648
                                                                                    CIP

Printed in the United States of America
Set in M Plantin Regular
Designed by Leonard Telesca

PUBLISHER'S NOTE
This is a work of fiction. Names, characters, places, and incidents either are the products of the author's imagination or are used fictitiously, and any resemblance to actual persons, living or dead, events, or locales is entirely coincidental.

This book is printed on acid-free paper. ∞

As for the truth of his word,
the Russe (Russian) for the most
part maketh small regard of it . . .
so he may gain by a lie and breach
of promise. And it may be said
truly that from the great to the
small the Russe neither believeth
anything that another man speaketh,
nor speaketh himself anything worthy
to be believed.

Sir Giles Fletcher
circa 1589

MAXIMUM VELOCITY

PROLOGUE

The man who was dead sat drinking coffee with growing irritation in the Manhattan McDonald's, not yet knowing he was dead, not at all certain why this meal was taking so long or what it had to do with string.

The Russian next to him, expansive, stocky, probably muscular under the expensive American double-breasted, kept ordering cheeseburgers and fries, devouring them loudly.

Turning to his slender, weasel-faced companion, the Russian began complaining about the string. "It's *cheap!*" he repeated between engorged mouthfuls. "How can you prepare such a lovely gift for our friend here and wrap it in cheap string!" He pushed the little white box—the "present"—aside with a dismissive elbow, reached for more fries, head shaking. "Insulting. We'll have to find better."

Turning fawningly, he smiled at the dead man. "Now, Abul, tell us again about the bombing! About your brave friend's masterful achievement! And don't spare any delicious detail!"

Which Abul did, for the fifth wearying time that evening, not at all wanting to, wanting only to consummate the agreement with the big, silvery-haired Russian who looked like a blockier Yeltsin. Weary to his toes, Abdul wanted only to accept his token gift (gifts of appreciation were legend with this man), the little box with the inferior string, get to the site of the next target, and get on with the final arrangements.

Instead—knowing the attentive fawning was a way of flattering him into giving them information, proving himself to them—he told them, carefully, the story again. How he and the militant Muslim Mahmud Abbouhalima had concocted the scheme, together with the young Egyptian immigrant Nosaiar, as part of the ongoing holy war—the jihad. How they had enlisted a young explosives expert, Ramzi Yousef, a Pakistani-trained terrorist. How, in a dilapidated garage in Jersey City, using 105 gallons of nitric acid and 60 gallons of sulfuric acid they constructed The Bomb.

How, on a typical February Thursday in 1993, the tenant parking basement of the World Trade Center convulsed violently, killing six instantly, a new era dawning not only for the citizens of New York but for the FBI, the CIA, the president of that country, and countries all over the world.

The big Russian, Ivan Godunov, chuckled over his cheese-burger, wiped grease from his delighted chin. "Wonderful, just wonderful! Terrorism comes to America!" This said a little too loudly for Abul's comfort. Though the McDonald's was noisy with disinterested patrons, this was hardly the place to be discussing acts of aggression against America.

"It's just that I love the American hamburgers so!" the Russian had explained earlier, setting up the meeting here. "Especially the Big Macs! Incomparable! I prefer them to the finest Russian steak!"

"I think it's in the shipment of the beef overseas, something happens to it," the silver-haired Russian explained after they'd left the restaurant, gone searching all over the east, then the west side of Manhattan for an all-night hardware store, Godunov holding the present away from him as though it were tainted, not letting Abul even touch it until properly wrapped.

"Really," the dead man assured him, "the wrapping is not important. I was hoping we could perhaps see the site now? I have a full schedule tomorrow."

The Russian chuckled in reassurance there in the cab's back-seat, the other, ferret-faced one gazing moodily out at dark, neon-stippled New York streets. "We shall visit the site just as soon as my clumsy associate attends to this insufferable inconvenience!"

Godunov handed over the present with an air of disdain, turned back genially to Abul, asking for yet more details of the wonderful bombing.

Fully an hour later—stronger, more suitable string obtained—they rode a narrow, clanking workman's elevator through the darkened, red steel skeleton of a lower East Side high rise. Rode it nearly to the top floor, which was high and dark and mostly finished except for the dusty litter of workmen's tools, a few cement bags, cinder blocks, big X's taped to newly installed windows. The windows offered the only light from the silvery disk of moon, the building's electricity not yet operational.

The Russian knocked once contemplatively on the window glass in passing, nodded. "Tempered against high winds. Couldn't break this glass with a sledgehammer! You have to hand it to the Americans!"

He stepped confidently through pools of shadow that would one day be the Berber carpeting of a finely appointed office, explaining as he went exactly where this next bomb would be placed, exactly how the building would fall, approximately how many people would perish beneath its thundering rubble.

So that Abul, distracted by this mountain of exactness, forgot all about the small, newly wrapped present until Godunov proffered it, beaming in moonlight. "For you. With our thanks. And to a brighter future for Islam!"

Abul, smiling, accepted the present at last. He supposed it was either a cash advance of some sort or a valuable Pakistani antique. He didn't much care just now, so weary was he.

He pulled the new, thicker string free, the wrapper following, worked apart a simple pasteboard box to find inside—nothing.

He looked to the Russian's grinning bear face with dark almond eyes, perplexed eyes, then haunted. "It is empty."

Knowing suddenly, Abul dropped the box and ran.

Not far. The big Russian cut him off at the elevator gate, moving with a speed remarkable for a man his size, grabbing and hoisting Abul (who was not a small man, not light) as though he were a child's doll. Throwing him back across the dusty floor as a man throws a discarded garment, without thought or effort.

Abul landed on his back in a plume of white dust, scrabbled up quickly. But the big bear was somehow there already—so incredibly fast—lifting him again.

Then setting him down gently, even dusting his coat jacket, the smile in place. "Yes, my friend, empty. As empty as your stories, I'm afraid. Dimitri, would you be so kind as to remove our friend's trousers, please?"

Abul, his death no longer a secret but a thing bright and certain as the impassive eye of the moon, stood trembling in silence, skinny knees knocking, pressing back urine as the weasel did his master's bidding. Long, tapered fingers pulled down Abul's pants, his undershorts, retrieved the coarse string from the dusty floor, and tied it snugly about Abul's heavy testes.

"You know the names—the history—of your so-called conspirators quite well, dear fellow. But your dates lack authenticity. The Trade Center bombing took place on a Friday, not a Thursday, as you stated, and it was the public parking level that ignited—specifically Level B-2—not the tenant parking. The real Abul, assuming he exists at all, would have known."

Stepping back, fingers laced with satisfaction, he watched, contented, while his aide tied the other end of the heavy string to a nearby cinder block, hefted this, grimacing, placed the heavy block in Abul's trembling arms. "There."

Godunov guided the trembling Abul, cinder block and all, to the nearest window, pushed it up one-handed, admitting a cool night breeze, the sour symphony of Manhattan traffic twenty stories below. He climbed up and out, guiding, inviting the shaking, pantless man to share the narrow ledge, a cement shelf so small the front half of both men's shoes jutted over the edge.

"A man, even an enemy," the Russian told him softly, balancing both of them there among the stars, "should not leave this world without choices. Yours will be simple. You may drop the cinder block—which will wrench free your genitals but not immediately kill you—and try to make it back down to a hospital or emergency room before you bleed to death. Or you may simply jump with the cinder block, avoiding nearly all pain but not, alas, death."

And leaning gently as the steel canyon's wind, he kissed the dark-eyed man on the cheek.

The Russian climbed back inside the building, shut and latched the window. Tapped on it lightly. "Should you survive such a plunge," he called through the glass, "clearly an unlikely event, but should you somehow survive it, tell your friends that I do not suffer impostors gladly! That there is only one man worthy of hunting with Ivan Godunov! The American genius Frank Springer! Can you remember that, my friend? Frank Springer! Your associates will know the name!"

Below again on the street, stepping into the waiting cab—just shutting the back door against the cold and night, giving the driver the address of the New Amsterdam Hotel near the park—the two Russian gentlemen heard a sound nearby. A heavy, thudding noise as of something fallen from a great height impacted on the roof of a car somewhere on the dark street behind them.

Though whether this object was animal, mineral, or both, none of them could say.

PART I

CHAPTER 1

In his dream, Chris was running again.

The same frantic run, same frantic dream, through the old Ventura County neighborhood, across the Wilsons' sun-yellowed front yard, Chris's face bathed in sweat and terror, Matty's last words still ringing in his ears: *"The baby's out!"*

Racing through the cul-de-sac to the old couple's place across the way, starting to vault their iron fence, he caught himself—if he couldn't, a toddler couldn't. He darted next door to Rick Corman's driveway, yelling, *"Nicky!"* The baby rarely answered to his name, but Chris couldn't help himself. Nor pounding Rick's front door, knowing he wasn't home yet.

Spinning back, he swept to his own backyard again, even though Matty had just come from there. What lay beyond the nearly five-foot stone wall was a steep ravine. What lay beyond that was the neighborhood's busiest intersection.

Chris looked past the stony rim. The world beyond held a ghastly clarity, each leaf and twig of the big oaks etched in livid contrast. Somewhere past his vision a sudden screech of tires echoed the canyon, set his chest thundering. Vault the wall, check below—or try back up the street? He lingered in agony, time, a wall itself, pressing in from all sides. *"Nicky!"* his voice hoarse with terror.

Chris huffed back toward the cul-de-sac to find Matty lurching from the front again, her expression leaving him hollow inside.

"I was doing the laundry—he was right *behind* me!"

Why wasn't the goddamn door locked? But there was no time for thoughts of that now. "All right," he gasped, "he can't have gotten far! Dial nine-one-one! I'll do the neighborhood again!"

For a nanosecond, their eyes locked. He glimpsed—beyond her dysphasia—a crazed pleading for forgiveness, a demand that he make this right as he always had. It isolated him from the universe. He thrust her back toward the house, unable to withstand her eyes, hating and dying for her inside. *God*, please, he kept chanting under his breath, *please . . .*

He awoke in the aluminum glider beside the new house, face stippled in maple leaf shadow, wakened by the cooling afternoon breeze. No longer in Ventura County, California, but a few short miles down a winding mountain road to the tiny hamlet of Greenborough, Colorado. And it was early fall, not late spring. And Matty was inside the new kitchen (he could hear her singing happily through the window) getting ready for Rick and Sharon's first visit.

And the baby, Nicky, was alive and well. A dream.

He sat blinking upward at the big maple overhead, his favorite, beheld the first telltale patina of rich orange crowding out the green of summer leaves. Soon the forest all around them would be a riot of coruscating fall colors. They'd been here over two months in the new house, and it seemed like only yesterday since they were packing up the crowded little Thousand Oaks town house, heading for the country wilds. Time evaporates as you grow older.

He was having trouble with the third act of his play.

Perhaps worse, he was beginning to have trouble with the fact that he was a playwright at all, particularly in light of his dismal sales of late. That, and the fact that way out here in the Colorado wilderness, he couldn't use the old excuses of his lineman job not to work. The move had been made, the money spent, the commitment made. He either took the bit in his teeth and made it as a writer or threw in the towel.

Third acts were always the toughest. Starting was easy, but those damn endings.

Chris rubbed his eyes, sat up, looked across the wide lawn at the beautiful new A-frame. A wonderful house. The kind of house he'd never have been able to even dream about were it not for their recent good fortune.

It was great. But a little scary too.

Especially when he kept dreaming about Nicky that way, about what had happened. What might have happened. Hey, maybe that was the answer to the third act: have Ralph and Sheila's toddler run out the front door of their town house. That way she'd have a good excuse to divorce him, and Act One would have more punch.

He grunted, shook his head. Nobody but parents would understand the terror of nearly losing a child. The worst kind of terror he'd ever faced.

He pushed up from the chair, gave his attendant typewriter and stack of unfinished pages a jaundiced look, and headed toward the house to join his wife in waiting for the Cormans.

Rick Corman was exploding with enthusiasm for the new house, racing everywhere, vaulting upstairs, clattering down, red-faced and exuberant as a ten-year-old, flashing back and forth before a bemused but beaming Chris, himself grinning with vicarious pride.

"This is *fan-fuckin-tastic*!" from a breathless Rick. "A genuine log A-frame! Unbelievable! Sharon, *hey*, Sharon!"

"I'm right here, dear," his wife replied, calm by contrast, from the upstairs bedroom. She stood beside Matty, the two of them coolly absorbing the spectacular mountain view below, a lazily kiting hawk, the forever sky.

Rick, who knew about homes, used to build them, leaped through the sliding doors again to the cedar deck, calling up to the women. "Look at this truss work! Look at this floor. I-joints, Sharon! They've got engineered wood I-joints! None of that two-by-twelve floor joist stuff for these people! I mean, is this fan-fucking-tastic or am I crazy!"

"That's correct," Sharon offered, "and kindly shut up; the baby is napping."

Rick came back inside, goggle-eyed, shaking his head at the

beautifully appointed interior, then at Chris. "You dumb cluck, you don't even know what you've got here, do you?"

Chris, grinning, imitated Sharon's deadpan tone. "That's correct."

Rick touched the wall lightly. "Gypsum plaster, expensive." He nodded, turned to Chris again. "What about the roofing? You don't have a clue, right? Come on," and he headed out the front door.

"We're going outside again!" Chris singsonged to his wife. Matty, upstairs, watching Sharon's back, thought, *Great, now I'll be left alone in the new house with someone I was never comfortable with in the old house. Why doesn't this woman like me?* "Sharon? I think Chris put some coffee on down there. Would you like some?"

Sharon turned from the picture window, smiling, pleasant, pretty. But never to be a close friend. "That's sounds nice, thanks."

On the lower veranda, Rick strained upward on his toes. "What you've got there are composite shakes, not real wood."

Chris came up behind him. "Is that bad?"

"No, jerk-off, that's good. Real wood shakes are short-lived and combustible. These are made from concrete and wood fibers—lightweight, durable, good-looking. Someone knew what he was doing." He turned to face the woods, drag in a deep lungful of clean mountain air. "Christ, will you smell that."

Chris grinned, shoving coffee at him. "I hardly notice anymore, actually."

Rick would have punched him if not for the brimming cup. "Oh sure, you don't, you fatuous bastard. Jesus, look at that view!"

"You just got off the plane; you'll tire of it by tomorrow."

"Right, like *you've* tired of it. Is that a hawk or an eagle?"

Chris glanced skyward. "Golden eagle. Largest predatory bird in North America. Endangered, of course."

"Listen to him, knows the local fauna already."

"Read it in the third grade."

Rick headed for the flagstones, the front drive. "You and your trick memory. Let's go for a walk."

"You just got here. Don't you want to wash up or pee or something?"

"I'll pee in the woods. That's what they're for."

★ ★ ★

In the house, settling on the downstairs sofa, Sharon blew steam from her cup, mentioned again how much she loved the house.

She wants to like me, Matty thought. *She just won't quite let herself. Why is that?*

"How's the coffee? Did Chris make it too strong again?"

Matty shook her head. "It's fine."

Sheila looked about at the log-hewn room, the stone stacked fireplace. "Wish I had a rich uncle. . . ." Blowing steam again, avoiding Matty's eyes. "How come you never mentioned him before?"

Matty in the big green easy chair—the one piece of furniture they'd brought from California—sat framed in the picture window by emerald firs, backlit by golden afternoon glow. "I hardly knew him, really. Certainly didn't expect to be left in the will, which did not include quite a million dollars, despite Rick's speculations. Enough to buy this place and a little more, that's all."

"That's a lot."

"We were lucky. What's the matter?"

Sharon, caught staring, looked away. "Nothing. Sorry. I was just thinking how Rick is going to miss Chris so much. He misses him already."

Matty nodded at her coffee. "Yes. Chris too. Too bad about us . . ." immediately sorry she'd said it. Too late now; it was out there.

Sharon, trapped in the intimacy of the house, could hardly just let it go. "I . . . know we haven't been all that close, Matty. I'm sorry for that, truly."

Slightly surprised at even this much admission, Matty nodded agreement. "Me too. Why, do you suppose?"

Sharon sighed. "Timing? Bad karma? We really haven't known each other very long."

"Long enough, though."

Sharon sipped at her cup. "Yes. Oh, well. One of those things."

Matty nodding, moving to the kitchen: "Yes, one of those things. More coffee?"

"Thanks." And after a moment: "It's just that Rick and I knew Chris for such a long time . . . before you came along. I mean it was like . . . suddenly you were just *there*."

"I love him very much," Sharon told her, pouring coffee.

"I know. I know that."

"Do you?"

"Of course. Listen—"

"I didn't do this to take him away from you, because we weren't making it as a foursome."

"Matty, I know—"

"I did it for Nicky. For the family. The family has to come first."

Sharon nodded. "Listen, I understand. If Rick and I had kids, I'd probably do the same thing. That awful highway behind the neighborhood."

She turned, when there was no response from the kitchen, to find Matty, cup in hand, gazing, frozen, out the window at lofty peaks, tangerine sky, probably seeing none of it.

Sharon watched her silently.

Matty turned—finally—looked at her. She smiled apology for the silence.

"You never stop thinking about it, do you?"

Matty looked at her coffee. "No. Never."

On the gravel drive, Rick dipped into his Plymouth's trunk, drew back a beach blanket, withdrew a length of leather casing from under that, handed it to Chris.

"What's this?" Chris unwrappd the Remington, bright with newness and sweet oil smells.

"Housewarming gift. Like it?"

"Christ, I can't accept this!" But he was already sighting down the smooth bore, lining up with a Douglas fir thirty feet away.

"Okay, give it back."

"Go to hell. And thank you, it's beautiful. I assume you brought your Browning?"

Rick Corman, tall and smiling and athletic—a better shot than Chris, a better lineman too—already had the weapon in his hand, slamming down the trunk lid. "I've got empties in the backseat. Or did you already have something set up?" He grinned, already knowing the answer.

Chris grinned back. "Right this way, my friend."

They fired ten rounds apiece, Rick hitting all of his, Chris missing nearly half.

"Jesus, three weeks away from the skeet range and you've lost your touch already!"

"Up yours. I've been busy."

"Doing what, adjusting to the clean air?" Rick drew in deeply, sighing wistfully, setting up the cans again on the slug-gouged stump.

"Never mind the cans, I want to show you something. Look here." Chris gestured to a wooded trail left of the curving drive. "This leads down to the lake."

Rick genuflected, dropping a can, face stricken. "Bullshit."

"Didn't I mention the lake?"

"Not bass. Where—show me."

"What—the lake or the lake *and* the boat?"

"You complete bastard."

"Didn't I mention the boat?"

"Jesus, how rich was this uncle?"

Chris unlocked the boathouse doors, pulled them aside, revealing the trim Chris-Craft rocking lazily in shadow, musky odors of lake water and cedar.

Rick stepped in, happy as a kid with a new train set, ran his hand across polished mahogany decking. "Jesus, real mahogany!"

"Is it?"

"Yes, you dumb ingrate, it is."

Rick stepped aboard gingerly, sat grinning behind the wheel, snapped his fingers at Chris, who dug deep, handed him the keys. "You ever drive one of these things before?"

"Just shut up and get in." He started the big Evinrudes with a coughing burble, reversed expertly, and piloted them out of cold shadow, into fading sun. Rick shoved the throttle forward and headed for open lake. "Christ, this is beyond beautiful. And this uncle lived here?" His voice just audible above the whine.

"In the summers, I guess, but even then not for years. It was a windfall, kiddo. I have never experienced a windfall. It's weird."

"God, look at that shoreline! Douglas fir! I'll bet that one's a hundred years old!" He pointed. "Is that someone?"

Chris had to look twice to see an old man materializing out of the fir-studded shoreline, silent and brooding as the trees themselves, swathed in deep shadow, unmoving as a cigar store Indian. An Indian, in fact, being what he was.

"That's John Antler Horn." Chris smiled. "Let's say hello."

Rick throttled down, nosing the boat toward the bank until rocks and flitting minnow became visible in the gradually clearing depths. The old Indian, shirtless and coffee brown even though the early evening chill was on them, stood rooted in scrub and bulrushes—as if growing there. He spoke without turning from the wide waters to see who he was speaking to. "Hello, Chris Nielson. I was coming to see you. Do you have a chauffeur now?"

"No, John. This is my friend Rick Corman from California."

Rick saluted.

The old man, face beaten as cracked leather now they were close enough to see, turned finally to watch them impassively through eyes that may have read World War I headlines. "I was in California once as a boy. It smells of fish."

"The ocean." Rick smiled.

Ignoring him, John Antler Horn held a book out to Chris. "I was bringing this to you, Chris Nielson. It tells of the ways of the iceboats. When the great water freezes, I will come riding across it to you and we will go sailing together. Soar like the hawk."

Chris accepted the paperback with a nod. "I'll look forward to that, John, thank you."

The old man turned to Rick. "You steer like a woman."

Rick smiled. "Is that a fact?"

"Your boat is well crafted but stinks of gasoline."

Rick shrugged. "Hey, it's his boat!"

Antler Horn looked at Chris. "When the snow falls, I will teach you to ride the iceboats. No gasoline. I will build you an Arrow. Smaller than my boat but very fleet. It will be an early winter. A cold winter."

"How do you know that?" Rick asked companionably.

The old man stared at him. Looked away, toward the woods and beyond. "I don't like the noises."

Rick was flabbergasted. "You don't like woodland noises!"

The old man ignored him. "It hurts my ears. Stings my eyes. I use much Tylenol now."

Chris nodded. "You mean all the new building in town, right, John? The hammering and sawing."

"It stinks of tar. It hurts my ears."

"Progress." Rick smiled.

The old man's face was granite, a face old, wise as the hills. "It is not a good thing. It is not a good thing that comes to the town. It is dark and low to the ground. It has the eyes of the spider."

"Sounds like progress to me!" Rick winked at Chris.

But Chris gave him a dirty look, turned to the old Indian. "Anyway, I'm looking forward to reading the book, John."

"I will teach you to sail the ice. Soar like the hawk. Did Montana play today?"

"Not today, John; the game is tomorrow. Anyway, I think he retired."

"Montana is a mighty warrior. I believe he is part Iroquois."

"Good to see you again, John!" Chris nudged Rick, who throttled away from shore.

The old Indian raised a flat palm. "Don't bend the pages. Don't soil the cover! I paid three dollars ninety-five for the book, Chris Nielson."

"Take care, John!"

Out of earshot Rick said, "Local color?"

"I ran into him one day in Greenborough—our local one-horse town—at the post office. He latched on to me."

"Why you?"

"'Cause I'm such a swell guy, of course."

"Where does an old Indian live on a Colorado lake?"

"Beats the hell out of me. Head over there and I'll show you where the big ones bite."

They cruised until the sun melted, a squished tangerine bleeding into the lake's opaque flatness. Chris became worried about finding his way back.

"What the hell kind of mountaineer are you going to make—can't find your way to a dock in the dark."

"I'm not a mountaineer. I'm a middle-aged Ventura suburbanite playing at mountaineering."

Corman scoffed. "Shit. I spent half my time in the 'Nam on nighttime river missions."

"Don't start, okay?"

"I'm not starting. What are you going to do for work out here in the boonies, sport?"

Chris didn't answer until he felt his friend's eyes on him. "Not a hell of a lot of telephone poles to shinny up, are there?"

"So?"

"Actually I don't plan to work, as such."

Rick throttled low, so they could talk easier, coasting toward the distant dock. It was growing quite chill—hints of an early winter? Maybe the old Indian was right. "As such?"

"He plans to write," Matty told Sharon evenly, running water in their cups, dropping them into the dishwasher. "He's going to be a full-time playwright now. And about time, too."

Sharon raised a brow. "And that—I mean, you can—"

"We're doing fine. Maybe he'll be the next Neil Simon, maybe he won't. But I'm damn sure going to give him his chance." Matty shrugged, looked out at the sinking sun, sky afire. "He's past forty. Accidents happen."

Sharon nodded, turned to watch the sun with her. "What do you do for shopping, by the way?"

"Greenborough is about thirty minutes from here. A kind of smaller Aspen before Aspen became 'that way.' "

Sharon sighed hugely. "God. Look at that sun."

"Come on, let's watch it from the deck. Maybe we can have a Maxwell House moment."

They stepped outside, Sharon inhaling heaven-sent pine, closing her eyes dreamily. "This could get addictive. Where are the boys?"

"Chris is probably showing off the lake."

"Oh, God, it doesn't have bass, does it? You'll never get rid of us."

Rick stepped out of the boat, turned to watch the rest of the sunset—what vacationers paid for and Chris would have every night—his former neighbor tieing up, closing the boathouse doors. Pausing then, arms akimbo, to watch with Rick the glorious lake, listen quietly a moment to the coming night, the beginning thrum of frogs, their craft's ebbing wake lazily slapping the pilings.

Chris was lingering a little too long.

"What's the matter, sport?"

Chris watched the lake, turned to head up the path. "Nothing."

Rick snorted. "Right. I know that kind of 'nothing.' The kind that's followed by those little dots—what do you call them? You're the writer."

"Ellipses."

"Whatever. Talk to me."

Chris sighed, swatted a pine cone. "Oh, I was just thinking, it would be nice if you two liked Matty."

They walked awhile.

"Well, I finally said something to shut you up."

"I like her."

"But not Sharon."

"Sharon is Sharon. She doesn't like me half the time."

Chris nodded. "Sharon thinks she's hard to get to know."

"She told you that?"

"No, but she thinks it. I envy you two."

"For what? You're the one with the Colorado A-frame."

Chris thought about it, gravel crunching beneath him. "You two have a history. You've known her most of your life. You have Christmas with her parents."

"The Inquisition part of our history."

"Matty and I have only the last three years and four months. In many ways, we're still strangers. Sometimes I wonder . . . if it's real. . . ." He trailed off.

They walked.

Rick said, "Signing of the Magna Carta?"

Chris sighed. "Not tonight, I'm tired."

"Signing of the Magna Carta?"

And Chris, without hesitation: "June 15, 1215."

"Where?"

"Runnymede."

"Birth of Jack London?"

"January 12, San Francisco."

"Year?"

"1876."

"First sale?"

" 'To the Man on the Trail.' "

Rick slapped his back, continued up the path. "Thought for a second there you'd lost it."

"My trick memory?"

"Your trick *mind*. Matty's the best—the *realest*—thing ever happened to your sorry ass. Even a dickhead like me can see that."

"That doesn't make it real."

Rick groaned impatience. "Don't envy me the lean years, pal. Just be glad you found someone as great as Matty before you cashed it in. Not that a loser like you deserves her."

"Amen to that."

"Looks like you've got company."

Chris looked up the gravel drive to the A-frame's cedar facade, a brilliant flash of crimson parked imperiously beside Rick's lowly Plymouth.

"Wow. Who do you know who owns a Lamborghini?"

Chris assessed the radical lines of the sports car curiously: radically low, radically priced, radically red.

He squinted, frowning. "No one."

CHAPTER 2

"**W**e're baaaaaaaaaaack!" Rick wailing from the foyer.

No attendant response.

Chris shut the door behind them, glanced around the empty house.

"See, I told you all this clean air was a mistake. Now they've gone off into the woods with some guy with a red Lamborghini." Rick turned to the picture window, saw the three figures conversing on the back lawn. "Who's that?"

"Mr. Lamborghini, I guess. Come help me."

"Help you what? I want a beer."

"I hate meeting new people. Come hold my hand."

"Jesus, he's a tall bastard. Is this an old school friend of Matty's?"

"Get your nose out of the fridge and we'll go see."

"Can't take him by yourself, that it?"

Matty looked up impassively when they slid open the French doors. Did she seem a little flushed, Chris wondered, or was that just the rosy sunset?

"Come meet Matty's cousin," Sharon enthused.

Rick swigged beer, burped lightly. "Rich uncles," he said softly, "now lost cousins. The girl's a plethora of surprises."

Chris smiled affably at the group below, suppressing a frown. "Is that my rifle he's got?"

Rick squinted. "Looks like it."

Chris sighed. "Why do I not like this guy already?"

" 'Cause he's taller and better looking than you?"

They descended the wooden steps with forced grins.

He *was* taller, muscular: thick blond hair, clear blue eyes that seemed to miss little. I wonder if I *could* take him, Chris found himself thinking strangely.

"—but the true golden age of Kievan Russia, of course, began in the year 980, when Vladimir became grand prince. Vladimir! What a man! Eliminated his brothers, you know, in a war of succession, and without a backward glance!" And Frank Springer turned to smile at Chris.

His grip, in Chris's, was restrained but firm, full of confidence and withheld power. "Chris, at last. Frank Springer, Matty's cousin." He looked apologetically to Sharon and Rick. "I'm afraid this was ill-timed."

"Not at all," Chris assured. "Frank, Rick Corman."

"Rick, a pleasure."

"How goes it?"

"And Sharon you've met."

"I have had the pleasure." Frank swept his arms toward the women. "With the company of two such lovely ladies I'd begun to hope you two had gotten lost on the lake."

Everybody smiled convivially. Sharon was clearly entranced.

"I think we're the ones who are interrupting," Chris said, nodding at Rick.

Frank waved it off indifferently. "Not at all. I was boring your lovely wives with my interminable stories of historic Russia. You know Russian history, Chris?"

"Not much. College."

"But he's a fast learner," Rick said.

"He has an eidetic memory," Matty offered. "Do you know what that is?" Was there a hint of rare sarcasm in her voice?

Frank Springer turned to her slowly, grinning. "Indeed I do, puss," and he winked, tapping her nose with a condescending forefinger.

"Nearly eidetic," Chris corrected.

"How remarkable!" Frank beamed. "You should really study mother Russia, fascinating land. Kitten and I have lineage there."

Chris turned with genuine surprise to his wife. "Oh? You never mentioned Russia, Matty."

Frank hugged her shoulder before she could speak. "It's depressingly far removed, I'm afraid. Still, there may be yet a drop of old Vladimir with us yet."

"Is he your main area of expertise?" Sharon—infatuated—wanted to know.

"One of many, my dear," Frank appraised her. "Old Vladimir was quite a guy. Brought Christianity to Russia, you know, put the nation on the road to Orthodoxy."

"I thought Russia was always a godless place," Sharon nearly flirted.

Frank smiled at her pert nose. "Did you, my dear?"

"Frank is from New York," Matty said.

Chris nodded. "Oh?"

Frank put his arm about Matty again, pulled her close. "Upstate. Rye. Haven't seen my baby cousin in years." He looked down at the coppery curls. "How long, kitten?"

Matty held her wide grin. "Years! I'd begun to think the Springer side of the family tree had disappeared," she told Chris, avoiding his eyes in the sun's dying glare.

Frank squeezed her once, kissed her cheek. "Can't keep a Springer down, little cousin! My goodness, Chris, this place is lovely." He assessed the grounds with an approving nod. "Just lovely." Put a finger under Matty's chin, lifted it. "You've done well for yourself, kitten."

Matty held the grin, frozen.

"What line of work are you in, Frank?" Rick inquired.

Frank turned to him. Smiled. "I'm what you might call a freelancer."

Rick stared at him. "Oh."

In the ensuing silence Chris nodded toward his rifle dangling in the big man's hand. "You hunt, Frank?"

"How's that? Oh. Say, you don't mind—?"

"Not at all," Chris heard himself say.

Frank hefted the rifle. "Remington, isn't it?"

"Yes."

"Fine weapon. Little light for my taste, but a good pheasant gun. You ever hunt pheasant, Chris? We've got some dandy ones back east."

"Afraid not. I was never into killing things much."

"Oh?" Frank lifted the rifle smoothly, sighted at the sky. Everyone followed the dark muzzle to the soaring blur of wings above.

Sharon started to say something, then jumped with the rest at the rifle's report.

The great eagle staggered, rolled, dropped spiraling behind distant firs. "Fine hunting weapon!" Frank declared, holding up the rifle affectionately, discharging the round expertly.

Rick leaned sotto voce to Chris, staring silently at the unbroken line of firs. "Now we know why they're endangered."

Frank glanced up at the deck, broke into sudden smiles. "What have we here?"

They turned in unison to see Nicky, in Dr. Denton's, gripping the railing posts, still sleepy-eyed.

"That's Nicky," Chris said, "our son."

Not looking away, Frank walked toward the deck. "Well, now! What do you say, cowboy?"

"Can you eat eagle?" Rick asked Chris.

Chris ignored him. He was watching the big blond man, who was kneeling down as Nicky came down the deck stairs gingerly, posts in a death grip.

Frank hefted the baby in one hand, the rifle in the other. To Chris's uneasy resentment, the child reached for the rifle. Frank showed it to him, grinning brightly, turned to the others. "Hey, this kid looks like me!"

"Is that thing still loaded?" Sharon wondered softly.

Chris stepped forward tightly. "Hey, partner," he called to his son. Nicky wriggled with outstretched hands, demanded to be put down, then rushed across the green lawn to his father.

They were seated in the dining room under the beamed ceiling and wagon wheel chandelier, just finishing rainbow trout Chris had caught the day before. It was black without. Beyond the curtained windows, every star was visible in the rarefied Indian summer night.

"Chris," Frank marveled between mouthfuls, "this trout is without peer, really."

"It's delicious," Sharon concurred.

Chris nodded across bone linen at his wife. "Matty's doing. All I did was bait the hook." Expecting a prideful smile from her, receiving only impassive silence. Was she pensive about something? Had he made some faux pas earlier?

Frank chewed reflectively, glancing around the spacious room. "I cannot get over this house. Just incredible. I really like what you've done with it, Chris."

"Thanks."

Frank shook his head, beaming. "Matty here gets the house and old Frank gets the sports car, right, kitten? Good old Uncle Arky!"

Chris paused in midbite, looked to his wife. "I thought your uncle's name was Thomas."

Matty opened her mouth to say something.

"Everyone called him Arky," Frank interrupted. "Why was that, kitten?"

Matty poked at her greens with a frozen smile. "I really don't remember."

Frank put down his fork, leaned across the table mischievously toward Rick. "Ricky!" He nodded at Matty. "Would you believe I once saw this gorgeous thing completely in the buff?"

Sharon dropped her water glass with a musical clink, not breaking it but spraying the table. "Oh, I'm so sorry!"

Matty was at it with linen napkins. "It's nothing, just water."

Rick and Chris stared at Springer.

Frank reached across toward Matty. "Let me help."

"I've *got* it!" she hissed, dabbing savagely. Then smiled nervously at them. "I'll get you another glass, Sharon."

Rick looked over at Chris.

Chris looked over at Frank. "You were saying something about 'buff'?"

"How's that? Oh! Good lord, it was *years* ago! On Uncle Arky's farm! Kitten and I used to go skinny-dipping! Couldn't have been more than six!" He tilted in his chair, called to the kitchen, "*Right, kitten?*"

Nothing from the kitchen.

Frank smiled and tilted back down, forking trout. "Beautiful little girl. Longest legs you ever saw. But you'd know all about that, Chris. Ricky, may I have the tartar sauce?"

Rick gave it to him, watching Chris. Sharon stared fixedly at her plate, chewing rapidly. "Sounds like Matty's loading the washer. I'll give her a hand."

* ★ *

On the deck under cool evening breeze, Frank shoved dark cigars at the other two.

"No thanks," Chris declined, "really."

"Don't be absurd," Frank insisted, shoving it into Chris's mouth. "That's right out of Castro's backyard."

Rick lit the big stogie gratefully. "Where'd you get them, Frank?"

Frank puffed, sighed pleasure. "I told you."

Rick squinted one-eyed past smoke. "You know people in Cuba?"

"Not people, Ricky, the old man himself."

Rick looked at Chris, back at Frank. "Castro?"

Frank leaned against the deck rail, studied the stars. "We spent some time together. Don't let anyone tell you that Nicaraguan crap is the best soil. Del still grows the best!"

Rick frowned. " 'Del'?"

"Castro. His close associates call him Del."

Rick looked at Chris, who shrugged.

Frank turned on the railing, looked outward toward the cloaking night. "You know, Chris, that's just about the most beautiful little boy I've ever seen in my life."

"Thank you."

"But a word of caution. Matty tells me there's quite a big river down the hill."

"A long way down the hill. We never let Nicky out of our sight."

"He was out of your sight earlier when you watched me shoot the bird."

"Hey!" Rick started, and Chris silenced him with a gesture.

"I appreciate your concern, Frank, but I think I can look out for my own kid."

"Don't get me wrong, I'm sure you and Matty are the best of parents—person can tell that just by looking at the child." He blew smoke at the stars, big cigar revolving slowly from jutting jaw, chiseled features glowing red when he puffed. "But let me tell you, there's nothing more terrible than to have your own child taken away from you. Nothing more terrible in the world."

Chris watched him. "You sound as if you speak from experience," he said quietly.

Frank puffed solemnly. "I'd just hate to have anything happen when you're not around. Makes a man feel awful bad. Dead inside. You come home, the wife is frantic, you search, you search—your gut tearing, the guilt building—and it all comes to an end with that still little body lying in the shallows."

"Listen, goddamn it," Rick shoved forward, "it just so happens these people have been through a lot."

Chris took his arm. "It's all right, Rick."

"The hell it is."

Frank turned innocently. "Did I speak out of turn, gentlemen?"

"You he-men ready for dessert?" Sharon called from inside.

Chris pulled back the glass, pushed a restraining Rick through it, and they went to join the women.

CHAPTER 3

Things got a little better after dessert.

Matty kept the wine coming, Chris the party rolling with accounts of his days as a staff writer at Metro before quitting movies to write plays.

But it didn't last.

Throughout coffee, a growing dislike—a cold war really—escalated between Rick Corman and Frank Springer, centering on the Vietnam conflict.

Rick, who had served during the war—nearly lost his teenage life during the Tet offensive—took umbrage at anyone who hadn't actually been there, slugged it out. He argued heatedly that the whole useless experience had been a kind of Greek tragedy—the outcome virtually preordained—a place in world history where such an inevitable folly could not possibly have been avoided.

Springer, the cool, soft-spoken intellectual, countered with his own view: that with proper understanding and application of military art, America would have influenced the outcome substantially.

And so, to the growing uneasiness of the other guests, the "war" at the Nielsons' dinner table escalated, Rick Corman adamant, Springer baiting and outmanipulating at every turn with quiet, cigar-puffing reserve.

"My dear Ricky. It is easy to salve one's conscience in the face of failure with the notion that nothing we could have done in Vietnam would have made any difference, that fate rather than direct action predetermined the end result. You blame our failure on the forces of history. But remember, sir, it was four North Vietnamese Army corps that conquered South Vietnam, not dialectical materialism."

Rick, ignoring you've-drunk-enough glances from Sharon, kept falling into the trap. " 'Dialectical'—what the hell is that? What's he talking about, Chris?"

"Why don't we pick a new topic?" Sharon suggested.

Rick cut her off with a raised palm. "What the hell does that mean, Springer?"

Frank Springer smiled benignly, puffed. "As Solzhenitsyn said, 'We must not hide behind fate's petticoats.' Our blunder was in assuming that this was a counterinsurgency war. We repeatedly defined the North Vietnamese guerrilla operations as a strategy in itself, believing all those 'people's war' theories Mao Tse-tung was espousing."

Rick blew out exasperated breath, sat back, and looked to Chris. "Do you have any idea what this guy is talking about, sport?"

"Where, in your view," Chris addressed Springer, "did the Americans go wrong in the war?"

Springer, watching Matty's butt as she cleared the table, turned smiling to his host. "We fought Vietnam the way we fought Korea. A major mistake. Like Korea, our initial response in Vietnam was defensive, a reliance primarily on South Vietnamese ground forces and limited U.S. air support. By the middle of 1965 it became obvious this wasn't cutting it. We needed combat troops to stabilize the situation. The First Cavalry Division—to which our brave friend Ricky here belonged—did a magnificent job of mopping up the Cong in La Drang Valley in central Vietnam. We had them on the run, and that's when the U.S. should have taken the offensive. Unfortunately, such action was not deemed within U.S. strategic policy, which called for the *containment* rather than the *destruction* of a communist power. Washington, fearful of starting a nuclear war, of Chinese intervention, backed Johnson, who effectively barricaded the one sure route to victory—a strategic offensive against the source of the war."

Rick slapped the table, making his wife jump. "A strategic offensive against North Vietnam was not politically feasible at that time, you effete snob!"

For a moment Chris thought Springer—a powerfully built man with no glint of retreat in his eyes—was actually going to vault the table and strike Rick.

Springer only smiled. "Perhaps not, Ricky, but we certainly could have taken the tactical offensive, isolated the battlefield. Instead of concentrating on North Vietnam, however—the source of the war—we played around with the guerrillas in the south— and lost. Counterinsurgency blinded us to the fact that the guerrilla war was tactical, not strategic. The enemy wore us down, laughing."

Silence at the table.

Until Rick just had to say it. "And where were you all this time, Frankie boy, smoking cigars with your pal Del?"

Springer, still smiling, put down his cigar slowly.

Chris—eidetic, not prophetic—nevertheless felt something bad coming, almost stood up to stop whatever was coming, when the evening was saved by the front door buzzer.

"I'll get it." Matty smiled gratefully.

The moment broken, Springer settled back, relit his cigar, turned companionably, and smiled at Sharon Corman.

"Hello, Chris Nielson."

Chris looked up to find John Antler Horn towering above him. He was fully dressed this time in plain blue work shirt and jeans, which still must have offered little protection from the growing chill outside.

"I have come for my book."

Sharon—apparently never having entertained a full-blooded Iroquois at dinner—sat gaping. Frank Springer puffed with mild interest.

"But, John, I haven't started the book yet."

"Not start?"

"John," Matty offered at his side, "would you care for cake and coffee? We're just finishing. Please sit down."

Antler Horn turned to her. "What kind cake?"

"Well, we have chocolate fudge or pumpkin pie if you'd prefer."

Antler Horn nodded his leathern face at her. "The Pilgrims shared pumpkin pie with the Indian at Plymouth Rock."

Matty smiled uncertainly. "Yes, that's right. I'll just get you some." She headed quickly for the kitchen.

Antler Horn, who was staring unabashedly at Sharon, leaned down softly to Rick. "Your woman has a firm bosom."

Corman smiled. "That she does."

"A keen observation, my friend," Springer noted, and Sharon colored appropriately.

In the kitchen, Matty poured a hasty shot of Old Grand-Dad, gulped quickly, held back the cough, gripping the lip of the sink. Her hands, she noticed, were shaking.

"I'd really like to finish the book," Chris told the old man.

Antler Horn nodded. "Don't bend the pages."

"No, I won't."

Matty returned with the pie. The old man took it from her, still standing, and headed for the door with it. "Oh," Matty said, taken aback.

"I am building you an Arrow, Chris Nielson," the old man called from the door. He paused long enough to appraise the table. "The smell is bad tonight." And he turned ancient eyes on Frank Springer.

Springer watched the old Indian coolly. "Smell?"

"He's talking about all the new construction work," Chris told him.

Springer looked impressed. "You can smell the town all the way from here?" he addressed Antler Horn.

The old Indian stared at him.

"I can't smell a thing," from a meek Sharon.

"It is a bad smell," Antler Horn told them. "It eats up the town. I must use much Tylenol from the headaches. Tylenol is best. Recommended by four out of five doctors."

Springer grinned.

The old man watched him, not grinning back. Then, taking his pie, turned and left the house.

In his absence the room was abruptly still.

"Well . . . ," Sharon Corman said at length.

And everyone laughed, perhaps to break the tension.

But not for long.

The moment the old Indian had departed, Rick picked up where he'd left off, goading Springer.

Matty, voice trembling slightly, sat down between them, a

convivial buffer. She turned to her husband. "Chris wasn't in the war, were you, darling?"

Chris, taking his cue, shook his head. "No. I was one of the lucky few who made it into the National Guard before they shut the doors. Saw a little action stateside when King got shot—a few riots—but nothing major."

"Were you always a playwright?" Springer wanted to know, and Chris, seeing the conversation thankfully going elsewhere, placated him. "I always wanted to write, I guess. I paid my early dues in Hollywood, actually."

"Tell us some of your Hollywood stories," Rick suggested, less aggressive now that he had the chance to brag about his hero.

Chris grinned, shook his head. "Hardly good after-dinner conversation. Besides, I always get acid indigestion when I talk about the movie-making business. I write plays now, not film scripts. It's apples and oranges."

Sharon shook her head. "It's too bad," she told Springer companionably, "Chris tells stories wonderfully. He has an incredible memory."

"He's anal retentive," said Rick. "How about you, Frank? Any absorbing tales of midnight raids with your pal Castro?"

Springer waved it off. "Enough talk of warfare." He grinned secretively. "But speaking of anal retentive, I do know a story that might amuse you. If I might bore you some more with ancient Russian lore."

"Please!" from an enthusiastic Sharon.

Rick groaned, rolled his eyes.

Sharon, covering, leaned toward Springer smiling, breasts brushing the white linen tablecloth. "Please, Mr. Springer."

"Frank."

Sharon colored again, Chris ignoring a sideways look of sarcasm from Rick.

Springer sat back expansively. "Well, as I'm sure you know, during the fifteen hundreds, Russia was ruled by the famous—or infamous—Ivan the Terrible."

"Sure, we knew that," Rick said, ignoring his wife's glare.

"Well, for a time it seems old Ivan forsook Moscow altogether, establishing his headquarters from a fortified palace at Aleksandrovsk, where he ruled this sort of weird parody of a monastery. One prince, Boris Teluipa, who was discovered to be a traitor in the emperor's eyes, met a rather unusual end."

Springer puffed smoke, glanced around to be sure he was the center of attention. "His punishment was unusual even for the time, especially in light of the fact that Ivan was a renowned anal retentive."

Springer puffed, everyone waited, Rick pretending to drift off until Chris kicked him under the table.

Springer grinned amusement. "Well, Prince Teluipa was dragged before his accuser. Stripped naked. And here's the amusing part. A particularly sharp stake was fashioned by one of Ivan's minions and inserted into the prince's anus."

Sharon Corman made a face.

"Inserted deep, driven up through his body and out the back of his neck, the poor soul languished in horrible pain for fifteen hours, quite alive in the monastery's dungeon."

Rick stared across the table, mouth open.

"Well, the prince's mother, the duchess, was brought in to speak with her son during the procedure until the prince finally expired. Afterward, the duchess, a good matronly woman, was given to over one hundred of Ivan's gunners, who—'defiled her to death'—I believe was the term. She was then thrown to the emperor's dogs, who devoured her."

The table was thunderous with silence.

Rick, unable—or unwilling—to hold back any longer, threw Springer his best incredulous look. "Is that your idea of an amusing after-dinner anecdote?"

Springer appeared genuinely taken aback. "Don't you see, it was his fetish. Ivan was anal retentive! Get it?" Shook his head, grinning, knocked back the remainder of his wine. "That Ivan, what a character."

Silence.

At length, Sharon Corman cleared her throat.

Matty wobbled to her feet, went to check on the coffee. In the kitchen, out of sight, her hand trembled toward the liquor bottle.

Chris was searching desperately for something to say when Springer suddenly got to his feet, fishing in his coat pocket. "Nearly forgot." He brought forth a small wrapped package, handed it to Matty, who was just coming back with the coffee. "Housewarming gift."

Matty took it tentatively, staring down at thin red ribbon on plain white tissue. "Thank you, Frank. You really didn't have to."

"Not at all." Springer retrieved the gift right back from her.

"May I?" and he turned to the stereo unit on the wall, peeling back the white tissue wrapping. "I think you'll all enjoy this. I listen to it day and night, whenever I'm at home." He snapped the CD from its plastic case, punched in the player, and turned knobs on Chris's Panasonic.

The room swelled with a light, rhythmic timpani. An organic sound not immediately recognizable.

Frank Springer turned, beatific, from the stereo.

"A rainstorm?" Sharon guessed.

Springer winked. "Guess again!"

Sharon frowned, listening to the soft rushing from the speakers.

"It's Niagara Falls," Matty stated tonelessly.

Chris looked up, surprised to find her at the base of the stairs. She looked wan, drawn. Ill?

"Kitten gets the door prize!" Springer enthused.

"Will you excuse me a moment?" Matty murmured, already heading upstairs.

The rest of them watching her silent back, Springer—as if worried Matty might miss the best part—cranked the volume knob higher, the rush of thundering water chasing her upward.

Sharon stood in Matty's absence, seemingly obliged to fill the sudden void. "More coffee, anyone?"

Matty climbed quickly—gripping the rail for support—to the second floor, the thunderous rush from below pressing at her back.

She came down the hall, took a quick peek at Nicky's sleeping form, came to the master bathroom, shut the door, locked it, picked up the bedside phone, and punched a number—punched twice because her finger wouldn't hit the proper buttons.

In a moment she told the receiver gently, "He's here."

Waited.

Then: "What do you mean, you already know that! What? Fine. Fine. Well, I want him *out* of here, now! No, *no!* Now!"

Pause, while she nodded exasperation, forcing herself calm. "Yes. I am calm. Fine. Then why wasn't I *told*?"

And again restraining her voice: "Fine. Fine. Make sure you do." And she hung up.

Not feeling better, not at all, hustling to the bathroom, too quick even to hit the light, throwing up the lid just in time and giving her dinner to the toilet.

She sagged, knees to carpet, tears tracing cheeks, waxen-faced, wiping her mouth with a palsied hand. A low, unearthly noise rose in the tight bathroom, a moan she finally recognized as her own. She pressed burning forehead to cool porcelain, closed her eyes. Why couldn't she just stay here, just melt here into the cool porcelain, become a silent slab of inorganic nothing like the wallpaper and tile?

No! Fight it!

Fight what? It was over. Over the moment she'd seen him coming up the drive.

How in the name of God had he found her?

Matty sat back, dizzily gripping the toilet's lip, listening to the slug of heartbeat in her ears.

She tried to stand, felt a familiar rise of nausea, fought it—there's nothing left to give you, toilet. But there was, and it hurt and burned more than before and was loud enough to make her worry they'd hear her down below. It left her slumped between toilet and sink, broken and drained.

Get up. You can't stay here. Maybe he doesn't want anything.

Oh, sure!

She watched the ceiling; the ceiling swam. They were going to get around to painting all the ceilings someday. And the kitchen, and that add-on studio for Chris. Well, not now. You took care of that, old girl. You took care of everything, including the marriage, Chris's career, Nicky—

Nicky!

A wedge of terror seared her, vicious enough to elicit a gasp; she bit back a fresh wave of vertigo.

God, please, God, do what you will with me, but do not let anything happen to my baby, not my baby boy, not my Nicky.

She hitched in a breath, the reek of bile, made herself sit up. *I will not sit here in my vomit and let anything happen to my child!*

After a moment, she ran cold water, stood before the mirror, gazed at her corpse's reflection.

She turned and rejoined her guests.

Matty came downstairs again on rubber legs, gripping the wooden rail with talons, hearing Frank's expansive basso from below.

Please don't let him ask to spend the night.

But Springer was already shrugging into his jacket, thanking Chris again, telling him for the fiftieth time how great his house was, how great his son was, what great good fortune it was that he had found and married someone like Matty.

He turned, spotted Matty coming down. "Kitten! You look pale! Chris, does Matty look pale?"

"Are you all right, honey?" Chris came to her, concerned.

"Fine. Too much wine, probably, the excitement."

Chris held the door for Springer. "Come back and see us, now."

Springer waved from the porch, looked again to Matty. "You can count on it."

Later, in bed, in darkness, Chris reached for his wife.

Matty stopped him with a gentle hand. "Just hold me awhile, please?"

He encircled her with an arm, kissed her hair, rich with the fragrance of her.

They were silent for a time.

"Do you ever miss the old neighborhood?" she finally ventured.

Chris thought about it. "A little, sure. But I love the new house, our new life." He turned to her in darkness. "Don't you?"

"Of course. It's lovely here. Lovely. Only . . ."

"Only what?"

"I don't know. I suppose I do miss some things. Not just the old neighborhood, but, you know, things."

"Hot Springs is within a day's drive. Kingston closer."

"Not exactly a cosmopolitan city either."

He was genuinely surprised. "You said you wanted to get away from the city, Matty. It was your idea. Because of what happened with Nicky."

"Away from that city, yes."

"But?"

"Chris, I'm glad we moved, I am."

"Well, are you or no?"

"Of course. It's just . . . I'm only saying that if we ever did want to move again, it wouldn't be that hard."

"Packing all our stuff wasn't hard?"

"Selling, I mean. It's such a lovely house, such a knockout view. We could be out of here like a shot. If we wanted to, that is."

"But we don't want to, right?"

"That's right."

They lay in silence for a time.

"I'm just saying it wouldn't be hard, is all," she murmured, not letting it go.

He lay there in sightless dark trying to decide if he really knew exactly what it was she was saying. Was about to turn and ask her something when the rhythmic rise of her breast against his arm told him she'd drifted off.

He sighed, not unhappily, but not yet sleepy either, thinking of the evening, of the Cormans, of Frank Springer. Of Matty. How much he loved her. What she'd brought to his life, what his life had been before her coming.

He'd been a lineman for Ventura County, the latest in a long line of jobs efficiently done if not deeply felt. Inertia until his true vocation emerged—mothlike—from a steadily aging chrysalis: He fancied himself a playwright.

Tall, athletic, gawky, and hawk-faced, with a nose he hated so much he made sure it got broken twice in the school yard, the young Chris Nielson had patterned himself (first in appearance, then in craft) after Long Island Library photos of Hemingway. He'd assumed, because he liked that giant's elusive simplicity, that a similar prose style would skate him through two New York colleges. His father, also like Hemingway—in love with the sea but constantly ambushed by matters of corporate law—neither encouraged nor dissuaded Chris's early writing aspirations, leaving it to the young man to find, upon graduation, that school was not the real world, and the real world was something he knew little about.

Taking his cue from Hemingway, Chris set out to find the world, his place in it. Which, to his dismay, proved not to be as novelist.

A reedy, implacable professor at Colgate had told him—to his chagrin and ever-after consternation—that his final essay lacked something. "What?" Chris had demanded, and the wan, effeminate reply had been that Chris would know it when he saw it.

Working odd jobs, cross-country, Chris in his twenties piled up reams of paper, novels and short stories, surpassed only by the reams of rejection slips received en route.

A one-night stand in Phoenix—an older woman, wiser than she'd first appeared—surprised Chris by staying up all night reading his latest rejected novel, telling him, before handing it back and rolling over, that it lacked something.

In San Francisco—when that town's dubious center was

Haight-Ashbury—Chris fell in with a group of actors and would-be Broadway stars, all of whom planned to leave the very next week for New York, study at the Actors Studio with Brando and Strasberg. Chris penned four plays there—just to try his hand at it—and, washing dishes in between, got two of them produced locally to not horrible reviews. When a friend suggested he try this in lieu of novels, Chris thought him insane.

By his early thirties, having landed in Los Angeles and looking less and less like Hemingway, an actor–would-be producer acquaintance who—like Chris—was currently waiting tables, read his newest book carefully, over late-night coffee, looked up, and told him it had terrific structure but that Chris lacked something as a novelist. "What?" Chris demanded cautiously.

A love of words, the acquaintance told him, and Chris thought about that. "You should try screenplays," the friend mentioned before letting Chris get the tab. "They're all structure."

Chris wrote five, all film noir suspense pieces, sold three almost immediately. On a roll, he milked his success for two financially rewarding years, years spent piling up dough and getting nothing else produced, a phenomenon peculiar to Hollywood. Four more months of this and he discovered just how much he hated the moviemaking process and at the same time how comfortable he found life in southern California. That and the format of the screenplay style. He decided, all alone one night over a pile of cheerily blazing scripts, to become a playwright.

During this entire part of his life, though he slept with a few, made friends with many, he had never fallen in love with a woman, never even casually considered marriage.

He had come close once, in college, lost her to a faceless someone, mantled himself in bachelorhood thereafter. The mantle grew to fit; marriage, the idea of it, rarely crossed his mind. He loved the out-of-doors, loved skeet and range shooting (not hunting or killing anything), was good with his hands, and prided himself on his self-sufficiency. Mostly he loved to write plays.

Which never made him rich (sometimes quite poor, forcing him to take odd jobs, become a lineman) but left him feeling complete. He stayed on the West Coast, where several of his plays had been performed by the local community theater. He had produced and staged the third, *Mating Season*, joined in happily constructing the flats, endearing himself to the crew, chosen the small cast, including a copper-tressed, lithe, demure twenty-eight-year-old Matty Springer.

He'd hardly noticed her during auditions. Onstage she came alive, something moving inside him there in the front row seats, her effect on him intriguing. He'd known she had the part after the first line. The others weren't bad, but this one could *act*. He couldn't believe she wasn't a professional.

He'd called that very night to inform her. She seemed pleased but not effusive. She knew how good she was. He found himself using the fact that he wanted to get the play going right away as an excuse to drop the script off at her place that night.

He'd really intended to drop it and get out of there. She'd fixed coffee and they'd talked, sprawled in her tiny apartment living room for six straight hours. Sleepy-eyed, strangely nervous, he'd finally bid her good night, turned at the door, and shocked himself by kissing her. She'd let him taste her tongue briefly, then grinned and pulled the door open for him, shooed him out.

He'd called when he got home to apologize. She'd laughed into the receiver, a tinkling of icy sound that thrilled him to his shoes. He'd felt foolish, irritated, stammering and clumsy as a puppy. She must have sensed it. What on earth is it you're trying to say? she wanted to know. When he didn't know either, she replied with a breathy sigh in his ear, "Come on back, I'll make another pot."

He'd walked in, and they'd stood in near darkness staring at each other. It was better already, just being near her again, the smell of her. He was shaking spastically, nearly vertiginous, she shaking her head with sympathetic smiles, cupping his cheek, a mother with a flummoxed child. In sudden anger he'd crushed her to him, bruised their lips awkwardly, pulled her down gracelessly on her lumpy couch; he had never wanted anything so badly in his life.

She had let him pull her breasts free, kiss them firm, let him see, even the pale, nearly invisible scar tissue tracing one of them. "A benign tumor," she'd told him directly.

"It doesn't matter," he'd whispered.

But she'd pulled the material completely away, thrusting herself at him. "I want you to know, to see it all now. If you find it ugly."

"Oh Christ," he'd whimpered, kissing her nipple, kissing the pale scar, "you're lovely." And reached, trembling between her legs.

Which was when she'd stopped him with a firm hand, stunned him with her next words: "Marry me first?"

He'd searched her green eyes, found no levity.

They'd driven to Las Vegas that weekend. Nicky was born exactly nine months later.

CHAPTER 4

Chris rose early, whipped pancake batter, and cut fresh fruit while Matty wrestled the baby. He ground coffee and laid it before her grateful eyes on the dew-smelling deck overlooking unearthly mist-shrouded Colorado. It was nice to be alone again, just the three of them, the Cormans having departed last night with tearful good-byes.

Across from Matty, over orange juice—Nicky bespattering himself in his high chair nearby—Chris and Matty exchanged looks of shared profundity, bottomless devotion, a perfect moment on a perfect morning.

In his room, Chris worked the morning through, knowing precisely when to quit. He had the first act done, the third memorized, was having trouble not padding the second to make it stretch. A jay tapped his window impudently, demanding he take lunch, which he found Matty setting atop the downstairs counter: steaming chicken noodle soup and grilled cheese sandwiches.

Munching a cracker, Chris said on impulse, "Let's take the afternoon off, go fishing."

She looked up to see if he meant it, saw he did. "And Nicky?"

"Bring him."

"Chris."

"We have life jackets, and I want him to get used to the idea of water. The sooner he learns to swim, the safer we'll feel."

"Well, I suppose."

"Winter's upon us."

She grinned. "You already talked me into it."

They packed a thermos and fruit snacks, toddled happily to their private dock, Nicky pointing at everything, having to know what everything was called. Chris took the Chris-Craft to the very center of the lake, Matty blissfully relaxed, the baby laughing deliriously in the breeze, sun-blonded hair whipping, eyes sparkling with wonder.

"He likes it!" Chris called above the twin inboards.

Matty nodded, winked.

But it grew unseasonably warm as the day progressed, and though Nicky could strip to only diapers, Matty was baking even under her wide-brimmed hat.

Chris, on a roll with three large bass, was loath to throw in the towel but started reeling in guiltily anyway, their lemonade-filled thermos empty.

"So stupid," Matty apologized, "I should have brought my suit."

Chris felt an adrenaline-pumping pull on the line but lost it. He craned, looking around them. "You know, there isn't a soul on this lake. . . ."

"Forget it, sweetcakes."

"Why? Listen, that bikini of yours is just a G-string anyway."

"I am not going nude in the middle of Lake Havasu!"

"Only with good old cousin Frank, huh?"

She shaded her eyes at distant shore to mask her expression. "There are other houses on the lake, people have binoculars."

"You'll be in the *water*, Matty! Anyway, what's the harm in giving some old fart on retirement pay a thrill?"

"You're a very sick man, Christopher Nielson. And the water's probably freezing by now anyway."

"All right," forlornly, "I'll reel in the rest of the way then. . . ."

But he did so want to fish, and she could never resist his whipped dog look. She sighed, arms on hips, not giving it to him easily. "The truth is, it's you who want the thrill."

He grinned impishly. "Her body glowed ivory in the midday sun. . . ."

"Who's that?"

"Christopher Nielson. Do it slowly."

But she did it quickly, graceful as an eel, leaving her clothes on the baking cushion, and into the water with nary a ripple, clinging gratefully to the gunwale, abruptly triumphant smiles. "Oh God, you were right, this is *marvelous*! Oh, honey, come join me!"

He nodded lustful irony. "And let Nicky handle the boat."

"You have a point. Oooo! This is delicious! Naughty but nice."

"You're making me very horny in front of my son."

"Save it."

"It's not going anywhere. Shit. . . ."

"What? *What*!"

He nodded and she craned in frantic foam, saw a white power-boat emerging from a screen of half-drowned firs near the north bank.

"Damn it, Chris, I *told* you!"

"Just stay under from the neck down. How'll they know?"

They roared nearer, four of them, voices loud even above the diesel's growl, beer cans glinting in fists, the angry whine of rock. One of them, in a red baseball cap and pot-bellied T-shirt, pointed at the Chris-Craft, maybe at Matty. Chris thought he heard the word "mermaid" then, a moment later, "cunt." Followed by guttural laughter as their wake slammed the smaller boat.

The Chris-Craft sluiced sharply. Matty clung tight but the heaving gunwale yanked her up and out, exposing pale, dark-nippled globes. She let go, swallowed water, choked, and, enraged, submitted to Chris's grasping hand until they settled. "They did that on *purpose*!" she croaked.

Chris watched their departing stern with slitted eyes. "Jerks."

Matty rubbed lake water from her eyes.

"God-*damn* it!"

She blinked hard, twisting in his grip to see the white racer leaning to a lazy U, sweeping around again.

"Give me your other hand."

"Chris, I'm not going to give those bastards the satisfaction!" She jerked free, kicked away from the boat. When the wake came, she ducked under nimbly, waited in murky green until the whining screws were past, rose, gulped air, ducked confidently beneath the next, smaller wave, and then they were gone.

Chris hauled her aboard, tossed her clothes. "Are you okay?"

"Of course. Assholes. Damn, you can't go *anywhere*, not *anywhere*!"

"Mommy *pretty!*" Nicky announced joyfully.

And that set all three of them laughing.

Chris, feeling good despite the incident with the powerboat, treated them all to dinner at the Florey Inn down the south shore, a sweeping redwood restaurant that was the best food to be had anywhere other than town.

They ate bass that Chris was sure was not as good as the ones he'd caught this afternoon, consumed delicious tiramisu for dessert, chatted, played the jukebox, observed the thinning tourist trade, and watched Nicky nod and finally go limp in his seat.

Chris carried him to the big, brightly lit dock, Matty laced in the crook of his arm.

The night was clear but brisk with winter's promise, cooler already than California nights, and the lake smelled not like the ocean but its own distinct inland odor, a pungent musky clarity Chris found clean and seductive. I have never, he was thinking as they stepped past cleats and coils of rope on the thumping dock, I have never been so utterly happy in my life.

On the moon-shimmered journey back to their own dock, Matty fell asleep against his shoulder, Chris at the helm, Nicky long gone under in his mother's protective arms. Chris let the feelings of sublime, peaceful happiness expand, probably to unrealistic boundaries, but what the hell. It gave him the chance to replay their too-brief past.

Marry me first?

It had been a big night for Chris, an excruciatingly nervous but thrilling first night for his *Token Relief* premiering at the Ventura Playhouse. All the more so because Gerald Reed, the Hollywood producer, was supposed to be in the audience.

Chris, hyper and fidgety behind curtain—plagued with last-minute doubts about the third act—peeked out at the converging crowd several times but never spotted Reed. He had high hopes for the show, though, even higher hopes for his leading lady–new lover, Matty. She looked radiant this evening in her special gown, all ready to sweep majestically into Act One, stun the local rubes with her beauty and skill. Chris had pondered, there amid first-night jitters, which he was the most proud of—his work or the beautiful woman he was secretly sleeping with.

Matty—never nervous—had surprised him by cornering him

minutes before curtain, a deep scowl marring greasepaint and liner. "Why didn't you *tell* me?"

Chris, tense and distracted, had blinked incomprehension. "Tell you what, Matty?"

"Norma Walker just told me Gerald Reed is in the audience! Gerald Reed the *producer!*"

It was the first time he'd seen her genuinely miffed, almost beside herself as if he'd forsaken some secret vow. "He *might* be here," Chris had defended, "it's only a possibility."

"Norma said she *saw* him!"

"So? I'd think you'd be excited. Here's your chance to break the chains of small town community theater, be a star. I'm quite flattered someone would drive all the way up from the Valley to see our little show."

"Well, I don't *want* to be a damn star!"

He'd stared blankly at her; it was all she ever talked about, when she wasn't talking about them.

"Pardon me?"

She'd seemed to stumble on it, cast about a second, then back to him, still angry but in control, a professional. "I'm not *ready* for that yet."

"Don't be ridiculous. You want to stay here and cast your pearls before swine the rest of your life? I thought you were an actress."

She'd looked away, cooling now. "I'm"—she put a hand to her forehead—"to tell the truth I'm happy just to be with you."

He'd put his arms around her. "Hey. Just pretend they're all naked out there, right?"

She'd smiled. A little. "I'm sorry."

He'd shaken his head. "I'm sorry. I'm a wreck. I wish I had your composure."

She'd stepped back, then, given him a complete smile, the old confidence back, then clouded again for a moment. "I just don't want anything to go wrong."

Chris looked down now as the rusty curls stirred, the boat rolling a moment in the trough of someone's stray wake.

The truth is, it had gone wrong, at least for her fledgling career. After their marriage she'd let it slip away, seemed, in fact, to forget all about it, concentrating on the marriage, on Nicky, who had come along nearly nine months to the day they'd met.

Nor did it seem in the slightest to bother her. She looked as happy and at peace as he. Maybe the clichés were true: happiness is not found in glorious, neon-lit career but in the arms of someone you hold dear.

He kissed the top of her head, elicited a sleepy murmur.

Lucky bastard, he thought, steering them home, you are one lucky bastard.

"Damn," he swore softly, but it was enough to awaken her.

She pushed up, Nicky asleep in her arms, and took in star-reflecting lake with the surprise of the freshly wakened. "Chris?"

He'd throttled down to a basso gurgle, drifting gently toward their dock, his posture tense. "Our friends are back."

She sat up rigidly, spied the pale hulk of the big powerboat parked before their boathouse. She frowned in the glow of amber dash lights. "That's a private dock," she murmured irritation.

Chris eased down farther on the throttle, aligned himself with the opposite side, thinking about but discarding the idea of coming about, taking a short tour until these jokers shoved off. Matty was tired and wanted a shower, Chris exhausted from the long day; he wanted a drink and bed. "Play it cool," he told her.

"Where do we park the boat?"

"We'll park it against the dock tonight; it'll be fine. I'm not going to start something out here late at night with these drunken bozos."

All four of them were sprawled on the deck around a seemingly bottomless cooler of beer. By now they'd be good and plastered; Chris hoped not dangerously so. He'd been wondering for ten minutes where the noisy music was coming from. Now he knew.

Still green behind the helm, Chris nosed the Chris-Craft as carefully as he could, still managed to bang the bow against the dock's tire guards. If the group wasn't already aware of them, it was now.

Chris had to climb out carefully, towing the boat, walk across the planks to the single cleat—his cleat—and stand before them.

"Ahoy there!" came a sloppy-lipped salute, followed by a chorus of giggles.

Chris assessed the group guardedly, smelling trouble, determined to head it off. "Gentlemen, it's a private dock."

More giggles. "That a fact?"

"It is. But may I suggest you sleep it off here anyway until morning? Lots of kids on the lake this time of year."

"Whatever you say, Captain."

Chris nodded. "Fine. You're welcome to stay until morning, then." He knelt and began to untie them.

The one in the red cap sat up hugely, heavy gut shifting, testing the limits of a beer-stained T-shirt. "The fuck you think you're doing, skipper?"

Chris didn't flinch. "Unlashing you. This is my cleat. Once I'm moored, I'll retie you on top of me so you can cast off nice and early in the morning." He felt his fingers trembling vaguely, found himself angry at this. Don't lose control, they're teetering already, waiting for an excuse.

"Suppose we want to 'cast off' before that, hot rod?"

Chris tied down, straightened, faced them. Big men, all of them, thick-shouldered and powerful, unshaven and smiling stupidly. "I'd think that unwise, considering your condition," he informed them.

"Think that unwise, would you? And what condition might that be, Captain?"

Chris felt rising heat, a pinch of adrenaline, ignored it. "You're drunk."

Now the smiles faded, in time with Chris's galloping heart.

"Come over here and say that, Captain."

There was the baby to think of, to say nothing of Matty. It was lonely and dark out here, and these men were doubtless tourists—away from homeland ties and laws—impressing each other with the bolstered confidence of combined numbers. Chris met it, unchallenging but firm. "Gentlemen, we can do this easy or with the help of the lake patrol. Your choice."

More giggles including a "lake patrol, my ass" from someone, and he was probably right. The lake cops would be few and far between at this late hour, and Chris had no radio on the boat, though this mob didn't know that.

He turned his back on them, walked to Matty and the baby, helped them from the boat, taking Nicky in his arms, thinking, Surely when they see the child—even one of these idiots must have children.

He was rewarded with catcalls and whistles. "Whoa! Would you look at the legs on *that!*"

They were all sitting up now, whooping and belching. "Hey, lady, I seen them big white melons in the daylight!"

Chris flushed, faltered, felt Matty's nails dig into his arm.

"Round 'n' heavy an' orange on the tips!"

Chris bit his lip, started to turn, let Matty pull him on.

"Hey, lady! When the kid's through, how 'bout lettin' us have a go! I been cravin' a milkshake all day!" Much laughter now.

When Chris turned, one of them was untying the Chris-Craft.

Chris dug in heels, yanked away from Matty. "Son of a bitch—"

"Chris!"

"That's *our* boat!"

Wishing for a gun, a lead pipe, anything, he strode furiously, and he knew foolishly, back to them, trying to make himself sound authoritative and dangerous. "Leave the fucking line alone!"

"You say something, putz face?"

Chris reached down, grasped a beefy arm, felt himself swept aside with breathless strength. He backpedaled, tangled with a coil of rope, crashed to the dock amid gales of harsh laughter.

He sat for an agonized moment, gazing numbly at his tangled legs, unable to face Matty, in for a pounding now, having no clue how to handle it. There were four of them, and they did this sort of thing all the time. Jerry Funcinello, a linebacker turned lineman with arms like coconuts that Chris had known and joked with back in Ventura, could maybe take these guys. Chris, stronger than most men from years on the phone poles, did not think he could.

Let the boat go, sue them tomorrow? Or put up a fight, get himself beat up, maybe killed for Matty?

He needed to think of the baby, but the idea of appearing a coward in front of his wife was killing him. He wobbled to his feet, fists doubled, and found them all staring somewhere beyond him.

Chris turned, hoping for a uniform, found instead Frank Springer moseying nonchalantly to the dock, grinning and winking at Matty.

"Evening, kitten! What's that on your pants bottom, Chris?"

Chris swatted dirt from his rear, grateful to his soul for any backup at all.

Frank, in sports shirt, slacks, and loafers—looking loose and casual—kissed Matty's cheek, patted Nicky gently, sauntered grinning toward Chris. "Friends of yours, Chris?"

Chris dusted his hands. "Not really."

Frank saluted the powerboat. "Evening, gents! Got a spare beer?"

"Not for you, turd face!"

Frank held the grin, laughed softly, appraised the dock. "Hey, Chris, that your Chris-Craft?"

"Yes."

"Well, it's untied." He knelt and took the mooring line in his hands.

When the beefy arms reached for Springer, Chris had a cry of warning on his lips but choked at the last second on phlegm. Frank was grabbed roughly, hurled sprawling across uneven planks, almost to the dock's lip, not quite into the black water.

Chris thought: shit. Far from helping, Frank had only made things worse. Now that the odds were less laughably uneven, Chris would be obliged to turn it into a swinging match.

Frank, for his part, rolled easily, came up unruffled on his buttocks, blinked. Wrapped his arms around his knees as if considering carefully, regarded the beefy giant above him with calm, impassive curiosity, as though the whole thing must have been some entirely excusable faux pas for which Frank was agreeably awaiting an explanation.

He nodded at the giant, even smiled there on his butt under the insect-flitting dock lights, beginning conversationally, unhurriedly. "You know, when the Mongols swept through Russia from 1237 to 1240, it was with a vengeance and brutality the likes of which that country had never imagined. It was awe-inspiring."

The beefy giant frowned perplexity, turned to grin at his friends: this guy is scared senseless.

Frank eased up with a grunt.

He found his feet. "The city of Ryazan, a holy place on the Oka River, was virtually annihilated. Even the great city of Kiev was gutted. The world had not seen the likes of the Golden Horde, as they were known."

The giant grinned, reared back, and smashed Frank in the face. Or would have if the face had been there. The giant missed, grunting with the effort of the miss, his big fist soaring over Frank's ducking back, Frank pivoting just right so the giant was just off balance, just beginning to pinwheel at the edge of the dock. Frank's spinning kick, which was faster than a blink and (from the sound of it) devastating in its power, caught the giant full in the solar plexus, drove him, beefy face white with surprise now, flailing backward magically as if from an explosion. He treaded air between dock and powerboat, pinwheeling wildly, no breath to curse with, hit the dark lake with a cannonball geyser.

There followed splashing and cursing and utter, amazed silence from the powerboat.

When everyone looked, Frank, smiling yet, was calmly retying the Chris-Craft.

Another heartbeat of silence.

Then, from someone, "Get that motherfucker!"

The biggest of the lot, sporting tattoos, came vaulting the white bow, landing squarely on the planks with an elephant thud in front of a just-straightening, unruffled Frank. The usurper hauled off with a haymaker, which Frank took full on the chin *and did not budge an inch*, even though the blow cracked across the lake like a broken bat.

He took it without wincing, only twisted his head a little under the big fist, his body barely swiveling, hands on his hips, feet planted.

"The Mongols, you see, were a nomadic lot, much preferring the grassy steppe to the forested northern country. In fact, they didn't really have the troops for such an occupation."

Tattoos was so nakedly shocked, he stood merely gaping, his laboring brain insisting he *must* have knocked the man down. The man could not have withstood that—no man ever had—so why was this guy standing here grinning at him?

But not grinning now as Nicky broke abruptly into sputtering wakefulness in his mother's arms.

The humor drained at once from Frank's face.

The tattooed man stepped back uncertainly.

Frank held up an admonishing finger. "Oh, dear, now you've awakened the child," and grabbed the man's groin in a blur of movement with his left, the striped T-shirt neck with his right, and (Chris did not believe this then, refused—having witnessed it fully—to believe it later) *lifted* the squirming hulk over his head and cast him back into his boat, where he landed with the delicacy of fallen timber.

Chris was aware of his open mouth, his own impotent fists.

Someone on board drew a knife.

Frank turned to him loosely, a patient pedagogue. "Despite their brutish appearance, the Mongols were not without brains. They first terrorized the Russians, then withdrew their troops to the lower Volga, remaining there poised and ready. At the first hint of defiance, they'd rush out and destroy the usurper." He grinned mirthlessly. *"Rush out like lightning."*

The man considered, dropped the knife, lunged for the throttle, the big Mercury mills coughing to life. Someone else retrieved the knife, leaped to the bow, and cut them free.

"Hey—hey!" They grabbed the man in the water, hauled him dripping into the already moving boat, powered away from the dock in a wall of foam that left the dock's barrels clanging with alarm.

Frank turned smiling to Matty, held out his hands for the baby, who was wide awake and quiet now, subdued as the others at the swift violence. Frank grinned, beckoned with his fingers and, to Chris's amazement, Nicky came grinning into them. He spanked Frank's shoulders with a flat baby palm, announced cheerfully, "*Strong*! Strong Frank!"

Springer grinned with delight. "Hey, he knows my name!"

He winked at Chris. "I tell you, Chris, the kid looks more like me every minute!"

CHAPTER 5

Over drinks, secure behind solid A-frame cedar, pressing back baleful night, pernicious memory, Chris admitted to Frank, not without admiration, "I've never seen anything like that in my life."

They were seated in the living room, relaxed and at ease, nursing highballs—something Chris didn't ordinarily indulge in but which seemed apropos considering.

Usually the perfect hostess, Matty seemed enigmatically distant, lurking always at the periphery. Attempting bravely, perhaps, not to make Chris feel inferior? Any more inferior than he already felt. Inferior but thankful: Nicky and Matty were safe and unharmed in cozy, cloistered safety again. He couldn't have prayed for a better ending.

"Really, Frank, where'd you learn to handle yourself like that, the army?"

Frank, watching Matty across the room, turned back to smile companionably at Chris. Patiently? "Just picked it up. Around."

Chris leaned forward in his chair, eager fan to big-league hitter. "Yeah, but that sock you took! I mean, how in hell . . . I've never seen anything like that! The guy was a bull!"

"He wasn't that big. Anyway, it's all done with mirrors."

Chris blinked. "How's that?"

Frank, eyes on Matty again, turned distracted to Chris. He's so blasé about the evening, Chris kept thinking, as if events like this happened to him all the time. Maybe they did.

Frank gave the coffee table his drink, stood, motioned Chris up with his hands. "It's easy, I'll teach you."

Chris stood wearily, warily. It had been a long night.

Frank motioned again. "Put up your dukes."

From the kitchen, coolly: "Chris? The baby . . . the noise . . ."

Frank waved her off. "This won't take a second." Took a stance, feet shoulder-width, frame loose, arms dangling. "Okay, Chris, hit me."

Chris hesitated, uncomfortable, made a wry face, threw a weak punch just past the other's chin.

Frank's eyes rolled. "No, no, *hit* me, Chris. Put something behind it. Don't worry, you won't connect."

Chris licked his lips. *Oh, I won't huh.* He'd boxed in college. "You're the boss. Ready?"

Frank smiled.

Chris swung with determination. Missed.

Frank heaved exasperation. "Look, are you going to screw around like some fairy, or do you want to know how to do this?"

Chris bristled, sensed goading, smiled reciprocally.

From the kitchen: "Frank, please."

Frank shrugged. "Hey, you want to be married to a pussy, it's your business."

No longer smiling, Chris dropped his hands. "All right, Frank."

Frank eyed him levelly. "All right, what? Maybe I should have let those guys squeeze Matty's tits."

Chris, with his best right, struck him, the sound cracking around the room.

Frank's head might have turned slightly, nothing more. He hadn't budged from his stance, smiling brightly at Chris. "See? A trick!"

Chris stared at his own fist. "I . . . did I connect?"

"You did not."

"But I heard."

Frank smiled, smacked his hands together below his waist and to one side, making the cracking sound. "Sounds real, no?"

Chris, impressed, showed it. "Then the guy never even touched you!"

Frank winked. "But he *thought* he touched me, or at least he was confused about it. Which made him an easy target. The trick is being somewhere you're not *supposed* to be."

Chris nodded in comprehension. Damn. His best right.

Frank took another stance. "Okay, hit me again."

"I'm going to take a shower," Matty announced, brushing past them stiffly, leaving a scented breeze that pulled both men.

Frank, cowed, dropped his hands. "Hey, don't let me keep you kids up." He consulted his wrist. "Christ, after eleven. I'd better find a hotel."

Chris leaped in like a lost brother. "Are you serious? Don't be silly; you'll stay the night."

Frank shook it off gallantly. "You weren't expecting company. I couldn't."

"Don't be silly," Chris heard himself repeating, "we wouldn't have it any other way, would we, Matty?" He half turned, stopping his wife midway on the second-floor stairs. "Right, honey?"

She paused impassively, one hand on the rail, smiled wanly, resignedly? She looks old, Chris thought.

"Of course," she echoed, gracious and nearly sincere.

From the pit of the living room the two men watched her, heads up, drinks in hands, backlit in fireplace glow, faces cast in protruding Adam's apples. Matty wanted, in her dragging exhaustion, very much to hurl something.

"Well, I'll take that shower now. See you in the morning, Frank."

"Hey, thanks, kitten." But she was gone.

Chris looked after her a moment, turned back to his guest. "She's worn out, poor kid. We had another little run-in with those guys earlier today."

Frank sat back, picked up his nearly empty glass. "Oh? And it seems such a nice, quiet little community."

"Yeah. Jerks. Let me get you a refill." He took Frank's glass, moved toward the kitchen. "Tourists. The price you pay, I suppose."

Franked nodded in sympathy from the living room. "I suppose. On the other hand, I'd give much for a setup like this!" He glanced about expansively. "And all because of good old Uncle Miltie!"

Chris, pouring, nearly slopped it, looked up. "I thought his name was Uncle Arky."

Frank never faltered. "Oh, yes, they called him that too. Some people called him Uncle Sam. Imagine? A lot of people, in fact. Good old Uncle Sam."

"How strange," Chris said, proffering fresh drinks.

"Isn't it? Almost like something you'd call the government."

"That he had so many nicknames, I mean. Why was that, do you think?"

Frank took a sip, shrugged. "Got me there. I only know I'm grateful as hell for my part of the will. I dare say you and Matty feel the same about the house." He smacked his lips appreciatively. "Good drink."

"Thanks." Chris settled across from him.

"Of course, of the two of us, you got the indisputably better bargain."

Chris raised a brow. "You think? I don't know, that's a hell of a car."

"Yes, but Matty . . ."

"Oh. You mean Matty. Yes. There's only one Matty."

Frank watched him, smacking. "Yes, indeed. Only one." He leaned forward on a sudden impulse, smile winning. "Tell me something confidentially, will you?"

"Sure, anything."

"I can be candid?"

"Of course."

"Is she a good fuck?"

Chris, choked, caught it, coughed, blinked, looked for the bad joke in the other's eyes, and didn't find it.

Yet Frank grinned disarmingly. "I mean, does she *like to* be fucked, as it were." He shook his head reflectively, leaning back again with the drink. "I always got the feeling she wasn't truly enjoying it with me."

Chris swallowed thickly, feeling drink and something more burning, the room listing slightly to port, barely aware of the glass in his hand. "What are you talking about?" he managed, hot-faced.

Frank appraised him innocently. "My first wife. Didn't I mention I was married before?"

"I don't think so."

Frank nodded, studied his glass contemplatively. "Marcia. Sweet little Marcia. And please understand me, it isn't as though the sex was wholly unsatisfying—for me anyway." He shook his head as if shaking away the unfathomable. "I just never felt she was really a part of it somehow, do you know what I mean?"

Chris cleared phlegm with another swallow. "I suppose . . ."

Frank nodded. "But for your part, Matty seems to enjoy it, does she?"

Chris set down his drink. "Frank, really, that's a pretty personal question, don't you think?"

Frank considered intently. "I'm sorry, I suppose it is." Then brightened. "But say, we're family, right?"

Chris, limply: "Well, yes, but—"

"I mean, Chris, let's face it, I practically grew up with that little freckle-faced kid. She was like a sister to me."

A sister you skinny-dipped with, Chris thought.

"I had her for the first part of her life, you have her for the second, right?"

Chris sat back. "That's not exactly the way I would have termed it."

"No? Listen, I think I know Matty well enough to judge whether she'd object to a harmless discussion about sex."

"I never said discussing sex per se was inappropriate—"

Frank held up flat palms. "You're right, of course. Sex *should* be a private matter between two people." He reached for his drink, then winked impishly. "Or between one person if the night is long and companionship scarce, right?"

Chris returned an uncertain smile.

"Just answer me this one thing, though, in all candor—and this is not something I would ask someone outside the family. I think you must know how fond I am of you, Chris."

"What is it?"

"In all candor now . . . does she suck you?"

Chris slammed down his glass, sloshing liquid across the glass top, *TV Guide*. "What the hell, Frank?"

Frank with the palms again. "You're absolutely right—that was indelicate. Compromising our friendship. A friendship that, believe me, I've grown to covet. I apologize. Sincerely. Forgiven?"

Chris mopped with a napkin.

Springer tinkled ice in his hand. "But you know, Chris," circling back, "there is one thing you'll have to concede. Without sex—and I'm talking good clean, wholesome sex here between consenting adults—without it, you two would never have had something as wonderful as that sweet little boy sleeping upstairs. Now, tell me I'm wrong."

"I'll grant you that."

Frank nodded enthusiasm. "I'd give my right arm to have a great kid like that. Who wouldn't? Aside from my dear wife, that is. Oh no, not her. Wouldn't have it, didn't want kids, not by me anyway. Didn't think I'd make a proper father. Now, I ask you, Chris, and be honest with me, do I look like insubstantial father material?"

Chris stalled. "It's really none of my—"

He broke off. Frank wasn't even looking at him. He was staring somewhere beyond Chris's shoulder.

Chris turned, followed the other's gaze. "What?"

Frank Springer rose slowly, eyes unwavering, strode calmly but purposefully to the west window. He stared out at what, to Chris, was flat blackness. "How far away did you say your closest neighbors were?"

Chris set down his drink, rose. "Miles away. You see lights?"

Frank said nothing. Stared.

Chris walked over, stood beside him, tried to follow his gaze. Blackness without. "What is it?"

Frank put his hands in his pockets casually. "Someone out there . . ."

Chris felt something turn in his stomach. He stared intently, until the pane congealed and he had to blink it away. "I don't see anything. How can you see anything in that dark?"

Frank turned from the window, retrieved his drink with a wave of indifference. "Well, maybe it was a deer. Or something." He swallowed, finishing the glass, handed it to Chris. "Still, I'd close those drapes if I were you. The house is well locked, I trust."

Chris licked his lips. "Well . . . yes. I sometimes don't bother. Way out here."

Frank nodded. "I'd start bothering if I were you." He stretched, yawned mightily, all smiles again, slapping his host on the back. "Chris, old man, I'm going to turn in if you don't mind."

"Of course. Your room is just down the hall, the far right."

Frank nodded, regarded the staircase. "Mine and Matty's, you mean."

Chris stared blankly at him.

Frank barked a harsh laugh, turned, slapped Chris on the back. "That expression! Chris, you're priceless. See you in the morning, old man." He paused at the foot of the stairs. "Really appreciate this, Chris. Truly."

"Don't mention it."

Frank hesitated, took a step back down. "Don't suppose you have an extra rifle? Thought maybe we'd get in a little hunting in the morning before my plane. If you have time, of course."

Chris considered. "Well, yes, I have an extra gun."

Frank winked. "Great, it's a date. Sleep tight." He ascended the stairs cheerfully.

Leaving Chris holding both glasses in the middle of the empty living room, wondering: What plane? To where? From where?

He'd never gotten around to asking.

When he climbed in, Matty was already long gone, sawing gently, exhausted.

Chris crept next to her carefully, kissed her cheek, felt himself stir at her perfume, snapped off the light, and touched her smooth shoulder, reaching down and around to the languorous swell of her breast. She stirred, did not awaken. He kissed her shoulder, lay back, arms behind his head. He'd wanted to talk to her about Frank.

But he really didn't know about what.

He lay quietly for a time, searching for sleep, not finding it, snapping the light back on, craning around and finding John Antler Horn's iceboating book.

He flipped through it desultorily: "*. . . when two yachts are running free with the wind on different sides, the yacht which has the wind on the port side shall keep out of the way of the other. . . .*"

Chris closed his eyes a moment, tried to imagine what the big lake would look like frozen solid. What the wind would feel like against his face, the iceboat whipping across the silvery surface . . .

He fell asleep that way, book in hand.

C H A P T E R

Sun in his eyes, Chris woke later than he'd have liked—past eight—thick-tongued and foggy: the highballs.

Matty was not beside him, her side cool.

He stretched in place, grunted, the good morning smells of bacon and coffee wafting up temptingly from below. Bless her. Trying to amend for last night's aloofness.

Chris kicked back sheets, sat to the accompaniment of cerebral ice picks. Jesus.

He let the picks have their way there on the edge of mattress, let them segue to dull throbs, pushed up finally, made his way to the bathroom. One look was enough. Okay, no more late-night drinking.

The others had probably been up for hours. Christ, had Frank mentioned something about hunting this morning? Please, no. He groped for his robe.

The spikes returned on his way downstairs, each step a not gentle reminder, but the coffee smell nearly intoxicating now. Where had Matty gotten it? It smelled fresh brewed.

He came into the kitchen and found Frank, bushy tailed and swathed in an apron, pouring bacon grease into an empty carton. "Top of the morning, old man."

Matty was not to be found.

"Come sit, the coffee's hot."

"Smells great." Chris shuffled to the butcher block.

"Cuban mocha, the best! These cups okay? I got them above the sink."

"Fine. Did you make all this by yourself? Where's Matty?"

Frank poured fresh-squeezed juice like an efficient waiter. "Sleeping, I assumed. Wasn't she with you?"

Chris shook his head, sipping gratefully. The coffee *was* superb. "She goes in with Nicky sometimes in the middle of the night if he wakes up. Falls asleep in there with him."

"I see. How's the coffee?"

"Fabulous. Is it yours?"

"Take it everywhere I go, can't do without it. How do you like your eggs?"

"Listen, you're the guest."

"Sunny-side up?"

"You really don't have to. I'm not that hungry anyway, Frank, thanks."

"Nonsense, can't hunt deer on an empty stomach. I make a huevos rancheros that will knock your socks off."

"All right. Listen, don't expect much out there. I haven't seen that many deer around here."

"Really? Saw some this morning. Pair of does."

Chris reached for the cream. "How long have you been up?"

"Oh, before dawn. Went for a long walk, hope you don't mind. Wanted to check around, you know."

Chris set down his cup with a clink. "No, I don't know. What do you mean?"

Frank doled out bacon. "For signs of our friends."

Chris tightened, regarded with sudden loss of appetite the sizzling meat. "And? Did you find anything?"

Frank savaged yolks in the steel pan, whipped expertly, added cheese, chopped onion, salsa. "I don't suppose you have tortillas on hand? Never mind. Hard to say. Very rocky ground around here. Human tracks, all right, I'm just not sure how old. Don't worry about it this morning; enjoy your breakfast."

Chris leaned back, head pounding, appraised the man's broad, aproned back. "What is it you said you did for a living, Frank?"

Back to him, Frank said, "I'm employed by the government. Occasionally. Didn't I mention?"

"Occasionally? How does that work?"

Frank turned to him with a grin, then a frown. "Say, you look dreadful. Headache?"

Chris nodded into his coffee. "A beaut. I don't usually drink that much, certainly not that late."

Frank snapped his fingers theatrically. "I've got the answer in my car. Sit tight." And he left the kitchen.

Chris sat listening to his stomach growl, then heave at the thought of the food that would relieve it. He looked to the wall clock: 8:30. It was weird being up like this without Matty and the baby. Maybe he'd better go check on them.

Frank returned, proffering an amber vial, extracted two pale tablets, placed them atop his host's neatly folded napkin. "The only true cure for hangovers."

Chris was in too much pain to argue. He swallowed, washing them down with the delicious coffee.

"Count to three and your troubles will be gone. What were we discussing, Chris?"

"You were about to tell me what you do for a living." He looked up just in time to see his Remington being tossed at him.

He caught it, miraculously, without breaking anything at the table, thinking, *That* was a dangerously careless thing to do.

"Locked and loaded!" Frank winked. "Eat up and we're out of here."

Chris leaned the black muzzle carefully against the butcher-block edge, checking to make sure the safety was on. How do you admonish a guy who probably saved you a great deal of grief the night before? He settled for: "I'll have to check on Matty and the baby first. And I'd like to grab a shower."

"Shower when you get back; you'll need it. How's the head?"

Chris paused in midthought. He looked up at his grinning guest. "Damn. It's gone."

Frank winked.

"What *was* that stuff?"

Frank laughed, shoveled himself bloodied eggs. "Old family recipe."

He couldn't find the new hiking boots Matty had bought him last week (he'd stuck the box *somewhere*), so he settled for his old tennis shoes. They wouldn't be going that far from the house anyway. He hoped.

He stood over Nicky's tiny bed, gazing at his wife, gold and pink as a glowing Delacroix, curled and cramped and perfectly content around their blissful son. Nicky snored softly in the crook of her arm, their skin lambent as marble in buttery morning glow. Matty, twisted in the blue translucent nightie he'd bought at Frederick's in the Valley as a joke, stretched soft and sleek, the silly outfit's feathery boa hem riding temptingly past bikini panties, long, bare legs coquette-lazy across rumpled sheets. Her tousled, burnished crown spilled over pillow and child. Matty the sexy mommy.

He kissed both foreheads, Nicky's damp with childhood dreams, mommy's cool and lingering with sleepy perfume.

I love you, he mouthed silently. Sleep tight, my precious babies, my life.

He straightened, eased shut the blinds, smiled proudly, then thought of investigating that deliciously vulgar nightie later tonight.

He turned, startled to find Frank framed in the doorway. "Everything okay?" Springer whispered with pleasant concern.

Chris stiffened at the intrusion. Let it go. Nodded, guided Springer out, shutting the door softly.

In the kitchen, Frank said, "What was it you were asking me before?"

Chris rummaged in the high kitchen cabinet, fishing behind canned goods for shells.

"Already got 'em." Frank grinned behind him, rattling the box. "My own brand."

Chris set his box atop the counter, turned from the cabinet not really surprised. "You were telling me what it was you did for a living."

He cradled his Remington uneasily.

He had never been on this side of the mountain before. Chris loved the out-of-doors but was no Boy Scout; the idea of getting lost lurked furtively at the back of his brain.

Frank, on the other hand, dressed to the nines in expensive Eddie Bauer outdoors attire, seemed in his element, the big rifle dangling confidently from his hand, eyes on the trail ahead. Which was no trail at all that Chris could discern, just a sort of narrow passage between fir and scrub and tumbled stone. The lake was somewhere to their north, blocked by ragged ridge. Or so he thought. Was pretty sure. Beyond the ridges Bale's Peak gloried in the season's first dusting of snow, blue-shadowed crevasses against deeper cobalt sky.

"And then after college," Frank continued his litany of the past forty minutes, detailed and exacting but coming no closer to revealing anything about his current state of employment, "I worked in a shoe store for a while. Got bored of that. Joined the army. Got bored of that, joined the navy. Got bored of that."

"Wait a second!" Chris puffed red-cheeked, mounting a steep rise, the tennis shoes already hurting. "How is it you managed to hop around to various branches of the service like that? Do you suppose we could stop a second, catch a drink?"

Frank was standing very still at the top of a rocky knoll—not winded, composed—sentinel-silent as the skinny pine flanking him. "You drink too much," he reflected softly, gazing at something out past Chris's range.

"Too much *water*?"

"It's getting hot. Water can blow you up like a pig."

"Well, what the hell are we doing, Frank, hiking or hunting?"

No answer, just a slow, authoritative rise of Frank's flat palm sending Chris into silence, making him abruptly aware of his own loud, clumsy stomping.

Frank stood motionless, part of the mountain.

Heart tripping, Chris struggled to his side, tried to get his breath. "What's the matter?"

Springer stared into vast, undulating canyons of rock, an unending vista of veridian and burnt umber.

Chris glanced about them. Saw only wilderness. He couldn't even spot the damn lake. "Is it a deer?"

Frank squinted.

A crow mocked the silence sharply, jabbing adrenaline into Chris's heart. "Damn birds."

Frank fingered his weapon's safety. "Someone's with us. . . ."

Chris felt his scalp tighten. He swallowed. "With us? Who?"

Frank said nothing, stared into emptiness. He turned, finally to Chris, face like stone. "Stay here." And walked off.

"Wait a second! Where you going, Frank?"

"Stay where I told you."

And then wasn't there anymore.

Chris on broken shale, sweating lightly, made a 180-degree

turn, saw nothing but pine, and rock and more rock. No Frank, and no one else.

He waited. The sun peaked behind a canopy of firs, flies making him quickly swipe his eyes, blink, rub. Still nothing.

"Frank?"

A rattle of stones behind him.

He turned to see Frank twenty yards off, pointing his rifle at him. "Frank? What?"

The report cracked through his skull a millisecond after the weapon jerked in Frank's arms.

I'm dead.

The thought begun but uncompleted as the round—an angry wasp—sliced the air beside his left ear. The shot's knocking echoes following. And Chris realized he was still alive, had not even been the target, because here came Frank full tilt over the rocky slope, rifle no longer in his arms but dangling in one hand. He was rushing past Chris now, rushing back to the top of the rocky knoll, crouched and loping, silent as a panther.

White as death, Chris faced him, frog-eyed.

Frank turned, shaking his head. "Missed him."

Chris, legs draining away, his own rifle a foreign anvil in his sagging arm, tried to form words. "You *shot* at someone!"

"Pretty sure I missed him."

Chris—flushed with adrenaline-induced fury—almost hurled his rifle to the earth. "You just took a potshot at somebody? What the hell? What if it was just some hunter?"

He trailed off under Frank's unwavering gaze. "Chris, he was drawing a bead on you."

The world was going white now. "What?"

"If I hadn't pulled down on him, we'd be picking up your brains right now. These guys mean business."

Chris swallowed constriction, bladder burning suddenly. "The guys from last night?"

Frank nodded. "At least two of them. I thought at first they only wanted me, but—*shit!*" face abruptly taut.

"What—*what!*"

"Matty."

"Matty?"

Frank seemed to consider a moment, then gripped the other man's shoulder until it hurt. "Can you find your way to the dock?"

"The dock?"

"Chris, stop repeating everything. Can you get to the dock from here? It's just down that gorge, through those trees, see?" and he pointed.

"I guess, sure. What are we doing?"

"Bastards. They may have lured us from the house so they could double back and get to Matty."

"Lured us?"

"Chris, I've been tracking them for the last hour. I didn't count on there being more than two of them. Now, can you get to the dock, or not? I want you safely out on the lake, if they haven't gotten to your boat, that is."

"Where are *you* going?"

"I can reach the house more quickly alone, Chris. Better get going now."

Chris turned, batting more sweat from his eyes, turned back. "Wait a second, I want to go with you."

"Chris, *think*. What if they surround us? We double our chances if we split up."

Chris was floating along with the nightmare now, a heady, spaced-out feeling. Like before when Nicky—"Well, what the hell am I going to do on the damn lake?"

"Don't you see, the boat is the quickest way to get help. Now will you for Christ's sake get *moving*?" This last a barked command that made Chris flinch, back up a step.

Finally he turned, trotted unenthusiastically away. A few pebble-strewn yards, then he craned back yet again. "This way?"

Frank sighed impatience, pawed through his wool-lined jacket, flipped Chris something silvery with glare that he caught one-handed: a compass.

"You know how to use one of those things?"

"Yes. Pretty much."

"The dock is due north. Just follow the needle."

"All right."

"Now, *go!*"

Chris ran.

He was still running, ten minutes later, when he realized he should have spotted the lake long before now, that, despite what the damn needle said, there was nothing around, before, behind, or near him but rock and more rock.

He came to a jagged crest, a high, morning-cool bluff. He stood leaning on his arms, breathing heavily, realized he was probably an open target, but *had* to get his breath, access his location.

He felt vulnerable and strangely out of sync with the living. Altitude sickness?

And then, there it was below and to the left, just the smallest wedge of blue lake, not north at all but nearly northeast. Could Frank have been wrong? He looked at his watch for no reason: 10:06.

Something not right.

It kept pulling his mind toward the house.

But where was the damn house now? Was that the south end of the lake or the west? You couldn't tell jack shit from up here. He cursed exasperation. Why the hell had they *moved* out here in the middle of goddamn nowhere?

Don't just *stand* here!

Better do as Frank says: Start formulating your own plans now and you'll screw everything up.

To his astonishment he found himself gazing into the black, fathomless eyes of a deer that might have been standing there forever. A whitetail. What they'd supposedly come up here for, its dun rump to him, head swiveled around, big ears pricked wide. When it ran, the tail would go up, a white flag to warn its brethren.

Chris tucked the compass away, hefted the rifle, started down the steep incline toward the distant, glimmering wedge of blue.

He knew, halfway down, that the incline was too steep for the tennis shoes, was composed of loose shale and gravel, not solid rock, and that he'd have to start running very fast now or throw himself down to get out of it.

He chose the former, arms pinwheeling, eyes wide, the cliff face like ice now.

No. Shit. "Stop!"

The shale ended not in level ground but yet steeper cliff. A deep gorge that—unless he could snag a sapling, a rock, something for purchase—he'd be spilling over.

Legs churning, he was caught in helpless inertia, falling in a rain of gravel and dirt, thigh and knee shredding under torn jeans. He tried to dig in with the tennis shoes—the worthless damn tennis shoes—but could not. Should have taken the time to look for the hiking boots. Here comes the edge of the cliff. Here comes the end of your life.

Matty, in morning light, kissing his cheek. *I love you, Christopher Nielson*, so lovely in morning light, and what would she do now and how would Nicky make it possibly make it without a father . . . ?

CHAPTER 7

Matty woke gasping, wide-eyed attentive, knowing all immediately, instinctive as a mother lioness.

She turned, checked the Aladdin clock on Nicky's bureau anyway, felt the attendant painful hitch through crusted lashes: 9:26.

And the baby was still asleep.

Something was dreadfully wrong.

She placed a trembling palm to his curly forehead, found it warm, damp but not alarmingly hot. Yet. She shook him urgently. "Nicky!"

Received a groggy blink, a slurred, "Pancake . . . ?"

Matty pulled him up to a sitting position, patting his cheek, heart lurching again at his dull pupils, lolling head. "Baby?"

And he was asleep again immediately. Shit, *shit*!

She scrambled up and found herself inside the silly nightie.

A cold chill, replaced immediately by a colder one.

She'd gone to bed in her flannels. Had Chris put her in this outfit?

God, please let it have been Chris.

She hit the hall running, already knowing the bedroom would be empty, which it was.

She floated down the staircase in a kind of dream, a nightmare, skidded on kitchen parquet to be greeted by more emptiness, lingering breakfast smells, two butcher-block chairs turned out.

She turned away. Turned back, eyes falling on the box of rifle shells atop the counter.

Adrenaline seized her. *Chris!*

She spun, swept to the front door, heaved it back with a wall-shuddering *whunk!*

In crisp morning light, Frank Springer's Lamborghini shone dully under a patina of dew, their drabber Volvo skulking in its shadow. Escaping her notice to the west, a black phalanx of clouds marched resolutely.

He's taken Chris into the woods!

With guns! Stupid! How could you be so stupid!

She whirled, replacing thought with action, lunged for the phone. Of course it was dead.

Matty stood trembling barefoot on the freezing floor, palsied as an old woman and as impotent.

Do something!

Nicky.

She lunged upstairs.

Must think. Must *think*. With Frank, the worst possible scenario loomed: Chris is dead.

Frank wants the child.

She hit the upstairs landing whining like an animal, skidded burning heels before Nicky's room, and made herself stop, made herself catch her breath and think, *think!* It's all you have now, your mind. Outwit him.

All right, all right.

The baby's okay, merely drugged.

As were you.

Not the orange juice—he hadn't spiked that—she'd kept that nearby last night, never let it out of her hand. He must have crept into Nicky's room late last night, administered a syringe.

She rubbed her arms absently for sore spots. God, did he know the proper dosage for a child? Would Nicky lapse into coma?

She ran to him again, lifted the tiny body roughly. "Nicky!"

The child blinked in lassitude, mouthed something unintelligible. She felt his forehead again, his wrists, ankles. He seemed all right, just out of it.

Get him out of here!

But Chris. Had he drugged Chris too?

Never mind, save the child! It's what Chris would want!

She rushed to the window, swept back the drapes, squinted into lancing sunlight. The drive—but for the cars—was empty, as was the side yard, what she could see of the back.

She spun, grabbed her robe, shrugging into it, stopped. No. Get properly dressed, get your purse and money; you'll need them.

She grabbed her tennis shorts, threw on the red knit sweater from Robinsons-May, braless, ignored socks, and shoved into old loafers, body shaking, shaking, she could not stop shaking.

Grabbed baby clothes in fistfuls from Nicky's bureau, found an old Toys "R" Us sack, stuffed it, swept the baby into her arms, and ran makeupless for the bedroom.

She snatched her purse, quick-checked for cash, found eight dollars, grabbed the checkbook (thinking of Chris again), shouldered the purse, and ran downstairs, baby in her arms.

She faltered on the stairs. Below, the front door was standing open.

Frank waiting on the other side.

She slowed, cradling Nicky, eased onto the hall carpet.

Matty stood staring at the trees without, the sky, the driveway, and two automobiles (escape) beyond.

Had she merely left the front door open herself? She couldn't remember.

Screw it, run!

Matty ran.

She hit cool morning breeze and starling song, lovely blue sky above. No one pounced at her from the sides of the house. Nicky blinked once in bright sunlight, turned his head, and snoozed in the crook of her arm. Just as well.

She couldn't hold him and juggle the keys at the same time. She must set him down somewhere.

She twisted in sudden panic, sure she'd heard a noise from the edge of woods, her heart jolting painfully again.

Nothing. Easy.

She lay Nicky across the sun-baking hood, dug frantically for her keys.

Which were not in her purse.

"Goddamn it!"

In the house? Upstairs? The bedroom bureau? The living room basket? Matty, Matty *think*! She slammed her fist against the locked door, and again, a weird whining sound formed deep in her diaphragm.

She studied a gray wren at the edge of the roof, still missing the approaching storm.

Think, now think. . . . Where did you leave them last?

Probably in the bedroom on the bureau.

"Come, baby!" She lifted the child again, turned, saw the lock tab was up on the opposite door. Considered it. She'd be to the house and back faster without the child.

She came around the Volvo's grille quickly, opened the door, laid Nicky gently across the passenger's seat, cushioning his sweet head. "Mommy will be right back."

He rowed air once with his legs, resumed snoring softly.

Matty dashed back to the house.

Up the stairs, breathless now, dizzy, in the bedroom, found the keys.

She had to make herself slow on the stairs this time.

Fall, break your neck now, and it will all be for nothing.

She cried out in shock at the cannon explosion of thunder shaking the house.

She crossed the living room again and jerked left with a now familiar stab to her chest. Something had surely moved there just at the edge of the woods.

She faltered. Looked out at the silent Volvo.

Came quickly and softly to the front door, shut it more softly. Spun and raced to the back of the house, nearly slipping and losing it on the big hooked rug.

She unlocked the back gingerly, sneaked down the back stoop, circled around the left side, eyes scanning the woods at the edge of the lawn, ears straining, stopping dead at the front corner. She peered carefully around.

Another jolting knock of thunder. Nothing else.

Go. Now. Run.

She sprinted for the car.

The first drops hit her as she yanked at the door.

She jammed in the key—the wrong one—yanked it out with a snap. Jiggled the ring, dropped it in the gravel, cursed, retrieved it, selected carefully with fingers that would *not* find the minute slot. Finally shoved it home and twisted, pulling open the door.

She had it shut again, had the engine started, and her hand on the shift before noticing that Nicky was no longer beside her.

"No!"

She leapt from behind the wheel, screaming his name.

"Nicky!"

She scanned the gravel drive, the wall of tangled brush and looming pine disappearing now in a curtain of rain. Dear God, he could be anywhere!

"Nicky! Baby!"

Matty raced to the edge of the woods, peered into the impenetrable shadow and secret dread. Snakes. Streams soon swollen to rushing torrents.

"Damn you to *hell*!" and she meant, mostly, herself.

She turned, hair matted, looking back over her shoulder. A child would be attracted to that which is most familiar. The house.

She raced back, skidding on rain-slick gravel, raking tender knees (Betty Grable knees, Chris had said, and now they were ruined), ignored pain, blood, racing, bounding the short steps, grabbing the bronze handle before remembering she'd locked it from the inside.

She collapsed back against the wooden frame sobbing, hitching with frustration, sputtering his name in a garbled shriek: "Nicky!"

Thunder snatched and flung her cry into distant timber.

Silence, but for her soft keening, the droning patter, chuckling eaves.

And, magically, the door opened behind her, nearly upsetting her, opening wider. She gained her footing, looking up, finding him grinning sleepily up at her—

"Mama . . ."

She swept him up, squeezed him against the damp, smelly red sweater, kissed his soft cheek, and saw behind him in the relative dark of the outside storm, the rangy silhouette of what she prayed was her husband but knew with knife-edge instinct was surely not.

Revived with the first droplets, then blinking back the ensuing torrent, Chris covered his face with torn fingers, rolled left on shrieking shoulder muscles, and found himself living still.

Living and even able to sit, eventually stand with the support of the rifle that Providence had divined should fall nearby. It had been a long drop—he remembered that much—but not a strictly sheer one as he'd feared.

He looked up into stinging rain, saw the branch-twisted, sapling-snapped path of his descent, and farther down, the crawling thicket of Rocky Mountain timber pine at canyon bottom that doubtless cushioned—and saved—his plummeting form. He ached in every pore. Yet he lived.

And walked, with some effort.

And, finally, began to remember the rest.

He checked his watch, found the crystal shattered.

He recalled, dully, Frank's plan, but having no idea how long he'd been out, dismissed it as moot. If Matty had truly been in danger, the danger was probably already to her. Going for help in the boat now (if the boat still existed) seemed fruitless and time-wasting. His best option was to return to the house as quickly as possible, assuming nothing was broken or badly sprained, which would be a miracle. Probably Frank and Matty were looking for him even now.

The fastest route would be straight up again, but at this vantage point that necessitated forbidding rock walls he had neither the strength nor experience to attempt. The next-quickest way would be straight across, but that held its own kind of problems: the vegetation was thick here, the rain making visibility limited. He could miss the house altogether, or worse, become lost.

The safest route was probably via the lake shore, even though this meant losing ground and time. With the familiar shore as guide, even in this deluge, he could find his way, circle around, locate their dock, be up the path and to the house within, what— two hours, three?

All right. That was the plan, then. Better get going before pneumonia set in.

He took a few gingerly strides. His legs seemed okay, though there was a terrible stitch in his left side that was either a superficial injury from a broken branch or something deeper and worse. There was no time to check now.

Blood pinked his forearms from a thousand tiny cuts the steady rain kept washing clean. He had a terrible headache, which was to be expected, he supposed, but he kept resisting the temptation to reach up there and feel about, maybe find part of his brain dangling loose.

The tennis shoes were a joke. Ripped and torn, one flap of sole made downward progress even more torturous.

He knew the lake was near but couldn't see it. If there were motor craft out in this downpour, the drum of rain on vegetation masked it.

He began reviewing old Boy Scout training, everything he'd ever read in the old, dog-eared manuals around summer campfires.

He knew the lake was near the lowest level of elevation, in his youth had studied and thus memorized the visible sequence vegetation undergoes descending a mountain, North American mountains at any rate.

The timber line is near the top, marking the zone of alpine tundra. Below that comes stunted, ground-hugging vegetation; a German word—krummholz?—something like that. Academic, anyway, he was well below that level surely.

He was surrounded by what he knew was mainly spruce and Douglas fir. They had a symbiotic relationship, these trees, the precise details of which he could not conjure: something about the slow-growing spruce living longer, the rapidly growing fir spreading seeds that help keep mountain slopes from erosion. Nature's unbeatable system. There had been a pen-and-ink drawing illustrating the process in the second chapter.

Farther below he'd find an abundance of ponderosa pine, and lower still the first junipers and broad-leaved trees surrounding the lake.

And in between rock and more rock.

Taking it slowly but also deliberately, rifle as crutch, girding himself with the conviction that Frank had probably already gotten there—protecting Matty and baby from any untoward incident— Chris picked his way down and down to the dancing surface of the lake.

Haggard and miserable, with no makeup and less incentive, Matty slipped into the nothing pink panties, pulled the sheer novelty nightie over her head.

In the downstairs bathroom reflection, she looked ludicrous as a saloon stripper: breasts barely veiled, hair still damp and matted from the rain, and no comb handy. Strange, that even under such bizarre circumstances, the urge to groom, look presentable, persisted.

She stepped into the fuzzy pink high-heel slippers, sighed resignation, opened the bathroom door, and went out to let him see it.

He was still in the tan Eames chair, rifle still across his knees, the long black muzzle in line with the sofa across the room. The sofa and Nicky's tousled head.

The child had awakened enough to open the door sleepily, recognize his mother, then drift off again in her arms.

Frank, cold and unheedful of her pleas, had administered another hypo into the child's slender arm. To Matty's horror, Nicky's sleep had thickened.

Matty stepped into the living room in her ridiculous outfit and faced him. "Now. Will you tell me?"

Frank took his time assessing her. "Turn around."

"Frank . . ."

"Turn around, I want to see the other side."

She did.

"Nice. You haven't gained a pound. I wasn't sure before, in the dark."

"You said you'd tell me where he is."

He leaned back, relishing the control, as he always had, smiling contentment. "Did you rouge your nipples?"

"There's no makeup in there."

"Well, where then?"

"In my purse. You said you'd tell me."

He shifted and the dark muzzle shifted with him. If it went off by accident, it would take the child's head and most of the couch. "He's alive."

Despite his propensity for lying, she felt herself breathe evenly again. "Where?"

Frank shrugged, gestured at the moving, gelatinous panes. "Out there somewhere. The lake, I suppose."

"The lake?"

"Your vulva looks terrific in that thing. Accents the pout. Did he fuck you in it often?"

"Why the lake?"

Frank sighed in boredom. "What do we have to drink?"

Matty looked to the kitchen. "What would you like? A beer?"

"God, no, your husband has no taste in ale. Any champagne?"

"There might be a bottle, I'll see."

He grinned. "And I'll watch you fetch it!"

She poured him his drink. "The men, last night. You knew them, yes?"

She looked up in time to see him nod, smiling.

"Pour yourself one, kitten."

She hesitated, didn't feel like fighting him, found another glass.

She needed to get him moved, get the bore of that rifle from Nicky's head.

"Who were they, Frank?"

He took the drink from her. "Now, who do you think they were?"

Suddenly she did need the drink. She swallowed, winced past bubbles. "You're lying."

"Okay."

She had another drink. "Why? Why would they?"

He crossed his legs, grinning wide, thoroughly enjoying it all, the rifle moving too but not out of the line of fire. "Seems I'm popular again."

She nodded to herself. As if he ever weren't popular. "They know, then. They know you're here, all about you."

"They're *why* I'm here, sugar. Does he fuck you in the woods as well? Out under the stars? The leaves sticking to your beautiful white ass?"

She set her drink on the wicker end table. "May I please get dressed? I'm cold."

"Really? I've been cold for years. Years, Matty. Do you have any idea what that's like?"

She turned on him. "A very *good* idea, yes."

He retained the good-natured grin. "You're saying I wasn't a warm lover? An attentive lover?"

"If attentive means ropes and leather and bruising."

"And phone cords." He chuckled liquidly. "You loved it."

"Sure, I did. It's why I ran away. Can I ask you to move that gun? It's pointed right at Nicky's head."

"I know exactly where it's pointed."

"Please. I'm not giving you any trouble."

"You're not giving me much of anything yet."

She turned away.

"Where did he fuck you when the baby was conceived?"

She hesitated by the big picture window, eyes on the rain-swept woods. Stay away, Chris. Stay away from here my darling. He'll kill you too. "I already told you; the child is yours."

Another soft chuckle. "And I'm supposed to believe that?"

"Believe what you like." But thinking, No, please believe that! If you believe that, you may not harm the baby.

Frank turned his head languidly, appraised the sleeping child.

"I don't have to believe anything, though, do I? Except a blood test."

She forced her voice steady. "That's true."

"And there's plenty of time for that. Please pull the curtains."

She turned to him. "Why? The neighbors are miles away."

"Pull the curtains. All of them. And turn off the lights."

She did as she was told, fighting back queasiness. "Can we put the baby to bed before . . . ?"

"Before what?"

She sighed. "Before we do it."

"Do what?"

She ground her teeth. "Can we at least put the child upstairs?"

He grinned. "And you'd carry him up, of course, and open the window, slip out, get that lovely get-up all wet with rain."

"Frank, for God's sake, come with me if you want."

He considered. "Can we do it in your bedroom?"

She turned back to the drapes, mumbling.

"How's that?"

"Whatever you *want!*" she hissed.

He chuckled. "You're being oh so cooperative. Are you buying time, is that it? Do you think you have time to buy, Matty?"

She sat wearily on the arm of the sofa. "I don't know what I have, Frank. Only what I don't have anymore."

He feigned sympathy. "Ah, poor thing. Five years with the wealthiest, most brilliant covert artist in the business—five years living in the lap of luxury in a style of wealth and glamour any woman would kill for—and you run off and find this idiot phone pole jockey and get yourself knocked up. You finally discover that motherhood and true love are really what life's all about. Is that the problem, poopie?"

She watched her sleeping son.

"I mean, am I supposed to feel sorry for you in this situation, is that it?"

She spun. "*No!* You're not supposed to feel a goddamn thing! When did you ever, Frank?"

His face melted to stone. "You incredible bitch. I loved you."

And she *had* to laugh at that, a kind of gagging chirp. Which she immediately regretted from his expression. She stiffened.

Don't push him. Ease off.

She sighed, as if the gesture would shirk the sudden tension. *Keep the conversation going, keep it going. . . .* Not sure at all what

she was stalling for. "I was tired. I was lonely. And I was not prepared to let that become the rest of my life. I'm not proud that I
ran."

"But you'd do it again?"

She shook her head. "What's the point of all this? Why don't
you just do whatever it is you intend?"

She jumped then as she heard him cock the gun.

He aligned the barrel precisely with Nicky's temple. "Did he
ever fuck you up the ass?"

"Frank."

"That's what they do where they sent me, you know. Among
other things. Many other things. One guy screamed for two days
solid. Not because he took it up the ass, but because he wouldn't
let them. Fine, they said, that's okay. And they sewed it shut for
him."

She closed her eyes. "Do you want me to beg, is that it?"

He shrugged. "I begged them. Doesn't do a whit of good. Not a
whit."

"He's your child, your *son!*"

"So you've said."

"Frank, I've told you I'll do anything. What is it you want me to
do?" She said it with every gram of restraint she could summon,
unable to take her eyes from the wavery black bore.

And, abruptly—in his silence—Matty jerked to Frank's
implacable expression with a revelation of dread. "You shot him,
didn't you."

Frank snorted. Cast his eyes heavenward. "Jesus. A loaded
weapon at your kid's head and all you can think about is adorable
Chris the mountain playwright. I did not kill him. I *will* kill him,
yes. Right before your eyes. And I will spill not one ounce of blood
in the doing. But for now, he lives."

He was around the bend, surely he was around the bend and
over the edge, talking in elliptical absurdities like he used to.

She had to think of some way to get Nicky out of here. If Frank
did make love to her, perhaps he'd go off guard, even fall asleep.

"Frank, he's just a baby, an innocent. Take the gun away. I will
not run, I promise. I'll do whatever it is you want me to. Just please
don't hurt the baby."

He looked placidly at her. "Your baby."

"Our baby!"

He shrugged. "Or perhaps *his* baby?"

"Just move the gun, *please!*"

"Maybe it isn't loaded."

"Please."

He was sipping the rest of his champagne, setting it daintily atop the coffee table.

"In 1584," he began conversationally, "when Ivan the Terrible died, there was no successor left to the throne. During one of his customary rages, the czar had bludgeoned to death his only promising son, Ivan junior."

Matty gazed dully at him, feeling herself draining away from within.

"He had, of course, two other remaining sons, but one—Fedor—was hopelessly retarded, and the other, an infant named Dimitri, had no real status in the line of succession. He was birthed, you see, from the philandering czar's seventh wife, and thus exempt from royalty according to canon law. In the eyes of God, it was unclear, as it were, who the baby actually belonged to. So idiot Fedor became ruler of Russia."

Matty stared at him.

Frank gave an imploring look. "You see, can't you, how capricious the fate of one's lineage can be?"

Matty closed her eyes, wrapping her arms about herself in the absurd nightie.

She needed, desperately, another drink. Was too ashamed to take one with the thought of Chris out there alone somewhere in the cold and rain.

Was thinking these thoughts absently, nearly exhaustion-dreamy, when someone rapped tentatively at the front door.

CHAPTER 8

Chris rapped at the door, having either lost his house keys in the fall or neglected to bring them on the hunt altogether.

He was trembling visibly, though whether from internal hurt, shock, simple chill from the rain-turned-drizzle or what, he could not say. He was miserable, long past exhaustion, maybe in serious need of medical attention. If someone would please just kindly open the door so he could come inside. Hopefully, Frank had already built a roaring, comforting fire (their first in the new home) and Matty had begun making Irish coffees. Most of all, he could just lie down on something soft and dry, a sensation he imagined akin to lying in heavenly pastures.

He rapped again, leaned on the buzzer, rapped harder, pounded, leaned and leaned. Finally shouted her name in a voice so hoarse it chilled him more than the cold drizzle.

Knowing, somehow intuitively, that despite the fact that both sports car and Volvo were parked just down the gravel drive, no one was going to answer.

On the fourth ring, Matty opened her mouth, despite Nicky, and—following the eerie wail of her name—started to shout a reply.

Frank cut if off with a look. "Just let it ring. Let it ring."

Inside, in her heart, she even agreed with him: Yes, let it ring. Let Chris go away.

Because if you somehow get in, darling Chris, Nicky will not be the only one to die.

You cannot fight him, Chris, you cannot defeat him. No one can. Others have tried. I've seen it. I've watched it. It's terrible. And not always swift. You cannot defeat him, darling Chris. You can only run.

And she bowed her head against the hammering and ringing.

I'm so terribly, terribly sorry, Chris.

After a while his bruised and blood-caked knuckles wouldn't take the hammering anymore, and he stepped back, out under the porch and into the cold drizzle again, craned around, saw that all the south-side drapes were drawn tidily together.

Funny. Why were the drapes drawn this time of day? He leaned right and saw the same was true of the north side. He felt a dread beyond even his internal physical pain.

Chris got himself off the porch and walked, then trotted, breathing fast with pain and something else, around to the back of the big A-frame house. Found that locked and draped as well. Felt the dread grow into a cancerous burning hole.

What the hell? . . . What the goddamn hell.

And for good measure he hammered away at one of the big picture windows (a funny kind of give to it, the window—strange he'd never noticed that) fearful at first he might actually break the glass, cut himself, but hell, he was cut up anyway.

Certain now he was not going to get in that way, he was rapidly becoming just as certain that if he didn't get in somewhere soon, he was going to pass out. And out here in the rain and cold that could be more than a little disastrous.

Nicky said, "Pancake . . . ?" eyes still closed.

Matty thought, Oh, Christ, don't talk, baby, don't make *noise!*

She looked apprehensively at Frank, saw his big index finger curl against the cold blue of the trigger.

And she blurted unthinking, unbidden, "He hasn't eaten! He's just hungry!" And slapped her hand over her own mouth instantly.

It did not stop Frank from rising (with that awful unctuosity and calm of purpose she knew so well, had witnessed so often), stepping gracefully as a cat around the ottoman to the sofa, where he carefully placed the black bore of the big shotgun to the child's tender, rosebud lips.

Matty ran to them.

She saw the black bore swivel (a fathomless, empty eye) look right into her, her chest—just to the right of her heart—coming to rest against her hard sternum, dead center between ample cleavage. Frank smiled a little, as though he'd been incredibly clever to align it there with such effortless dexterity.

Matty could feel the hollow knock of her heart reverberate the long barrel all the way to his trigger finger.

Nicky said, "Black bear . . ."

And went back to sleep.

Chris awoke under light rain again, the second time that morning.

Or had he really been asleep?

Everything was moving through thick gelatin now. Or he was moving through it, and everything else was standing still.

He looked down at himself. Bright drops exploded over his shirt front like crimson flak.

My head is bleeding again. I wonder if that's bad. Well, of course it's bad, but I wonder how bad.

He realized he was in the soggy yard on the spongy grass of the south side of the house. He could not remember coming here, could not remember it at all. His ass was freezing. Spinal meningitis! The old infantry scourge.

He struggled up, fell. Crawled to a large puddle still dimpled with occasional drizzle, drank deeply on hands and knees, like the big African cats on the *National Geographic* shows. The ones he used to watch in his warm, dry house in Los Angeles before moving out here to the lovely nightmare of the woodlands.

He felt a bit better for this. In a few moments he was able to make it up to his knees, then actually stand on rickety legs, wavering.

He turned, began to search about for a rock, something hard to do what he knew he must.

There were no rocks. In the woods, yes, tons of them, quarries of them, but not here on the neatly trimmed lawn. And Christ knew he hadn't the strength to walk (crawl?) back to the woods and look through the soaked and tangled loam for a damn rock.

Never mind. Matty had gathered a few large, smooth river stones last week, placed them in a lopsided pile near the porch in hopes of someday lining a garden. If there was any luck left to him, they'd still be there.

They were. And he seized one—nearly capsizing dizzily with the effort—a palm-size beauty with mottled flecks of raw sienna. He steadied himself, wound up with his best Nolan Ryan, and hurled it at what he felt was the smallest and therefore least expensive window to replace.

The rock struck dead center. And hurled back at him, thumped at his feet.

He stared, blinking at the unfriendly window, an ape confronting logarithms. Damnedest window he'd ever seen.

He found himself suddenly sprawled in the wet grass again, not quite remembering falling.

He waited, not impatiently, for the wave of vertigo and nausea to pass, for the woods to quit spinning.

How could a rock of that size not at least crack a simple plate glass window, thermal-paned or not? Hard to say. Things were getting pretty dim out here in the drizzle. Severe contusion of the left frontal lobe perhaps (he'd read it somewhere) or maybe just the weather, a second front moving in, darkening the already darkened sky. It was good that they had moved out here, though, he thought with mocking humor; certainly a good thing Matty's uncle died, left them this wonderful A-frame beauty out here in the middle of god-damn nowhere. Where the neighbors and police and firemen and hospitals are so *wonderfully* far away that a man could *freeze* to death in ten minutes if he gets locked out of his own home! And he heard himself laugh, a gargled croak. And the sound of it scared him.

He sat up again, this time only to his knees, survived another wave of vertigo and surging nausea, found himself on the heels of his hands again, throwing up blood.

He looked down at the spattered red grass before him. And he thought, If I fall down again, I will not get up.

He forced himself to a sitting position, from where, by degrees, he managed to regain his feet and go looking for the next thing he must do, which was find the rifle.

He found it, half submerged in muddy water, sucking up rust. He'd need an oil tanker to clean and store it now. Chris stood there, wobbly and sick, blinked his eyes into focus, took aim with wavering barrel at the arrogant window, and pulled the trigger.

He cursed, thumbed off the damn safety, aimed again, rocking on his heels. He pulled the trigger.

He was knocked back and over with the recoil despite deliberately tucking the stock snugly into his shoulder in anticipation.

He struggled up again and just stood there staring stupidly at the window, which had a few small nicks but no more, certainly not blown inward the way a normal cooperative window would be.

Matty jumped at the shot—too close to be thunder—nearly cried out, catching herself.

Frank merely smiled.

The sound that immediately followed was like a fistful of stones, a sudden summer hail against the dining room picture window. Matty wasn't at all certain what had actually taken place.

Nicky stirred sleepily but that was all. I must get food into him, Matty thought absently, the concussion still ringing in her head. Or water, at least, so he doesn't dehydrate. Or did Frank supply that with the syringe? God, please don't let my baby die. She looked to Frank as if for answers.

Found him across the rug, peering through a slice of drapery, muzzle ever in line with the baby. "Our mountain playwright!" He grinned.

Matty felt an inner hitch.

Frank winked. "Down but not out!"

The coldness, which had heretofore nagged only his numbing epidermis, was beginning to make inroads to his center, clutch greedily for his heart, his soul.

Chris's mind framed it with utter simplicity: This is what death feels like. Now you know.

Not so bad really. Not nearly so full of the terrors he'd always imagined.

Until he thought of Nicky. And her.

Terror bloomed then like living petals. The cold fingers of death retreated a centimeter, and he wrestled back the comforting complacency long enough to care a little about living again.

He looked at the damn window.

He didn't think it could have been a faulty shotgun shell, though he supposed this was possible.

He had taken a terrible fall, though, and lost all his remaining shells in the doing, except for the one that remained in the other barrel. Try the impregnable window once again?

Christ, he could barely heft the rifle.

Or (and he turned now to look down the gravel drive) try something else?

There would be no key in the car, of that he was almost certain. Not unless either he or Matty, in a rare moment of distraction, had managed, blessedly, to leave one in the ignition. That was possible too, he supposed, there being a lot of distractions of late. But fat chance, really.

Still.

He fell down twice getting there.

He didn't even bother glancing past the big Lamborghini's sexy side windows, which he was sure were locked. He just used the shiny red cowling to rest against for a moment until the next wave of sullen vertigo rose and ebbed.

He stumbled on to the next car, found it locked tight. Naturally.

This time he placed the butt of the stock against his chest and literally leaned against it at a right angle to prevent being catapulted backward again. He pulled the trigger.

The driver's side window evaporated in rainbow spray, taking the passenger's side and some interior roof batting with it. The blow had such force, there remained only a handful of tiny hexagons of safety glass sprinkled across the sun-baked dash, the sculpted seat. A good thing, because he had no strength to sweep them aside, barely enough to tug up the lock tab, swing open the rusty door, and drop down half dead behind the wheel among the fluttering motes of batting.

Out of the damn rain at least.

There was hardly time to think before darkness swept down and pulled him under again.

"Sure, you can look," Frank permitted companionably.

Matty came to his side, peered through the slice of curtain, saw nothing out there but drizzle and wet forest and empty yard.

"He's in the Volvo."

Yes, she could just see the dark silhouette of his head now. "Why's he just sitting there?"

Frank went to make himself another drink. "I think he fell down."

Matty turned from the window. "Fell down?"

Frank poured, nodding. "Down the mountain." He grinned. "Or ran into a mountain lion. You have panthers up here in the Rockies? Of course you do. Anyway, he's covered with blood."

She started for the door in jerky strides.

Was stopped, of course, by the click of the rifle.

Matty froze, closed her eyes, still facing the front door. "Please, let me. He may be dying!"

Frank knocked back the drink, set the glass on the tile counter with a smacking of lips. He looked at her a contemplative moment. "All right, you can go to him."

She spun toward him with a shock of hope.

He held up a cautionary finger. "Or you can stay here and help me revive the kid. I think I might have overdone that last shot. . . ."

Matty's heart seized up.

Frank poured another quick one, watching the tousled head on the couch contemplatively. "He really does look like me, in a way. Don't you think?"

"Frank, please!"

He shrugged. "Choice is yours, kitten," he belched softly. "The playwright or the kid."

His chattering teeth woke him this time.

Chris clamped his jaws tight, appraised his surroundings.

Oh, yes . . . that's right, I managed to drag myself to the car.

And the car has a mirror.

He sat up stiffly, pain flaring inside. (*"Something broken in there for sure, Mr. Nielson. We'll know more when the X rays come back."*) He reached out, adjusted the mirror, found it not as bad as he might have expected. There was a lot of black, clotted blood around his black eyes and matted hair, maybe hiding the worst of it.

If only he had the ignition keys.

A low grumble of thunder, fairly loud but mostly bluff, the storm was moving off to the east on legs of lightning.

You have to get out of here somehow. Get out, get looked at, and find your wife and son.

He found himself staring idly at the glove box.

Nearly gasped aloud on remembering. Bent forward with a hiss of pain and punched the silver button. The lid flopped, little interior light winking on. There was a half-eaten Hershey's chocolate bar with almonds he'd left wadded against the maps and other paraphernalia a week ago. It had congealed within the steamy daytime interior to a kind of paper-sticky paste, and it was the most delicious thing he'd ever consumed. It lasted two bites.

He leaned out the shattered window to catch a mouthful of clean mountain rain to wash it down and actually felt better.

The glove box. His mind kept returning to it.

There was a little yellow button in there that would open the trunk. If Matty hadn't taken the earthquake emergency kit out when they'd packed to leave for the mountains . . .

His legs were so stiff when he tried to swing back out of the front seat, he had to sit impatiently and roughly massage his thighs and calves with tender fingers. One entire nail was missing from the left index, he noticed mildly, that same finger completely without feeling or sensation.

He hobbled to the trunk over cantankerous gravel, hefted the lid with shrieking back muscles, began to riffle through maps, paper cups, McDonald Happy Meal toys—discarded footprints of their short life together. Three short years and they'd accumulated so much.

Here was a deflated beach ball from past trips to Santa Barbara beaches, here a sandy blanket from same, here a Raiders baseball cap he'd forgotten about.

And there, under the tire iron, was the scuffed white plastic box with the red cross emblem: CALIFORNIA EARTHQUAKE EMERGENCY KIT. He flipped up the lid. A bottle of antibiotics. Band-Aids. Rubbing alcohol, aspirin (he instantly downed a handful), a tube of Cortisone-5 creme, bandages, penknife, a packet of instant coffee, and a small bottle of drinking water.

Even before applying the medication, he dumped the packet of coffee in the water, shook the little bottle vigorously, and drained it. He'd need it badly if he was to navigate the steep, downhill hairpin turns to come.

He lay back against the headrest a moment, let the caffeine and aspirin bite into his system. Better. He caught the raspberry jam mess in the mirror that was his face. He didn't dwell on it. He wasn't dead yet.

Chris took a deep breath, reached wincing under the dash, gripping the penknife in one hand, feeling for the appropriate connections with the other. He'd watched a neighbor kid hot-wire a car when in his teens. How hard could it be?

"Oh Jesus, Frank! He has a *fever*!"

Springer sauntered unhurriedly to sofa, whiskey glass in tow, bent with the urgency of inspecting a hangnail, and placed a big palm over Nicky's small, damp brow. "Umm. Maybe a touch."

"What did you give him?" Matty demanded, not the least fearful of the rifle just now.

Frank grunted in superiority. "Would you know if I told you?"

She ran a hand under Nicky's shirt, pressed it to his thin chest. "He's sweating! You've got to help him!"

Frank was already setting the drink atop the coffee table with a grunt, bending before the couch, and casually sliding out the black valise that Matty had no idea was hidden there.

He snapped it open, tossed back the dark leather lid, which shone dully, smelled wonderfully of rich leather. The inside was lined with dropper bottles and plastic disposable syringes, a box of them, the bottles held against the side of the case with loops of elastic. On the back of the lid was a small black handgun similarly attached. Matty looked at it a moment, looked away.

Frank sighed, taking his time, ran a finger across the bottle labels, selected one with pursed lips, and withdrew it.

He held it up and squinted. "You want to switch on that lamp, please."

Matty jumped up obediently, snapped on the Tiffany knockoff she'd bought at Best Company, throwing rainbow light through art nouveau mosaic. Frank nodded at the little bottle. "Yeah, this is the one."

He tore apart a cellophane syringe pack, withdrew the plastic syringe, popped the protective tip from the stainless needle, fitted that into the bottle's rubber stopper. He drew off amber liquid carefully.

He turned to Matty. "Got any alcohol in the place?"

She pointed stiffly. "What is that stuff?"

The familiar smile. "Would it help if I told you?"

"Goddamn it, what are you putting into my son?"

Frank lowered the needle, sat back patiently on the carpet, in no particular hurry. "Thought he was *our* son."

"What's in the syringe?"

"Well, *is* he our son or not?"

"Please don't start that. You know he is."

"Then I'm not likely to give him anything that would injure him, right? I mean, assuming you believe I believe that this lovely child lying here before us is indeed my progeny."

Matty watched him for a second. Then rose and headed quickly for the stairs. "I'll get the alcohol."

But in the bathroom she hissed a curse, slammed her trembling fist against the shiny porcelain sink before the open medicine chest. The tall plastic bottle, murkily opaque, still stood beside the toothpaste and cold cream but was deceivingly empty. She'd kept meaning to replace it.

Down the stairs again, the ridiculous nightie fluttering about her, she called, "We don't have any alcohol."

Frank sighed, bored. He reached for his whiskey glass. "Never mind." He took a hanky from his shirt pocket, dabbed it in the drink, rubbed it over Nicky's impossibly slender triceps. Springer picked up the syringe.

"Wait!" Matty ran the back of a hand across her mouth shakily. Then, as if she'd reached a decision, she rubbed both hands on the carpet quickly, a drying motion. She held one out. "Let me do it."

Frank appraised her curiously. Finally heaved his shoulders, handed over the syringe.

She reached past Frank and picked up the half-empty dropper bottle, fitted the needle into the rubber stopper again, and withdrew the rest of the amber fluid.

She dabbed whiskey on her left forearm and inserted the needle slowly, until the fluid was half gone. When she withdrew the needle, she cocked her arm and set the half-empty syringe atop the glass coffee table gingerly. She held the arm that received the shot against her, crooked it in case of blood.

Frank regarded her expectantly. "What now?"

Matty swallowed, felt her son's fevered brow again. Turned to sigh, gaze distrustfully at the half-empty syringe. "Now we wait awhile."

Frank laughed good-naturedly, an almost pleasant sound under the circumstances, straightened, laughing harder now, and moved to the closed drapes, peering out. "My trusting, loving wife!"

Matty watched him saunter to the entertainment unit, twist knobs and flick buttons on the stereo. Acid rock flared into the living room, which he adjusted to a bearable level.

"What are you doing?" Matty asked him.

Frank pulled one of his dark cigars from his jacket, lit it, settled back in Chris's deep green easy chair comfortably, crossing his legs, puffing at the ceiling. "Dance for me, kitten."

Matty managed a disgusted sound, looked away.

Frank grinned. "Dance for me."

She glared at him.

"Hey. Whatever you just put into your system will react more quickly to an active metabolism! Get up and move around! Dance for me!"

She started to say something, glanced over at Nicky's shallowly moving chest, the line of perspiration on his brow. She felt him quickly. He was hotter.

"It's your kid," Frank informed her between puffs.

Matty got to her feet. Yes, he was a maniac, but what he said made sense. Eyes on her son, she began to sway lightly.

"Come on! You'll never get it into your system that way! Shake a tail feather!"

She dragged in breath, lifted her arms, revolved her hips, breasts swaying heavily. She kept her eyes on Nicky, knowing exactly where Frank's eyes were. Fine. The smug prick. Let him look good. And while he was doing that she might just make a dive for that gun strapped inside the lid of that black valise, a gun he'd apparently forgotten all about.

She jerked her eyes away from it instinctively. Frank never forgets about anything.

She turned to look at him now, forcing a wan smile. He *was* watching her, watching her crotch, to be precise. He had a few drinks in him, had been out traipsing in the woods with Chris this morning. He must be tired.

She swayed wider, thrusting out her chest, giving it the old college bump and grind.

Frank clapped encouragement. "Atta girl, work that serum!"

She moved her hands to her breasts to further distract him, faked a groan as she pinched her nipples, stepping absently closer to the black valise in the process.

"Pump it, baby, pump it through the old pipes!"

She bucked, turned, shoved her ass at him, bent, hands sweeping the carpet, inches from the valise. Grabbed her ankles, giving him a nice full moon, wiggling to the tempo, hair cascading, face flushing. She could almost reach out and touch the shiny black revolver.

A motor coughed to life in the driveway.

Matty straightened, gasping.

Frank, abruptly sober, moved quickly to the curtain, peeped through.

"What is it?" Matty whispered. Then louder, above the thumping rock: "What *is* it?"

Frank took the cigar from his mouth. "Your husband. Looks like he got the car started."

Matty dived for the revolver.

Snapped it free of the lid with a clean jerk, clamped both hands around it, and was up and aiming at Frank's head with a smoothness that surprised even her.

Except that there were two Franks now.

She blinked, shook her head.

She was perspiring profusely. Much more—she realized with sinking insides—than from the simple effort of her dancing.

Matty swallowed sudden nausea.

She pulled the trigger at his swimming form.

Nothing happened. The safety. Maybe the safety was still on. She knew that much about guns.

Only she couldn't seem to remember exactly where a safety would be on a handgun. Or exactly its purpose.

She stared dully at the shiny gun, fascinated by its blue sheen, in its own way quite lovely.

Frank took it away from her leaden arms as effortlessly as candy from a baby.

A baby.

Nicky. Mommy did it for you, baby.

She was looking up, at an odd angle, looking up from *under* the glass coffee table (how had she gotten down there?) with fast-glazing eyes, looking at the shiny length of half-filled syringe.

Chris!

She was seeing his face there under the glass table. Chris's sun-burned face smiling at her that first day on the little Thousand Oaks suburban stage.

Though it was Frank's echoing laughter that accompanied her into darkness.

CHAPTER 9

He nearly drove off the mountain on three different occasions.

The last was the worst. He had actually passed out completely. The pilotless Volvo skidded in cliffside gravel, fishtailing sickeningly.

Chris awoke with a gasp, wrenching the wheel frog-eyed, mouth a terrified rictus. The canyon lip loomed close, closer—surely the car would dip sharply any second now, surely he'd be gone. But then roiling dust was billowing past, and he was still clutching the plastic wheel with bloodless knuckles, heart slamming.

The car, though, was pitched at the very brink, pointed in the wrong direction now, going up the mountain instead of down, engine still idling obediently.

He saw his choices in clear definition: Either he stopped now, pulled over, shut it down, and rested (with the very large possibility he'd never wake up again) or gritted his teeth, tromped the pedal and barreled the rest of the way to Greenborough.

The problem was, he had no realistic idea how far the trendy little postcard hamlet was. He'd only been through it twice (overpriced boutiques, too-cute designer clothiers, art galleries) only been up this narrow mountain road twice, hadn't paid the distance much mind; thought, with that razor memory of his, it was about an hour-and-forty-minute trip.

His watch was ruined so he couldn't judge from that, and blood kept running into his eyes, making watching the odometer a good trick.

Screw it. He wheeled around, put her in second, and screeched away, spraying shale.

He had to get help, reach the authorities. He knew enough about police work to realize that time was everything. The colder the trail, the less likely the chances for success. He kept telling himself, of course, that there was nothing to worry about. The real danger lay in his own worsening condition. Matty and Frank and Nicky were fine, had gone looking for him when he didn't call. The police were probably looking for him right now.

That was why he sighed with grateful relief—despite the fact he was speeding recklessly—when red-and-blue lights flashed in his rearview and the big black-and-white bore down on him wailing its eerie warning.

He really had every intention of discussing the situation with the nice officer after the two cars pulled to the rocky shoulder. But by the time the patrolman, in his crisp brown uniform, dark leg stripes, Smokey Bear hat, and Sam Browne belt came around, Chris couldn't seem to get the door handle of the Volvo open to greet him. He was so weak.

He didn't even have breath left to explain all the broken glass and buckshot patterns on the dash and roof. Didn't have the strength to reassure the officer that he really didn't have to frown suspiciously like that or draw his shiny service revolver. I'm not drunk, or dangerous or anything at all. Except maybe dying.

He awoke in glaring brightness, eyes slit. Angry little needles assaulted his brain.

"It's very bright in here, isn't it?" A calming, country voice (New England? Vermont?). The voice was attached to an even brighter white blur, so Chris had to squint painfully at that too.

"Walls supposed to be off-white, what they call eggshell. Clean and reassuring without being antiseptic. But I think the painters got the wrong swatch. Let me draw the blinds a little. There. Better?"

Chris nodded gratitude.

"Can you talk, son?"

He tried, managed a croak.

A friendly chuckle. "I'll take that as an affirmative. Fell off our mountain, did you?"

And this time a yes that was more intelligible.

"Thought so, get a lot of that around here." The white blur became a watery Arrow shirt now, inside a whiter lab coat, and above that a bushy mustache, bushy eyebrows, thinning silvery hair, black-framed glasses. A patient, almost paternal smile. "Look like a damn country doctor, don't I?" Another warm chuckle as the lab coat busied itself with gleaming hospital things. "That's what they all say, and that's what I am, so that part fits pretty well, don't it?"

He came around now to the stainless-topped table Chris realized he was lying on, looked down through the big black-rimmed glasses. "What don't seem to fit so well is you. Got a name, son?"

"C-C . . ."

"Take your time now; we got lots of time. Here." He handed Chris a glass of something that tasted like plain water.

No, Chris was thinking, we don't have time.

"Th-thanks. Chris. It's Chris . . ." And it actually took him a second for the rest. "Nielson."

The warm smile widening with the nod. "That's good, that's fine. And I'm Doc Holiday. Hallicur, really, but the local boys like to pretend it's the Wild West out here, so I oblige them. Where do you hurt most?"

"Jesus. Everywhere. My wife—"

"You were alone in the car, Mr. Nielson."

"I know. I think my wife and child may be in danger. Do you have a phone?"

"All right, all right, we'll get hold of them; you just lie back. You're not as bad as you look, and I only say that because you happen to be just the second lucky recipient of X rays here in my humble country office, my shiny new machine being only two weeks old. Been trying to get this cow town to buy me one for three years. People always falling off that mountain, busting legs. You fared better than most, nothing broke. How's the head?"

"Fine. Pain's gone."

Holiday winked. "It'll be back. I put some Demerol in your IV, shot you up with antibiotics, took some stitches near your crown. How far'd you fall?"

"A hundred miles."

Holiday chuckled. "Well, you must have bounced all the way. North peak?"

"I really don't know."

"Okay. Anyway, nothing serious far as I can see." He grinned again. "You looked surprised!"

"I tossed up some blood."

"Bit your tongue. No stitches needed there. No internal nasties, I'd have seen them. You're going to be stiff as a poker, ache like hell when it gets cold, which it will soon. I'll give you some pills for later. You allergic to anything, penicillin? Ampicillin?"

"No."

"Good. Probably won't need it anyway. You feel well enough to talk a spell?"

"On a phone, yes."

Holiday moved to his office door, opened it. "Officer Clayton would like a word with you. He'll see to it your calls get put through." He leaned out. "Buck—"

The crisp uniform, sans the Smokey Bear hat, entered soberly, came to Chris's table. "How're you feeling, sir?"

"His name is Nielson, Buck. Chris Nielson. Says his family might be in some trouble. I'll leave you two to talk. Not too long, Buck." And the kindly Doc Holiday shut the door behind him.

Chris faced imposing shoulders, blocky, tanned face, requisite service mustache, mirrored shades, a beefy, extended hand that wasn't particularly firm because it didn't need to be. "Officer Clayton. Call me Buck."

"All right, I'm Chris."

"Fell off our mountain, did you?"

"Yes. Clumsy."

"Uh-huh." He was watching Chris's eyes closely. General procedure or suspicious? "You'll want to try hiking boots next time."

"I was in a hurry."

"Oh? And why was that, Chris?" Companionably he shook out a smoke, offering one to Chris.

"No, thanks. Look, about my wife—"

"They were hiking with you?"

"No, no. They were at home."

Officer Clayton consulted his pad now, flipping it open with a practiced snap. "That would be Thousand Oaks, California?"

"No, that's the old address. We live here now."

"Uh-huh." Ready with a pen. "Where would that be, exactly?"

"Up the mountain. It's . . ." He suddenly realized he couldn't think of the address. And him with a perfect memory. Maybe that stuff Holiday had given him.

Clayton waited, pen poised patiently.

"We just moved in a few days ago. I can't recall the address just now." He absently rubbed his head, feeling for the stitches.

"Take your time, Chris."

This was going nowhere. Going *too* slowly nowhere. He needed to talk to Matty now! "Listen, the number's in my wallet."

"We didn't find a wallet, Chris. Just the registration in the car. With the California license. You know, Colorado state law requires you to register new plates within thirty days."

"I've been meaning to. Listen, please, to what I'm saying! I have reason to believe my wife and child may be in danger."

"What sort of danger, Chris?" Not quite patronizing nor quite suspicious. More like maybe this guy's okay, just took a bad fall. Shook up his brains a bit.

Chris was thinking, Back up a notch, give this by-the-book gendarme something to hang on to. "The other evening, my wife and I were returning from dinner on the lake. I have a Chris-Craft."

Clayton jotted.

"And a private dock. Well, these guys, a group of them, party types—we'd seen them earlier when (and he thought he'd better leave out the part about Matty's nude bathing), when we were fishing. Well, they came by fast in this big boat, caused waves, made snide remarks, you know."

"What kind of remarks?"

"Just . . . Look, it isn't important. They were drunk."

"No drinking on the lake. New law."

"Anyway, as I said, we had dinner later up the lake, and on the way back, as I was docking, here were these four guys parked in front of my boathouse. It's a private dock, as I said."

"Uh-huh."

"Well, they started trouble."

"Assaulted you."

"Yes. No. Well, lipping off. They pushed me."

"Pushed you."

"That's right."

"Uh-huh. And you pushed back?"

"No. My wife's cousin was there." Was this going to get Frank in trouble? "He took care of the situation."

"How?"

"He just handled it. Called their bluff. They went away. Anyway, the next morning, Frank and I—"

"Hold it. 'Frank'?"

"Matty's cousin."

"Matty, your wife."

"Yes! I have a wife, Matty, a boy, Nicky, he's two. Well, Frank and I went hunting the next morning and—oh, I forgot! Frank thought he saw someone near our house that night. Outside in the dark, prowling around."

Officer Clayton scribbled. "Prowlers."

"Anyway, we got up early, went out to look for deer. Someone shot at us."

"Who?"

"We couldn't see."

"Uh-huh."

"They nearly hit me."

"Uh-huh."

Chris regarded him wryly. "You look unconvinced, Officer Clayton."

"Buck. Not at all. You're sure it was intentional? I mean, there are other hunters, lots, happens all the time."

"It was deliberate!"

"Take it easy, Chris. I have to sort this out my way. Go on."

"Well, Frank—we both—got worried it might be those guys at the dock. We decided to split up. Frank would go back to the house, look out for Matty and Nicky; I'd get to the lake, try to get help."

"Split up."

"Yes. It seemed like—we thought it'd double our chances, in case something happened to one or the other of us."

"I see. Too bad you didn't have a cellular phone."

"I tried one once. The mountains, too much interference."

"I understand. Go on, what happened then?"

"Frank went back to the house. I started for the lake. That's when I fell. Listen, didn't anyone notify the police here? It would be under the name of either Nielson or Springer."

"No nine-one-ones for several days now, Chris. So after you fell . . ."

"I was out for a while. I made it back to the house. The place was locked up tight, all the drapes drawn."

"Nobody home?"

"I can't be sure. I lost my keys."

"The windows?"

"I tried that. I was pretty weak."

"Sure."

"I hammered and yelled, got no response. Frank's car was still in the drive; that's what's got me worried."

"But the place was locked up."

"Tight as a drum."

"You checked all the doors?"

"No one had tried to get in that I could tell, but as I said, I was in pretty bad shape."

Officer Clayton nodded, scribbling, flipping over a fresh page. "And these guys at the dock, they're the ones shot out your car window?"

"No. I did that myself."

Clayton looked up at him.

"I had no keys. I had to get in."

"I see." Scribbling. "And how'd you drive the car without keys, Chris?"

Chris looked at him a moment. "I hot-wired it."

Clayton didn't look up. Scribbled.

Chris waited him out this time, feeling a vague tightness pressing into the room.

There was a badly framed Norman Rockwell print over the sink, showing a little boy on a chair with his pants down, bare butt, studying a diploma in another doctor's office while the doctor, back to him, prepared a syringe. Chris wondered if it could be this picture—an old *Post* magazine cover probably—that had inspired Holiday to become a GP himself.

Officer Clayton finished scribbling, looked up for more.

"That's about it," Chris said. "I was coming down the mountain when you stopped me."

Clayton nodded, tapped the pen and the pad reflectively. Chris could see it in the mirrored lenses.

Tap tap tap.

After a moment, Chris pressed: "So you see, I'm very concerned about my wife and child."

Officer Clayton nodded. "I can certainly understand that. Now, let me see if I've got this straight, Chris. You say you and this"—he consulted his pad—"Mr. Springer, saw someone prowling on the premises last night."

"Frank saw them."

"Why didn't you call us then?"

In fact, Chris had thought about it. Somehow, though, with Frank there, it had seemed an overreaction, even though the thought had pecked at the back of his brain most of the night. "I don't know. I should have."

"Might have saved you a lot of trouble."

"Yes. It was thoughtless. Do you suppose we could try to contact my family now?"

If Officer Clayton was about to reply, it was interrupted by Doc Holiday's ringing office phone. The place was too small to have an outer office secretary. To Chris's surprise, Officer Clayton moved to the wall and picked up the call.

"Yeah. Uh-huh. Right. Nielson, yes. Fine." He stood over a spotless, stainless-steel sterilizer. Used to use them to sterilize syringes, Chris thought. Now they're all in disposable packs.

Officer Clayton hung up, came back to Chris cinching up his belt. Chris didn't understand why it was necessary for him to retain the damn mirrored shades here in the office. It wasn't *that* bright, eggshell white or not.

"Sorry," Clayton apologized, "procedure. How's that address coming?"

Chris, patience gone, pushed up on an elbow, felt the dragging weight of his own body, like pushing through wet sand. "Look, I told you they weren't home!"

"So far as you know."

"I want you to start looking for my wife and kid!"

Clayton studied him calmly. "How would you suggest we do that, Chris?"

He hadn't really thought it through. You're the goddamn police! he felt like barking but didn't. Better to remain collected. His veracity was begging credence as it was.

"I think the best thing to do is have you rest awhile, Chris. Maybe you can come up with that address."

"Christ, it's a new A-frame practically straight up the mountain! How many A-frames you got in this area?"

"A number. And which road are we talking about?"

"The one you stopped me on!"

"Settle down now. We're trying to help. There's a hundred

access roads off Cameron Trail. You recall which one leads to your house? Give me that and I'll dispatch a car right away."

"What about the damn phone? Can't you get the address from the operator?"

"Just tried that, Chris. You're not listed yet. Apparently." Something in his tone.

"What do you mean, 'apparently'?" Chris bristled, despite himself.

"This is the sticks, Chris. It takes longer here. We should get a tracer on it in a few hours if—"

If what? If it really is my home? But again he held back. Pushing this oaf would gain him nothing, he could feel it. But he had to push somewhere.

He threw back the sheet covering him, found himself swathed in bandages and johnny smock. "I'll take you up there myself."

Doc Holiday poked in, frowned bushy brows at what he saw. "Whoa! Where you goin'?"

Chris was up to a sitting position, biting back the pain so they wouldn't see. "I can't recall my address just now. Buck is going to take me up there."

The good doctor looked to Officer Clayton.

Before they could exchange words, Chris blurted, "You said nothing was broken!"

"You're weak, been through a lot."

"So have my wife and child, I'm afraid."

Holiday softened a notch. Looked to the cop again as if for confirmation. Clayton shrugged. (*It's your call.*) Holiday finally nodded. "All right, if you must. I want you back here within two hours. Buck?"

"You got it, Doc."

Chris pushed off the table, masking the attendant grunt. A small victory. "Where are my pants?"

The headache returned with slamming force, but of course he masked that too, wishing fervently, however, he had those pills the doctor had promised him, whatever they were.

"Turn left here," Chris instructed Officer Clayton.

It was so strange. Chris had lived his whole life without once riding in a police car. Everything was clean and new and eerily detached; even the upholstery reeked of officiousness, no-nonsense professionalism. Not quite cold. More like personalityless. Like Officer Clayton. Mirrored. I can see out, you can't see in.

Up the narrow road then, the gravel drive, and there was Frank's Lamborghini.

"Nice car."

"It's Frank's."

"I see."

Clayton pulled past it, nosed the squad car before the A-frame's porch, cut the engine, microphone already in his hand. He mumbled something, the radio crackled, mumbled something indecipherable back, and he hung up the mike.

Chris was looking at the big service rifle planted between them, wondering if Officer Clayton was going to unlock it, figuring—rightly, it turned out—he wouldn't.

They got out.

Officer Clayton carried a checker-gripped .45 police special at his left hip. A southpaw. But he didn't unsnap the holster guard on this either. He looked very calm and collected as they approached the house, something about his easy, dawdling gait angering Chris.

But not as much as the shiny new address plate affixed to the porch: 1944 Sycamore Dr.

It had not been there before; Chris was sure of it. And sure too that Officer Clayton had taken ample notice of it. It was pretty hard to miss, all bright and freshly painted like that.

When they reached the door, Clayton turned to him expectantly. Chris tried the knob again, found it still locked.

Clayton knocked sharply. "Police officer! Open up, please!"

Nothing, to Chris's despair.

He was about to turn to Clayton with an I-told-you expression when there was movement from within. Chris, heart leaping, heard a click, and then the door pulled inward and there stood Frank Springer looking blankly at them. "Yes?"

Chris started in: "Frank! How's Matty!"

But Springer held the door firm with his right hand, did not step aside. "Excuse me?"

Chris looked at him. "What's the matter? Is Matty hurt?"

Springer was looking at Officer Clayton now. "Is there some kind of trouble, Officer?"

"You are Mr. Springer?"

"Yes." And Frank looked blankly at Chris again. Then back to Clayton. "What can I do for you?"

"You're this gentleman's wife's cousin?"

Frank frowned, started to smile then. "Pardon me?"

Chris pushed forward impatiently, trying to see past broad shoulders into darkened foyer. Was halted by Officer Clayton's big hand on his triceps. "Hold on a minute, Chris."

Chris tore away. "Goddamn it, Frank! This isn't the time for your fucking games! Where's Matty?" He pushed ahead, and this time it was Frank who pushed him back, down off the lintel.

"Hold on here! Who is this man, Officer? I want to see some ID."

To Chris's astonishment, Clayton was dutifully producing it, his deference to Frank obvious. "Greenborough Police Department. This man claims he lives here. Do you know him?"

Claims.

Frank looked Chris up and down. "I see. This is some kind of welcome wagon joke, right?"

"Do you know this man, Mr. Springer?" Clayton reiterated with authority.

Frank appeared genuinely flummoxed. "Of course not! What the hell gives here?"

"Goddamn you, Frank!" Chris sprang past him, past both, rushing into the house, calling at the top of his voice: "Matty! Nicky!"

Clayton was right behind him. "All right—"

Chris whirled on him like an animal, face tight, forgetting all promises to himself about calm resolve. "Don't fucking touch me! Just don't touch me, okay?"

Officer Clayton came up short, held up his hands in a calming gesture. "All right, Chris. Stay frosty, now. We don't want to upset these people."

Chris glared at Frank. "Where the goddamn hell are they?"

Frank turned innocently to Clayton, but Clayton would not be nudged from command here. "Mr. Springer, if I could see some ID of your own, please. A driver's license, perhaps."

Frank nodded cooperatively. "Of course." He produced his wallet, opened it, handed it to the officer.

Clayton glanced at it, then up quickly to Chris. Motioned stiffly to him.

Chris came over cautiously, Clayton handing him the wallet. The address was the same as on the new plaque outside. "This is bullshit! That plaque out there is brand-new! Ask him who else lives here."

Clayton took the wallet, handed it back to Frank with an inquiring look.

"My wife and child are in town, shopping."

"Wife's name?" from Clayton.

"Matty Springer. My son is Nicky."

"You bastard!" Chris seethed. "You can't get away with this shit!"

Clayton held another calming hand to Chris. "Mr. Springer, I assume you have a marriage certificate somewhere. I'm just trying to establish things."

Now it was Frank who held up consolatory palms. "It's quite all right. I have them right here. Just a moment." He walked to the living room, to Matty's lacquered Chinese desk.

He's doing it all with such style, Chris was thinking, such incredible conviction. Jesus, I could almost believe it myself.

But his insides were chilling over. What had this madman done with his family? If he'd gone to such lengths as the new address plaque and the phony driver's license, anything was possible. He'd been a fool to let him stay the night, to go out "hunting" with him, after those weird soliloquies at dinner, those lewd intimations about Matty afterward. He'd been a fool.

Yes, and Frank had taken every advantage of it.

"Here we are." Frank came back to them with a brown, string-wrapped file folder, opening it as he came, shuffling paper within. "Officer Clayton, was it?" He handed a dog-eared sheet to the big cop.

Clayton looked it over, looked up again at Chris with those fathomless mirrored eyes.

Chris, already imagining it, had to see for himself anyway. He took the marriage certificate from the cop's hand, glanced at Matty's familiar cursive, Frank's alien scrawl.

Something moved inside him.

Despite the insanity of all this, the certificate, the date, the age of the paper, it did appear genuine. Certainly it did to the big cop.

Who was turning now, crossing the room to the foyer mirror, the teak table beneath it. Upon which rested a new gold-framed photo of a smiling couple. Chris felt his chest lurch.

Officer Clayton turned with the photo, held it up so Chris could see clearly. It showed Matty and Frank, pressed cheek to cheek, grinning brightly. Matty just a shade younger, but indisputably her despite that and the different coif, lighter lipstick. Frank's hair seemed a bit thicker.

"When was this taken, Mr. Springer?" Clayton wanted to know.

"Five years ago. Just after our marriage."

The cop turned to Chris again. "You know this woman?"

Chris was looking at the staircase. "What difference would it make if I said yes? He's got you convinced already, he's so damn clever."

And with that Chris bolted for the stairs. "Matty!"

"Hold it!" Clayton yelled, and Chris, showing them his back, imagined the shiny service revolver being yanked from its creaking leather holster.

"It's all right," Frank was soothing calmly, "let him. I want this over with now."

Chris thumped the upstairs hall, glanced in Nicky's room and went straight to the master bedroom, not so much because he expected to find his wife but only some familiar part of her, some article of clothing, a perfume bottle, a reminder that she had ever existed at all.

He yanked open the bedroom closet.

All of his clothes were gone. So were Matty's. At least the ones of hers he remembered. There was women's apparel here, all right, rather expensive from the look of it, but nothing he'd ever seen Matty in. And on the far side, a whole new wardrobe of men's things.

Of course.

Buy all new clothes, and there's no possibility of tracking down anything with a receipt.

Chris turned and found himself staring at the bed.

He could look in every closet, of course, in every nook and cranny, but he knew instinctively he would not find them in the house. He had no idea how or where Frank had secreted them, but it wasn't here.

His mind began to race.

You must calm down. You must not let him win this or carry it even a single step further. All the odds are on your side as long as you don't panic. He's expecting you to panic. But the odds are with you. You can't just wipe out a couple's past history, even a brief history, just like that. There were things beyond marriage licenses and addresses. He just had to stay composed and think of them.

He came back down the stairs swiftly but in control, hand on the smooth pine banister. He felt unreal, as though his feet hardly touched the carpeted stairs at all. He might have been hurrying down to see if these two visitors would like a drink.

Officer Clayton was on the alcove phone, hanging up as Chris hit the hooked rug. A hallway picture was missing, he noticed. The one of himself grinning and tanned, holding up a bass from two years ago. Matty had taken the picture at that little lake north of Ventura.

Officer Clayton, in a voice that seemed immune to anger, asked, "How's the head, Chris?"

He'd almost anticipated it. "I'm fine."

Frank was eyeing his bandages. "Were you in a fight, Mr.— what was the name again?"

Chris told him, "Fuck you, Frank." He turned to the cop. "I want an all-points out for my wife and child, and I want it immediately. We both know there's nothing physically or mentally wrong with me. A man who loses his wallet and license in a fall doesn't by association go insane. I want you to phone headquarters now and locate my family. If you don't, and this is a promise, I'll have every attorney I know in Los Angeles up here and you'll be trading in that Smokey Bear hat for a janitor's cap."

This said evenly, authoritatively, with all the cool but outraged taxpaying citizen demeanor Chris could muster.

Officer Clayton remained an impassive block behind mirrored lenses. "I just spoke with Sheriff Bradley. He'd like a word with you. I know you're going to cooperate with me, Chris."

"Of course. And you're going to cooperate with me, right?"

"We're going to do everything in our power to see this thing gets settled. You have my word."

Chris nodded curtly. "That's good enough for me." Just to show how compliant he could be, he opened the front door, and waited courteously for the big cop. "My attorneys will be in touch with you, Frank. And of course I'll explain to them your penchant for practical jokes, though I doubt they'll share your sense of humor. Are you coming, Officer Clayton?"

Clayton replaced his round-brimmed hat, turned to Frank. "Sorry for any inconvenience," Chris heard him say softly.

Frank shook his head, mumbled something with a forget-it air.

By the time Clayton reached the door, Chris was already halfway to the patrol car, moving in stiff, deliberate strides, shoulders back and rigid.

The sun was out, clear and bright, having already dried every trace of the previous day's storm, as though it had never rained at all, as though yesterday had not existed.

CHAPTER 10

Sheriff Bradley was also Judge Bradley and the owner and sometimes salesclerk of Greenborough Taxidermy, the town was that
small.

A sign declaring these various vocations was posted, black type
against frosted glass, on the door to his small office in the Greenborough County Courthouse. It was the oldest building in town,
perhaps the county, its Civil War vintage stone walls having survived generations of six-foot drifts and golf ball hail. A lone black
cannon—from which war, no one was certain—faced outward
toward the Colorado peaks.

Joe Bradley was short and stocky and balding and seemingly in
a perpetual sweat. He sported a tieless tan shirt and slacks, a large,
silvery cowboy-style buckle, black, immaculately shiny boots.

On the cracked plaster wall behind him was a framed sepia
photo of Greenborough's turn-of-the-century police department,
taken during mining years: broad mustaches and muttonchops,
period uniforms studded with rows of buttons. Next to that hung
an aerial drawing of the little Colorado town, watermarked, faded,
with impeccable, draftsman lettering: 1962. Neither picture hung
evenly.

Bradley sat behind his metal desk, which was an antique from the fifties, solid and heavy as a Buick, beneath the dragonfly hum of a portable fan, though it was cool enough inside. He gestured for Chris to sit, asked if he'd like a cold drink.

"No, thanks."

"No? Coffee?"

"I'm fine, thanks."

Officer Clayton remained standing near the door and was not invited to share in the partaking of beverages.

"Now then," Sheriff Bradley grunted affably, unhurried and casual with small-town demeanor. Chris was becoming accustomed to it. "Let's talk a spell, Chris." He swiped a beefy hand across his desk as if clearing away old business. "Buck, open that goddamn door, will you? It's hotter'n' hell in here. I've got some cold pop in the back, Mr. . . . what was it?"

"Nielson. Chris."

"Can't drink beer when I'm on duty." The sheriff winked, lowered his voice as though not to be heard by Officer Clayton, though obviously he was. "I fudge sometimes on Saturday nights. Don't tell no one."

"You have my word."

Bradley leaned back with a grunt and sigh, adjusted the fan to hit him more squarely. "Now then. You were out to the Springer place, Buck tells me."

"It's my place, Sheriff."

"Call me Joe. Your place."

"That's right."

"Uh-huh. Well now, Frank Springer claims it's his place."

"Frank Springer claims a lot of things. Like being married to my wife, for instance, and being the father of my child."

Bradley nodded. "Uh-huh. Well. Now, this is a hell of a thing, isn't it?"

"It is that."

"And you're saying the A-frame up there off Cameron is your place."

Easy, Chris assessed, don't get riled again with these people. "Look, Sheriff—Joe—clearly the quickest way to settle this is to contact my wife and boy. Now, Frank Springer doesn't deny they exist, so why don't we just go back up there, find out exactly where it is he claims they are, contact them, and get this over with?"

Sheriff Bradley nodded, took it all in with patient concern, licked his broad lips, sat back in his chair, closer to the electric thrum of fan blades. Not riled, never had been riled, never would be. He let his eyes drift toward the easy movements of Main Street, whose sunny sidewalks forced a squint. "Well, wouldn't surprise me. Wouldn't surprise me if two people in this town did get their houses mixed up. Tell you one damn thing, this burg's changing. Changing fast. You know Aspen, Chris?"

Chris puffed impatient cheeks. "I've been there, yes."

"Used to look an awful lot like this place, Aspen did. Small town, provincial. Nobody in a hurry. Then the movie stars moved in." He shook his broad head as if in deference to the immutable. "Now Greenborough is looking more and more like Aspen. Not just tourists. People actually putting down stakes. Escaping city smog, city crime. We got *art* galleries now. Shit. They don't make a dime, don't see as how they could. But they're here for the long haul. Town is definitely changing."

Sheriff Bradley broke his reverie, glanced up at his deputy behind Chris's shoulder. "Now then, Chris, as I understand it, you have no current ID with you, is that correct?"

"As I explained to Officer Clayton, I apparently lost it when I fell."

"Yes, Doc mentioned you took a spill off our mountain. How's the head?"

"Fine. I do have ID, of course, but it's—it *was*—in my house. But naturally that would necessitate going back up there and searching the place."

"Well, we'd need a warrant for that, of course."

"If you believe it's Springer's place."

"Well, it's somebody's place for damn sure!" He barked a laugh to keep everything light and amicable. When Chris didn't join him, he glanced over at Officer Clayton.

"Now, what about mortgage papers, bill of sale, that kind of thing, Chris?"

"Again, they'd be at the house, with the rest of my things."

"Uh-huh. Now, we've checked with the real estate people, and they claim the house is listed under the name Springer. Matty Springer."

"My wife. The house was a gift from her uncle."

Bradley nodded, picked up a pencil. "And would you have his number and address?"

"He's dead."

Bradley put down the pencil. "Uh-huh. Any relatives living that would know this uncle?"

"Look, Sheriff—"

"See, the thing is, Chris—can I call you Chris?"

"Please."

"The thing is, Chris, Buck here tells me he saw mortgage papers, marriage certificate at the Springer place, under the name of Frank Springer."

"Sheriff Bradley—"

"I've put a tracer on them. They check out with New York State bureaus."

Chris thought about it, ignoring the sudden pang. Smarter than they looked, these people. "Papers can be forged, Sheriff. Easily."

Bradley raised brows. "That a fact?"

"Of course."

"You've had personal experience with that, have you? Law work? College, maybe?" Still friendly, in the way Officer Clayton had been friendly, the way a cobra is friendly until it bites.

Chris sat back, not knowing what exactly was transpiring here, only very certain something was.

He was holding fewer and fewer cards, it seemed. But there were still aces among them. "I repeat, Sheriff, find my wife and child and ask them, point-blank, who their husband and father is. What could be simpler than that?"

Bradley patted the metal desk top once, confirming he'd already reached that conclusion. "Makes the most sense to me. Buck?"

Chris could feel Officer Clayton nodding behind him.

Bradley grinned winningly. "And I've instructed Mr. Springer to call this office the moment his wife—this woman and child— step through the door. Meantime, we've already run a check on you, Chris—pardon the intrusion—with the Ventura County Police Department. And you check out just fine. Your address in Ventura County, your car registration—"

"Wait a second. If you've checked my residence there, then you know Matty is my wife."

Bradley frowned, shuffling papers on his desk, looking under files. "According to our reports—where is that damn thing?— according to our reports you're a male, Caucasian, age forty-two, single."

"That's ridiculous."

"Says so here." He handed the printout to Chris.

Chris glanced, tossed it on the desk. "Look, Sheriff—"

"How long were you married to this"—he glanced at his papers—"Matty person, Chris?"

"Three years."

"Married three years." And now Sheriff Bradley was scribbling notes. "And where did this marriage take place, Chris?"

"Las Vegas."

"Uh-huh. The year?"

"1992, August. Look, we'd be on file there, wouldn't we?"

"Where is that, Chris? Name of the church?"

He had to think about it a moment. It had been a hastily arranged affair, a last-minute, adolescent frenzy.

Marry me first?

He remembered the motel outside the strip a lot more clearly than the little Vegas office that served as a church. "Church something. Little Church of the West. Something like that."

Bradley scribbled. "Uh-huh. You wouldn't recall the address?"

"Christ, wouldn't we be on file somewhere in the county clerk's office?"

Bradley scribbled, nodded. "Could be. We'll certainly check it out. Wife's maiden name?"

And Chris, knowing damn well Bradley knew it, only wanted Chris to say it aloud, obliged him evenly. "Springer."

"That's it," Bradley scribbled.

The desk phone rang.

Sheriff Bradley cradled it to his shoulder, still jotting. "Uh-huh. All right. Thanks."

Hung up, looked past Chris. "That was Doc Holiday. Says he needs to see Mr. Nielson in his office pronto. Says it's urgent."

Chris could hear Clayton moving behind him, probably putting on his hat, his pride and joy. He never seemed to wear the hat indoors.

"This is a small town, Sheriff," Chris told him. "An attractive redhead and a little boy of two can't be that hard to find."

"And we've got every available man out looking, Chris; you can bet on it. Now, for the moment I want Buck to escort you back to the clinic and see what's got the doc all puffed up. I'll call you from here the second we get any kind of word. You can rely on that. Believe it or not, this is not the first missing-persons case our little hick town has dealt with. Leave it to us, Chris. Buck?"

Officer Clayton's hand was atop Chris's shoulder even before he could rise.

Doc Holiday already had the X ray of the head's profile. A translucent ghost of Chris's inner self, it was tucked beneath the metal catch of the glowing light box on the office wall.

Holiday was on the phone as Chris and Officer Clayton re-entered the office. He hung up, turned with his warm country smile. "Ah, good. How's the head, Chris?"

Chris stood stolidly, telegraphing no interest in sitting down— this would be a brief stay. "My head is fine, Doctor," he lied. It throbbed dully.

Holiday grunted. "In fact, it may not be so fine, I'm afraid to say." He indicated the glowing X ray. "Switch off that light and you'll see better."

"I can see it fine."

"All right. Can you see this . . . ?" He pointed with his little finger. "This little blur of silver above the left temporal lobe. That's a cranial fissure, Chris. Not necessarily a problem in itself. It's this grayish area below it here I'm concerned about." And he indicated with the pinky again.

Chris stood his ground. "Yes?"

Holiday sucked a tooth. "X rays are immensely helpful tools, but hardly perfect. This is a new machine and I may have muffed it, but I developed two plates. This is the clearer of the two."

None of this matters, goddamn it! My wife and child are missing! Can't you idiots see that?

But he didn't say it.

Because of course they could see it. And evidently, so much more. How much more, that's what Chris had to find out. And he had to stay very cool and be very careful in the finding. Otherwise they'd let him deal with the broad-shouldered Officer Clayton, and everything would be so by-the-book he'd never find out anything.

Very cool, very collected: "From the hip, please, Doctor."

Holiday nodded. "Well, this gray area we're talking about, it does not have the earmarks of a tumor, so put that from your mind right away. It may be merely an extra convolution, excess tissue. It happens, means nothing, nothing to worry about."

"Or?"

"Or it may be an area where internal bleeding is collect-ing. Again, if it stabilizes, nothing to worry about. I'd rather it not be there, but people have lived perfectly normal lives with worse things in their brains. It becomes a problem if and when it develops into hematoma. That can cause pressure, and complications."

"Such as?"

Holiday shrugged. "In its present location? At the least, chronic headaches. At worst, blindness, epilepsy."

Chris poked his hands on his hips. "Why didn't you mention this before?"

Holiday consulted the X ray, avoiding Chris's eyes. "Just missed it, I reckon. I'm a bit new with this machine, as I said."

"I see. So what do we do about it, Doctor?"

Holiday pushed the black rims to the bridge of his nose, consulted notes absently atop his cluttered desk. "Well, bore through the cranium if need be, into the offending area, drain it like an abscessed tooth. Or nothing, if it doesn't grow and if you don't develop symptoms." He looked up at Chris. "Any dizziness at all? Nausea?"

"No. I'm a little hungry."

Holiday smiled. "Any strange odors? Smell of oranges, for example, where there are no oranges?"

"No."

"Good. That's good. Good sign."

Chris watched him a moment, bit back a sardonic smile. "So what do you think, Doc? Could something like this affect my memory? Make me believe events occurred that didn't occur at all, that sort of thing?"

Holiday cleared his throat, shuffled papers. "Well, it certainly is a possibility in cases like this. Anything's possible where the brain's concerned. Best to be prudent, not jump to conclusions. As I said, it may be nothing at all. We'll have to wait and see."

"And how do we do that?" Chris asked, beginning to recognize the signs of a definite pattern.

Holiday sat in his worn swivel chair, eliciting a protesting squeak. "Depends. I'd certainly like you to stay with us for a spell. Preferably in a bed."

Stay with us.

"You have that kind of facility in this little clinic?" Chris asked amiably.

Holiday shook his head, anticipating it. "No, but I have an arrangement with Kelsie Baxter down at the bed-and-breakfast.

She has a room we use sometimes. You'd have complete privacy, much better than an ordinary hospital room, hell of a lot better than the damn Mayo Clinic. You'll get three hot meals a day, and I'll be close by to pop in, check on you." He winked. "And Kelsie's a pretty lady!"

Chris nodded, glanced quickly at Clayton's direction, saw himself in mirrored eyes. "Sounds ideal."

"Lot cheaper than you'll find in the city. And if it turns out to be nothing—which it probably is—you can be on your way no worse for wear and with a clean conscience. Any luck finding your family?"

"We're working on it," Officer Clayton put in.

Chris rubbed his chin as if in genuine consideration, though he'd already made up his mind. "Well, Doctor, I certainly appreciate your concern. The bed-and-breakfast sounds like good advice; I'll give it serious thought. By the way, would I be able to make the necessary arrangements there myself?"

Holiday nodded. "Just tell Kelsie to buzz me for confirmation." And he glanced at Clayton, then quickly away again.

Chris continued to nod agreeably. "I'll need a place to stay anyway while Officer Clayton checks into finding my family."

Chris moved quickly to shake Holiday's hand, put an end to it, get out of there. "Thanks again for all your help. I'll certainly give it serious consideration."

"It'd be for the best, Chris. You oughtn't to be moving about with that head. Especially driving."

"Uh-huh. Well, thanks again. I'll be in touch."

Holiday scribbled on a notepad. "Here's a prescription for something that will make you more comfortable. Use Peterson's Apothecary on the corner; Pete's the cheapest. Generic brand will do." He looked up. "Oh, you don't have money."

"I've got plastic as soon as I call for a new card."

Holiday nodded, handed the prescription to Chris, who tucked it in his shirt pocket. "Don't fret about my bill for now, or Kelsie's. Main thing is to get you off your feet as soon as possible."

"I suppose I'd have time to grab some lunch first?"

Holiday smiled. "Of course. Just have Kelsie call me when you're all checked in. She's a nice lady, take good care of you. Buck, you help him if he needs to carry anything."

"Will do, Doc."

"I'll have Billy send over the paperwork later."

"Paperwork?" Chris raised a brow.

Holiday waved it off. "Insurance forms, that stuff. Pain in the butt. The state makes us check you in just like at a regular clinic. You sign a couple of sheets, nothing to it. You have insurance?"

"Yes."

"There you go."

"Fine. Well, thanks again. You'll be hearing from me." And before Clayton could say anything, Chris, to maintain control, turned to him. "Can I see you for a moment outside, Buck?"

"Sure."

On the sun-glaring sidewalk, Chris pretended to study the prescription with great concern. "Now, where's this pharmacy the doc mentioned?" he asked the officer helplessly.

Clayton was tugging on his hat. "Just there on the corner. Can't miss it."

"Fine. Listen, Buck, sorry about before. I'm a little stressed out." He held up the prescription. "Now I know why."

"Forget it. Understandable. We'll have plenty of time to sort out the details after you've had some rest."

"Right. Thanks." Chris heaved a noticeable sigh, as though having settled a great struggle within himself, looked around the trendy little main street with weary eyes. "Well, I'm going to grab a bite to eat, then hit that bed-and-breakfast. Head's beginning to ache a bit. Where's a good place for a burger?"

"Maxine's down the block. Homemade fries."

"Sounds great." He extended his hand. "Thanks again, Buck. And you'll contact me the moment you hear from Matty and my boy?"

Clayton took the hand. "We're on top of it, Chris. We'll find them; you have my word."

Chris started away. Officer Clayton, not easily rid of, slapped Chris gently on the back. "I'll just tag along with you to Maxine's. Time for my lunch break anyway."

Over a dripping red cheeseburger that was probably quite good but which he hardly tasted, Chris mentioned to Officer Clayton conversationally, "Doc Holiday seems a very conscientious man."

Clayton, his Smokey hat riding the back of his chair, was wolfing down the blue plate special, something that required no articulated order, just a routine nod when they walked in. "Oh, Doc, he's the best. Saved my bacon more than once."

"How's that, Buck?"

Clayton talked around enormous mouthfuls. "Snake bite. Big rattler down by Wicket Crick. Got to watch where you step around here."

Chris watched to see if the cop was being clever, not able to tell.

"And what you step on," Clayton added. "Doc had the antivenin. I carry it with me now in the squad car."

The restaurant, small and homey and full of original stainless fittings, real leather booths and good smells, was nearly empty. Not yet lunch hour. The few morning stragglers—mostly elderly cronies—eyed Chris and Clayton curiously from red leather stools, as though Chris were getting preferential treatment dining with the sheriff's deputy officer.

"I don't suppose you see a lot of major crime in a town this size," Chris went on for something to say, stalling, thinking of Matty and Nicky, trying to figure a way to dump the big cop, wondering where to look first and how, knowing the answer lay with Frank Springer but not knowing how to get back up there yet, not discreetly anyway.

"More than we used to. Lot of people moving in. You'd be surprised how many from California like yourself. Them earthquakes. But we still spend the majority of our time digging tourists out of ditches," he looked up smiling, "or off mountains!"

Chris smiled back obligingly. "You don't like all the newcomers to your fair city, huh?"

Clayton shrugged, chewing. "Hell, I don't mind. I just got a raise. More people, more money. You see that big mess of construction down north of Main?"

"Yes, I did."

"Building one of them multi-plex theaters. Hell, this town never had even a single little movie house, now they're building a multi-plex. People tire of skiing and hiking, they want something to do at night besides watch the stars." He nodded down at the table. "You're not eating much."

Chris studied the barely touched burger. "My head. Little nausea."

"You want to take the Doc's advice, get off your feet, let Kelsie take care of you over to the bed-and-breakfast."

Chris was gazing out the front window, past the backward red and green MAXINE'S lettering, at Main Street, wondering where Matty might be out there. "Well, Buck, to tell you the truth, I'm a bit torn about that. I have some unfinished work back home, you see."

Clayton looked up from his fries. "Ventura?"

Chris nodded. "Thousand Oaks. Just some unfinished stuff with the phone company back there. I was a lineman before we moved here to Colorado. Mostly I just need to tell them where to send my insurance papers, social security number, that sort of thing."

"Couldn't you do that by phone?"

Chris looked as though he hadn't given it serious thought. "Well, I have some equipment to give them, stuff in my trunk I forgot to turn in."

"You could mail that."

Chris conceded: "Maybe. They're a little picky about company property going through the mail." He rubbed distractedly at his head for effect.

"Hurts, huh?"

Chris nodded. "I suppose I really should get off my feet. I just hate worrying about unfinished business." He craned around. "I wonder if I could make a call from here. Try to reach my office."

"Sure. Maxine's got a phone there in the back, next to the johns."

Chris didn't get up too fast. "Yeah, I suppose that would be best."

Clayton chewed fries, oblivious of intrigue. "You go make your call; I'll take care of the tab here."

"Oh, I couldn't let you."

Clayton held up his free hand. "I insist." He leaned forward as if the courtesy had pushed them past some crucial point in the relationship, made them old friends. "Maybe the Sheriff wouldn't like me saying this, Chris, but to tell you the truth, everyone would feel a lot better if you stayed in town, let us take care of you. I'm not saying you're the type, mind you. But well, in the past, some of these tourists, some of these clowns who get themselves in what they refer to as accidents, well they end up suing the city in the process, if you see what I mean. We're a small town, despite the newcomers. What money we make is still dependent mostly on the tourist trade. Sheriff Bradley might not like me saying this."

Or maybe he instructed you to say it, Chris thought, just in case I needed added inducement. "I understand, Buck. It probably makes the most sense for me to stay right here in Greenborough."

"I really think it does, Chris," Clayton assured sympathetically.

Chris pushed up. "I'll just make that call. Here. Let me get the tip, at least."

But Clayton held up both hands. "Taken care of!"

"Well, thanks, Buck, I appreciate it."

The phone was located, thankfully, in a narrow, remote hallway, not within easy earshot of the dining room.

"Operator, I want to place a collect call to Thousand Oaks, California." He gave the name and number.

Waited.

"Hello?"

Operator: "Collect call from Chris Nielson. Will you accept charges?"

And Sharon Corman's deliciously familiar voice answered, "Yes, of course. Chris?"

Operator: "Go ahead, sir."

"Sharon."

"Hi! How are you? Is everything okay?"

She'd find out all of it soon enough, not now. "Just homesick. Honey, is Rick home for lunch yet by chance?"

"Yes, he's in the den, watching the game. Is Matty okay?"

"Fine! I'm on kind of a tight schedule, though, sweetheart. Let me speak to Rick a sec, huh?"

And with an edge of concern Sharon answered, "Sure, hold on. . . ."

In background void that was the Cormans' kitchen or family room, Chris heard the hollow sound of Rick's name being called. Chris imagined his former neighbor, sprawled in his favorite threadbare easy chair, sandwich in hand, trying to decide whether to get back to work or stay for one more touchdown. Good money in being a lineman these days.

Sharon, meanwhile—intuitive, wise Sharon—probably unconvinced this call wasn't serious, made no attempt at idle chatter while her husband stuffed in a last mouthful of sandwich and came to the phone.

"Homesick already, huh? All right, you poor country hick, you can have the spare room."

"We're in trouble, Rick. I have to make this fast."

And Rick, abruptly sober, swallowed food. "What? Shoot."

"It's crazy. I can't start way back at the beginning. You'll have to trust me."

"What can I do? Is it Matty?"

"Yes, and Nicky. I think they're all right for now, but I need you to get up here."

"Was it an accident? Are you hurt?"

"Not yet. I'd like to leave Sharon out of it for now. Is that impossible?"

"Tough, not impossible. I have a conference in Chicago tomorrow night, something about fiber-optic cable. Chicago's close to you anyway."

"What about the conference?"

"Screw it—they'll survive without me. It's my best excuse to Sharon. Is it soon enough?"

"It'll have to do. Now listen. I want you to stay clear of the house when you get here. Don't go near it."

"Where are you, Chris?"

"Just listen. You're to check into the Greenborough Bed-and-Breakfast on Main as a Mr. Adams. If they ask for ID, you lost your driver's license or whatever. Pay cash. Pay cash for everything, so bring plenty. Can you do this without Sharon knowing?"

"I can do it. Where will you be?"

"I'll be at the bed-and-breakfast. But don't, and this is important, do *not* try to contact me. I'll contact you. Try for an afternoon flight. But *no* phone calls. You don't know me; understand what I'm saying?"

"Jesus!" There was excitement behind the concern in Rick's voice. An adventure was beginning, the kind Rick had missed since 'Nam.

"Did you write it down?"

"Greenborough Bed-and-Breakfast."

"Go down to the restaurant at six sharp—that's Colorado time. Be sure to adjust your watch. Pick a double booth and order a big meal. Keep your big mouth shut. You're a tourist. Don't screw it up. I'll be along soon."

"How long am I staying?"

"At least a week. And listen, bring enough money to buy some hardware. Can Sharon hear you?"

"At this point, yes, uh-huh."

"All right. Bring enough for at least a couple of deer rifles, handguns if we can get them."

"That will be fine, yes, Chris." Rick's eagerness was barely contained now.

"Okay, on your horse."

"Well, good hearing from you. You take care now."

"Six sharp."

"Same to Matty. Bye!"

Officer Clayton was forking into a thick slab of cherry pie when Chris, smiling, sat down again.

"Everything okay with the phone company?" he asked between bites.

"Just dandy," Chris said, and now he tackled the cheeseburger.

Feeling—if not actually better—less alone.

PART II

CHAPTER 11

Matty awoke in her own bed at her usual time, ocher light sweeping through billowing north window curtains, birds singing, the wake-up smell of rich coffee wafting from below. That meant Chris must already be up. Bless him for letting her sleep.

Then she remembered it all.

My God.

Her first collected thoughts: *I'm still alive.*

She sat up without even a headache, brushed back burnished curls, caught herself in the bureau mirror opposite the bed, startled and laughably owl-eyed. She wore her flannel pajamas, not the ridiculous see-through nightie.

God in heaven, *could* it have been a dream?

She kicked over the mattress edge, grabbed her robe, shrugged into it, not bothering with her warm wool slippers until she'd checked first on Nicky.

She found him snug and sleeping easily in his blue plastic racing car bed, hugging Black Bear in a death lock. She touched the cherubic forehead: warm but not sweating. He did look pale and wan, though. Or was that the morning light?

She came to the hall.

"Chris?"

Matty cautiously descended the stairs to the living room, the kitchen. Hot coffee was warming on the counter. Everything neat and clean. Spotless. Her curious reflection watched her in the hanging stainless skillet over the stove.

"Chris?"

Clutching the robe's bodice with hopeful fingers, she hurried to the front door, found it unlocked, pulled it to her.

It was clear and bright and cool outside. The big maples were beginning to show color now. The shiny Lamborghini gleamed at her from the drive. Chris's Volvo was gone.

She stood there, breeze lifting a strand of hair across her eyes. She retrieved it, chewing her lip. Chris's car was gone, yet Frank seemed to be gone as well.

It's your chance! Get the baby out of there!

She jerked reflexively at the thought, caught herself. She'd been fooled by this before. Many was the time he'd appeared to be gone, only to show up at the last moment, in the least possible place, with that grin. That grin.

She shut the door.

Called at the top of her lungs. *"Frank!"*

Nothing.

And the house did *feel* empty.

It's a trick. A trap. One of his games.

She had to think. Don't rush this, don't blow this, there's a logic to it somewhere. Figure it out.

Never mind that, goddamn it! Get Nicky out of the house!

Her animal instincts took over. Yes. Get Nicky safe. That was the only important thing.

She turned, hesitated, turned back. She saw a vision of herself fleeing with the sleeping child—the eventually *heavy* child—through dew-flecked woodlands, tangled, exhausting brush.

Try the phone again.

She did, and of course it was still dead.

She stood listening to the empty nothingness in the receiver, whatever feelings of normalcy about the morning she'd allowed herself to indulge conveniently erased. She recognized the familiar edge of panic, felt it building.

Matty threw open the door abruptly and hurried down the walk, the rough gravel drive to the big red sports car. It was useless, a waste of time, she knew, but she had to check, had to know.

She bent to the silvery handle, pulled. To her amazement it

came open easily. To her further amazement, Frank's car keys dangled in the ignition.

Too easy. Too inviting.

Yet there it was.

She had only to dress, gather Nicky in her arms, and make a break for it. He might be out there somewhere, might be right down the road, waiting for her with a shotgun. But so what? She'd push Nicky low in the seat, duck down herself behind the wheel, floor the big engine, and blast past him somehow.

It was a chance.

A chance you've had before.

But still a chance. She sprinted up the stairs. Grabbed shorts and halter top from the closet, not bothering to dress this time, lifted Nicky gently (he looked so terribly pale). "Come on, baby," and ran with him back down the stairs.

Frank would be there, waiting at the foot of the stairs. Or the front porch. Or sitting in the red sports car. Smiling. Smiling.

But he was not.

Not even thinking of the keys to the house, she swept down the drive, cradling Nicky in her arms, reached for the silvery handle again, jerked it open, and placed the baby carefully in the seat beside her.

You've done all this before.

Reached for the ignition—mouthed a silent prayer—and twisted.

Click, thunk. Nothing.

No roar of massive Italian engine, no comforting rumble of the seat beneath her. Nothing. Just the light, soughing breeze, the mindless arguing of sparrows.

And then something more.

"Doe, a deer, a female deer . . ."

She looked up, trembling now violently without the big engine, saw him coming through the screen of woods directly before her. He had on the plaid hunting shirt she'd bought Chris last year, a spring buck across his shoulders, a big one, its antlered head dangling loosely. And yes, smiling as he sang.

". . . ray, a drop of golden sun . . ."

Matty sat back, abruptly drained of all resolve.

You couldn't beat him. You could not beat him. God knows she'd tried.

Frank came level with her side window, bent to wink ". . . me, a name I call myself . . . Top of the morning, kitten! Had breakfast yet?"

He carried no weapon, no weapon she could see. Probably, somewhere, he had the big hunting knife hidden under his jacket. Or maybe he'd merely run the deer down. Impossible as that sounded, it was entirely probable where Frank Springer was concerned. Frank Springer could do anything. Anything.

He grinned down at her, looked over at the sleeping child, took one of the deer's dangling forelegs in his hand, and waved a muddy hoof at Nicky. "Hi there! How we feeling today?"

Matty didn't even look at him. "What did you do? Why aren't I dead?"

Frank turned to her, seeming not to feel what was surely a massive amount of weight on his broad shoulders. "How's that, kitten?"

"What was in the syringe, Frank?"

"The syringe? Oh, the syringe! Just a sedative. You were pretty much in shock from exhaustion anyway." And now his expression, when she finally turned to look, was one of shock itself. "Matty, you don't think I'd have put anything lethal in it. Not to my own son."

She turned away, absently studied the traces of reddish gold lining the maples beside the drive.

She could sense him smiling again. "He *is* my son, right? I mean, we've established that, have we not?"

She let her head fall back, closed her eyes in submission, hands still on the useless wheel. "What are you going to do, Frank? Chris will be back here with the authorities any second."

"Really? You think so?"

"Of course."

"Whatever for?"

"Must we play games?"

"I'm not playing games. I hope Chris isn't. You're my wife. We've already established that Nicky is my son. The house is in your name, which also makes it my property. What game is there to play?"

For a moment she thought it was just another of his absurd ramblings. Then a pang struck. She opened her eyes, turned. Found him smiling.

"What in God's name are you up to, Frank?"

He beamed, patted the dead buck's flank. "For later, some fine venison stew. For now, a little surprise. You're going to love it. Like a second honeymoon."

Matty grimaced inwardly, remembering the first honeymoon, the first time she'd realized just exactly how insane he was. The things he said. The things he made her do.

Her plans—even back then—had been to run someday.

"Just let me get this strung up and drained, and I'll be right with you, kitten."

He headed off jovially for the back of the house. "Fa, a long, long way to run! . . ."

Matty gazed over at her innocently sleeping son.

A long long way to run.

She could attempt it now. Say to hell with the damn car, grab Nicky while Frank was busy with the deer, and bolt for the woods.

Yes, she could.

She could also be caught. Springer ran like the wind. And that would be the least of it. His true way of punishing her would be through the child. It was an unspoken agreement between them. As long as she did not try to flee, did his bidding, Springer might— *might*—agree to not hurt the child.

He was capable of the worst; she must never forget that. Not that she could. It wasn't hard to conjure old memories. The Honeymoon from Hell. The little mist-flecked cabin near the railed parapet, the constant, distant thundering of the falls. His hands in the dark. His hard-muscled body. The things he'd asked her to do. The places he'd asked her to touch. Lick.

". . .women are all bitches. Oh, it's true. Their cruelty is legendary. Zingua, for instance, queen of Angola, cruelest of all women. Killed her lovers as soon as they'd come in her. . . . To flatter her ferocious spirit she had every pregnant woman of less than thirty ground in a mortar before her eyes while she fucked. . . .

". . . make it hard, Matty (grunting). . . . Make it hard, you simpering bitch, or I'll kick you again. . . ."

She swallowed back the memories, the terror and revulsion.

Yes, he would kill the child. Then start to work on her. She was walking a delicate line. Their only chance now was Chris.

But, of course, he'd kill Chris as well. That too was part of the plan.

In the boat, Frank was ebullient.

Blond hair swept flying in the wind, white teeth smiling fiercely beneath Chris's captain's cap, he commanded the Chris-Craft's wheel as easily as he'd mastered anything she'd ever seen him touch, as though he'd been driving powerboats all his life. For all Matty knew, he had.

"I think it was just marvelous of good old 'Uncle Arky' to buy us this wonderful craft, don't you, dear? That's a genuine mahogany deck; did you know that, kitten?"

She was staring at Nicky, still asleep, curled on tan cushions beside her, wrapped in the afghan Frank had allowed her to bring along, jouncing with the bow's spanking beat.

Nicky had been asleep for hours now, perhaps more than a full day. It was becoming dangerous.

Her dread had gone past the possibilities of brain damage and epilepsy. She feared coma now, the dark sleep of forever, feared she'd never see her son's bright green eyes again, hear his musical laugh.

She turned to grinning Frank with the beginnings of an imploring expression. But what was the point? Every time the child's name was even mentioned, the clouds descended over the sharp Nordic features; the air took an almost palpable shift of energy. All she could hope now was that he had not brought them out here on the chill, deep waters to dispose of the child.

Murder was second nature to him. A friend. He'd called it that once. "Life can be treacherous, kitten, deceitful, but there's real inner peace in murder."

Even in the execution of an infant. A sociopath knows not of guilt, of boundaries. Frank could as easily drop Nicky over the gunwale into the rushing foam as swat a fly, without an inkling of self-recrimination. He could lie in bed later that night and describe in relentless detail his personal vision of the child's demise: the terrified descent into blackness and cold, the cruel water rushing into tender lungs, the gasping convulsions, final trickle of bubbles, innocent, glassy eyes sinking into dispassionate silt, unheeding muck.

Frank could tell it all vividly, coolly, unblinkingly. Tell what the fishes would do later with the tiny, pale body. Tell it with the vivid clarity of the insane. While Matty ministered to him on the sheets, labored before him as he made her do things to him, grunting and laughing.

But not yet. First he'd have his little game. Punish her with the waiting, the not knowing. Then, when she least expected it, when he'd lured her into a sense of false security, he'd strike. Swift, deadly. With utter finality.

Even so, she could not stop herself. "Frank?"

"Yes, my love?"

"The baby, Frank. Please! He's been sedated for hours. He has a fever. He's had no food or water. He must be dehydrated. He'll die, Frank."

Frank smiled. "Just look at this lake, would you?" He beamed. "I used to *dream* of a place like this. Those days in the Funhouse, I used to *masturbate* thinking of a place like this. With you. With a little boy of our own."

He turned beguiling eyes on Matty. "I never dreamed it would all come true someday, that we'd be here, just the three of us, on this beautiful lake, in that beautiful house. I never dreamed you'd give me a son, kitten."

She was feeling Nicky's wrist with thumb and forefinger. "Please, Frank! His pulse is weaker."

Frank looked down at the sleeping child. "A Springer doesn't have a weak pulse. We all have strong, powerful hearts. A northern people. The Caspian Sea. Our ancestors fought the Mongol hordes."

He turned to look at her with black, unyielding eyes, a face gone abruptly to stone. "Assuming, of course, it is my son."

An air horn barked to their left, fifty yards across windswept whitecaps; a lake patrol boat, khaki-uniformed arm waving a friendly greeting.

Frank smiled obligingly, waved back: just a family outing on the lake.

Matty watched the big cruiser pace them for a moment, pull slowly away.

She jerked reflexively, almost stood in the Chris-Craft, almost waved frantically at them. Once they'd pulled alongside, they'd see the wan, sick little boy. She wouldn't even have to tell them this was not her husband at all but a madman who'd kidnapped them.

And she almost did it.

Except she knew how it would end. Her standing helplessly by as Frank, still grinning, not even breathing hard, killed both the nice officers with his hands and sank their boat. All without losing more than a few minutes or attracting further attention on the mostly empty lake. It was fall. The tourists had gone. The Chris-Craft was at lake's center, far from the probing eyes of the few beach houses. Frank could do it all, quickly, neatly (relatively) and without event.

She watched the patrol craft dwindle in the distance.

Something was coming.

She could tell from the look on Frank's face. It had changed. The usual sardonic smile replaced by intense anticipation.

He was going to drown the child.

But no. She could see what it was now, looming toward them out of shroud of late morning north shore mist: an opening. An entrance, flanked by knee-high bulrushes, jagged granite islands, and fallen juniper. A river.

The lake held a secret, something she'd never seen or heard about. A narrow river mouth, hardly twenty feet apart. But widening gradually now as they plummeted down it, Frank not throttling back at all but surging recklessly away (was there another way with Frank?) as though he'd been here before.

And smiling, smiling.

What on earth was he up to?

Matty looked askance at him, her head snapping hard as she did. The boat lurched nearly out of control, then swept back to the river's center under Frank's steady hand.

He winked at her. "Rocks hitting the keel. Water's shallow here. Sorry about that."

Another spine-jarring thump, less severe. Frank craned over the bow to watch for sunken obstacles. She wished to God he'd slow the goddamn boat before they were all killed. A heron flashed by in a blur of drumming wings, squawking alarm.

Another bump, sharper, the craft sluicing. Frank regained control with his tight grin. He was loving this, loving terrifying her.

Matty looked out across the raised bow, higher now that they were out of the whitecaps and Frank had increased speed recklessly. The opposing riverbanks seemed to be closing in again. Forty feet . . . thirty . . .

There was a sound like nails on blackboard. A black-taloned branch clawed across the passenger's side, reaching for them. Matty cried out, stretching for Nicky. Too late to prevent a dark-clawed twig raking his pale forehead with a tracing of red.

"Goddamn it, Frank! Slow down!" She pulled Nicky to her, wiped the scratch with her elbow. It wasn't a deep wound, and not bleeding much from his pasty, colorless forehead, but the idea of it filled her with a white fury.

Frank glanced at them a moment, pushed the throttle forward gleefully, the boat leaping.

The riverbanks closed in on both sides. Twenty feet. Fifteen.

"Frank!"

A gray boulder, larger than a car and dripping lichen, rushed at them.

Matty could see it all in an instant: the bow splintering, twin engines ripping through polished mahogany, their bodies flying forward.

"You *bastard!*" she screamed above the engine's whine.

She dropped her son on the cushions, grabbed the wheel. Frank chuckled, grip like steel, the wheel unyielding.

"Turn it, *turn it!*"

He backhanded her hard, knocking her across Nicky's fragile, doll-like form, the child producing a sibilant *shuuuu* sound. Matty glanced up to see the big rock filling the sky, the sun, cold shadow rushing to take her head off. Rushing inches past instead, her hair lifted in the backwash.

And now they were slowing, Frank throttling back.

Slowing rather quickly. The twin Evinrudes growling to a burbled purr over which another sound became immediately audible. A rolling, familiar noise she could not place.

Matty sat up. The river before them disappeared into a rising plume of roiling mist. "Frank?"

He idled down as the river widened again, nosed the Chris-Craft toward the right shore and put her in neutral. They bumped the muddy bank gently, and then they were there, the roar deafening now. A waterfall.

Frank twisted off the ignition and grinned triumphantly at her. "Didn't I tell you it was a surprise? Just like Niagara Falls, huh, kitten?"

He vaulted the gunwale, grabbed the mooring line, and tied them to a sapling. The swift-moving current already was pulling the stern about, making the line taut.

Then he bent and reached for Nicky.

Matty moved forward, forgetting for just that microsecond how swift he was. She never saw the blow coming, never really felt it, only her back hitting the hard transom, neck snapping forward, knuckles scraping painful metal.

When she'd pushed up again, reeling, they were gone, Nicky in his arms, moving toward the thundering falls.

"Frank!"

She scuttled from the boat, colors dancing before her eyes, fell in sucking mud, pushed up, and stumbled after him. "Frank! Please!"

He's going to throw him over the falls.

Matty, head in a vortex, ran, ignoring searing pain in her back, her legs.

It had been his plan all along.

She ran, tripping, gasping, as in a dream, slow-motion and ethereal, in which the forest, the river, the roaring of the falls all congealed into one hideous undulant entity, through which she could not possibly push, not in time to stop him. "Frank! For the love of God!"

Ignoring her, not even looking back, Springer moved into the water, to his ankles, thighs, bucking the surging current at the very lip of the thundering falls. He balanced himself precariously with his precious cargo, the river tearing at his knees, the slime-covered rocks slippery beneath waffle-soled boots. One slip. One little slip . . .

Matty ran. Skidded, fell, tearing a bare knee, pinwheeled, still running, up again running, running, to the very brink of the falls. She gazed over the chasm, the cascading river hurling its tons of sun-dancing liquid, the dizzy drop—fifty feet if it was an inch—to flat, immutable rock, churning spume, the roar so loud it blotted out the world.

Frank!

She waded out into the rushing water, instantly snatched away by the impossible force, a mammoth hand swatting her. Matty screamed, twisting, grabbing, branches, rock, shoreline. Clawing, digging, she dragged herself drenched and hacking back among current-bent bulrushes.

She looked back to see them. Frank held Nicky at the very center of the falls.

Frank braced like a pit bull, thick-muscled thighs bulging beneath the jeans plastered to them, back corded, forearms bunched. A Viking sacrificing a child. Her child, her baby, her life. She saw him lift Nicky over his head.

"Frank!" A silent wail welling unbidden from deep within her soul. She sank to her knees in the mud.

All gone. All ended. Everything she loved.

There was movement behind her. *"Hey!"*

Someone was shouting loudly, deep and basso, full of anger and disbelief.

Matty looked up, saw them standing there behind her on the shore: two boys in hiking boots and backpacks, and a girl, long straight blond hair streaming, fringed skirt, calf-high Indian moccasins, no makeup and buxom, like a hippie. She'd been sucking a lollipop, had taken it from her mouth now as she stared in astonishment at the bizarre sight at the edge of the falls.

Frank, his inexplicable reverie broken, turned at the sound.

The deep basso voice again, from one of the boys. "What the fuck you *doin'*, man!"

Frank gazed calmly at them. Smiled.

He began to wade back to shore, Nicky still in his arms.

Matty stood shuddering on rubber legs, daring to hope.

They came ashore, dripping, the unconscious child dangling, Frank smiling pleasantly at the young people, especially the long-tressed girl. "The golden age of Kievan Russia," he began, "was ruled by Vladimir, one of three sons of Svyatoslav. Vladimir became grand prince."

The two boys looked at each other blankly. One of them drew off his backpack carefully, in slow, almost rehearsed gestures.

"It is not for his political or military success we remember Vladimir, however, but for the part he played in religion."

Frank, still holding the child, watched calmly as the hiker set the pack gingerly on the ground. The boy's eyes never wavered from the dripping figure before him. There was a sense of something coming, of a line crossed never to be retreated from.

"In 986 representatives of the then current faiths attempted to convert him. The Khazars, of course, tried to teach him of Judaism. But when Vladimir asked them why the Jews had been driven from Jerusalem, their lame reply was, 'God was angry at our forefathers and scattered us among the gentiles because of our sins.' Well, clearly Vladimir had no interest in the religion of a dispersed people."

The tallest boy, the one who had not removed his pack, looked dubiously at the others, then back to Frank. "Man, what the fuck are you talking about?"

Frank offered a patient expression. "The Volga Bulgars

approached Vladimir next. They tried to get him to accept Islam. 'Mahaomet', they told him, 'in the next world, will give each man seventy fair women.' Now ordinarily Vladimir—a man who was not beyond lust—would have entertained such a proposition. The problem was, the Mohammedans added a caveat. Abstinence from wine as a condition of their faith. Naturally, Vladimir would have none of that. 'Drinking is the joy of the Russes,' he told them. 'We cannot exist without that pleasure.' "

The hiker on the ground was reaching casually, deliberately into the pack, eyes still locked on Frank. Springer no longer seemed interested in him, so committed was he to his lecture.

"Ah, but the Roman and Byzantine churches were something else again. Christianity had already been around awhile in Kievan Russia, in Vladimir's own family, in fact. The Cathedral of Hagia Sophia in Byzantium was a particularly glorious sight. Prince Vladimir therefore"—Frank held out the tiny dripping figure to them like a present—"not only became a full-fledged Christian, but decreed that all the people be baptized immediately." And he sat Nicky, soggy and fragile, and apparently baptized, at their feet.

Matty darted to her son, swept him up, felt with a surge of relief his faint breath against her cheek.

Frank turned to Indian Girl, her long blond hair wisping like spun gold in the breeze off the falls. "The *Primary* Chronicle tells us, however, that before—and perhaps even after—his conversion, the new prince was 'overcome by his lust for women.' He had at least seven wives, three hundred concubines at Vyshgorod, three hundred at Belgorod and two hundred at Berestovo." Springer smiled gently at the tall blond girl, her green oval eyes appraising him with sophomoric wonder. She seemed more fascinated than frightened. Frank smiled engagingly. "Tell me, as a matter of confidence, dear heart. These fine young men, do they fuck you one at a time, or both together?"

The girl pulled her slick lollipop from her mouth with an impudent pop, the astounded, open mouth revealing a delicate pointed tongue, paved Day-Glo green with confection.

The kneeling boy came up with a wide stainless hunting knife that caught and threw back sunlight. He held it loosely at his side.

"The attraction for the intermediary female is obvious here," Frank edified. "Though she lacks, of course, the male prostate, the woman's anus is still considered an erogenous zone, its contractions acting in tandem with those of the vagina, procuring a very satisfying orgasm in all three participants. The attendant males, of course, benefit further by the added sensation of their members rubbing together between the thin anal wall of the woman, though this, clearly, is an acquired taste some men find distracting."

The glinting knife came up slowly to a port position and the other, a darker-haired boy, stepped back a foot as if from a psychic signal, his left hand pulling the girl along with a will of its own. The hiker with the knife stepped between the two of them and Frank. "I think you'd better just get the fuck out of here now, mister."

Frank smiled.

The hiker, knife before him, turned eyes but not head toward Matty. "Are you with this guy, ma'am?"

Matty had backed up two steps of her own—Nicky tight against her chest—already seeing the not distant future as clearly as through prophetic crystal. "Run," she instructed them evenly.

All three looked at her as if confronted with the unfathomable.

"With the three of us, of course," Frank continued casually, unbuttoning his flannel shirt, "we would need to utilize the single, unemployed orifice. I would suggest the two men act in chorus, encunting and sodomizing her, while I labor over that bountiful chest and proffer my organ to her lips."

The hiker with the knife leapt, ignoring Matty's shrill warning. *"No!"*

Frank received him gracefully, guided the deadly blade easily away, locked them in embrace. A brief scuffle, a carelessly flung foot, and the backpack went sprawling, a silvery transistor radio flying from the open end, striking a rock, and blaring into life. The O'Jays: "Love Train."

Frank hugged the boy tighter. "Wait! Wait! I *love* this song!" He whirled about and began to dance with him, the silvery blade hidden somewhere between them.

"Run!" Matty screamed at the other two.

But they stood speechless, dumb and uncomprehending, though the blonde with the long hair shaped the beginnings of a word with her delicate oval mouth, her funny green tongue.

". . . *people all over the world—join hands . . .*"

Frank whirled the boy round and round, locked tight, their soles throwing up little clouds of dust and briars.

Frank laughed gleefully, the boy's face beet red with fear and dizziness and something else.

Faster round and round.

The blond girl screamed abruptly, tongue glowing green in sunlight, lollipop dropped and forgotten. A thin ribbon of blood had started at the dancing boy's lips, tracing the determined chin. Frank let him go.

The boy spun one more lazy time, a wobbly, vertiginous circle, head bowed, uncomprehending face accessing his shirt front, the blossoming patch of sepia.

Frank cavorted—oblivious or unconcerned with his late partner—clapped his hands to the thumping beat. Matty saw now it was Frank who had possession of the knife, safely belted and put away. The blade not even red.

The hiker staggered to a bowlegged crouch, ripped at the baggy front of his shirt. Ripped and moaned like an animal as the wet, gray snake of his intestines spilled free. "Oh no . . . ," he said simply. "Oh no oh no . . ."

The blond girl screamed louder, piercing, but still she did not run. She stood rooted, watching her young friend's futile attempts to gather his slippery insides, a waft of fecal stench reaching them from where the blade had bit deep and deeper, the blood making a waterfall of its own.

The other boy, ignoring screaming girl and eviscerated friend, bolted at last.

Frank reached him in four easy strides, tore back his head with a handful of black hair, brought the youth back on his knees, Adam's apple protruding, sliced through that with indifferent facility.

"The Assyrians believed," Frank told the hysterical blonde, "that if you fuck a man while beheading him, it produces a mutual orgasm, the victim's penis completing ejaculation even after the neck has been severed."

Matty found herself in deep woods, Nicky to her pumping chest, her legs churning with a will of their own, ignoring whipping brambles, cutting limbs.

Directionless, unthinking, she fled. As she had fled once before.

Behind her, over distant waterfall cacophony, she heard a

tandem crashing of foliage. The blonde, galvanized at last. Then a high, inhuman shriek, like a gutted horse, that broke off as abruptly as a record from a lifted needle.

Then there was only the sound of Matty's laboring lungs, the crunching beneath her flying sandals.

CHAPTER 12

Chris stalled around in the little restaurant, drinking cup after cup of Maxine's hot fresh coffee until what he hoped would happen finally did: The pager on Officer Clayton's black service belt beeped and he turned to retrieve it.

"Yeah, Clayton here. Uh-huh. All right."

Clayton belted the pager and took a final sip of his own coffee. "Somebody stuck in a snowdrift; they need an assist. Shit, I don't see why Harvey Hendricks can't handle it. He's the one with the damn snowplow."

"It's snowing already?" Chris asked with concern.

"In the higher elevations. Nothing for you to worry about yet. I have to go, Chris. Can you can get checked into the bed-and-breakfast all right?"

"I'm going there straight from here," Chris lied.

Officer Buck Clayton adjusted his wide-brimmed Smokey the Bear chapeau just so, twisting deftly back and forth until the desired effect was achieved. "Well, this little run up the mountain shouldn't take more than an hour. Call the office if you need anything."

"I will, Buck, thanks."

Clayton stood, dropped a wad of one-dollar bills. "And don't fret none about your wife and boy. They can't be far. We'll find them."

"I hope so, Buck."

"You count on it." He tipped his brim. "Stay loose."

"See you."

Chris sat quietly until the broad-shouldered uniform had moved past the glass door and into the black-and-white parked curbside, started the engine, and pulled away.

He sat awhile longer after that, too. He was thinking: Was the call real? Was Clayton parked down the street watching, waiting for his next move? What about the other officers in town? Had they been alerted to keep an eye on Mr. Nielson, the crazy man who claimed he lived up at the big A-frame when another man was already living there?

Chris cursed himself inwardly. If he'd only gotten into town sooner, showed himself around, made himself familiar with the locals, none of this would be happening. As it was, he was a complete stranger here. For all they knew, he really could be some out-of-town nut needing watching.

But why didn't it feel that way? Why did it feel like something else?

He got up, moved back to the pay phone, and dialed his number. He was rewarded with a busy signal. Really busy or disconnected?

He dialed the operator, told the local lady his problem.

"That's reading as a disconnect, sir."

"Well, it shouldn't be. I live there. Can I get someone up there right away to check on it?"

"Certainly, sir. Your address?"

Chris gave it to her, remembering Frank's newly painted plaque.

"That's listed under a Mr. Springer, correct?"

Chris didn't argue with her. "Yes."

"We'll get right on it, sir."

"Thank you." He hung up, strode from the café.

He stood blinking a moment later in the bright afternoon sun, checking his watch: 3:45.

He looked around the little town, the trendy shops, spotty areas of construction work. The cobble walks, nookery shops reminded him of Carmel, California, sans the reconstruction work and—of course—the attendant sea.

He lingered, thought about checking in at the sheriff's office but sensed instinctively it was a useless move: Sheriff Bradley might indeed know something by now. Might have known it for hours already, but he wasn't going to inform Chris of it. Something weird was going on in this town.

So how to play it?

A side-street office front had caught his eye earlier. He started for it now, feeling invisible eyes at his back.

He shifted direction with what looked like a casual move and crossed the street instead. He strode—still unhurriedly, hands in his pockets—two blocks to the Greenborough Bed-and-Breakfast.

It towered amid stately pines, a refurbished Victorian, most of the antique filigree looking original and well cared for, newly painted in blinding white. Three stories of pampered gingerbread, red tiled roof, cupolas and turrets and dormers, white lace curtains peeking out. It reminded him of those few remaining seaside hotels from the turn of the century.

The foyer was a symphony of muted crimson: red brocade curtains, wine red carpeting, ruby red crystal chandeliers that would cost a fortune now. All of it nearly too much red for the eye but offset by the warmth of oak paneling, the polished-to-gleaming wide oak front desk with its Jack London brass lamps and trim.

"I'm looking for a Kelsie Baxter," Chris told a red-uniformed girl behind the shiny service bell and leather-bound register.

"Are you Mr. Nielson?" the girl asked.

"Yes."

"You're all set up in room three-ten, sir." She turned, took a key from the rack behind her, handed it to Chris. "Any luggage, sir?"

"No, not for now, thank you."

She smiled her official bed-and-breakfast smile beneath freckles and red pillbox hat. "Elevator's that way. Restaurant's over there. If you need anything, just dial one."

Chris nodded, inwardly chagrined, that creeping sensation his life was being orchestrated for him. "Well. I guess I'm all set, then."

"Enjoy your stay, sir."

He approached the black wrought iron cage-style elevator at lobby center. Pressed a brass-framed button that lit softly. The interior, spotless and meticulously maintained like everything else in the hotel, lifted Chris roofward with a light vertiginous bump and comforting, well-oiled purr. He shared the lift with a dark-eyed beauty in green who smiled at him. Inviting? Chris nodded back without overdoing his own smile: He had other things on his mind, and the woman in green appeared to need little encouragement, looked to be on her own in the little resort town.

The hall on his floor was—to his relief—a demure beige, though the carpet remained the requisite red, the doors boasting cut-glass handles, big brass keyholes.

The room was smaller than he'd have expected but pleasant, with a working fireplace, though gas only and probably new. The bed was soft but comfortable—brass railing head and foot—the cabinets knotty pine and smelling of polish. Paintings of mountainscapes in oversize frames flanked the walls, and real marble sinks graced the bathroom with new, but antique-style, brass fixtures. Only the black eye of the TV with its attendant HBO card looked out of place; the phone had a French-style receiver, which was mixing cultures but at least old-fashioned. Someone had tried.

Chris washed his face and hands, dried them on fresh-smelling towels. He opened the bedside nightstand, found the thin Greenborough phone book under the Gideon Bible, flipped quickly, and dialed a number. "Hello, my name is Chris Nielson. I'm new in town and need some advice. Would you have some time this afternoon? I see. How about tomorrow morning? Good. Ten o'clock? Fine. See you then." And hung up thinking: no secretary, no receptionist. But it was a small town, after all.

He sat back against the brass headboard, found that uncomfortable, and slid down to the mattress. Exhaustion found him with almost frightening abruptness. He wanted—needed—desperately to close his eyes for a few minutes. But sleep seemed an act of betrayal. Were Matty and the baby sleeping now? Was Springer letting them? Even *with* them?

Hurting them?

He rolled to his side, found himself staring at one of the framed prints of mountain peaks, a badly rendered knockoff by a nobody artist. He turned again to his back, allowed himself to nudge off his shoes, release some of the tension that had knotted itself into his lower spine.

Impatience dragged at him. He should be out there looking for them, not lying here in bed. He should be in his car, heading back up the mountain with a fireman's ax, something to break through those goddamn bullet-resistant windows.

But they'd see him and follow. If not Officer Clayton, then some one of Bradley's crew. No real confrontation would be possible.

He had in mind instead a nighttime assault. The element of surprise. He would do this either by keeping Rick here in the room to field any possible phone calls—the door conveniently locked from prying eyes—or with Rick as a partner in crime, scaling the mountain together, mounting the assault against the A-frame and the demented Frank Springer.

Those were the options at present, anyway.

He closed his eyes a moment.

Maybe sleep, if it would come to him, wasn't such a bad idea at that. God knows he'd need his rest, his strength. He tried to convince himself, against his exhaustion, that he was doing everything right. That—under the circumstances—it was all he could do.

He could think of nothing, and thus remained impotent and doubtful and staring at the ceiling, seeing Matty's lovely face.

Marry me first?

Who else, besides Frank Springer, was lying here?

And how much?

Was helpless little Nicky the only truly innocent victim in the game?

He was lying there on the bed, eyes on the ceiling, seeing his son's laughing face, when sleep crept up on him.

He dreamed he was back in the old house, the Thousand Oaks house, and this time the dream was as vivid as the events when they occurred, unraveling in precise sequence.

It was hours since Nicky had first disappeared, since Chris had pulled into the driveway to find Matty running toward him, mouth agape, eyes shell-shocked.

In his mind and heart, Chris had given up. The baby was gone.

He turned from the French doors and moved through the darkened house toward the kitchen; neither he nor Matty had bothered to turn on the living room lights. Another unconscious effort to hold back the night? She had her back to him, drying dishes, still coppery, still slim, more lovely now than when they'd met. He sensed the gulf, already widening rapidly between them, made an honest effort to go to her, close it. God knew she needed him, now as never before. He could not do it.

He did not hate her, blame her, but so much black, fathomless heartbreak after three years of such incredible, shared happiness was inconceivable. Part of him, perhaps a large part, was still accepting none of this. Such perfection cannot tarnish. He didn't want to touch her because it would all be different and he wasn't sure he could withstand that too. In his selfish terror he needed everything to be as it was before; until it could be, they were strangers. Probably he was wrong. Yet he could not go to her. He could not. He turned from the kitchen.

He knew he was beyond exhaustion, that it colored everything, made it gray and suffocating as river mud.

Yes. But how to shut down the mind?

They'd need something tonight if they were to sleep at all. He knew the importance of sleep, of oblivion. He'd call Dr. Ramsey, get something from the pharmacy.

He kept finding himself in Nicky's room, unsure why. Maybe because being there made the child seem alive. Maybe because he'd have to come here eventually and putting it off would make that event impossible. Yet he didn't want a stranger disposing of the toys, the clothing, if it came to that.

He stood by the Aladdin lamp atop the dresser and watched his son's ghost gambol about the room. The pain was so acute it reminded him to breathe, a desperate wheezing sound that pushed him to tears he nearly succumbed to. Chris reached down and retrieved a fallen Golden Book from the crayon-stained carpet, stuck it with its fellows in the lower shelf.

The room was a typical mess. Matty was always after the child to pick up, which Nicky was not quite ready to comprehend as logical. He was such a good kid, such a beautiful child. In the delivery room, Chris had not wanted to give him up even when Matty smiled and demanded the baby needed to nurse eventually. The child, like Matty, was the second miracle in Chris's life; he never wanted to let it go.

Now it had been taken.

Red Bear, shiny and still new, glared at him upside down from the corner. Chris scanned the room. Black Bear, eyeless and threadbare, was nowhere to be seen. Chris straightened on impulse. And now went swiftly to Matty in the kitchen, checking the hall carefully as he came, a glimmer forming.

"Black Bear isn't in his room. Did you know that?"

She turned from the sink, eyes puffy and red as her dishwater hands. "No." She had to clear her throat and try again. "No." He never seemed to be near her when she was crying, yet clearly she had cried a lot.

"He might have taken the teddy with him when he got out," Chris pressed. It wasn't much hope but anything was more than they had.

She nodded, not getting it. "And?"

"It might be important. If he dropped the bear—if they find it, it might be a clue."

She looked unconvinced but didn't pursue it with him.

He stared at her a second. "I'll phone Calley." Calley was the young cop.

She waved him off wearily, drying her hands. She looked as translucent and fragile as fine crystal. "No. It's my turn. I'll do it."

They had taken turns calling and answering the police all night, the police and neighbors and friends and relatives. It had become an act of accepted agony, one she insisted on sharing. It always amazed him the things she found tolerable, sometimes what would, to him, have been the hardest things. She moved to the wall phone, dialed.

When she hung up, she turned and stared through him. "He had his last booster today," she said desultorily. "He only cried once in the office. Dr. Brauch said he was as healthy as a horse." She seemed a wraith, ready to melt into nothing, taking the last three years with her. If he blinked she would be gone, a vanished dream.

Chris wandered back toward the living room, already placing too much weight, and hope, on the bear.

He was brushing his teeth before the master bath mirror, watching himself with hooded eyes, waiting, with her, for the pills he'd fetched from the pharmacy to take effect, wondering if they would.

His gaunt reflection was no one he knew, and the fact of it sent a bolt of dread through him. Could he—could they—possibly live the rest of their lives with it? It seemed inconceivable. Something, sometime he knew would change. But would it be enough. And in time?

His heart slammed at a croaking scream from the bedroom. Matty!

He slipped on tile rounding the corner, pajama bottoms flapping, trailing toothpaste spittle. He found her on the thick shag beside the bed, hands pressed to red temples, expression surely that of the deranged. He flew to her side with a compassion of guilt that was almost rage. "Matty, what?"

She sagged against mattress edge, legs drawn up, nightie tangled, shuddering with laughter and tears. He grabbed for her, tried to draw her tight but was shoved away with her newfound strength. She could hardly stop the hysterical laughing. But when he found her eyes they were alight and clear, and his chest leapt.

"I couldn't find my slipper! I was reaching under to look for my slipper!"

It took him a moment; then he dropped her and grabbed at the sagging coverlet, bending low.

Beneath the bed, beside the slipper, Nicky lay in fetal bliss, rosy-cheeked and breathing fine, Black Bear under his chin, far away and safe from sterile-smelling offices and doctors' needles.

Chris pulled him out gently, as though he might disintegrate, woke him with rude kisses, held Matty and rocked her and rocked Nicky between them and listened gratefully with her to the delicious shrieks of their son's sleepy indignation.

The doctor had said the shots would make him drowsy; Matty had forgotten until this moment.

The nightstand phone burred, and Chris caught at it, still laughing with her. It was Rick next door, just checking in.

Chris pulled in the first clean breath since afternoon and told him.

Later, the baby safely between them, Chris lay in now comforting darkness, arm around her, and thanked God in a long and silent prayer.

Matty turned gently to him. "I want to move from here," spoken softly but with the strength of finality. "To the country, maybe. Someplace far away and quiet with no cars. And I want to do it soon."

He said nothing, not to argue with so much conviction, but lay wondering: How? On what?

"I will never let this happen again," she whispered resolutely.

And Chris, finally—held by her—allowed himself long-held tears.

He was awakened from the shattering memory at eight o'clock by the shrill of the phone. "Chris. Sorry, did I wake you? It's Doc Holiday."

"Hello, Doctor . . . what time is it?"

"I did wake you. It's just after eight. You okay? They taking good care of you there?"

"Fine. What have you got for me?"

"Nothing yet, I'm afraid. Just talked to the sheriff. But they're on it, Chris, never you fear."

"Good. That's comforting."

"How's the head?"

"Okay. I was really out."

"You need the sleep. Get back to it. I'll check with you again in the morning."

"Thanks, Doc." He hung up, stared into darkness.

He awoke in sunlight, as refreshed as if he'd slept under a sedative.

He checked with the desk for phone calls. There had been none.

He showered, dressed, and came down to the restaurant for a light breakfast, ordering a cinnamon roll and coffee. He thought about it over the slim local paper (no mention of Matty or Nicky or anyone missing) and finally gave in to intuition, ordering ham and eggs, figuring he might need the energy later.

In midmeal he looked up to find Doc Holiday sitting down across from him. "How's the patient this morning?"

"Fine. Coffee?"

"Thanks, had mine." Holiday could read Chris's expression. "No word yet, Chris. I checked with the sheriff on the way over. You could have ordered breakfast in bed, you know. I instructed Kelsie."

Chris nodded gratefully. "It's okay. I needed a break from the room. You think a short walk in the sun would do me any harm after breakfast?" He said it with deliberate nonchalance, as though the thought—a harmless one—had just occurred to him.

Holiday hesitated. "Well, I'd prefer—"

"Just around the block, keep my circulation up."

"All right, if you must. Then hustle back upstairs and get in bed. If you feel any dizziness—any at all—you hightail it back here pronto."

"Will do."

"I'll be back to check on you early this afternoon."

"Thanks, Doc," he said between bites of ham. "I really appreciate all that Greenborough is doing for me."

"It's our pleasure and our duty, Chris."

Chris smiled at him. Grinding his teeth.

When Holiday had gone, he threw down his napkin, signaled the waitress, signed a credit bill quickly, and walked to the back of the hotel to the bathrooms.

Which he bypassed, slipping past the bathrooms out the back way.

He worked his way around a large courtyard and gazebo, past several guests, along the back of the building to the adjoining alleyway. He came up the alley quickly to Main. Stopped and looked both ways for black-and-whites, familiar faces. Chris took his chances and walked casually across Main to a gift shop selling mainly silvery necklaces and rings with blue stones in them. He smiled at the clerk, browsed over the display cases, asked if he might use the rest room in the back. He went back there, bypassing the rest rooms and out the rear door. He crossed over two more streets via the alleys. He felt exhilarated and silly.

Goldstein and Sons, Attorneys-at-Law was sandwiched between a bakery and a shoe repair shop on Gorge, a side street off Main.

The office, like Sheriff Bradley's, was one room, simply appointed, with a faded couch, several rusty steel file cabinets, shelves upon shelves of law books, a scarred wooden desk. Mounted on the otherwise bare wall was a small glass case harboring what looked to Chris like a vintage German Luger. In front of that sat a balding, bespectacled man in a gray suit and tie, reading—through thick-lensed glasses—a faded paperback. Mickey Spillane, Chris noticed. Mr. Goldstein looked up when Chris entered.

The paperback came down. "Yes?"

"Mr. Nielson. I called yesterday. Mr. Goldstein?"

The balding man, very short, rose high enough to extend a pale, hairless hand with not much of a grip over the desk. "I'm the only one. There are no 'sons.' I just thought it looked better on the shingle. Sit." The bland, oval face cried out for a beard or mustache.

Chris sat back in the single wooden chair. It was hard and uncomfortable.

"It keeps out the little nuisance claims," said Mr. Goldstein.

"How's that?"

"The chair. You get a lot of poor-paying nuisance claims in a town this size. You won't sit long in that chair unless this is something important. Call me Abe."

Chris nodded. "Chris. Does everyone in Greenborough go by first-name basis?"

"Part of our small town élan. How can I help you?"

Chris thought about it a moment, crossed his legs. "Are you acquainted with Sheriff Bradley, Mist—Abe?"

The desk phone rang. Goldstein snatched it up officiously. "Yes? Uh-uh. Not now, no, I'm with a client. That's right," he said with some exasperation and hung up.

The diminutive attorney smiled at Chris. "Sorry. You were asking if I was acquainted with our local sheriff."

"Yes."

Goldstein laced his fingers, nodded behind owl eyes. "Interesting. He comes into my office, and right away he wants to know not what I charge, not am I any good, not why a smart Jewish lawyer would stick himself in a poor-paying hick town, but if I know the local gendarmes. Interesting."

"Do you?"

"How could I not? As I said—"

"It's a small town. Do you like him?"

"Bradley? A redneck shmuck. Worse, a bigoted redneck shmuck. Next question."

"Is he now or has he ever bribed you?"

Abe Goldstein smiled, a latter-day Humpty Dumpty with glasses. "Are you a cop?"

"Why? Are you hiding something, Abe?"

"An increasingly large bald spot just back here at the crown. Other than that?" He shrugged hugely. "A few small items the IRS probably wouldn't deny me anyway; who can say. You are, if I may say, Chris Nielson, one interesting fellow. One obviously intelligent, badly dressed, radiantly paranoid but interesting fellow. I can no longer contain myself. What incredibly interesting case have you brought to my humble offices?"

Chris decided to tell the lawyer everything, found himself opening up, leaving out no details, glad to unburden himself like this with a total stranger, a seemingly trustworthy total stranger. But that was just intuition.

Goldstein took notes now and then, mostly just listened and nodded. "And where is our friend Mr. Springer now, Chris?"

"Up at the house, I presume."

"With your wife and boy?"

"I'm pretty sure. Though they didn't appear to be home when Officer Clayton and I were there."

"And it's your contention that you're being held a virtual prisoner here in our lovely hamlet."

" 'Detained' would be the polite word. Though no actual words to that effect have been spoken. Or any effect. The question is, *why* am I being detained? On the face of it, one would suppose suspicion."

"Of murder?"

"As I said, no words are being spoken. It's been *suggested* I stay around. Out of medical precaution, not law enforcement. But there's something in the air. You can feel it. Or, anyway, I can feel it." Chris smiled sardonically. "Unless, of course, you believe that spill I took really did scramble my brains."

Goldstein nodded, scribbled, then tossed the pen aside, sat back again as if just finished with a meal. "Why'd you come to me, Chris?"

"Why not?"

The attorney glanced out his office window. "There are two other law firms in town. Bigger law firms. Did you think to save money with a guy like me?"

"No."

"I didn't think so. Why then?"

Chris followed the other's gaze out the window. A group of construction workers were tearing into a small shop across the way. "This is Colorado, but it's still very Midwestern in many ways, very provincial. It's a white-bread town. There are two churches and no synagogues. Rich people are moving here, mostly patrician types from New England, some Californians. It's becoming—if you can believe all this urban renewal—a rich man's playground."

Goldstein watched him. "You're trying to say—in your delicate way—a vaguely antiseptic playground."

"If such a thing can ever be called 'vague.' "

"Your thinking being, one persecuted soul might aid another persecuted soul."

"Something like that."

Goldstein sat back, smiling. "A very interesting, bright young man."

"Abe, can you help me find my wife and kid?"

Goldstein thought about it. "It's a small town. Everyone knows everyone. You need a detective, Mr. Nielson." Mr. Nielson now.

"There aren't any."

"Bring one in."

"Takes time and money and they'd be out of their jurisdiction."

"A private dick, then."

"You mean another stranger? Like me?"

The attorney smiled, conceded the point. "I see. What is it you want me to do, exactly, Chris? Assuming I believe your entertaining but decidedly improbable story."

"Do you?"

"Well, assuming I do, what would you have me do?"

"Handle the legal end. Let me know what rights I have, if any. Look through those shelves of books of yours for local loopholes, zoning restrictions, obscure property rules, anything that will help prove the place is mine and not his. Mine and Matty's." He withdrew a slip of paper from his breast pocket, handed it to the attorney. "Make phone calls I can't make. This is the name of the church we were married at in Las Vegas. Bradley's supposedly checking with the county clerk's office there, but let's not depend on him."

Chris reflected a moment. "Two days ago no one could have convinced me I wasn't married and living in that house up the mountain. Now I'm not so sure."

Goldstein took the paper. "Anything else?"

"Check with Westlake Hospital in Ventura; get Nicky's birth certificate. The problem is, all my records are in that house."

"And you and Mrs. Nielson don't go back very far."

"Right. And to make matters worse, she retained her maiden name. Springer."

"Why?"

Chris drew a deep breath. "I never really thought much about it." He shook his head. "Christ, our marriage—our relationship—has to be on file somewhere."

Goldstein nodded at the paper. "What you're asking me to do is be your attorney without letting anyone know I'm your attorney, is that correct? A kind of undercover lawyer."

"You could call it that."

"Interesting. Anything else?"

Chris hesitated. "Well, do some extracurricular snooping around locally, if you have the time."

Goldstein's eyes danced, acknowledging—perhaps savoring—the challenge: "Nerve" was what Chris really meant, not "time." Goldstein had the desire, certainly, if not the nerve. Chris sensed—hoped for—past personal grudges between the lawyer and the local police.

Goldstein glanced at his notes, leaned back in his chair. "Shall we be frank then? In the vernacular of our youth, you suck in the legal department, the rights department."

"Does that mean you won't take me on?"

"You already know I will. We'll do it strictly by commission, forgo the usual retainer in light of your current financial embarrassment. When this thing's resolved, however, you'll find me not cheap."

"That's fine. I have credit card money I can pay you with now."

"Better keep what money you have. You'll probably need it. In a pinch, I can be a soft touch, but don't spread that around."

"I won't. Thanks."

"Meanwhile, want some free, nonlegal advice?"

"Yes."

"Things legal take time, even the little things. Sometimes those take the most time of all. Don't wait, Mr. Chris Nielson. Don't wait for the law. Their law or my law. The longer your family is in jeopardy, the more you have to lose, both physically and legally."

"I understand. I'm taking care of that."

Goldstein lifted a brow. "How?"

"Do you need to know?"

The bespectacled man shrugged. "I suppose not. All right. I like you. More, I like your strange case. Worse even than the anti-Semitism up here is often the boredom. This I like. Interesting. James Bond." He saw the expression on Chris's face. "Please. I am entirely in earnest, wholly sympathetic. I know your suffering. I'll do everything in my power, you have my word."

"Or you might go straight to Bradley."

Goldstein nodded, held his hands palms up. "That's good. A little paranoia can be a good thing. But somewhere along the line, it seems to me, you're just going to have to go on faith with me. Can you do that, Mr. Chris Nielson?"

"I just have, haven't I."

Goldstein smiled. He jotted again, handed it to Chris. "My

home phone number. I'm ten minutes from here. Use the pay phones."

"I understand."

The attorney nodded, laced his fingers. "James Bond. Yes, this will be interesting. Tell me, are they relatives?"

Chris looked at him. "Who?"

"The other men you trust. The ones you're going back up there with."

Chris watched him. "Only one, not a relative. How did you know?"

"You wouldn't attempt it alone, surely." He assessed Chris's lanky form. "Only one. My goodness. Do you have guns?"

Chris thought about it. May as well tell it all. "Yes."

Abe Goldstein smiled. "How exciting. James Bond. You've been appraising my German Luger, the one in the glass case behind my head. Were you thinking of asking to borrow it?"

"No."

"A good thing. It never leaves this office. Do you see the small crack on the hand grip?"

Chris squinted. "Yes."

"Belonged to a Nazi officer, that gun. My Uncle Tunis gave it to me."

"Sounds like an interesting story."

"A brief story. My uncle was a child when he, his father and older brother were standing in the cold rain and mud of the Dachau camp. His older brother was twelve, a precocious but gentle child. They had been standing for hours, at attention, for no reason other than humiliation, when my uncle's older brother, tired and very thirsty, tilted his head back to catch a few drops of rain. One of the German officers yelled at him. He lowered his head again but not soon enough. The officer—a nice looking young man with flaxen hair—took out his pistol and blew the boy's brains out. He then turned it on the sobbing father, but it apparently stove-piped—jammed—so he beat him to death with it. The Luger, apparently assumed worthless now, was cast into the mud. When the G.I.'s liberated the camp, months later, my uncle found the gun near one of the stalags. My step-aunt was so afraid—years later—my uncle would use it on himself, she threw it away in the trash. I retrieved it. Beautiful weapon, isn't it?"

"Beautiful as death," Chris said.

The little man smiled, nodded. "I think you'd best leave my office now, Chris Nielson. Did anyone see you come in?"

"I don't think so. But—"

"But who knows for sure. That's part of it, isn't it. Well. Deep intrigue comes to little Greenborough."

Chris glanced outside; they were hammering and sawing across the way. "Not so little for long."

He stood, shook hands with the little bland-faced man, and went to the door.

Turned. "So. Tell me, Abe, what is it you do?"

The lawyer glanced up. "How's that again?"

Chris grinned, nodded at the paperback on Goldstein's desk. "Why don't you just refer to yourself as a private eye?"

Goldstein might have colored slightly with the smile. "An old Hebrew proverb has it that there are two people in every man. The one who walks about, and the one who's trying to get out. I can't think when I've enjoyed someone's company more, Chris, but for safety's sake—your family's sake—you'd best make yourself scarce around this office until I have something concrete. I'll find a discreet way to contact you."

Chris paused at the door. "You don't think I'm being overly paranoid, then, thinking my phone might be bugged?"

The attorney shrugged. "I think prudence is the initial shield against all things untoward."

"Hebrew proverb?"

"Goldstein invocation."

Chris nodded. "Right. And thanks again."

"Thank me when I've earned it. Ah, here's trouble . . ."

And Chris, heart tripping, turned to see an almond-eyed, dark-haired young man in his early twenties come through the door.

"Mr. Nielson, my irrepressible nephew, Hershel. Hershel, Mr. Nielson."

The young man shook Chris's hand, smiled beguilingly. "Are you a client, sir?"

Chris started to answer when Goldstein interrupted. "He is a friend, Hershel and that's all you need to know. A lawyer doesn't just ask questions, he asks the right questions. And by the by, I'd appreciate a few less phone calls when I'm with a client."

"You just said he was a friend," the young man corrected.

Which caused Goldstein to smile. "What do you think, Mr. Nielson: Will this boy make a decent attorney someday? Close the door, Hershel. Mr. Nielson is a busy man."

Chris let himself out into unfriendly streets.

C H A P T E R 13

Matty hadn't gained twenty yards before exhaustion reached up to drag her down.

She stumbled in rocky, steep-sloping soil and brambles, her instincts to break the fall thrusting her arms out. This, in turn, nearly threw the child from her.

She clung to him instead, crashed heavily amid weeds on her right shoulder, endured lances of pain through her lumbar vertebrae, the utterly futile sense that she had done this all wrong again, had always done it wrong, would continue to do it wrong until both she and Nicky were dead and the maniac had won. She should have trusted her initial instincts. You can't outrun Frank Springer; no one can.

Yet how could she simply continue to sit and do nothing?

Well, she'd done it now. And Nicky would be the price of her folly.

She should have run the moment she had the baby safely in her arms again, the moment she saw Frank dancing with the hapless hiker. She should certainly have run long before he had slit the other, taller boy's throat.

Now Frank was killing or had killed the poor blond girl, perhaps raping her first, giving Matty a few precious seconds instead of the several minutes first offered her.

She lay in tangled brush, trying to get her breath, trying to decide which way to go, which was an absurdity itself because she had no real idea where she was.

She knew (approximately) where the river was, and ordinarily it would make the most sense to follow that back to the lake, and eventually, the house. But Frank would, of course, be anticipating such a move, and besides, what good was the house anyway? What good was any hiding place against him?

Matty looked down at her baby. So pale, so terrifyingly white, the tiny chest rising in shallow hitches now.

He'll be dead before nightfall without aid.

Shut up!

She would not listen to taunting inner thoughts. She would get him to a hospital somehow. She would find a road, flag a car, something. She would not let her son die in the woods.

She searched the thin wrist desperately for a pulse, found feeble fluttering. When she thumbed back his left lid she found eggshell-white orb, tendrils of veins like red lightning, the pupil rolled back. Coma?

Nicky, Nicky my sweet baby.

Goddamn you to hell, Frank!

She sat up, clutching Nicky to her breast, trying to get her bearings. Outsmart him. What would he be doing now, this second?

If the blond girl submitted, he'd have cut her throat straight-away and been done with it. If she put up a good fight—which he reveled in—he might rape her more than once just for the thrill. Which would buy Matty time.

Time bought from another soul's misery.

Shut up! I'm trying to think!

What would Springer expect her to do?

He'd expect her—panicked and exhausted and carrying a burden, even a relatively light burden—he'd expect her to follow the river. All right, then she must choose otherwise.

Matty turned to survey the surrounding woodland.

Trees. Elms, she noticed. Brush, rocky soil, slabs of granite and shale, an increasing amount of dry, fallen leaves. Winter was coming on fast now, warnings of a bite in the air. To her east—at least she assumed it was east—lay a balding area of gray stone flanked by pine and fir. Few leaves had fallen there, blocked by a phalanx of evergreens. Without leaves she would make less noise, less of a trail.

She struggled up, looked once behind her apprehensively, and struck off for the bald spot.

Every ten yards or so she stopped dead still, cocked her head, and listened.

Birds. An occasional scurrying of something not human. But no sound of footfalls. Yet.

She grinned mirthlessly at herself. Foolish. Stupid. She would never hear him coming. No one ever did. He was just suddenly there.

She pushed on, dead leaves crackling beneath her no matter how lightly she tread. Finally came to the barren area of mostly rock, felt some small comfort when the crackling ceased. If she could just get a good lead on him, just get beyond the radius of his tracking ability.

She stepped on something that squeaked.

Matty jumped back reflexively, eyes darting to the rocky humus. Nothing but pebbles and weeds.

A fat bramble caught her eye, then something more. Movement. She bent closer. Found herself gazing into mottled fur, the round agate eyes of a kitten.

A kitten. Out here?

She nearly bent to pick it up. But she had her own troubles. She gave a backward glance, passed it by. The poor thing.

She cast another glance across her shoulder. Nothing. Only woods.

She was nearly to the other side of the bald area. If she could get some distance beyond that—it was probably wishful thinking—but she might have a chance of losing him.

Yes, then all you'll have to worry about is surviving a night alone and unsheltered in the woods. If exposure doesn't kill you, thirst will.

She bit her lip hard, not feeling the pain or tasting the blood. She'd had a sudden horrific picture of herself down on her knees, alone in cold, unforgiving forest under towering, malignant trees and black, starless sky. Digging a tiny grave with her bare hands.

She broke into a panicked run, heedless of her thudding footfalls, of the crunching leaves, running, running. Twisting back now for a final glimpse before the forest closed in behind her again.

". . . doe a deer, a female deer . . ."

Matty skidded to a heart-jolting stop, nearly spilling the child. A sob broke uncontrollably from her lips.

". . . ray, a drop of golden sun . . ."

She could only stand there, heart lurching, shoulders shaking with hopeless sobbing, ears enduring the awful tune, which might be before her, behind her; she had no idea. He was good at that.

He had found her. Of course he had found her. She had always known he would. It's just that, even under impossible odds, you can't help trying. So she had tried. And now the child would die.

". . . me, a name I call myself . . ."

She held Nicky close, kissed the pale forehead lightly, whispered, "I love you, baby." And she waited.

Springer came smiling from the woods directly behind her, exactly over the path she had come, as though she'd left a clear and easily readable trail for him to follow, as though—hands jammed casually, jauntily, in his pockets—he hadn't had to try at all.

"Hi, kitten! Going my way?"

She turned to look at him.

There was not even a single drop of blood on him anywhere: his clothing, his hands, his stupid grinning face. Yet he had killed. And killed.

It came to her. The deaths of the hikers, on the breeze, wafted toward her off his body. No blood, but he could not hide the smell of their last moments on this Earth.

"How about we go home now for a nice Thanksgiving dinner? What do you say, Matty?"

Thanksgiving. Now isn't that odd, she thought dreamily, not having even considered it before. Could it actually be Thanksgiving already? Could the holidays be here, come into this nightmare, just as they had every time this year, unaware that anything—that everything—was different this time? Could it be true that within this insanity some people, somewhere, still lived lives that could be considered normal?

She'd all but forgotten the meaning of the word.

He was not more than fifteen yards from her. "Say, kitten, I've got a great idea for a Thanksgiving supper—!"

It happened so fast, with such astounding swiftness, that not even Frank—indomitable Frank—saw it coming.

A dun blur to the left of him, a flash of tawny fur, and a throaty scream almost like a woman's, and Springer was abruptly down, something having knocked him over and back, a huge clawing something that Matty finally realized was a puma, a mountain lion.

Of course, it all made sense now. The kitten! Probably one of a litter of kittens, hidden beneath that bramble bush. Matty'd disturbed them, probably set up an urgent mewling the thundering falls had masked from their ears but not that of the alert mother cat. And she, a great, lithe thing of muscle and fang—flush with alarm and fear and the hated smell of humans—had returned to the bramble den to find Frank nearest to her brood. Returned and struck.

And it was Frank who was screaming now.

A very strange sound. Matty never having heard Frank scream. His enemies, yes, but not Frank.

A strangely delicious and satisfying sound. Frank screaming and kicking and the tawny snarling thing atop him.

Matty hugged Nicky tight and ran.

The growling and screaming fell behind her, farther and farther. *Run! run! run! run!*

Wouldn't it be just wonderful, wouldn't it be just the sweetest kind of poetic justice, if all that man had failed to do, nature accomplished in a single violent moment?

Of course it was too much to hope for.

She shouldn't have even been thinking about it. She should have been looking ahead for signs of a path, a road, even a car. Instead she twisted back one final time, hoping—praying—to see the big cat disemboweling her ex-husband—ripping out his eyes and liver. She looked back instead of forward, so that the big oak, by the time she'd turned around again, was squarely in her face. Hard, unyielding, implacable.

She lay in her own bedroom. She ached from head to foot but was warm and dry, covered with a blanket, aware instinctually that it was night and that some time had passed.

She remembered, with startling clarity, everything from before. She was pretty sure it was the same day now turned to evening.

Jumping up, head throbbing hugely, she rushed in the gloom to Nicky's room, finding his blue sports car bed empty.

Matty ran to the stairs, down them, across the cold floor, the foyer, to the kitchen, where she was assaulted by a combination of sights and sensations so traumatic they took her breath away.

Frank was leaning against the stove, fiddling with something in a saucepan, humming a soft tune. The kitchen was radiant with delicious smells of roasted chicken or turkey or something. He sported a white apron over gray slacks, a kelly green velour sweater, and Chris's house slippers.

Nicky was in his high chair in red Dr. Denton's.

Awake in the chair and *eating*! He looked up with a bright smile that broke his sweet face, broke her tortured heart. He squealed in delight, cried, "Mommy!"

That made Frank turn from the stove. "Well, Happy Thanksgiving. Up and at 'em, are we? Come join us, kitten? Smell wake you up?"

Matty came, dreamlike, into the bright kitchen, found a chair beside her wonderful son, and slumped, unable to take her grateful eyes off the pink, healthily smiling baby shoveling mashed potatoes into his mouth with his red plastic Power Rangers spoon. "Nicky, baby."

Frank shuffled fried, crackling veggies, turned back to her. "Hungry little bugger, isn't he?"

Matty pressed back tender curls, put a palm to the perfect, convex sweep of forehead. Cool, normal. She turned heartfelt eyes to Frank. "Thank you."

He raised curious brows. "For what? Hey, the child has to eat, yes?" He put down his spatula and came to her, bent and kissed her, which she permitted, even allowed the brief trace of his tongue over her sensitive palate, so grateful was she, so caught up in the moment, too famished and exhausted to repudiate.

Springer sat grinning beside Nicky—the child between them—helped him when Nicky got too much on his plastic spoon. One big happy family. He turned with earnest excitement to Matty. "Listen, kitten, I've been thinking over the whole thing. What do you say—after this glorious Thanksgiving dinner with just the three of us—what do you say we blow this joint? Pack it in. Pull up stakes and head for the hills."

She could not stop her eyes from drifting to the table, the shiny china plate casting her own warped reflection, her stomach roiling in impatient anticipation.

Frank slapped his forehead admonishingly. "You're famished, of course! Here!" He pushed up swiftly, hurried back to the stove, and with the propriety of a fastidious German hausfrau, ladled nourishment onto her plate with dexterous ease, carrying steaming plate, wineglass, and condiments all in one trip, laying them carefully, uniformly before her amid sparkling flatware. "Eat! *Mangia, mangia!*"

Matty forked in greedy mouthfuls, the sudden rush of blood sugar almost intoxicating. She quaffed the entire glass of wine, and Frank was right there for the refill, towel wrapped around the bottle, smiling a curiously warm, benevolent smile.

"What do you say, kitten?" He gestured ceilingward. "This place isn't us, not really *us*. We're city folk. Don't you miss the shops? Tell me you don't miss the shops—New York, Dallas, San Francisco?"

Matty reached for fresh warm biscuits, another helping of the sweet-smelling turkey. "God," she found herself saying, "this is wonderful. Did you cook this yourself?"

"Dig in, there's plenty. What I've been thinking about is a new start. In a new place. A new old place. New York, specifically."

Matty nodded, chewing, energy and stamina spreading warmly through her vitals. Let him talk. Just eat while you have the chance.

"I've been thinking about it ever since—what's wrong?"

She'd been staring unconsciously at his shirt. "What? Nothing!"

A suspicious crease formed on his brow, soon faded back to another beguiling smile. "The panther. The mountain lion. You're wondering why no blood, no scratches."

"Well . . ."

"No, it's okay. It's a perfectly normal thing to wonder about. Anyone might wonder about that. I'm not the paranoid individual some would have you believe, Matty."

He rarely called her Matty.

"I know," she offered.

"It's the Kevlar." He grinned. "The vest. I never go out without it. You should remember that."

"Of course." Of course. Never go out without your bullet-proof vest.

"I hope the screaming didn't bother you. I was never in any real danger. I've fought mastiff, kitten, animals that weigh far more than that scrawny cat. I had my knife, of course."

Of course.

"The screaming was to distract it. I took a couple of scratches on the thigh before the blade went in. Nothing more. Were you concerned?"

"No." Just eat. Get your strength back. Let him ramble, sit here quietly, and eat his delicious dinner; he hasn't poisoned it, so put that out of your mind.

"Anyway, I've been thinking. Remember New York? Remember Niagara Falls? Of course you do. How could either of us ever forget that? Well, I sat up there in your bedroom earlier, after I'd carried you home, and I began to think about it. And do you know, kitten, I honestly believe—what's the matter now?"

She swallowed hard. "Nothing!"

The sly look again. Then the attendant smile. "It's those hikers, am I right? You're concerned about those kids."

"No, I—" She looked fearfully at Nicky; he was spilling applesauce on his pajamas. Frank, without looking, wiped it off with a napkin, the kind of gesture a father might make.

"Yes, you're concerned about those kids I killed."

"No, really."

"Don't lie to me, Matty." Abruptly cold.

She made herself keep eating. "All right. A little concerned."

And now the big smile was back. "They weren't kids. I think you must know they weren't really kids, kitten."

"No?"

He made a scoffing sound. "Of course not. You know what they were. You know my life is in constant danger, that everywhere I turn there is always the chance of sudden, inexplicable death. I couldn't very well let that happen now, could I? I couldn't very well let them kill me and leave you and our son out there alone in the woods. Matty?"

She jerked her eyes to his. "What?"

"He *is* our son. Right?"

A thrill of dread. "Of course. Yes."

The smile back again. "Exactly. So you can see why I had to do what I did, can't you?"

"I can see it, yes."

"More wine?"

"I'm fine. Thanks."

He laced his fingers, leaned toward her eagerly again. He was about to continue when Nicky hit his head with the plastic spoon.

Matty felt her heart lurch.

"Don't," Frank told the child evenly without looking.

Nicky said, "Phamm!" and hit him again.

Frank started to turn to him.

"He's through!" Matty blurted. "Through eating."

Frank regarded the child. "Where's your toy, Nicky? Where's the nice toy Daddy got you?" He bent and retrieved a plush toy—a stuffed tiger—from the carpet, handed it to the boy. Nicky grinned, kissed it, pounded it on the table.

"Our mistakes," Frank began again to Matty, "all of our mistakes, all of our misfortune can be traced back to the same place. Upstate New York. Niagara Falls, where we were married, where it all began." He looked down at his hands, rubbed absently at his ringless ring finger. "I didn't do well by you, Matty."

Matty watched her son chew the tiger's ear. "Frank, it was a long time ago."

He slapped the table so hard, Matty jumped with a small cry, a scrap of food dropping from her mouth. Nicky gasped.

Frank recovered quickly. "I'm sorry. But it was *not* that long ago. It was practically yesterday. By the standards of the universe it was less than the smallest part of a second. Matty, I wronged you. I know I did. I wronged the marriage, handled it badly."

She stared at her plate, swallowed thickly.

"And I want you to know how sorry I am."

When he said no more for a time, she glanced up and was utterly astonished to see tears tracing his cheeks, his head bowed, hands clasped atop the bone tablecloth as if in prayer. "It was the business, the job. The fucking job." He blinked and the tears fell, splashed his big knuckles.

Matty felt something coil within her.

"You can't imagine the things they ask you to do. I know you think you were a part of it—saw part of it—but you don't know the worst, kitten. You can't know the worst, the depths, the utter depravity."

He looked up at her, eyes red, face drawn. She had never seen such a look on his usually imperious face. "They can *change* a man, Matty. They can twist a man and tear him apart with the things they ask. And ask. And keep on asking. Because once you're in, you're in. Forever. There's no coming out again. It's what you become. And what you become is worse than evil. What you become is . . . nearly divine."

She watched him, breathless.

"The worst, of course, is you begin to like it. You begin," and he choked, and pressed his eyes tight so the tears ran in rivers, "begin to *crave* it."

He reached out a trembling hand, covered her own with it.

Matty had to will herself not to pull away. His palm felt like a hot carapace, the skin of an alien thing.

"I want it to stop, Matty. I want it to all go away now. I want us to start over. Start where it first began to go bad. I want to take you—both of you—back. To the falls. To the place where we wed and conceived this wonderful child."

Matty heard an unnatural sound from somewhere, realized it was herself whimpering.

"I want to make it all up to you, to give you the life you deserve. Both of you. And I *can*, Matty. I have discovered that I have it within me to do this. Will you help me? Will you come with me back to the falls, back to a fresh start? I'll quit them. I swear to you I'll quit them. And I'll change. I'll be again that man you fell in love with."

She was trembling so violently she actually had to grip the table edge surreptitiously with her left hand. "Frank, can we talk about this? I need to think."

He kissed her cheek gently. "Of course. Take all the time you need. We have all the time in the world now. Did you get enough to eat?"

"Yes. Thank you so much."

He reached for a steaming saucer. "Here, have some more."

"No, I'm full, thanks."

"Please, you need your strength."

Don't fight him.

She forced a smile. "Very well."

He beamed, forked giblets onto her plate.

Matty picked up her fork, thinking of the white thundering falls between New York and Canada, their spray-flecked cabana, long walks along the mist-shrouded cliffs with a man she thought was someone else. A man she thought she could love. Did love.

The pungent food rose to greet her nostrils. She poked at a giblet. Hesitated.

Matty turned the wedged-shaped meat over carefully. She forgot for a moment to breathe.

She stared dully at the telltale swath of Day-Glo color on the meat's bumpy surface, cooked, but still lollipop green. In her mind's eye she saw the blond tresses, the look of horror.

Oh, dear God.

Her chair crashed backward as she lurched up, stumbling,

racing for the downstairs bath, Nicky so unprepared for this, his pink mouth formed a startled O.

The toilet lid was down and she could not wait; she gave it to the tub.

In a moment she knelt, trembling at the cool, porcelain lip, shaken and rigored with nausea. Swimming visions of a tongueless blond head swam before her, ants already at the lovely eyes. . . .

Matty pushed up, sobbing, gave another wracking spasm to the john, so gut-wrenchingly forceful it produced a tandem squirt of urine.

Insane! He's completely insane!

His high-pitched lunatic laughter mocked her from the kitchen.

CHAPTER 14

Awaiting Rick's arrival below, Chris dozed away most of the torturously long afternoon, or rested, anyway, in the too soft hotel bed, real sleep eluding him.

Or perhaps he didn't actually seek it, though he acknowledged the need for it. There was much to be done in the hours ahead. He would need his rest, his strength. He'd started doing push-ups, situps, other freehand exercises. He was far too stiff, though, and growing steadily stiffer, from the fall. Push-ups especially produced blinding headaches, and, besides, it was too late anyway. You couldn't hope in a few desperate hours to get into any kind of decent physical shape, not after months of indolent living.

He was going to be depending on Rick for a lot. Maybe too much. It plucked at his conscience. He kept envisioning Sharon's accusing face.

Chris hadn't scaled a line pole, braced himself high above the earth in leather straps and harness, in nearly a year. He still had most of the lineman's equipment in the Volvo's trunk the last time he'd noticed, but he hadn't touched it since summer before last.

He lay in the strange hotel staring up at the white, immaculate ceiling with its ornate moldings and Victorian scrolling, experiencing a sensation at once amusing and alarming. He couldn't seem to clearly remember his wife's face. Not distinctly, not with the flawless definition his memory usually afforded.

He lay against the detergent-perfumed hotel pillow, quietly considering this. He had read somewhere that lovers, recently parted, sometimes have difficulty describing each other. It isn't that, though, he told himself ruefully, not at all. It's something else. You knew her, yes. But you never really *knew* her.

The past few hours seemed to amplify that theory.

Never really knew her.

We're all of us, in the end, strangers to each other. Who had said that?

He rolled to his side, regarded the bedside phone bleakly. Another odd sensation: He'd never distrusted a telephone before, other than in the way those phones he'd repaired below countless high-tension wires had earned his distrust, with their scrambled circuits and weather-corroded amplifiers. But having listened in surreptitiously to countless calls himself—afternoon confidings, bored housewives waxing endlessly about nothing of consequence, screaming toddlers in accompaniment while Chris labored dangerously high, sweating, dodging wasps, trying to secure a better connection for the oblivious parties—in all that time he'd never feared another listening in on himself.

He rolled onto his back again, feeling the steady chug of his heart through chest and pillow.

In the end, of course, it wasn't she—the two of them—that mattered most. In the end it was Nicky that mattered. No matter whose son he may be. Nicky was innocent.

After a time, he gave up the thought of real rest. Rest was something that would come only when this ended.

Chris came down to the restaurant at quarter past the hour.

It was imperative that Rick come to him, not the other way around.

He saw his friend the moment he entered the large, oak-paneled café, the big, blocky redhead bent over a menu, the athlete's build, the loud Hawaiian shirt and khaki slacks. A bit overdone touristy look.

Chris smiled amiably at the hostess and asked if he could sit anywhere. She said that would be fine, and Chris found a table across from and about twenty feet away from his former neighbor.

He sat, picked up his menu, and waited patiently for Rick to notice. When he did, Chris met his eyes a moment, then looked immediately away. This must look unrehearsed. After a time, he glanced up again, nodded nearly imperceptibly, and Rick got up.

When Corman came to his table, Chris looked up from the menu as if in surprise, reached out a hand, and made a show of what a coincidence this was, gesturing toward the chair opposite.

"Do you think that anyone bought that shit?" Corman smiled softly, scooting his chair in.

Chris shrugged, kept the stupid smile in place for show. "Who knows? This seemed less attention-getting than me inviting a perfect stranger to dinner. Let them think we're old friends. Any trouble getting into town?"

"No. Kingston's got an airport the size of a Kmart, and the bus up here to Greenborough moved like a jet turtle, but I've got skis strapped to the rental car for show. Did you know it was snowing outside?"

"No. Damn."

"Not heavily. Where's Matty?"

"The house, I hope. I think she's all right, Nicky too. But I'm in the dark, really."

"What the hell's going on?"

"Our pal Frank Springer."

"He's back?"

"*Moved in.* Claimed the place. And my family."

"What the hell are you talking about?"

"Sh!" Their waitress had come over. Chris ordered the pot roast, Rick a cheeseburger. The two men sat watching the Bic pen take careful orders in that unhurried, small-town way, a wad of gum revolving in a pretty adolescent cheek. Chris thought: she's eighteen, nineteen, hasn't a care in the world except whether or not her boyfriend will press sex on her again this weekend.

When the waitress left, Chris said, "I know how this sounds, believe me. Christ, you should see how it *feels* from over here. But Springer's in earnest apparently. And somehow he's managed to get the law on his side."

"The law?"

"The local law, anyway. Either through design or a set of fortuitous circumstances or both. Anyway, he's in and I'm out. Out in the cold. And they're watching my every move, every phone call to see I stay out for a while. Probably watching us now."

"Why, for Christ's sake?"

"That's the question."

"And Matty's okay, you think?"

Chris shook his head. "Not sure. My gut tells me they're up there at the house with him. Probably safe, for now. Springer has a very legal-looking certificate that says he and Matty were—are—man and wife."

"Yeah? So do you."

Chris sighed. Seeing, listening to Rick again, was making all this seem the more unreal. "Yes, *inside* the goddamn house! Along with everything else I can prove is mine, except the car, which I have. Frank was generous with that. Nice of him. Probably it's easy to trace a car license and registration."

"But the license shows where you live."

"It shows my old address, Rick. Look, I've covered all the bases, don't you think I'd have thought of everything by now!"

"Keep your voice down."

Chris willed himself together. "I've thought of everything. Problem is, someone else has thought of everything too."

Rick looked off absently a moment. "I knew that prick Springer was no good from the start." His quick blue eyes darted over the restaurant, as if assessing the situation in one confident sweep. His expression read: It's okay, I'm here now, don't worry about anything. "All right, what about the state police, the mayor?"

Chris shook him off again. "They'll just refer it to local jurisdiction and we'll be right back playing footsie with these good old boys."

"Okay, just checking on you. You realize you're talking some kind of weird conspiracy here."

"I don't know what I'm talking. I do know I'm not going to just sit idly by, wasting time pretending to be a good little boy for Sheriff Bradley while the trail to Matty and the baby grows cold. Playing it legal is also playing into their hands."

"Christ, it's hard to believe the whole goddamn *town* is in league with this maniac!"

"Stick around a few days. I'll make a believer out of you. Something's rotten in Greenborough; I just don't have the time or inclination to find out what. I want my family back. *Now.* I'm going back up there tonight. If Matty and the baby are there, I'm bringing them back with me, worry about the rest later."

"And I'm going with you." Rick slapped his arm.

Chris looked away with self-reproach. "Sharon thinks you're in Chicago."

"Don't worry about that."

"I do worry about it. So should you. These guys—these so-called country yokels—don't let their looks fool you. They're smart. Smart enough. Not to mention Springer himself."

"I can handle Springer."

Chris wondered about that. Rick's great fault in life was his overconfidence. Being a war hero who collected guns and was a good shot and terrific friend didn't make him indomitable. "Springer may have help up there, Rick."

"We'll have help too."

Chris looked at him. "What did you bring?"

Rick, in his element now, could not suppress a tight, imperious grin. It was cowboy time. "FedExed all the hardware straight to the hotel. Waiting for me at the desk when I got here. Nobody suspected shit. Don't worry; we're loaded for bear."

"I want to pay. Just give me all your receipts."

"Screw that. Let's just get Matty and the baby back."

Chris felt a spreading warmth. Maybe, with Rick here, it could actually be done. "The stuff's in your room now?"

"Trunk. Locked and loaded, oiled and ready. Whenever you are, old buddy."

Chris glanced at his watch. Felt it beginning. "As soon as it gets dark."

In a far corner of the hotel parking lot, under an aluminum street lamp he'd made blind with a rock, Rick opened the trunk of the rental Acura. Moonlight spilled across a trunkful of dark blued metal, checkered wood stocks.

"Christ," Chris stepped back, "this is an *arsenal*!"

Rick grinned. "We won't use it all, but better safe than sorry. Any of this stuff look familiar?"

Chris gave him a jaundiced look. "You know damn well I know next to nothing about firearms outside of skeet rifles and the occasional target pistol."

Rick smiled. "Don't worry. Okay, quick lesson." He pointed at each weapon in turn. "What I brought mostly are shotguns, and

I've eliminated pumps and semiautomatics for the sake of speed and simplicity. I also left out the single-barreled break-open jobs because they allow only one shot before reloading. That leaves us with the side-by-side and over-unders, hunting and target guns. These big twin bores have a marvelous psychological effect when aimed between the eyes."

Chris glanced around them, feeling open and reckless and desperate and scared and pumped.

"This is my favorite, the Rossi coach gun, imported from Brazil. You can fire several hundred rounds of full-powered buckshot and rifle slugs all day with this beauty, and the weapon will still remain tight and function reliably. Forget all that special chokes crap. We'll be firing, most likely, at close range, and at twenty feet any shotgun pattern will do for our purposes."

Chris nodded as if he were absorbing all this instead of thinking of Matty and the baby.

"For ammo I brought—with you in mind—low-powered skeet loads. These are quite lethal, good man-stoppers at close range. The barrels are all over eighteen inches, which will keep us within federal laws and allow us to look like innocent quail or rabbit hunters in case johnnie law comes calling. Okay so far? You look dubious."

"I'm okay," Chris told him.

Rick Corman grinned. "No, you're not; you're scared shitless. Good. So am I. That'll keep us on our toes, keep us from shooting each other. Anyway, don't sweat these technicalities. I just wanted to brief you a bit in case of emergencies." He reached lower in the trunk and withdrew a sleek, shiny handgun. "Ruger P-94. One of the best nine-millimeter handguns around, and one of the newest models. This is similar to the P-89 you fired at the range back home, without the ergonomic problems of that model. Here." He handed it to Chris.

Chris took it, hefted it. It felt good.

"Notice the new and improved grabbing grooves. That means even if your hands are slick with sweat—which they will be—you should have no trouble at all operating it. The safety-decock levers are also more user-friendly. Feel that Xenoy grenade-checkered grip? Slimmed down from the old model. Feels good, no?"

"Yes."

"The redesigned magazine still holds a full fifteen rounds. She's thirty-three-point-one ounces unloaded, the recoil mild enough for a kid to handle. I've fired it with my SIG-Sauer P-226 and the scores were comparable."

Chris suppressed, here in the open, the urge to sight down and aim the gun. "Ammo?"

"Black Hills full-jacket nine-by-nineteens, one-hundred-forty-seven-gram subsonic hollow-points, specifically designed for the gun's parabellum chambering. Shoot the tits off a gnat." He reached lower into the trunk, withdrew another rifle. "I'll be lugging this little sweetheart. Mauser Magnum action, prewar collector's rifle. Takes the longer cartridge. I prefer it. Okay, that's it. We ready to rock?"

Chris stuck the Ruger in his belt. "Ready."

Rick smiled, eyes lit in the parking lot's glow. "Let's waltz!"

The snow was building up, blanketing everything rapidly, including the narrow mountain road. Not a fortuitous sign, Chris thought.

Rick, behind the wheel, turned to him with one of his confident grins, reading his mind. "Don't worry about it. I've got chains in the trunk, in case."

Chris looked over at him. "You thought of everything."

Rick grinned wider. "Even to renting a white car so we'd blend with the weather."

"How'd you know it would snow?"

"Newspaper gave it a better than sixty percent chance. I gambled. Gambling's part of it."

"It," Chris knew, meant part of the game. Which Rick was clearly relishing. He was, in fact, a whole new Rick, boring studio work and suburban house behind him. He was back in guerrilla-infested forests again, basking in the heat of battle. Or enjoying the Rocky Mountain chill of battle, as it were.

Halfway up the mountain—ghosts of firs against pale white, nearly lunar hills pacing them in the Acura's headlamps—a low-beam's flare bloomed suddenly in the rental car's rearview, like the glowing eyes of a nocturnal beast.

"I see it," Rick said before Chris could. "Doesn't look like a black-and-white, but I don't know about these country patrol cars. Let's be prudent."

They pulled to the shoulder. Rick got out, threw up the hood, and pretended to poke around. A Chevy sedan passed them, the passenger side lit briefly in the Acura's glow: a pasty, cherubic face under a floppy hat festooned with lures. Then it was past, red firefly taillights retreating into black woods. Rick slammed the hood and slid in again. "Fishermen."

Chris looked at him. "At night? In the snow?"

"It's been done." Rick looked unconcerned.

He pulled back onto the narrow mountain road, tires making crisp sounds in the deepening snow, and they drove on without incident.

Though a moonless night, the landscape—swathed in snow—nevertheless glowed distinctly about them. Chris was certain that even without the car's lights they would see the road ahead clearly. And in turn be seen clearly themselves.

A wedge of apprehension formed at his middle, spread. All his plans of sneaking up here under cover of dark were rapidly dissipating.

He noticed Rick was slowing down considerably. A precautionary measure on the steep, slick road? Rick suddenly had an apprehensive air about him.

"Any cutoffs before we get to your house?"

Chris shook his head. "Not that I remember."

Rick nodded. "Me either. Well, we'll just have to make a cutoff of our own, then." He jerked the wheel over and turned the car so sharply it made Chris's breath catch.

"What the hell are you doing?"

The Acura bounced over the snowy shoulder, dipped bumper-first at a steep angle. Chris's safety harness cut into his shoulder. The vehicle plunged into a copse of trees, a sharp metallic scraping vibrating under Chris's feet. "Christ!"

The car bumped along, scraped back a pine bough, exploding powdery snow, and jerked to an abrupt halt. Rick killed the lights.

"What is going on?"

Rick shut down the engine, rolled down the window on his side. Sniffed the air.

Chris frowned. "What are we doing?"

Corman held up a gloved hand. "Shut up."

Chris sat, obediently quiet, surveying through powdery windshield the glowing, alien landscape. Minus the car's headlamp glare, it was nearly phosphorescent now. Winter wonderland, he thought absently. Then he imagined their dark shapes moving contrastingly against it. Open targets.

He turned back to Rick. "What gives?"

Corman was appraising the woodlands past the Acura's hood. "Doesn't feel right."

What the hell did that mean?

Rick glanced in the rearview, then ahead again, turned the handle gently, and climbed out quietly. "Come on. Easy."

Rick shut his door softly, came around to the trunk, opened it, reached in, and withdrew a gray duffel. He extracted bone-colored material from it—hooded jumpsuits, Chris saw—threw one to him. "Put it on."

"We're going on foot?"

"We are."

Chris began stepping dubiously into the pale material. "Is this rayon? Where'd you get these?"

"Army issue. Don't ask."

Chris grunted. "I assume you can find my house from here."

"In this brightness? A cub scout could."

Chris nodded to himself. A cub scout maybe, but not me. He'd be lost out here, luminescent snow or not. Lost without Rick. Rick's strength and confidence, Rick's army training.

He zipped up, buckled in front, tucked the Ruger in the belt. Rick was already showing him his back, striding confidently ahead through calf-high drifts, ever the platoon leader. Chris hefted the rifle and hurried to catch up.

They trudged uphill for maybe ten minutes, Rick's hooded head swiveling continuously, sweeping the forest on both sides with his eyes. He paused, vapor fluttering from his mouth, leaned toward Chris. "If we get separated, try to stay due north." He indicated with his rifle. "Twenty feet the other way and you'll fall off the mountain. Straight drop, half a mile."

"I'll struggle to remember that."

Rick smiled. Started ahead again, froze.

"What is it?"

Corman held up a quieting hand, head cocked.

Chris leaned toward him, whispering. "Hear something?"

Rick lifted his chin. "We're not alone."

Chris's scalp tightened. "How do you know?"

Rick tilted his head back. "Smell that? Cigarette smoke."

Chris sniffed. He didn't smell anything.

Rick handed Chris his rifle, rummaged at his belt, withdrew something from a left zippered pocket.

"What are we doing?"

Rick took the object, a coil of translucent wire—like fishing line—and began wrapping one end about the fat bole of a pine tree. When he had it secured to his satisfaction, he walked the line across an open area perhaps twenty feet wide, began anchoring the other end to a tree of similar size. "Stand over there by the wire, Chris, in the middle."

Chris did.

Rick came to him, nodded at the wire just below Chris's Adam's apple, and slapped him on the shoulder. "Good, that'll do. Let's go. Quietly. As quietly as you can."

Chris grabbed his rifle and caught up with his friend.

"If we get ambushed," Rick whispered, "run back this way; just follow our tracks. Try to remember where the line is. Memorize the area with that famous memory of yours. Try to run back under that wire before you get shot. It should catch an average-sized guy at the throat, a big guy in the chest. Either way, running at full tilt, it'll knock 'em on their ass." He winked at Chris. "Just a little security measure. Don't worry. We won't get separated."

Chris trudged on warily, thinking, Then why did you bring it up?

The mountain became momentarily steeper. Chris's calf muscles ached dully under the constant, trudging rhythm, his breath more and more labored. I will not slow down, he repeated to himself, I will not show Rick that I am tiring, no matter how much it hurts, no matter how much this goddamn snow tugs at my boots.

Eventually the ground leveled somewhat, the trees thinning.

Rick halted abruptly again.

Chris, thankful for the chance to get his breath, refused to lean against a sapling for support. Christ, he was miserably out of shape, breath vaporing like a fog about his head. "What's the matter now?"

Rick ignored him, sniffed the air. Then he smiled. "Well, well . . ."

Chris waited, growing cold, impatient. In the car they would have reached the house by now; he'd be at Matty's side. Was this tramping about in the cold really the best way? What the hell good would it do if he was too worn out to be effective in a confrontation?

Rick nodded. "Yes."

Chris drew deep breaths, felt somewhat better. "Yes what?"

Rick smiled. "They're here."

Chris glanced around quickly. "Who? Where?"

"All around us."

Chris squinted, feeling his hand tighten reflexively on the rifle stock.

The snow-mantled forest was still.

Just snow and trees and hills and black sky and more snow. And silence. The all-consuming silence of the great outdoors.

And then, to his right, about two o'clock, movement.

Chris lifted the rifle, knew instinctively he was too late.

"Just put it down," the emerging figure commanded. A figure that a moment ago was a tree. And Chris could see, with sinking heart, the dull gleam of the man's own rifle.

Heart suddenly tripping again, Chris thought: a forest ranger. Maybe just a ranger or a cop. Maybe.

But the approaching man, Chris could see now, wore no uniform, just a deep red mackinaw, jeans, and waffle-soled boots. The rifle was a single-barrel job that looked mean. "On the ground," the man said evenly.

Chris hesitated. "Who are you?"

"On the ground, asshole, or I take you off at the knees!"

Chris dropped his rifle.

The man kicked it out of the way with a grunt. He wore a thick beard, breath smelling vaguely of steak sauce. Something about him . . .

"Now, where's your friend?" He motioned with the barrel for Chris to raise his hands.

For a moment Chris didn't understand. Rick was right beside him. But turning his head carefully, slowly, he found that he was not. "I'm alone," he attempted.

The man grunted. "Right. And who left that other set of tracks?"

Chris squinted at him. "I know you."

The man smiled in sardonic acknowledgment. He radiated self-confidence, the rifle held almost lazily in his arms.

"From the dock. You were one of the guys haranguing us at the boat dock that day."

The man stuck his rifle barrel under Chris's chin sharply, a sensation like icy heat. "Your pal, dickweed, where is he?" he demanded with less patience.

"I'm right here," Corman announced.

The man spun quickly and fired into the night. A sharp, thunderous report that echoed distantly over alabaster hills. Rick's voice had seemed to come from nowhere, everywhere.

The man swiveled the rifle before him. "Show yourself! *Now!*"

"Don't shoot anybody."

The man shifted his rifle to the right, saw nothing, turned quickly, and struck Chris sharply between the shoulders. Chris went to his knees. Before he'd even gotten over the shock of that, the cold rifle bore was ground into his temple. "Come out *now*, motherfucker, or your friend is dog meat!"

Chris looked up with slit eyes to see Rick, hands raised above his head—left still clutching his rifle—step from behind a tree way on the other side of the clearing. Exactly opposite of where he—and apparently the stranger—had anticipated.

"Drop the artillery, jerk-off!"

Rick hesitated, glanced at Chris, dropped his rifle to the snow, hands stiffly above his head.

Jesus, Chris thought. Jesus oh Jesus, what have I done.

"Now get over here with your friend."

Corman came toward them cautiously. "Who are you?"

The man aimed his rifle at Rick's gut. "State trooper. Who the hell are you tramping around up here at night?"

Rick drew closer, face impassive in starlight. "We're hunters. We have permits. They don't distinguish between night and day."

"Smart guy. Being a smart guy can get you killed."

Rick said, "So can impersonating a trooper."

The man leveled the rifle.

Don't, Chris thought, don't be a smart-ass now!

Corman was twenty feet away. "Let's see some ID."

"Fuck you, pal."

Corman was twelve feet away. He smiled. "Troopers don't fire on unidentified targets. You shouldn't have been so trigger-happy, asshole. You gave yourself away."

Chris's eyes went wide. *What the hell are you doing, Rick?*

The bearded man raised the rifle butt over his left shoulder, prepared to send it crashing down into Rick's face.

Chris—as in slow motion—saw the rifle butt tremble on the brink of descent, the man's shoulders bunching for the blow beneath the red mac—saw Rick standing there confidently—*smiling!*—not even flinching, as gunfire cracked across the clearing. A purple hole appeared magically in the bearded forehead. The man was flung backward violently as if thrown, arms splayed, rifle flying.

Chris jerked around in bewilderment. *Who had fired?*

Rick stood easily, pulled the zipper down on his jumpsuit front, revealing the hidden, still smoking automatic, gripped in his "third" hand.

He came before the silent body, pointed the automatic a moment between the wide-open eyes, seemed to satisfy himself, stuck the pistol back in his belt.

Chris watched him shrug off the jumpsuit top, remove the length of supporting fir branch from the sleeve and glove, toss the branch to the snow, slide his real arm back into the sleeve. Neat trick. Where did you learn that? Chris thought. The army, one of those macho soldier of fortune magazines?

Rick crouched over the body, rifled the man's mackinaw, found a slim wallet, held it beneath a thin penlight. "We are," he muttered to Chris, "graced by the presence of one Andrew J. Spanning, recently deceased. Mr. Spanning hails from Virginia. His license number is VR 222-7694. He carries American Express when he isn't busy being dead. Mr. Spanning is minus the beard in his driver's license photo."

He flipped through the man's wallet. "Hm. This is interesting." Turning, he handed the open-faced wallet up to Chris. "Isn't that our friend, third from the right?"

Chris took the wallet, appraised a Polaroid of six grinning fishermen holding a string of walleye and bass against autumn backdrop, the man in the middle the corpse at his feet. Chris's eyes shifted third from the right: Frank Springer. Slightly heavier, younger, but Springer, no mistaking it. "What the hell?"

Corman was patting down the corpse. "What the hell indeed."

Chris shook his head. "This doesn't make sense. This guy can't be a friend of Springer's. I saw Frank beat the crap out of him the other day."

Rick looked sharply at him.

"He and some of his pals gave Matty and me a hard time one day on the lake. Springer came along and broke it up. Saved us, really."

Rick's eyes slitted. "Sure it's the same guy?"

"It's the same guy."

Rick thought about it. "Hm. I smell a rat."

"I smell a setup."

"What kind of setup?"

Chris gazed fixedly at the photo. "That's the question."

Rick grunted, hefting the man under the armpits. "Wanna give me a hand here, sport?"

Chris had to think a moment to get his legs to work. "What are we doing?"

"Take his legs. That's it. Now let's get him over here."

Chris regarded the edge of the precipice.

"What are we *doing*, Rick?"

Rick maneuvered to the rocky edge. "I don't know about you, pal, but I'm going to do my best to make this look like a hunting accident. On three now . . ."

"Wait a second." Chris dropped the legs. "We can't just throw him off the damn cliff."

Rick watched him patiently. "No? Where does it say that on our hunting licenses?"

Chris looked anxiously at the body. "Cut the shit. This is a human being we're talking about! Someone with family, friends!"

"Yeah! One of his 'friends' is terrorizing your wife up at that house right now."

Chris shook his head. He felt disoriented, vaguely sick, compelled to slow down that which was moving too fast, out of his reach. "No. No, it must be a mistake."

Rick put his hands on his hips, blew vapor. "Well, is he the guy in the wallet photo or not?"

Chris sighed. "Yes."

Rick grunted. "Then fuck him." And he hoisted up and out with another grunt, pushed before Chris could blink. The body flopped outward over the snowy crag—a nodding marionette—dropped away.

Chris turned, not to have to see it disappear into the gulf.

"What do you think?" Rick, in mop-up mode, was already retrieving the man's rifle. "Looks like he was wandering around here at the edge, tripped, and shot himself to me." And he tossed the rifle after the spiraling body. "Eleven eighty-seven Remington. Good weapon."

He turned to Chris, became concerned. "Your first dead one?"

"Yes."

Rick nodded. "First one's the toughest. Take deep breaths; you'll be fine."

But I am fine, Chris was thinking, finer than I'd have guessed. His legs were vibrating slightly. But I'm not scared. Isn't that amazing? he thought. I'm not as scared as I thought I'd be. Just vaguely sick, empty inside.

He looked over at his busy ex-neighbor. Not Rick, though. Rick is charged, in rare form. Rick is thriving on this. And no wonder, Chris mused with distant chagrin, he's *good*! The guy really is good! It wasn't just talk all these years.

Chris turned back to stare at the lip of the cliff where the body had disappeared. A moment before, a living, breathing man. A man with a past, with emotions, maybe a wife and kid, had walked these snow-mantled woods. Something at once cosmic, profound, and unsettlingly prosaic swept through him. The man was there, and then he wasn't there. But the cold and snow remained, and he, Chris, still breathed, still lived, still *was*, struggling his way through the *now*. Until, like a brief flicker of movie frame on the vast, eternal screen, he was gone too, removed forever, unremembered and insignificant—

"Hey!" Rick squinted at him. *"Hey!"*

Chris blinked, looked over.

"Deep breaths. Feeling sick?"

"No."

"Put your head between your knees."

"I'm okay."

"Have to pee?"

"No."

"Don't be embarrassed if you have to pee."

"I don't have to pee."

Rick nodded satisfaction. "Well, this confirms what I already knew," dusting his hands, reaching for his rifle. "We're dealing with a psychotic. Maybe a group of psychotics."

Chris endured pestering light-headedness, like a relentless gnat. He couldn't shake the giddy sensation he could dance across the snow without leaving tracks. *"Invasion of the Body Snatchers,"* he muttered.

Rick looked at him. "What?"

"Ever see that movie? No one could trust anyone. Everyone was against everybody else."

He felt something thrust into his hand, looked down: a flask. "I don't want it."

"Drink. One swallow."

"I'm okay."

"I know, drink it anyway."

Chris took a swallow, winced, the whiskey blooming inside him, pressing back the vertigo.

Rick collected their gear. "Better get moving before more of his fishing buddies show up."

Chris looked at him numbly, felt a distant thrill of fear.

"Still want to try for Matty?"

"Of course."

"Okay. We split up from now on. Until we reach the house. It's going to get hairy; I guarantee it. They'll try to make it look like an accident too. You up to it?"

"I told you I'm okay."

Rick smiled. "So you did." Slung the rifle over his shoulder, pointed at the forest. "Your house is due east, about three-quarters of a mile. You can't miss it if you follow the tail."

"What tail?"

"Scorpio's tail." He glanced skyward. "It's that constellation over there—"

"I know where it is. Why can't we stay together?"

"Because this doubles our chances of getting to Matty and the baby. If one of us gets delayed, the other still has a chance to get your family out. Any objections to the plan?"

Yes, plenty. "No." That feeling of apartness remaining.

"On your way, then."

Chris hesitated. Stalling? he wondered at himself. "You're positive. About where the house is?"

"Leave the reconnaissance maneuvers to me." Corman grinned tightly. The eager warrior, humping happily through mine-infested rice paddies again. Chris wouldn't be able to talk him out of this now even if he wanted to. And part of him wanted to. He started up the mountain by himself, feeling very open and alone.

"Hold it!" Rick tossed him something. "For close-in fighting."

Chris caught a thin, beautifully designed eight-inch knife sheathed in leather. "Nighthawk. Stick it in your boot in case the Ruger fails you. The handle's Kevlar-reinforced Zytel, which helps again with those slippery hands. The blade's four-twenty-five steel, blackened to kill glare, sharp and strong as hell. I've sliced double shoulders of cowhide with it. Like going through warm butter."

"What about you?"

"I've got a Cold Steel Tanto. We're old friends. Wait a sec—" He walked back to Chris, pulling something from behind him, from his belt.

He held up a thin strip of dead-gray metal, no bigger than a nail file, that caught no reflection. "This is what we call a Folsum Special. Prison shiv. So thin it'll break with longtime use but save your ass in a tight spot. Here's the real beauty. . . ." He bent down to pull at the lip of Chris's left boot, exposing the inner lining. "Now, the Nighthawk you stick in here, against the calf, right? If we get stopped, patted down, it's the first place they'll look, and they'll take the knife away from you." He put the razor tip of the smaller shiv against the boot's lining, shoving down smoothly until only the top of the wrapped grip was visible, and then not without looking hard. "So we put this little baby right next to it, hidden in the lining. Once they find the Nighthawk they won't be looking for the shiv—pass it right by—but you'll still be armed. Works like a charm. Okay. We ready?"

Chris swallowed involuntarily. "Listen a sec—"

"Don't even start. We're in it now, up to our asses. No turning back."

That tripped it. Chris felt an unbidden rush of pent-up fury. "Which delights the shit out of you, right?"

Rick regarded him coolly. "It had to be done, Chris."

"You don't know that! He was going to hit you, not shoot you!"

"Hit me first, shoot me later. Both of us. Trust me."

"Yeah, I *am* trusting you. This is dangerous as hell and way out of our depths. Certainly mine. We've killed a man! We're firmly outside the law, in case you haven't noticed, so just quit playing marine for a minute and listen. This bastard Springer may be crazy, but in the eyes of those moron townies he's doing nothing illegal. You have to understand they're just waiting for us—for me—to pull something stupid and reckless so they can put me away with just cause. I've worked like a bastard up to now, ground my teeth and bided my time to avoid irrational moves."

"We're not making irrational moves, Chris," Corman assured him patiently. "We're making necessary ones, and we'll continue to if you let me lead. And please lower your voice."

"I just—it's moving too fast. I have to *think!*"

"Do that. Think of Matty."

"She's *all* I'm thinking of! Think of Sharon, goddamn it!"

"I have. I told her I loved her the night before I left, kissed her forehead, screwed her until we were both sore, and now I'm up here with you and ready to follow through. It's started, Chris."

You started it, Chris thought but didn't say.

Corman watched him a moment. "Chris, you want me to go this alone? I will. You don't have to be ashamed."

"Don't be ridiculous."

"I work well alone anyway. You can wait it out in town."

"They're my wife and kid, goddamn it!" Then, faltering: "I just . . ."

Rick watched him quietly. "What is it?"

Chris regarded the baleful tangle of forest. "I'd just prefer it if we stuck together."

"No. This is the way. I take the back of the house, you the front."

"What, just walk up and ring the bell?"

Rick's face was pale with reflective light, impassive. "That's exactly what I want you to do. Maybe Matty will even answer it. But if Springer does, play it cool. Ask calmly to see your wife; you just want to talk with her; you're posing no threat. Keep the gun in the small of your back. Look loose and frosty. Mainly stall him, keep him talking so I can get in the back way. If Matty and Nicky are there, I'll find them. I know the house top and bottom, remember? If Springer won't let you in, don't argue with him. Stall him with talk, but don't let it get physical no matter how much you hate the prick. Tell him your lawyers will be in touch with him and walk away peaceably."

"I already did that."

"See? You're learning."

But it still didn't feel right. "We should have some sort of emergency signal," Chris offered unenthusiastically.

"Okay. If you do get lost, fire one shot. Wait five seconds so I can get a location fix, then fire one more. No more. Absolutely no more. If you get into trouble, two shots in rapid succession. Got it?"

"Yes, Sergeant."

Rick grinned, slugged his shoulder. "We'll have Matty back in your arms before the night's out. Get moving now before we talk it to death."

Chris slung the rifle, turned resignedly, headed into shadowed, unfriendly woods.

CHAPTER 15

Ten minutes later, cut off, open, and alone, Chris found himself stumbling though deeper and deeper snow, the mountain ever more treacherously steep, the rifle digging into his shoulder, his spirits flagging.

Breath labored, exhaustion clawing at him, he fought back a persistent conviction that this was all a massive mistake, that a faster, cleaner, less reckless route to rescuing his family could have been found with more time and patience.

But you're out of time. And you've thought of everything.

He had thought of everything. Hadn't he? A nighttime assault was the only answer. Right? A nighttime assault was the only answer. He kept repeating it like a mantra, in tempo with every muscle-aching step against the dragging snow, throat raw from gasping frigid night air.

Yet doubt remained. A cloying resentment built within his gut.

Resentment for himself, his own stupidity at not recognizing the signs earlier. Even a little resentment for Corman, their only probable savior. Rick and his impulsive, cavalier disregard for danger or law; his little-boy naïveté, turned loose out here in the wild.

But it wasn't the wild, not really. The laws of man didn't stop just because they were surrounded by the laws of nature. Rick only wanted them to. Pretended it was so.

He trudged through heavy drifts, the top millimeter already frozen so his boots made crisp muffled sounds. He stumbled occasionally, catching himself with outstretched hands, face buried momentarily in the wet snow, cursing, sometimes losing the rifle. Then he'd have to go through the effort of stopping again, pulling off his gloves, shaking the snow from them, replacing them over numbed fingers, trudging on. In what he hoped was the correct direction.

It had started snowing harder. If this kept up, he'd have to stay on his toes for hidden drifts. Deceptive and lovely, they could swallow a man, bury him alive, or so he'd read. Something else to plague his already crowded mind.

He heard a noise behind him, spun quickly.

Nothing.

A squirrel or hare.

He stood in the deepening cold, wet flakes clinging to his lashes, blinked them away, studied the landscape for any more trees that stopped being trees and became something else. Thought of hot soup and his warm bed in the big A-frame, Matty curled beside him, the soft length and sleep-musky fragrance of her.

He thought of Springer sleeping next to her.

Tore his thoughts away from that.

But not completely. Not ever completely. Keep them just at the periphery of consciousness. They'll keep you angry, resolute. And that will keep you brave.

Chris felt himself twitch.

The clear, rarefied mountain air brought a sudden new scent wafting across icy peaks. The sweetly pungent odor of machine oil.

A car? Passing on a road somewhere? But he'd have heard it, surely.

He stopped trudging, forced his breathing to slow, and listened.

Not a sound. You could hear a pin drop, if a pin would make a sound in the deepening snow.

He shivered involuntarily. Deep in his soul he felt a sudden, inexplicable sensation of nakedness, as though exposed on all sides. Some part of his brain began to convince him it was not a squirrel at all he'd heard.

Just ahead and to his left—thirty yards maybe—a massive outline of boulder squatted between silhouettes of towering ever-greens. Something about its bulk was sharp and slightly unnatural. Chris blinked.

There was an abrupt guttural roar that must be a grizzly, fol-lowed—too quickly for him to react—by the painful, piercing glare of headlamps, the crunch and thud of treads over snow.

All but blinded, Chris staggered back, arm across slitted eyes. He thought: a car? Out here in the trees?

A whining gasoline growl made him jump. Something was *shushing* toward him, the lights growing brighter, blotting out all night vision, blotting out the world. A snowmobile.

They'll try to make it look like an accident.

He raised the rifle to the all-consuming glare, squinted watery pupils at solar brightness, couldn't seem to make himself squeeze off the shot, unwilling to kill as swiftly, as effortlessly as Rick had.

Maybe it was a park ranger. A real one this time.

But the vehicle wasn't slowing. He could feel the snow shudder beneath his boots. *Shoot them!*

He'd forgotten the safety. He had to pull the rifle down again to find it, and by then the vehicle was on top of him, the world drowned out by white roar. Chris leapt sideways, felt smooth metal smack his left boot, lift him almost gently into a graceful looping somersault that left him time—in midair—to contemplate between retaining the gun or falling on it, discharging it into his gut. He opted to let go.

He landed in soft snow, scrambling for the weapon as the vehicle and its shadowed driver etched a tight U-turn as antici-pated. In the darkness that preceded the passing glare, the rifle—the whole woods—was lost to him in opaque ocher, his retinas shrunk to pinpoints. Then the sweeping headlamps returned, throwing surreal, elongated shadows. He picked out the weapon's shadow from surrounding rock and brush and dove for the stock.

He had it in his hands, had it to his shoulder, up on his knees, as the bright lights enveloped him again, the engine screaming death in his ears. He sighted carefully despite this, got off a round that whined tunnel-long off chrome cowling. He tried to leap side-ways again, slipped in wet snow, screamed as a heavy runner passed over his right leg. Chris waited in agony for the grinding tread to follow.

It didn't. He apparently had rolled far enough from the scouring undercarriage.

He held on to the rifle this time, despite the burning agony in his leg, got up on one knee, and was sighting down the barrel at the retreating machine when fresh headlamps washed over him from the south.

Two of them.

Chris swiveled the rifle—hearing the first vehicle making its second whining turn—sighted on the second one with trembling arms, squinted into the coming glare. He had a sudden inspiration as the piercing lights blotted out the night.

He hesitated in apparent confusion, trying to look dazed. Then, at the last moment, he feinted left, pivoted like a basketball player, and jumped right. As the vehicle swept by, he pointed half-blind at the passing cockpit and pulled the trigger. A quick pressure at his shoulder, a white face lit whiter by the muzzle's flash, an instant of reddish spray, and the lights were by, plunging everything into blackness again.

A heavy, metallic *crunch.*

Chris leapt forward, found the snowmobile had collided with a big aspen, pinned there, motor racing, spewing greasy fumes, a dark torso canted over the bars. He dropped the rifle, straddled the back of the vehicle, and pulled at the shoulders of the all-but-headless corpse, gloves slipping in warm red.

Chris pulled hard, cursing the vapor, pulled and yanked with straining back muscles until the body dragged free. He hefted it over the cowling and into the snow like a sack of cement mix. I'm doing this, I'm running and I'm killing and I'm doing this, doing it rather well. Rick would be proud.

He vaulted into the seat as the first machine bore down on him, yanked the bars, wrenched the throttle, felt the vehicle shudder, whine resentment, finally tear free of the tree in a spray of chips, the odor of bruised bark. The machine bounced once over rocks and roots, then sailed effortlessly over blessedly smooth snow.

Chris killed the lights—no sense making an even brighter target— kept the black rubber grip at full throttle, tried to remember the path up, rocks they'd passed, familiar crags and trees. Two trees in particular. If he crouched low, and if his pursuer's high beams didn't give the plan away, the wire should pass over the snowmobile's hood, into the driver's face. In theory. If he could find the wire again.

An insect buzz sliced past his ear. He didn't immediately associate it, then did. They were firing on him, his engine's whine masking the explosion.

It gave him an odd sense of elation that nearly overrode his fear. They were firing on him because they could no longer afford to try to camouflage it as an accident. That meant they could be made desperate too, perhaps as desperate as he. That meant they could be beaten.

The next shot caromed, whining, over his cowling, and the next took his windshield away in a shock of spider-webbed Plexiglas, making his fear blossom anew. He began to weave, his vehicle leaving a serpentine path for the bullets to follow.

It seemed to work—he didn't hear any more of the angry insect buzzing—but it also put him in jeopardy of losing his way.

Or maybe he'd already lost his way.

Nothing looked familiar now, and even in bright starlight he could not pick up his and Rick's tracks without the headlamps. Regrettably, he switched them back on.

Nothing ahead but pale, undulating alabaster. The relentless snow had covered their tracks.

He was off the path, maybe way off, maybe already past the trees with the wire strung between them.

Ahead and to his right, a geyser of snow kicked up silently: another bullet.

Chris began to weave his vehicle drunkenly—madness going downhill at this speed—but what choice had he? He had to find their tracks again, had to find the wire.

The black wedge of stump came out of nowhere.

When he finally saw it, Chris gasped, swerved hard, leaning into the bars with all his weight, thought for a moment he'd pulled it off. But his left runner caught a black, projecting root, caught it just barely but enough. An echoing *spraaaang* of protest. The vehicle sluiced sickeningly, the impact jarring his neck into sharp pain, then alarming numbness. The machine listed helplessly to port—Chris compensated—but the fork was suddenly sluggish, and he could tell from the vibration through buttocks and heels that the runner was damaged. How badly he couldn't know. But without proper steering—especially at this speed—he'd be an accident waiting to happen. He needed to slow down, and he couldn't slow down.

He remembered the Ruger against his back, thought about trying to maneuver it from his belt, but was too leery of letting go of the wildly jinking bars. The black grips were alien under his hands now, living things straining to tear free. At any moment the machine would wrest control from him, dash him headlong into a rock, an implacable aspen.

Another insect buzz, then another, and the vehicle lurched, spun out of control. They'd shot the other runner. The bastards knew what they were doing.

Teeth gritted, shoulders knotting, Chris held on, control gone as he barreled into the spin, irrepressible g-force pinning him helplessly against the panel. He was skidding sideways down the ever steepening mountain, turning, turning in a lazy, terrifying arc, until he was almost heading backward.

Then, magically—at the apex of tipping over—the right runner bit the snow again, and he was leveling out, still plunging down a nearly vertical grade at more than fifty miles per hour, but the machine was reacting to his commands again, if resentfully. Chris saw his teenage self, fighting icy Long Island streets on his first motorcycle, an old Indian. *Always turn into the slide.*

He regained control but lost speed, the other vehicle's lights blazing across his dash. He was an easy target. The next shot would surely be through the back of his skull. He could feel it coming.

When it didn't, he glanced back and saw why. The other snowmobile was just behind him, gaining fast on his crippled vehicle. Still a chance for them to make it look like an accident.

He had to do something and fast.

To his right the cliff edge dropped away to sheer disaster. He could try riding the edge of that, swerving dangerously close to the brink, hoping they'd swerve farther, topple over.

But they were probably experts at the snowmobile, and he was suffering crippled steering as it was.

To his left, there were only flashing trees and rock formations, the occasional deadly drift, but he could not lure them into one of those without killing himself.

Just ahead at eleven o'clock, a rocky shelf extended twenty feet above the mountain floor, between them a copse of Douglas fir.

He *might* survive driving off the end of it. And anyone who didn't absolutely have to would probably not attempt it. They'd see what he was up to, probably try to swerve around the shelf, but the firs would impede them. He might lose them in the woods. Might.

Chris hesitated. Yanked left.

He'd need all the speed he could muster for a smooth landing—like a skier leaving a ramp—the more altitude, the farther he'd fly, the softer the landing.

In theory.

He opened the throttle.

He was twenty yards away from the shelf when the next slug smashed into his dash, inches from his shoulder. They were on to him, didn't want to follow in his wake, attempt this suicidal leap.

Chris ducked low, gripped the bars, and pointed for the middle of the shelf.

His vehicle began to shudder under small, then larger rocks, hidden beneath the snow. A good-size, invisible boulder would rip him apart now. He was thirty feet from the lip of the shelf. Twenty feet.

Another bullet spewed a geyser of snow just past his bow. He whipped around, saw the other vehicle closing fast, not slowing as he'd hoped. *Shit!*

He turned back, saw the lip rushing toward him, a heart-swooping drop beyond it—thought, No, I can't make this, this is my death—nearly yanked over at the last second. Then said, "The hell with it," set his jaw, and powered over the rim.

Vibrationless, nearly sublime weightlessness followed. He was soaring, the only sound the engine's surprised whine and the screaming wind in his ears. He was a hawk, an eagle, that lovely, wide-winged creature Springer had shot that first day.

Chris closed his eyes, waited.

Felt himself slammed rudely into the hard dash—backbone compressing painfully—the vehicle reconnecting with the cacophonous finality of a car wreck.

Chris opened his eyes. He was still moving.

For a terrifying instant he thought the crippled left runner would leave him, sheared away by the terrific impact. But it held, and the snowmobile, groaning and shuddering, was still in one piece. A second ground-shaking *whump* astern told him he had not completed the leap alone.

So much for diversionary tactics. He had further stressed his vehicle and all but crippled his own spine and for what?

He'd have to maneuver around somehow and return fire with the Ruger, his only out.

And then there was something familiar about the landscape

speeding toward him. That copse of scrub pine to the north, the snow-capped rocky ride flanking it.

There. Just to the left. Rick's twin firs. The thin metal wire strung taut and invisible between them.

Chris wrenched left, heard a warning grind from the undercarriage, felt tugging resistance. Gradually he maneuvered the flying vehicle toward his target. When he had the bow directly aligned between the two trees, he held fast.

Something slammed him without warning from behind, plowing him into the dash again. Blood squirted from his nostrils. The world went black for an instant. Deep purple, magenta.

They'd struck him from the rear, trying to knock him into a tree or boulder.

He looked up dazedly, saw he was off course again, heading away from the center of the wire. Heading—if he kept going—clear to the other side of the left tree. Could the sons of bitches have detected the wire?

Chris wrenched the vehicle again, found it would not move, the steering gone. No. *Not when I'm this close!*

He grabbed the right bar in both hands, yanked hard. The wheel held stubbornly. He was yards from the tree now. In a moment his headlights would pick up the thin length of wire, and it would be too late.

He tore off his gloves for better purchase, gripped the bar in his hands, set his teeth, and leaned right with the last of his strength. The vehicle drifted two feet to port. Not much, but enough.

The left tree was coming up fast on the driver's side. He'd narrowly miss it at this range—might even graze it—but he thought he could clear it and he'd be into the wire. The question was, would the shattered windshield of the vehicle pass under it, even with him ducking? Would his pursuer catch on and dodge aside at the last instant?

No time for speculation. Here came the tree, his lights picking out the details in the bark now, the wire still invisible. My God, it *was* the right pair of trees, right?

Chris felt another thudding impact behind him as his pursuer's cowling smashed his tail. His vehicle fishtailed, straightened. The tree loomed and in the instant before he crouched low, Chris saw the wire highlighted in the headlamps' glare.

Then the tree was past and he was under.

He turned to look over his shoulder.

A dark shape in the pursuing cockpit was aiming a pistol at his head. Chris imagined actually seeing the coming bullet as it sped into his forehead, blew out the back of his cranium.

Something zipped past his left ear. At the same instant the figure behind him suddenly disappeared: winked out like a TV image, the pursuing snowmobile, pilotless and slowing rapidly.

Chris squeezed the brake on his vehicle, brought it to a lurching stop, leapt out running, reaching behind him for the Ruger.

He found a parka-clad man behind the wire, lying on his back, leg twisted beneath him, front of the parka sliced scalpel-clean where the wire had received him. The man struggled up, straining for a silvery automatic just out of reach in the snow.

Chris brought the Ruger around and shot the man twice in the chest.

He waited a moment to make sure the man didn't move again.

Then he turned, vapored breath enveloping him like an enamored wreath, walked to the man's vehicle canted against a snowbank, still thrumming with life.

Chris climbed aboard, turned the machine around, and started back up the mountain to his house. Everything was suddenly easier, the concept of some kind of success becoming a substantial part of his consciousness.

He parked a safe distance from the front of the A-frame.

He cut the vehicle's motor, climbed out with the Ruger. He had no idea if Rick had arrived yet or not. He guessed, though, with the aid of the snowmobile, that he had beat Rick up here. Especially if Rick had encountered trouble as he had.

Chris stood for a moment in the falling snow regarding his house.

The upstairs was dark, the living room and kitchen windows glowing. There was slight movement from behind them, though at this distance, with the curtains drawn, he could distinguish nothing.

He walked through the snow to his gravel drive, passed Springer's half-inundated Lamborghini, kept on going—an easy gait—to the front porch.

On the stoop, beneath the darkened porch light, he stuck the gun behind him again and rang the bell.

Springer opened the door as if expecting visitors. He wore Chris's robe and pajamas.

"Chris! What an unexpected surprise!" He looked like it wasn't unexpected in the least. "We were just talking about you. I didn't hear your car." He craned past Chris's shoulder to the empty drive.

"Cut the shit, Frank. Where's my wife?"

Springer turned. "Kitten, look who's come to visit!" And back to Chris: "Come in, come in. We just put the baby down and were about to have a nightcap. What can I get you?"

Chris stepped cautiously across the lintel, the Ruger pressing the small of his back.

He hadn't expected it this way. The best he'd hoped for was a stalling tactic at the front door, if even that. Now he was actually inside the house.

He didn't like the sound of the door shutting behind him, didn't like the feel of this, despite the warmth of the familiar house, the cheery glow from the fireplace.

Matty's slim form curled on the sofa before it.

"Matty's a bit under the weather," Springer said. "Worn out. Nicky's had the flu."

Chris felt a bright heat, suppressed the urge to blow Springer's back apart with the Ruger.

"Scotch and soda okay?"

Ignoring him, Chris came to the edge of the living room, looked down at Matty's long legs trailing the couch, the flimsy novelty nightie he'd bought her as a joke. He felt his gut tighten.

Play it cool, keep him talking. Rick was probably already at the back door. "Matty?"

She turned with lidded, desultory eyes, the curvaceous length of her lit from the hearth's pulsing glow. "Chris . . ."

He came to her quickly, knelt beside the couch. Started to sweep her into his arms when he saw the blood.

"You have no idea how hard it is to get a new place in order," Springer said from the kitchen. "We've been unpacking, moving furniture, getting Nicky's booster shots. These kids. And then he still comes down with the flu. Can you beat it?"

It wasn't a lot of blood, but it was matting the flimsy nightie above her left breast. "Jesus," Chris whispered, again repressing the urge to reach for the gun, "he's hurt you!"

He looked into his wife's eyes.

Christ, she was drugged.

"I think the place is shaping up nicely, though, don't you, Chris? Here's your drink. . . ."

Chris appraised the bigger man balefully, hoping his trembling didn't show, guessing it did. "What have you done to her?"

Another of Springer's practiced looks of astonished innocence lit his face. "Done? Well, I've tried to take very good care of her. Her and the boy. They are my wife and son, after all."

"You'll die for this, you son of a bitch." *Come on*, Rick; what the hell are you doing? I'm taking this bastard on my own.

Springer came around the couch, set Chris's drink on the coffee table, sat on the edge of the sofa next to Matty, his weight making her roll slightly toward him. "Oh, of course, the blood. How stupid of me. You're concerned about the blood." Scoffing. "It's nothing." He reached up to draw the filmy negligee away from her breast, withdrew a hankie from his robe pocket, and patted the soft tissue above the areola. Matty made no move to interfere.

Chris would have leapt on him, screaming, out of control, if the sight of what was imprinted there hadn't stayed him. The pale white scars were gone, covered now by a carefully crafted tattoo, still fresh and weeping lightly. "What the hell?" he whispered.

"Beautiful, isn't it?" Springer beamed, settling back expansively. "Of course, I administered a topical anesthetic, Xylocaine. She didn't feel a thing. Still a bit drowsy, however. The bleeding will stop in a few hours."

He tenderly patted the trickling design again, and something in his expert, nearly medicinal gesture stopped Chris from shoving him away violently.

"You're wondering about the design. As you see, it's a kind of beast, a very singular creature, the mythical siren. A beautifully plumed bird with a woman's face. She has, since classical times, lured mariners to their doom, so they say."

Springer straightened, cocked his head, admiring his handiwork. "The basic pattern, of course, goes back hundreds of years. You can still find them decorating houses built along the Volga River. Shutters, lintels, friezes and the like. The artisans, in preparing a panel for carving, drew the design on paper first, placed that flat against the wood, the outline perforated with a needle and the paper sprinkled with coal dust, thereby creating a stencil on the wood. The paper was then removed, the remaining dots connected, followed by the actual carving. The modern tattoo artist follows a similar technique. I picked up the trick while in the navy. Not bad work, would you say?"

Chris reached up, pulled the nightie over Matty's breast again, patting her pale cheek. She'd drifted off. "Matty. *Matty!*"

"She's very tired, I'm afraid. Your scotch is growing diluted."

Chris ignored him, Matty's eyes on him now, black and unreadable. "Chris . . . please go. . . ."

"Kitten!" Frank cried. "How inhospitable."

"Shut up, Springer," Chris said. Then to his wife, "I am going, baby, with you."

"No . . ." Her eyes were fighting to focus on him.

"Can you walk, honey? Can you sit up?"

"I wouldn't advise that," Springer said.

"Matty? Answer me. I'm taking you out of here. Where's Nicky?"

Her lids drooped. "No . . ."

"Sound asleep in his room," Frank obliged, swallowing scotch. "Check for yourself if you like."

"I intend to." To Matty, "Shall I carry you?"

She looked away. "Please. Go."

"Can you walk?"

"Chris . . . you must leave. . . ."

"I'm taking you and the baby out of here."

She shook her head weakly. "No . . . don't want that. . . ."

Chris shot Frank a look. "What the hell did you give her?"

"Me? Simple sedative. For the tattoo."

"Matty—"

"No!" Firmer this time, her eyes more focused. "I'm his wife . . . his wife. . . ."

"Like hell."

"Certificate genuine. I belong to him. Go now. . . ."

"Matty, stop it! He's rehearsed you with drugs."

Frank set down his drink beside Chris's. "I can see you two have a lot to talk over. I understand. These things can be delicate. I'll just leave you alone for a bit." He strolled toward the kitchen convivially. "Help yourself to anything in the bar, old man."

When he'd left, Chris sat beside her.

In Frank's absence she seemed slightly more attentive, less fearful.

"Jesus," Chris breathed, and it hung between them like a glass wall, all that could be said for a moment.

She looked beyond him for a dreamy time, as if recapturing something, the old Matty face back, briefly, the sweet curve of nose, the lovely round forehead. Then tightening, the urgency back. "You have to get out of here, Chris."

"Matty—"

"No, you have to leave *now*! I'll try to get in touch somehow. A few weeks, months. You must go, baby, you must, you must. Terrible danger here!"

"I'm not afraid of him." Though he was.

She was fading again. "Get in your car . . . go away from here . . . begging you. We're okay . . . baby fine. I can do this better alone. Trust." And her lazy eyes focused a moment. "He's a killer, Chris. You can't know. He's *insane*. Please. If you love me. If you love the baby."

His throat moved thickly. "Not without you."

Eyes narrowed, anger behind them, mind fighting sleep and him, Matty made a face he'd never seen before. "Don't *need* you to be brave! Need you alive! You can't help here . . . can only get us killed. He's covered all the bases. Has the law with him. He's more clever than you can imagine. Can't make you understand it all in two minutes. Just trust me. Leave!"

She held his eyes more steadily. Was the drug wearing off?

Chris looked down, saw a half-filled cup of coffee on the table— sniffed it—held it to her lips. Matty took it in small, then bigger gulps.

Her eyes—pupils still expanded—gleamed nonetheless.

Chris set down the coffee, suddenly in no hurry, a bigger fear than Springer plucking at him.

Heart knocking, he lifted her chin, made her look directly at him. "Do you love me, Matty?"

She shook her head, turning away. "There isn't time."

Chris pulled her chin back. "There's time for that, damn it."

Matty licked her lips.

He watched her, heart thundering now, something breaking apart inside him. The end was coming—was here now—and it was not the end he'd anticipated. He felt sick to his knees.

"Matty?"

She couldn't look at him. "I'm sorry, Chris."

He stared back, insides collapsing. "Do I take that as a no?"

She sighed, trembling with it.

"So that's it. I was a . . . convenience. Someone to run to, escape to. From him. Is that it?"

She stared somewhere past him, face saying it all.

He had the sudden pressing urge to use the Ruger on himself. "Answer me, goddamn it!" He surprised himself at the depth of his anger. "There's a child's life at stake here!"

Matty looked down at her hands, shoulders slumped in submission. "I was scared, Chris. I was scared." She closed her eyes as if having said that was quite enough. Sighed a sigh that seemed to go on for a long time. "Scared. Confused. Panicked. You could never understand." She looked up at him. "You saw what he did to me. Well, he's done worse. Far worse. I had to run. But I had nowhere to go. So I ran anyway." And she couldn't meet his eyes for this next one: "And you were there."

She shrugged wistfully but perhaps guiltlessly, everything but self-pride seeming to have been wrenched from her.

He studied her a moment. "I don't believe you."

She offered an almost smile. She studied him wearily. "All right. Believe this, then: If you don't leave now, he will definitely kill you. You cannot, *cannot* beat him. No one can. After you—his blood up—he'll doubtless kill me. And after that . . . the baby."

Something in her tone turned the room to stone, the cold, unyielding finality of marble. This tone—he sensed—had been there before, witness to terrible things. Things buried somehow and moved mechanically past. Petty lies and deceits were the least of what lay between them.

Chris stood, mouth acrid with fear again, the impossible tonnage and implacability of an avalanche descending on him. He said, despite this, "I'm taking my son."

She reached for him and he tore free. Plunged up the stairs, three at a time, raced the darkened hall, threw back the door to Nicky's room.

The baby was sleeping peacefully in his plastic racing car bed, pink and restful and, to Chris's relief, seemingly healthy. Chris swept him into his arms and raced for the hall again.

He was certain the couch would be empty when he reentered the living room.

Yet Matty was there, sitting stiffly, hands folded in her lap, staring into nothingness. Springer was not to be seen.

Chris stood over her, the child dangling from his arms. How the hell was he going to do this? Where the hell was Rick?

He laid Nicky down gently at the opposite end of the couch, turned, and pulled Matty to him again. *"Matty!"*

Before she could respond, there was a muffled blast from outside. Another. A shotgun. Rick.

Chris whirled, the Ruger in his hand before he even realized it, raced for the front door, flung it open.

A single, terrible scream pierced the night. A sound like no other, that reached inside and ripped at the heart.

"Rick!"

He stepped down to the porch, Ruger before him, squinting into the gloom, his night vision gone. "Rick!"

Chris hesitated, torn with indecision.

Don't leave them. Don't leave them inside. You'll never see them again.

A low, terrifying moan from the woods.

Chris leapt from the porch, gun waving before him, trotted toward what he guessed was the source of the sound, heart tripping in his throat. "Rick!"

Outside the penumbra of the porch light, the night—the woods— were black. He stood in the damp grass, head cocked, listening.

He might have heard a low, distant groaning.

He stepped forward cautiously, distracted by the sound of his own labored breathing, the Ruger trembling in his fist: It felt small and silly and useless.

He must have been insane to let Rick talk him into parking the car so far away. He'd never find it now.

A low moan just to his left.

He turned with the sound, stepped into thick brush.

"Rick?"

His boot kicked metallic hardness. He bent, retrieved a long, silvery flashlight.

Chris clicked it on, feeling his breath catch. The leaves and grass before him were mottled red. There was a trail of it leading in dark droplets away from where he'd found the flashlight.

Chris followed quickly, flashlight in his left hand, gun in his right, something inside warning that the flashlight was not Rick's, that it belonged to someone else, had been placed there deliberately to be found, to illuminate the crimson trail.

He swept the beam before him.

Ghostly tendrils of limbs and foliage, chiaroscuro patterns crisscrossing the dark night.

A misshapen bulge, out of place in the orderly tangle, caught the edge of the beam. Chris directed the cone of light higher and found Rick turning lazily, dangling upside down from a stately Douglas fir, supported between ankle and bough by something indiscernible. Both knees, slick with wet, were crooked at improper angles, the arms hanging loose and outstretched as if beseeching the earth below. The eyes, closed—probably in death—were bloated, as were the cheeks, from gravity-driven fluids. Twin rivers of black blood oozed from a mouth hung open and supplicant as if awaiting dentistry.

Chris dropped the light, scrambled toward the big tree, whipping the knife from his boot. He climbed, cursing, fell, reached again with torn fingers. Three torturously long tries to scale the rough limbs above the swinging body, reach down with the Nighthawk and sever the length of belt that held his friend, letting him drop heavily the ten or so feet because there was just no other way.

Chris leapt, stumbled to the motionless form, cradled it, found himself weeping, blubbering, "Jesus."

Rick Corman opened his eyes, regarded the night with dull wonder, a little boy slapped for no reason he could understand. "Grogghhh," he burbled, and a fresh gout of blood dribbled onto his chin.

You're all alone now, an inner voice told Chris.

He knelt there in the dark and cold, rocking his friend, smelling the blood, the fear.

CHAPTER 16

Chris found himself in a mauve, antiseptic-smelling tunnel—a hospital corridor—staring listlessly at a single proclamation taped to an otherwise bare emergency room wall: WE CAN BEAT AIDS IN OUR LIFETIME.

He sat, hands in lap as though he'd forgotten them, ankles crossed, on a hard wooden bench, experiencing nearly preternatural sensory overload. Everything was heightened, everything too loud, too bright, too busy. He was at the heart of it all, stronger, smarter, and just slightly ahead of the world about him, cranium buzzing. Despite (or because of) the evening's preceding trauma and attendant exhaustion, he teetered giddily on razored exhilaration. In this pumped, altered state, he felt absolutely confident that he could do anything. That—should it be needed—he could easily substitute for any brain surgeon who might suddenly be called away. Could take the doctor's place and perform effortless, exacting incisions in the oculomotor nerve with no danger whatever to either the medulla oblongata or the pituitary. Mop with a flourish and leave the sewing-up chores to some lesser minion while he, Chris, went for coffee break.

People passing kept looking askance, sometimes outright

staring; he was covered in leopard spots of blood from the chest down, Rick having spilt a great deal, mostly from his mouth.

Chris knew, on the long drive here to Kingston emergency (having studiously avoided Greenborough and the ubiquitous Doc Holiday) that both Rick's legs were broken—probably shot away—at or just above the knee. A glistening spear of silvery bone had tented and finally poked through his friend's right jeaned thigh, the leg and foot below twisted and turned wrong.

Chris had removed both his and Rick's belts and applied crude tourniquets to the upper femur at the superpatellar bursa of both legs. He had applied the tourniquets at what he was pretty sure was the femoral artery of each leg. Indeed, most of the bleeding there had stopped, though so had the circulation—the nearly hour-long drive to Kingston (Greenborough would have been far closer) putting nagging doubts about gangrene and the loss of lower members plaguing his fevered mind—fists white-knuckled on the sports car's wheel in a sweat-slick death grip, eyes glued to the high beam's glare as though willing the miles shorter, the emergency room closer. There had been no time to search for the stupid rental car. He had stolen Frank Springer's Lamborghini, having found the keys dangling unattended within.

He had stopped just once during the frantic drive, canted at a gravel shoulder, reached back, and loosed each strap quickly, letting some blood flow into the lower extremities and over the seat cushions, then pulled the belts tight again and driven on. Rick had never regained consciousness or really lost it, hovering, open-eyed and open-mouthed in glazed (painless?) detachment that Chris prayed was not shock, though it certainly should have been.

There had been nothing Chris could do about the horrible black mouth. Blood glistened in a sluggish, oily stream. He considered stuffing a rag there, rejected it for fear of cutting off breathing or possibly, inadvertently, drowning his friend in his own blood.

He drove into the unforgiving blackness of night and fear and anger and guilt and the eerie whimper of his own terrified voice.

Drove and drove and drove, and then was suddenly there in the bright emergency parking lot, leaning on the horn, men in white coats whisking his wounded friend from the backseat—too impersonally abrupt, really, after what Chris by himself had accomplished—leaving him alone and feeling empty in the mauve corridor with the AIDS sign, the trembly adrenaline high, the skulking shadow of his shame.

His attention kept drifting to the pay phone on the wall, his mind attuned to who was at the other end of the line, of the awful duty he must perform, should have performed the moment they'd brought Rick in.

Sitting there, dreading the call, Chris stared stupidly at the emergency corridor floor, its multicolored directional lines leading off and away to this room, that station. He found himself ruminating absently about—of all things—his best friend's wife's nipples.

He'd glimpsed them once, several summers ago on a camping trip with Rick, Sharon, and Chris's perennial date but never-quite-wife, Janey.

It had been a bright, hot August day, the air sweet as athletic sweat. Chris had left the others momentarily, climbed the short fir-studded knoll to the shared cabin, stepped inside to retrieve a fishing lure—having assumed it empty, the others frolicking at the dock. Walked in, turned, and found Sharon knotting a green bikini string from the front, cups behind her, exposed breasts and surprised face lit golden and fetching from the cabin's north window.

"Oh," she'd offered calmly with pear-shaped smile and no particular hurry, routinely finished fastening the halter, permitting Chris a clear, nearly leisurely look at imperiously large nipples, bumpy Orange Crush areolas—holding her smile and her eyes on him so he had to look away first and wonder later and ever after exactly why she'd done that. Certainly not an invitation. Were they just such old, close friends they could share this kind of intimacy with neither embarrassment nor undue curiosity? Pardon my little faux pas, but I'm glad it was you, dear Chris, who had the opportunity to see how lovely I am.

He stared now at the white hospital phone, dread fluttering impatiently in his middle. A night of dreads. This just one more. There'd be no smiles from Sharon tonight. She'd not only never forget this bloody, tragic night, but dissect—over the days, in fine detail—every nuance of it, eventually come around to asking him questions about every minute, every second, until it arrived at this moment and the final question: *Why did you wait so long to call me?*

So he rose, at last, shouldered the receiver, shouldered his responsibility, and made himself place the call.

Her cheery "Hello?" came on the line. Followed swiftly by an octave shift as he unfolded it. And, finally, the black, bottomless well of her silence.

He found himself wishing—receiver burning his ear—he'd thought this through more carefully, but supposed he had. Really, there just wasn't any way else to tell it. Your husband's been shot. Shot bad. She didn't ask how and he didn't volunteer. That would come later. There was going to be a lot of later.

He hung up, stared at the silent phone, silvery cradle, everything looking as it had moments ago but everything different.

He regained the wooden bench, stared at the AIDS sign, could not stop the conversation from echoing back, unbidden, unwanted.

"How bad?"

"I don't know, Sharon. He's in intensive care; they're doing everything."

"Conscious?"

"I think so."

"Bleeding?"

"Some. I have a good feeling he's going to be all right." And to move ahead, avoid details: "Let me give you the address of this place."

"It's Kingston, Colorado, right?"

"Yes."

"Then the cabbie will know where the hospital is." Composed. Too composed. Suspicious?

Chris heard footsteps, looked up at Dr. Werthem striding down the hall with deliberate clicks, stethoscope looped around his neck the way they wore them these days, not by the earpieces.

Chris stood, expectant.

Werthem looked tired but content enough. "Strong man, your friend. Lost a lot of blood and never even went into shock. Athlete?"

"He works out. He's out of danger, then?"

"Oh, I think so. Never really lost consciousness, if you can believe that. His tongue was nearly torn from his mouth; did you know that? We stitched the best we could, but he may lose some sensation at the tip. What the hell happened?"

"Hunting accident."

"I see. . . ." Skeptical but not pressing. Let the police do that if they showed up. "Bit his own tongue, I suppose."

"I guess. What about the legs?" Chris pressed.

Werthem lit a cigarette, offered one to Chris, was declined. "A goddamn mess. The left one especially. How'd you know about the femoral artery, army training?"

"Yes," Chris lied, not to have to explain. "Will he walk?"

Werthem gave a wry look, picking a shred from his tongue. "Not before a lot more operations, and maybe not then." He noted Chris's expression. "But probably, yes. I'd say the chances are good. Depends on how extensive the nerve damage is, and we won't know that for a while. You going to keep him here?"

"I don't know, his wife is on the way. Why?"

Werthem shrugged modestly. "We're a good surgical shop for a small-town hospital, see our share of shotgun wounds—quail hunters. Our rehab wing is top-notch, new whirlpools. I'd keep an eye on him personally."

"I'll pass it along, thanks. When can I see him?"

"Give us a few minutes. It'll have to be brief."

"I understand."

Werthem nodded, looked Chris up and down once, turned back down the hall, white lab coat fluttering, the AIDS note stirring in his wake.

"Hey . . ."

Stirring from a sleep he hadn't remembered surrendering to, Chris stared up owl-eyed at Sharon Corman, mind just behind his open mouth, racing to catch up. She was shaking his shoulder lightly.

He was asleep in a hospital. Rick had been hurt. Matty and the baby were still in danger.

He sat up quickly, found himself in near darkness, neck stiff from the chair's hard back. Rick's curtain, closed, glowed softly beside him. The black opaqueness of the window told him it was not yet dawn. Sharon's presence seemed to crowd the room. She stood in near silhouette, her perfume warring with the crisp-smelling outside that had followed her in.

He could hardly see her face in the gloom, but he could imagine the details.

"He's sleeping," she informed him, as though he might not know, as though Rick were the only subject on either of their minds.

To show her he already did know, Chris answered, "Yes."

Sharon straightened, stood there for a time, and just stared down at him, saying nothing and speaking volumes. Her fear had dissipated while he slept, questions and suspicions surfacing.

Chris rubbed his eyes. "When did you get here?"

"Few minutes ago. Are you hurt too?"

He looked uncomprehendingly up at her, then down at his mottled shirt, the dried blood. "No. No, I'm okay." He nodded at the curtain. "How is he?"

"Stable."

Chris nodded impotently, suddenly more alone than even before in the great woods. "That's good." It sounded insincere somehow and he didn't know why.

He kept expecting, hoping, Sharon would sit on the edge of the empty, adjacent bed, but she wouldn't oblige him. She loomed, looking down darkly and saying nothing. Then finally, after what seemed too long: "Where's Matty?"

Chris licked his lips against terrible, insistent thirst. "In Greenborough. In the house."

"What happened?"

"Rick told you nothing?"

"No." But her distant tone confirmed she suspected something more sinister than her husband lying about a business trip, a convention.

Chris rubbed his thighs absently, wishing desperately for a drink, anything to drink, even plain water. "She and Nicky have been abducted." It sounded ridiculous no matter how many times he said or thought it. It sounded unreal.

"Abducted?"

"Yes."

"You said she was at the house."

"It's—Sharon, I can't tell it in here."

She looked at him a moment more, then turned to the curtain, parted it a fraction, then turned back. "I need to check into a motel. Do you want to take me?"

"Of course."

She already had her purse in her hand, a clipped, curt movement achieved with stiffened shoulders. She was blaming him. She didn't know the whole story, and already she was putting it at his feet.

And—he supposed—not without justification.

Razor-sharp Sharon Corman.

"Come on," she told him. "We can talk in the car."

★ ★ ★

Chris drove, talking, explaining, Sharon listening quietly, looking straight ahead, expressionless, streaks of passing car lights in her hair. Expressionless and silent. All the way to the motel.

Chris insisted on checking her in, carrying her luggage, getting her squared away.

It was a small, dowdy affair, chipping plaster and smelling vaguely of mildew. All the bigger chain concerns were booked; ski season had begun.

Chris opened a window for her, despite the bitter breeze, to clear out the stuffy room, adjusted the thermostat, parked her luggage against the wall, acutely aware of her ominously silent presence at his back. He had already told her most of it in the car, including his relationship with the police in Greenborough. Sharon had responded with stony silence.

She stood squarely in the middle of the little room, arms folded, watching him.

He could feel her eyes on his back as he busied himself, procrastinating. Until his utilitarian unpacking movements began to feel silly and forced, the excuse to stretch too obvious. Finally he straightened and turned to her and awaited from her he knew not what.

The entire scene held an aura of unreality: the late hour, this strange room, the sinister something burgeoning between them, an inert explosiveness that would not happen. He had the sudden, baffling urge—in the tragicomic absurdity of the moment—to laugh.

He'd kept hoping—despite the tragic circumstances—that Sharon's very presence would lend an air of comforting familiarity to his topsy-turvy world, bring the warmth and comfort of known reality with her. It had not. Alone and cut away from Rick this way, she seemed less even than a stranger, a new woman entirely, with whom he shared no rapport, hardly any recognition. A chasm had opened between them that neither would ever quite bridge. There was more than anger in her stiffened shoulders. There was the posture and quiet balefulness of the deceived. That chiseled edge of coolness she'd always reserved for Matty, Sharon now extended him.

"What are you going to do now?" she asked, arms still folded tightly, as if keeping something pressed behind her breast.

Chris stood impotently, hands in his pockets. "Go back, of course. Get Matty."

"How?"

"I'll think of something."

To his relief, she turned away and perched on the edge of the mattress. "What about Rick?"

He didn't understand. "Well, you're here now."

"He's your best friend."

"Sharon. Matty and Nicky—"

"He may not walk again; did they tell you?"

He needed to come to her and dared not. "Dr. Werthem said he had a very good chance—"

Her curt nod cut him off. "Even a better chance before you called him."

Chris sucked in a trembling breath, feeling all his terrible exhaustion now, which no amount of sleep could offset. "What can I possibly say, Sharon? You know how I feel."

She looked up sharply. "No. Tell me. How do you feel? I'd like to know."

"Honey—"

And finally—to his relief, really—she let it go. "He *worshiped* you! Would have done anything for you! Probably died for you. Nearly did!" She was giving in to the anger at last (probably a good thing) voice tremulous with it, in danger of going shrill unless he intercepted this.

"I didn't know where else to turn, Sharon! I told you—"

"You didn't tell me! You didn't tell me *anything*, Chris! If you had, I wouldn't have let him come! You know that! You knew it then!"

"Rick was—"

"Rick was a big overgrown Boy Scout! He was an infantryman past his prime! An old soldier scared of growing older! He was a kid playing in the woods! He was your best friend! My *husband*! The only one I've got!"

"Matty's the only wife I've got."

"Is she?"

He stood regarding her in dull amazement. "Of course," he whispered.

Sharon made a sharp sound and looked away at the rug, purse clenched in her lap as though fearful of theft.

Chris stared at her a moment. Then found a chair, sat back.

"You just . . . ," and he shook his head, flummoxed by what he was thinking. "The simple truth is, you just never really liked her, did you?"

She rolled her eyes, didn't bother looking up.

"Did you?" He nodded at what he perceived as the obvious. "And you've liked me a little less since the day I brought her around. Brought them both around. It was never the same, not like the old days at the cabin. You just never warmed to them."

She glared at him. "Don't be an idiot! You know how I feel about that boy! And you didn't 'bring her around'! Rick and I *met* her, the same way we met Janey and Susan and all the other women in your long bachelor's life. I liked them all, Chris, all of them, Janey especially."

"But not Matty. Never Matty."

"I never got to know Matty! You whisked her off to Vegas before she even said boo!"

"You've had two years to know her, Sharon! More! You didn't try!"

And she threw the purse at him with such surprising contempt he barely had time to block it with his hands, the metal buckle searing his knuckles. "*Damn* you, Chris, *damn you*. Why didn't you marry Janey? She loved you! She still loves you!"

He just stared uncomprehendingly at her, slowly shaking his head. Then he got up, heading for the door. "I can't do this, Sharon."

She lunged from the chair, nails digging into his arm. "Where are you *going*, you son of a bitch!" Her impetus drove them both into the door.

He caught both her hands before she could slap him. "Sharon, stop."

"You're staying *here* goddamn it!" kicking at him now.

She needed a slap—something to shock loose her terror—but he just couldn't. "Sharon."

"Even now you're thinking of her!"

He shoved back hard, gripped her wrists until the fine bones there ground together and she winced. "What the hell am I supposed to be thinking about, for Christ's sake?"

"Me! Us! Who your friends are!"

"Matty's my *wife*!"

She wrenched free and slapped him so hard he didn't really feel it. They stood there gaping at each other, still hearing the slap echoing around the room, the shock having worked on her just as well this way.

With haggard breath Sharon said, "She's *his*, Chris! For God sake, can't you see that? She was *never* yours; she's Springer's! She and . . ."

He waited for it.

". . . and Nicky." And she stood breathing hard, wiping back her hair with a stiff hand, face beet red, eyes dark hollows of fear.

Chris found himself gripping the knob to quell sudden trembling. "No."

Sharon sighed hugely, turned, unseeing, collapsed boneless to the bed, hands covering her face. "Chris, Chris, Chris."

He gripped the knob until it hurt; the trembling remained. *Wasn't someone supposed to get you a drink at a time like this? Where was the someone with the drink?*

Sharon pulled her hands away, looked into the palms as if for answers, shook her head in wonder. "You have this, this incredible memory thing, all this knowledge stored up, and you know nothing, nothing."

"What did she tell you?" he demanded warily. "What did Matty confide?"

She gave him a hopeless look. "She didn't tell me *anything*! That's precisely the point. She never told me anything. Women talk to each other, Chris. Women bond through verbal exchange the way men bond through, oh, fishing or shooting things or whatever. Women *talk*! Especially women who care about each other. They tell each other *everything*. Do you know Janey's mother's maiden name?"

He didn't. "That doesn't mean—"

"I do. And I know her favorite color and her favorite movie and who she saw that time for her yeast infection and how bad her PMS is. And how sweet you are, Chris, how giving. I know you, love you, through Janey."

"And nothing from Matty, is that it?"

Sharon puffed air, slapped her thighs. "It isn't that simple. Matty's sweet. Maybe she's even—despite all this—somehow a good person. But she only lets me get so far, so deep, like there's this level she deigns entrance to, but no further. Everything else is locked up. She's pleasant enough. But friends, real friends? Chris, it isn't I who didn't try, it's her! Two years and I know no more about her now than I did the day you introduced us."

"She's shy."

"She's walled off!" She looked at the rug again. "And now I know why."

He clung to the knob, feeling that to let go would be to float away and never see the end of this cruel, compelling conversation. Never see Sharon or Rick or any of what had once been called his past again. "You're saying," he began hoarsely, "what in essence you're saying is, our relationship is a lie."

She looked up with genuine tenderness. "Chris, you're so sweet. But you don't understand women at all. You're just this big puppy where women are concerned."

When she continued, her tone was almost resigned. "She's making a fool of you, Chris. Worse, she's going to get you killed. I'd be sorry for that, and so would Rick."

Chris turned to the door. "I want my wife and child back, goddamn it."

Waited. But she said nothing.

When he turned to look, she was staring at nothing.

Her left eye, caught in cheap lamplight—the other half of her face dark—this eye, Chris noticed for the first time with genuine surprise, was not truly brown at all but dark hazel, with a pencil fleck of green, a flaw. Turning that half of her face into a lie.

He seemed to be viewing her with a clarity he'd never glimpsed before: a lovely, impregnable chrysalis beneath which the ugly worm lay writhing in threads of envy and regret. Poor Sharon. Poor Rick.

You're wrong, he thought. I'm sorry—shocked—that you and Rick have lost it, that it isn't very important to you anymore, but you're wrong.

"All right," he heard himself saying, "I'll stay. I'll find another cabin down the court. We can have breakfast together in the morning, then go see Rick."

She looked at the wall noncommittally, gone from him.

"I promise," he said to wake her up.

She closed her eyes, still sitting rigidly.

Chris shut the door softly behind him, the bitter air lighting up his head. He stood there on the motel porch for a moment, letting the cold wash him clean.

Then he got into Springer's Lamborghini and drove out of town.

He sped into the night, back to Greenborough, thinking, I *should* stay. I should be there in the morning when Rick wakes up.

Thinking also that, in light of what his life had become, promises—like sex, like Sharon's eye—had taken on a different hue.

CHAPTER 17

Matty dreamt she and the baby had indeed escaped the maniac at last, had fled to the boathouse on a lovely spring day.

She had wrapped Nicky securely in his little orange life jacket and maneuvered the Chris-Craft to the middle of the wide lake where no one on earth, not even hard-muscled, fast-swimming Frank Springer could ever catch them. But then she'd looked up to see that he was, after all, cutting through the water toward them in long, even strokes, his effortless Australian crawl, and would be there soon. And so, she supposed, there was only one recourse, the one she'd known all along. She held Nicky a moment, kissed him, then picked up the small hand ax and began chopping the hole in the hull of the boat. Never thinking once through each successively exhausting swing that it would have been far simpler—and faster (Frank was getting close)—to merely take the baby in her arms and leap overboard and leave it all behind, the horror and the dread. Leave it all above and far away as she and her child sank into green and greener and finally sunless depths. And when this idea did at last begin to take shape, when she straightened, pausing with the ax to consider it, a cold wind came rushing at them abruptly across the lake, turning flat surface to rutted field, making her tremble violently, freezing the water hard, drowning Frank, which was good but too good because the tangible aspects of the dream were slipping away now . . . lost to the languid, prosaic pull of reality, drawing her up and finally out and alone. . . .

She woke on the couch downstairs, trembling—no blanket over her—in darkness but for the pale starlight from the north living room window.

Matty blinked, readjusting to the world of reason and dread. Not her first dream of suicide, hardly. She closed her eyes again against too much reality too soon.

She was stiff to soreness from the cramped position on the sofa, the impending cold. Frank must have forgotten to turn the heat on. Or not forgotten. Certainly he hadn't bothered to cover her.

She sat up in clinging webs of sleep, blinking dully at the pale glow from the kitchen, the neon counter lights above the stove that were never turned off.

Her throat was raw from vomiting. She remembered little of what had followed the unspeakable dinner, except the green swatch of tongue; she remembered that clearly enough. Oh, yes, and Frank coming into the bathroom behind her, kneading her shoulders gently as she heaved again and again into bright porcelain, murmuring with his best reassuring tone, "Oh, come now, kitten, it isn't all *that* bad. Why, the early settlers feasted upon each other as a matter of course. Those hard, unendurable winters you know." It caused her to retch again, doubtlessly to his delight. And then, holding her limp, trembling body by the sink, wiping her stinking mouth with a warm washcloth, he'd clucked, "Tut-tut, kitten, you don't think—you can't possibly think—I'd serve something like that to our child. Our only child." And he'd smoothed back her hair, running the warm cloth down her neck, across the globes of her breasts, the still angry tattoo reflected there in the sink mirror. "It was just my way of reminding them, you see. Mum's the word. Talk about what you find up here, and you get your tongue taken away. There now, you look better. Shall we finish our meal?"

He held her up as she stumbled back through the house, making it no farther than the sofa, which seemed to reach up and pull her down into its softness, its promised oblivion. Springer sat beside her as she drifted away, stroking her brow. "We have so many enemies, don't we, kitten? The girl was lovely. I hated doing that; I really did. But they often put pleasing features on the faces of the enemy these days. It's their way of putting us off guard." He kissed her cheek gently. "But we'll never be off guard, will we, Matty dear?"

Turning then, he stooped, admonished the baby: "Oh, dear, look here, you've dropped your little present again. That won't do." Springer retrieved the little plush tiger from the floor. As Matty looked listlessly at the two of them, Nicky reached out with a grin and Frank handed him the stuffed toy.

Matty looked more closely at the toy, at Nicky's hands, arms, the brownish streaks, on the tablecloth too. Heart thundering as she bent forward, she appraised the stuffed tiger closely. Not a tiger at all: a kitten, a mountain lion kitten, newly dead, newly stuffed. Nicky giggled obliviously, rubbing the stringy fur in his face.

She'd faded to black after that.

She sat in the darkened living room, thinking of Chris. Wondering about the gunshots outside, wondering if he'd survived after plunging recklessly from the house. He had a gun in his hand, an automatic. She'd never, in all their time together, known him to carry such a weapon. He was a crack shot with a rifle, but he loathed handguns, would never carry one unless he meant to use it.

Had he used it last night?

Were those distant shots another of Frank's tricks, luring Chris outside where he could finish him off without bloodying the house? His precious goddamn house.

Matty put her head in her hands.

She should have done it differently. Somehow she should have thought it out, made sure Chris didn't come back, knowing he would. She should have taken the child and run.

But where in these woods and this cold?

And Chris would have come anyway, and Frank would have killed him.

Still, she couldn't help thinking it was all her fault.

Well, of course it's your fault! You're the one who got him into this. . . . You're the one who lied, who deceived. . . . Chris did nothing . . . nothing but give you a home and food and shelter and a father for your child. . . .

And to thank him, she'd gotten him killed.

She sat upright, shook her head violently once. All right, this is accomplishing nothing. You've no proof he's dead. Frank liked to tease, to drag things out. He could have killed Chris long ago and he didn't. There must be a reason for that, if even a sick, twisted one. Assume Chris is alive, trying to get you out of this. Now try to do something for him by staying alert and attentive. If only for Nicky.

Nicky.

She pushed up, grunting, to search for him, hoping it would be a quick search, ending in his bedroom, Nicky in his plastic car bed.

Which he was. He lay in scarce moonlight, limbs thrown trusting-wide in innocent slumber, the room secure with the purring snore of his baby's dreams. Matty crept closer, bent to kiss the pale head—hesitated at the sight of the flung left arm—bent closer, unable to stifle a gasp. A tiny purple hole at his creased crook still wept a drop or two of pinkish fluid above the thread of vein. Sedated again.

Bastard, *bastard*!

She sat beside her son a moment, gently pressing back his fallen locks, knowing a full-piece orchestra would not awaken him. Matty cupped his cheek, mouthed, "I love you."

And watching him, was reminded of the dream. . . .

She had, in her deeper recesses, always hidden suicide away as a last desperate measure, though of late it had begun to seem less distant and even less desperate: just common sense.

There was certainly no escaping Frank. He was waiting for her to run, *wanting* her to run, so he could catch and humiliate her. Shoot her—and the child—full of sedatives, make the game go on as long as he could.

And that might be a long, long time.

She had long since given up on the authorities. Something was wrong. They should have been here now. If not the local cops, then the office. The office would know the lines were dead, that she was in trouble, would know and come swooping down on Frank to end this. But they weren't swooping down. That meant only one thing: She'd been lied to. Not only by Frank—least of all by Frank—but by the higher-ups. Lied to and deliberately used.

No, the authorities weren't coming. No one—except perhaps for poor Chris—was going to get her out of this. Only herself.

And the single way to do that was to kill Frank.

She looked down at her beautiful child. A cold fury swept her suddenly.

Frank was, after all, just flesh and blood. He *could* be killed.

And she was the closest to him, had the easiest access. She couldn't just lie down and let him kill her only son, slaughter the only man she'd ever loved.

There must be a way.

She couldn't outsmart him. He was always a step ahead. Not outsmart, no. But she might be able to surprise him somehow. . . .

Something Chris had told her once: *I know no one will guess the ending to this play because I don't know the ending myself yet.*

Get a knife. A kitchen steak knife, one of the sharp ones. Put it under the mattress. He had to sleep sometime. Fight the sedatives he was slipping her in her water or coffee or wine, fight them long enough just to stay awake long enough for him to drift off, lower his guard.

Then slip the knife from under the sheets.

It would be dangerous, but she could not bear this feeling of uselessness any longer. Anything was better than this, even risking the child's life. Frank might very well kill him anyway. This biding her time was only begging off the inevitable.

She would do it. She'd get a knife and kill the bastard.

She bent, kissed Nicky's nose, nuzzled his cheek.

Wondering, even then, if she had the will, the nerve for it.

Or if the gulf of her exhaustion—the drugs he'd lined her veins with—were simply robbing her of her sanity.

She came down the hall softly to the master bedroom, knife against her buttocks, held by the elastic band of her panties.

Frank would be there, asleep but never really asleep. A roach walking could wake him. He never even bothered locking the downstairs doors. He knew she wouldn't attempt escape again because there was no escape, no path to outward normalcy, unless he deemed it so.

He would be lying there peacefully in the big hand-carved bed—hers and Chris's bed—waiting to see if she'd come creeping in with him just to stay warm. He would not touch her, not even make the beginning overtures to sex. Of that she was sure. Oh, he might insist on the flimsy nightie again, even pull the bodice apart occasionally to admire his handiwork above her breast, but he wouldn't touch her, kiss her, even put an arm around her.

Until she said it was time. Until she came to him. Asking for it, begging for it.

It was the agreement between them, unspoken but fully

acknowledged: Sleep with me, dearest kitten, spread your legs for me, do all that I bid and more, and maybe, *maybe*, I'll let the child live.

And it would have been a small enough sacrifice for the life of her child. Easy just to lie there, endure it.

If not for the memories. . . .

She had been a senior at Radcliffe, her whole life laid out before her, neat and orderly as her tidy dorm room.

She was pretty, bright, buxom Madeline Wilcox from Kansas, riding high on a scholarship in Byzantine history. But she was Salina, Kansas, shy, awkward in what she was certain were very important eastern social graces and the cotillion manners of the other coeds. She hadn't left Kansas so much as escaped her life there: a standard drunk and abusive father, a standard weak and acquiescent mother.

Her worst beating came on the night of her fifteenth birthday, when, pretty and already burgeoning in her high school sweaters, she'd stayed too late at the local theater to catch a double feature with friends. The beating had hurt, humiliated, but come an hour too late. The second feature had been Inge's *Picnic*, and Matty's path was fixed. Like her new heroine, Kim Novak, Matty had already decided that she too would flee Salina, albeit without William Holden. She accomplished it with a scholarship.

To shake off Salina dust, acquire Novak grace, she'd minored in theater, trying desperately to overcome a timidity others found only charming. "You look like you're walking over plowed ground," her uncle Emmet had once told her as a child, crushing her girlhood even more than the brief brush with polio that left her outwardly limping just the slightest, inwardly haunted a good deal. At Radcliffe, with the help of old Marilyn Monroe movies, she'd turned the limp into a swish that got her looked at.

She'd done well in her studies, excelling in history which was a snap for her and surprising herself with the ease at which she slipped effortlessly into acting, achieving minor stardom in the school Experimental Wing and flowering wondrously in the big musical extravaganzas and Williams epics, during which her Blanche Dubois brought tears and cheers to jaded New England audiences. She just had a knack for it.

A nervous virgin until her sophomore year, she had submitted to clumsy petting and clumsier (and eminently unfulfilling) fucking of her Stanley Kowalski costar (a handsome, fumbling lad named Rink who worshiped The Method, actually had Brandoish looks without Brandoish talent, and made love worse than the worst farmboy) in the backseat of his father's Mercedes, getting a little of it into her but most of it on the shiny new upholstery.

Two more minor trysts (one pretty bad, one really awful—both mercifully fleeting) until Ancient Russia and Professor Springer, first semester of her junior year.

She had admired Springer's incredible knowledge of Russian peasantry and religion, his grasp of every aspect of the classical setting. He had admired her classical features and long legs.

Jason Allen, two rows behind her had admired them first, however, had shocked and delighted (taken her breath away, actually) by offering her his Delta Tau Delta pin on their second date, then taking her breath away further at the off campus Holiday Inn with some very enthusiastic, deliciously prolonged and gently explosive fucking, during which none of it got anywhere but way up inside her and then inside her again, until she knew she must jump up soon and let it out, wipe it away for fear of pregnancy, then groaning under him yet again and not caring if she was because she knew immediately that she was going to marry this handsome young attorney-to-be with the marvelous wit, marvelous smile, have many of his children and live out there on Long Island not far from his parents whom he talked about incessantly but never quite got around to introducing her to.

Matty, on the other hand, got around to introducing Jason to her roommate, Cloris, and they doubled-dated (with past flame Rink of all people!) all that winter and into glorious spring (Matty's grades suffering oh just slightly because she was by now far less interested in getting into Russian History than Jason getting into her) glorious spring and right up to the end of final semester during which Jason, at their favorite motel, and directly after pushing her determinedly and deliciously between hard motel headboard and flowered wall until she screamed with pleasure and near-swooning, mentioned—while she was still coming down from it all—casually mentioned that he had decided to marry roommate Cloris whom he'd been seeing (and enthusiastically screwing) since early winter and by the way could he please have his pin back?

Matty spent the summer in a state beyond depression, bordering suicide, especially when she thought for a few fleeting weeks she might be pregnant (wishful thinking—she was so far gone she'd have settled even for Jason's child), had somehow survived the insufferable Kansas heat and a maddeningly complacent, lassitudinous mother (father had blessedly died, succumbed to alcoholism that spring) to go limping indifferently back to campus the following autumn, limping into Professor Springer's advanced Russian history class, nodded desultorily at semester's end when he'd told her she was flunking, openly admitted to him one day after class that her heart just wasn't in it.

She'd submitted to his invitation to dinner, submitted further to his gentle probing about home and seemingly endless fascination with her distant Russian lineage. Had submitted further yet to his equally gentle advances on his apartment sofa, Mahler swelling accompaniment on the stereo, let him feel between and finally get between her legs, winced and actually cried out at his bigness, then clamped tightly to him, and come with a grateful release of breath and soul. You fuck like a lynx, he'd breathed on her, and she'd absently assumed that a compliment. Then, still in her, he'd mentioned, almost in passing: "Have you ever tried this . . . ?"

The first of many ideas, some of which bothered her, some of which even frightened her, but none of which, in her lifting depression, she eschewed. Professor Springer, she was convinced, was saving her life. If the sex—as the months went by—got a little kinky, if he liked doing certain unconventional things, that was okay, she supposed. He was tender and considerate and always grateful. And he stayed. She was satisfied enough, if not truly fulfilled. She did not, had not, and—she knew—would not ever love Frank Springer.

By midsemester, Springer began to speak ever more seriously of an after-graduation marriage, Matty nodding over dinner or on lakeside walks, rootless now, free and clear and as indefinite about her future as she had been sure of it just months ago, Jason and the old gang a distant, sophomoric past.

And, she supposed, after all she could do worse than a muscular, blazingly intelligent, eminently respected, sexually charged older professor who constantly doted on her, constantly reminded her of the greatness of her Russian ancestors, constantly hinted of his "other" work—better work—more *important* work awaiting him after his college tenure. Of travel, a great deal of travel, the magical places she'd see, wonderful, sophisticated people she'd meet. And, eventually, the kids they'd have. All in all a life that would certainly be stimulating if not her girlhood romantic dream.

They were wed the day after graduation at Niagara Falls, something he'd dreamed of, apparently, all his life. Matty sailed above it all, never quite there but there enough, made love to him with great gusto if not passion, held his hand in the misty moonlight against Niagara's throaty roar. She supposed that this was what real love was.

No one she knew had attended the wedding. Matty's mother, a walking corpse since her husband's death, showed no interest. She would eventually—thanks to Frank's funding—be put in a very fine midwestern nursing home, last exactly two weeks, quietly wither, and die.

As for Frank's flamboyant promises, he certainly kept one of them, a spacious home in Rye, where Matty spent her days at the hairdresser or the mall (wondering vaguely if she might run into distant Jason—maybe get to meet his elusive parents), spent her nights alone in a big bed in a big house while Frank was out "working." Government work, so he said, never saying more than that, never showing her his office ("It's really mostly freelance, kitten") and never letting her forget that he did not like the subject brought up.

And that was her life.

At first she complained that he was never home (some company being better than no company) and soon she complained (inside— never to him) when he was home. Because Frank wanted only one thing when he was home. And he wanted a lot of it. And he insisted it be lurid. And ugly. Often grotesque and, finally, painful.

She'd struck back only once. And that had taught her a fresh threshold of pain.

And so she bottled it up, endured. A caged animal.

"What in the name of God—," her gynecologist had begun one afternoon. And she'd never gone back to see him.

She knew, deep inside, that if this kind of sickness kept up, she not only would not be able to have children; she would no longer want children. Not with this man.

Then had come that other thing.

They had been alone together one night in a darkened parking lot when two men had attacked them. Or attacked Frank, at any rate. They had guns. They had knives. They were the size of linebackers.

And she saw what—without breathing particularly hard—Frank did to them.

Saw too what he did to them afterward, to their bodies.

There in the dark lot, he arranged them, naked and dead, one behind the other, one *in* the other, a grotesque tableau quite obviously for someone else's eyes. But not before he'd emasculated them, sliced off their testes, stood grinning happily at Matty, and tenderly, savoringly, swallowed them.

"The Incas believed that to achieve the inner power of the enemy, you must devour his—" But Matty was already retching there in a black alleyway, beyond his patient attention.

Still, she'd heard enough. And more than that, she heard the *way* he'd said it, done it as though he were calmly lecturing her class back at Radcliffe. As though any blasphemously unspeakable act could be justified through intellectual enlightenment.

She truly saw him for the first time that night. She saw that his sickness, his appetites were as boundless as his great strength and cunning. The schoolteacher guise was a pleasant front to something far bigger and more insidious. It went well beyond the limits of depravity, to the dark soul of the insane. Only a quiet, diabolically insane mind could conceive of them. To understand, truly understand and appreciate and thus respect death, Frank believed he had to wallow in it, ingest it.

There were those who would give him the opportunity, all the opportunities he could wish for. Even pay him for it, pay him handsomely.

Meanwhile, her ever more foreboding and unfathomable husband enjoyed an almost surrealistic immunity from the law she never quite comprehended.

He was so smug about it, so above it all. Above God.

While the sex, the sickness of his needs, became ever more bizarre and loathsome.

Sash cord around her neck, choking off her breath, the full weight of him atop her, the great burning member already spouting deep within her, he'd hiss in tempo with his climax, "Orgasm through suffocation . . . is the most . . . sublime . . . art of all." His nightmarish grin swimming liquid red before her as she passed out, praying distantly not to awaken.

Thus battered, thus bruised, it was sometimes weeks before she dare leave the house. Sometimes months.

So the madness that had become her life grew, expanded like a cancer. And so too the first glimmering hopes of a plan to leave him. But knowing now what he was, what he had become, realizing her leaving would have to be swift, final and irrevocable. She would not get a second try.

She planned it, with meticulous attention to detail, for six torturously long, methodical months.

Then threw the whole plan out when the men in the dark gray suits with dark, grim eyes came to their door one Sunday morning and took Frank away for her.

They told her all about the legendary Frank Springer. Who he worked for and why. Why he had once been so valuable to them, why he no longer was.

They told her where he was going and how she would be cared for. For the rest of her life. She need not worry. Ever again.

And they did not lie. Not then. They provided well for her. So well she couldn't stand it any longer.

And, eventually, escaped them . . .

Matty now came quietly down the hall of the big A-frame, knife against the hollow of her back, pushed gently at the bedroom door. She found the bed empty, still made, Frank nowhere to be seen.

Playing his little games?

She whirled at something behind her.

Only shadow and an empty hallway and the painful crashing of her own heart.

Easy. Don't lose it now.

He's somewhere in the house. He wouldn't leave you. You just have to find him is all.

She turned back toward the hall and heard the distant chopping.

She came back inside the bedroom, to the window, parted the translucent curtain gingerly, and gazed down at him there in the snow-mantled backyard. He was naked to the waist, big red-headed ax swishing a deadly arc above him, wood splinters flying. Making firewood for them. For their cozy little winter home. How sweet and considerate.

She stood gazing at him for a long moment, at the swift sureness of the strokes, the thick, corded back, muscular shoulders, deadly precision with which he placed the whirring blade.

And she had this silly steak knife.

Matty sighed hugely, let herself rest miserably against the cool

window molding for a moment, the inequality, the absurd dispro-
portion of it settling over her. She had no more chance against him
than a fly with a—

She pushed up abruptly, not allowing herself to complete the
thought, marched resolutely from the bedroom back down the hall
in stiffened strides. She must do something!

Grab the baby now and run while he's outside!

Sure. Run where, into the nearest snowdrift? That wasn't the
way; panic never was.

Yet there *was* a way. There *must* be. Don't outsmart him, surprise him.

She found herself on the darkened staircase, padding into the
deeper shadow below, mind racing, the sharp, even *thok* of his
blows echoing from the back. He probably wasn't even breathing
hard.

She came to the front door, found it unlocked (of course), staggered back at the first icy gust, and promptly shut it again. How in
hell did he stand it without his shirt? He's not human, that's how
he stands it.

She came back across the living room rug, head in her hands—
temples throbbing—and managed, in the dark, to collide painfully
with the corner of the coffee table. *Shit!*

She spun away, hands fisted—*damn you, Frank*—lashed out
impulsively with her foot at the teak deco bureau against the north
wall, heard a plate fall within and something else. She started
away, then looked back to find the something else was the black
valise, fallen out from between bureau and wall.

Matty stood gaping at it a moment, plans and good fortune coa-
lescing into a single thought.

A quick glance over her shoulder at the chopping sound, then
she was lunging excitedly for the valise, unsnapping it as quietly as
possible, holding the contents out to scant moonlight.

There were at least a dozen little dropper bottles of various
drugs, full and unused. Nearly a dozen clear packets of plastic
syringes.

She smiled in the moonlight.

Not a knife. A syringe! That was the way. A syringe loaded with
sedatives. Enough to kill him if she could. If not, then put him out
long enough for her to get to the ax.

Yes, a syringe. Under the mattress, tucked just inside, where
her fingers could pluck it loose quickly.

She reached into the leather valise, withdrew one of the little bottles, squinting at the label: Seconal.

She hesitated, trembling suddenly.

But would he miss it? And the syringe?

Had he counted all of them, every single item in the case? It was entirely possible. Frank was nothing if not methodical, paranoid beyond all reasoning.

She rolled the bottle in her hand, picked up one of the syringe packets, tore it open before she could back out. Do it! It's a chance you'll have to take. What's he going to do if he catches you, kill you?

She jabbed the steel needle into the rubber stopper, withdrew a syringe full of the clear liquid, held it up to the feeble light, and froze. The chopping had ceased outside.

The door opened with a shock of cold, and Frank walked in.

He didn't see her at first, where she was crouched there on the floor. Then he did see her and hesitated in midstride on his way to the kitchen. "What the hell are you doing down there, kitten?"

Matty, not skipping a beat, dropped the syringe and empty bottle in the valise, shut the lid silently behind her. Here's where the old stage training comes in handy, Matty.

She put her hand to her head to distract his eyes from the floor, pushed the valise beneath the rattan chair with the other hand, stood on wobbly legs in deep shadow. "I fell *down* is what I'm doing here, goddamn it! From whatever that crap is you put in my tea!"

And she stumbled toward him, faking a convincing weave, or so she thought.

Frank regarded her quietly, smiled. "Christ, you look awful."

"Thanks so much. Maybe if I got a little something to *eat* around here besides sedatives." She pushed past him into the kitchen, suppressed a huge sigh when he followed. Had he seen?

She knew Frank wouldn't say if he had. He'd play along for a while, humiliate her with it later. Humiliate and torture her with it.

"You kept throwing up," he offered behind her. "I was trying to calm you down. It was just over-the-counter stuff."

She wove histrionically to the refrigerator, pulled down milk, poured a glass, not looking at him as he moved to the sink faucet for cold water, beads of sweat glistening on his shoulders. "What're you doing?" she asked, as if innocent of all.

He gulped, refilled the glass, gulped. "Ahh. Chopping firewood. Want to help?"

"Thank you, no. Your sedatives are making me sick. Can we stop that, do you think?"

"They help you sleep."

"They help me stick around, you mean."

He poured more water. "You're free to leave anytime, kitten. I'd take a warm coat, however."

She poured more milk to keep her hands from shaking. "I've been considering your proposal," she began companionably.

But she knew the moment she'd said it that it was too soon, the wrong tack, that it wouldn't work. It would only make him suspicious.

"What proposal was that?" he gulped suspiciously.

Think, Matty, *think.* "About staying with you, going back to Niagara Falls and all that. Remember?"

He put down his glass carefully. "Oh? And?"

She closed the milk carton, replaced it in the fridge. "Well, I've thought it over very carefully."

He turned to her to study her expression. For lies. To watch her eyes.

She avoided his. "I've come to a decision."

"Yes?"

"Yes. I think it would be just lovely, Frank, if you were to take Niagara Falls, all of upstate New York, in fact—and let's not leave out Canada—take them and shove them squarely up your skinny ass."

He barked a laugh.

Matty sipped milk, praying.

Frank shook his head, dried his hands, and headed for the front door again. "I'll be finished in twenty minutes. I'll come up to bed then and see if you've reconsidered."

"Don't bother."

He grinned, shut the door behind him, leaving a waft of frigid air across her already trembling knees.

She'd made it. But it was close. Patience, that was the key. Next time she'd do better.

Matty pushed the glass aside, hurried through the kitchen, turning off the light as she went.

She knelt by the rattan chair, withdrew the valise. Withdrew the syringe and bottle and knew instantaneously that it wasn't going to work. Even if he didn't discover the missing bottle and syringe—even if he wasn't counting—he was the one who emptied the trash, he was the one (in his vast paranoia of being tapped and bugged) who tidied up, peeked and dusted in every corner. And there was just no place to hide the evidence. No place at all.

Except maybe the toilet.

Matty replaced the valise carefully, felt around the rug to make sure nothing else had spilled, picked up the filled syringe gingerly, the empty bottle in the other hand, dashed upstairs again.

In the master bedroom she eased up the edge of the mattress on her side, gently slid the loaded syringe beneath, let the material down again. A tiny, nearly indiscernible lump.

No. To Frank, nothing was indiscernible.

She inserted her fingers under the mattress, poked the syringe deeper. Stepped back and appraised it. Yes. It looked fine.

At least she thought it did.

CHAPTER 18

Driving back to Greenborough into bloody dawn, Chris had feared he'd drift off to sleep behind the wheel, glide across the divider headlong into another car. Or into hard, crusted-over banks at the opposite, ash-colored shoulder, not yet softened by morning sun. But he was wide awake, brain tingling with alertness, as though he'd had more than his customary two cups of morning coffee, when in fact he'd had none.

The big red sports car felt strangely comfortable under his hands. Alien and twitchy as a young mare for the first few miles, it soon settled under him, Chris getting into the quickly jinking wheel, the tighter turning radius, tremendous response. He saw why people—men especially—coveted them, those who could. He could even grow lazily envious, adding another envy to everything he already envied of Frank Springer's.

Springer liked the best. Which is why he'd picked—perhaps even married—Matty. Why he'd continued to pursue her when they'd separated. Like men of good taste everywhere, he had not been immune to the deep green eyes, the sexily languorous mechanism of her body in motion, the quiet confidence counterpointed by the unabashed quickness to laugh, even be charmingly silly.

The soft, golden length of her, the sweet taste of her inner mouth, the way she tasted back, unhesitating, regally urgent.

You can stop this now.

But, of course, he couldn't. There was no longer any real reason to believe that—even in her captivity—she was being faithful to him, forced or no. Had ever been faithful to him, in fact. Had ever told him the truth about anything.

Lies had been a part of their lives from the beginning. How many, how far-reaching, he'd yet to learn. If he ever could, ever could get that close again now that Rick Corman was out of it. But there were many lies, certainly, perhaps more than truths.

Yes, but no one comes into a relationship without some lies, he told himself. We only come into the world lieless. Only birth is immaculately free of deceit.

Depending, of course, on whose birth we're discussing here.

Chris regarded the sudden adrenaline pang dully. He'd grown nearly inured to it, the same pang he always felt when he thought of Nicky now. One day you have a son. The next day you have a son and something else. The truth was, the baby did bear a passing resemblance to Frank Springer.

Chris braked for an old Buick out here in early morning light on the plowed but still treacherously patchy highway. An old green bulbous tank with chrome-rimmed portholes like his second-hand college car. Chris employed the low center of gravity and wide treads of the Lamborghini and shot recklessly around, not sliding an inch on the deceitful asphalt. As he passed, feathery clods of snow flew from the antique's hood, exploding behind them like broken stones. Chris glimpsed a weathered, determined face within. Was the old green Buick going to Greenborough too? To loved ones? To a happy, normal, comfortably prosaic life?

Something else to envy.

He glanced down at the shiny car phone. Plucked it up, one hand on the sensitive, leather-wrapped wheel, and punched the hospital's number, asking to speak to Dr. Werthem.

"Dr. Werthem's off duty now. Dr. Michaels can help you."

Chris said, "All right," and waited. He eventually received a youngish voice, munching something, early breakfast probably. "I'm a friend of one of Dr. Werthem's patients, Richard Corman," Chris told the voice. "I'm inquiring about his condition this morning."

"Corman . . . the gunshot wounds, yes?"

"Yes."

A rattling of papers in Chris's ear. "Patient is stable . . . vitals good . . . Blood gas fine this morning; they just took it. Passing some color in his urine earlier, cleared that up. Yeah, he's doing well, responsive."

"When would I be able to talk to him?"

There were red and blue lights flashing in the sports car's rearview.

"Oh, this afternoon, if his count's still good. But I doubt he *can* talk. He's undergone mouth surgery, you know."

"I see," lamely from Chris. "Thank you, Doctor."

"Anytime."

The big highway patrol car closed in rapidly, filling Chris's rear windshield. Chris smiled.

He replaced the receiver, pulled the big red sports car obediently to the shoulder, having expected this.

Chris didn't know this trooper—Officer Colgon from his breast pocket plaque—didn't even know if he was from Greenborough County, one of Sheriff Bradley's boys. He was young and blond and big and clumsy, much the way he'd envisioned the invisible doctor on the phone, and he seemed to regret putting the cuffs on Chris rather than not.

Chris didn't receive the cuffs until he'd followed the lone officer into Greenborough's quiet, early morning downtown, but the minute they'd parked in front of the sheriff's office, the blond trooper in his crisp brown uniform came officiously around the big patrol car, asked Chris politely if levelly to put his hands behind his back, cuffed him, and led him firmly into Sheriff Bradley's office. Like a TV movie, Chris thought, seeing Matty's face concentrating in bluish cathode light.

The office was empty. Chris wondered if Officer Colgon was going to put him into a cell. But the tall young man motioned to a bench beside the sheriff's desk and left Chris there for a moment. Colgon made rummaging noises in a back room. Chris supposed that Colgon supposed he wouldn't run far in cuffs on a bitter, slate-gray November morning.

Officer Colgon returned in a moment and made a fresh pot of coffee, offered Chris a cigarette, was refused, lit one of his own, sat down in an antique hard-backed chair on the other side of the sheriff's desk, got up again immediately when a young boy brought in a box of doughnuts. The officer offered the box to Chris, was again declined. Chris didn't see how he was supposed to eat with his hands behind him. Colgon paid the boy, sat down with the doughnuts and coffee, and ate and said nothing for nearly an hour until Sheriff Bradley came in with a chill breeze and a puffy look of sleep on his face.

Bradley pulled off his creased leather uniform jacket with its wool collar, hung it on the single coatrack, rubbed his hands together, and proclaimed it colder than a witch's tit. He went straight to the coffee, poured himself a cup, looked over his shoulder at Chris. "You want some?"

"No, thanks."

Bradley sipped, steam caressing ruddy cheeks, smacked and grunted, and took the first deep breath of the workday. He came to his desk as Officer Colgon reentered the room. Bradley glanced over, saw Chris's cuffs, made an impatient gesture, and the young officer uncuffed him.

Chris rubbed his wrists, thought of offering thanks, but didn't. Bradley was already shuffling papers on his desk, sipping gently with his free hand.

"Keep you waitin' long?" he said to the room, and Chris realized he meant him.

"No. Under an hour."

Bradley nodded. "Goddamn plow couldn't get up to my house. Goddamn driver couldn't get his car started to get to the plow!" He grunted a short laugh, selected a paper from the pile, and fished for his glasses. "Now, then. You've been a busy boy, Chris. . . ."

Chris watched him from the bench.

"How's the head?"

"Fine, okay."

"Been down to Kingston, have you?"

"Yes."

Bradley looked down his nose at the paper, through bifocals. "Uh-huh. Well, what I'm wondering—what we're all wondering— is why you elected to take Mr. Springer's shiny red sports car instead of your own."

Chris said nothing.

Bradley put down the paper, the glasses, turned to him, suddenly wistful. "Had me a sports car once. Green Alfa. You familiar with the Alfa Romeo?"

"Yes."

"Italian car. Pretty little thing. Always in the goddamn shop. Pretty little thing. Not much for icy weather. Got an APB out on you here, Chris." He rattled a slip of paper. "You aware of that, know what that is?"

"Yes, I do."

Bradley scooped up the papers as if they were of small consequence. "Well, just a formality, really. Don't often get the chance to follow big-city SOP in a town like Greenborough, so I punched in an APB just to see what it was like. Don't think it'll be on your permanent record. Why did you steal the car, Chris? Or would you rather wait for Springer?"

Chris raised a brow. "He's coming in?"

"He's the one filed the charge." Bradley nodded, sipping unhurriedly.

Of course, Chris thought.

Bradley smacked fat, confident lips. "Of course, we all know you got a good explanation," just barely patronizing, "though you're likely to take a worse shellacking from Doc Holiday than from me. As I recall, he requested you stay put in that bed-and-breakfast and rest. Sure you're okay? No headaches?"

Chris looked out the window at Main Street coming alive in gray light. "I'll wait for Springer," he said.

Bradley shrugged, moving back to the coffeepot. "Well, it's a free country. Might think about getting your attorney's number handy though, be my advice."

Chris thought of Goldstein, whom he hadn't thought about in some time.

"Or the court will appoint you one if it comes to that. Course, no one believes it will." Bradley sipped, smiled.

Chris looked over at him, Bradley happily munching a doughnut now. For Bradley, it was going to be a great day.

Chris, after more than an hour, finally had a doughnut himself, and some coffee, and then Frank Springer walked in with Matty in tow. He too was smiling. Chris thought he'd never seen so much smiling in a single morning.

Matty, unsmiling, was bundled in a heavy silver fox fur he'd never seen before. She looked once at Chris, then away.

Springer came over, shook Chris's hand, found a bench opposite him, beneath a pane-drifted window. "Coffee smells good," he announced companionably, and Sheriff Bradley poured him a cup with grinning acquiescence. Then he took his official place behind his big desk, settled himself and shuffled papers again.

"Tough drive down, Mr. Springer?"

"Not bad. Had to wait awhile for the cab. Most of the roads are clear now. Going to be a nice day, I think."

Bradley nodded. "Sky's starting to blue again." He shuffled papers, reaching for the glasses. "Now then, about this here car theft business . . ."

Chris kept looking to Matty, who would not meet his eyes. She looked slightly wan but not alarmingly so. Where was the baby? He studied her face for an answer, found no undue concern etched there. Springer's gotten someone to watch Nicky. If Chris could get to the house right now, he could walk right out the door with the baby.

He studied his wife's face. Drugged? She didn't appear so. Apathetic? Not quite. Something behind the eyes. A secret? He knew her too well. She was harboring something. Something Frank knew too? Or something Frank did not know?

"—a warrant here in my hand for your arrest, Chris," Bradley was saying.

Chris drifted back to him. It would be a closed case now; they had him just where they wanted him. A car thief. He'd be tucked away for as long as they could stretch it. And Matty would be Springer's. Time would pass. And pass. Until they became strangers again.

Bradley was watching him expectantly. "You want to make a statement about this thing, Chris? Call that attorney?"

"What kind of statement?"

Bradley smiled, looked to Springer, who returned the smile, looked back to Chris, who shrugged and smiled too, just to make it even. "Well, for instance, did you or did you not steal Mr. Springer's automobile?"

Chris sat back, already feeling the interior of his cell. "I borrowed it."

Sheriff Bradley grinned wider as if anticipating it, scratched something on a pad with a yellow stub of pencil. " 'Borrowed,' uh-huh. And when did this 'borrowing' occur, exactly?"

"Last night, around eleven p.m."

"You were with the Springers?"

Chris folded his arms. "No, I was with a friend, Rick Corman."

He watched and saw Matty start to react, catch herself; her cheek twitched once, face remaining impassive.

"At the Springer residence," the sheriff jotted.

At my residence, Chris thought, not saying it, saying instead, "We were nearby. In the woods."

Bradley scribbled by rote. "And what were you doing up there in the snowy woods at eleven at night, Chris?"

"Hunting."

Bradley looked at him. He hadn't expected Chris's quiet composure. He'd expected shouting and leaping and spittle-flecked accusations. So had Frank, who was smiling admiringly at Chris now. Wouldn't it be funny, Chris thought, if I got out of this by simply telling what was essentially the truth?

"Hunting."

"That's right. I know the property. Good deer hunting up there."

"At night?" Frank interjected, holding the admiring grin.

"Why not?" from Chris, not looking at him.

Bradley jotted. "Hunting in the woods. And what happened?"

"Rick—my friend—was shot."

There was an audible rasp from Matty. Everyone but Chris strained hard not to look in her direction.

Bradley's jotting slowed. "How was that, Chris?"

Chris folded his arms matter-of-factly. "He was shot. With a rifle, I'd say."

"And who shot him, Chris?"

Chris made a face as if explaining the obvious. "Why, another hunter"—he looked at smiling Frank—"I'd suppose."

Bradley jotted, almost glancing up at Frank, not quite. "And you saw this happen, did you?"

"No. I was some distance away. I heard it. Came running. Rick—my friend—was already wounded when I got there."

Bradley nodded. "And you didn't see this other hunter?"

"No."

Bradley jotted. "And what transpired at that point?"

Chris thought about Rick's mangled mouth, the black blood, decided to leave it out. This was working rather well. "As soon as I saw my friend was hurt, I picked him up, fireman-carried him over my shoulder, headed back for the car."

"Your car."

"No, the rental car. Rick is from California. He came up to hunt with me for a few days, rented a car."

"Why do that, Chris, when you already had the Volvo?"

"Rick wanted a set of wheels of his own while up here, to get around and all."

"Uh-huh," Bradley jotting less enthusiastically. "And so you were carrying this friend to your car . . ."

"Yes, and I came upon the"—and he said it deliberately—"*Springer* property, and saw Mr. Springer's car, saw the keys inside, and decided that would be the quickest way."

"Why didn't you knock on Mr. Springer's door for assistance?"

"It was late. He might have been in bed. The car was there; why wait for an ambulance to plow through all that snow? I figured the sports car was the quickest way." And saying it out loud made it seem all the more so. Chris was becoming very satisfied with himself. He was actually turning this thing around. It showed in Bradley's face, his jotting hand.

"Yet you drove all the way to Kingston when we have a fine physician right here in town. Why?"

Chris considered for an instant. "The wounds appeared extensive. I thought the patient might need a full medical facility. As it turned out, I was right."

Bradley jotted, dotted an *i*, and sat back. Finally he looked up at Springer. "Any more statements you'd like to make, Chris?"

He pretended to think about it. "That's about the extent of it. I'm sorry if Mr. Springer was inconvenienced. I certainly had no intention of stealing his car. It was an emergency situation."

And it settled, sound and reasonable, within the quiet room.

Bradley sat back, squeaking his swivel chair, tapping his stub of pencil on the yellow legal pad. "Well, Chris, that's quite a story. Trouble is, as I recall, just a while back here you were accusing Mr. Springer of moving into your house. Even abducting your wife and child. Sounds to me like your motive for being on the Springer property is subject to conjecture."

"I was hunting," Chris said simply.

Sheriff Bradley, no longer amused, looked at him levelly. "Are you saying you're no longer making these wild accusations about that house on the mountain, about Mr. Springer and his wife here?"

"I'm saying," Chris told him, "that I was hunting with my friend Rick Corman. Hunting. I'd be happy to undergo a polygraph to that effect." And of course he'd pass it, because he had, in fact, told no lies. As everyone knew.

Frank Springer was grinning ear to ear, a grin of admiration, of an opponent bested. Temporarily, at least.

Bradley tossed down the pencil. "Well, Chris, I'm afraid we're going to have to hold you a few days for further questioning."

"Oh, I don't think that will be necessary," Springer said, standing now, hands casual in Docker pockets.

Bradley looked to him obediently. "Well, Mr. Springer—"

"It's okay, Sheriff, I'm not going to press charges."

Bradley appeared confused.

Springer appraised Chris as though Bradley no longer mattered, was no longer in the room. He intoned with quiet patience, "If I don't elect to press charges, then you've no reason to detain Mr. Nielson, isn't that right?"

"Well . . . technically."

"So there you are." He was still ignoring Bradley, focused enthusiastically on Chris as if seeing him for the first time. "Obviously just a misunderstanding. I wouldn't want to in any way impede an emergency situation, as this clearly appears to have been. I assume you have the number of the hospital in Kingston, Mr. Nielson, and the patient's room?"

"Of course."

Springer nodded. "Well, then. That's all there is to it. If we're finished here, I have work to do."

He stood staring amiably at Chris until Chris realized he still had the keys to the Lamborghini. He stood, fished them out, and handed them to Springer.

"Thank you. I hope your friend wasn't seriously hurt."

"Me too." Another glance at Matty, who was just looking away, mouth tight.

Springer reached forward and offered Chris his hand. Chris took it, felt the firm, decisive grip, read "Congratulations, I'm letting you have this one" in it—felt the pressure exceed what was normal decorum for just a moment, then release.

Springer shrugged into his coat, nodded to the sheriff. "Sheriff Bradley." He turned to Matty, took her arm, and they were out of there in a rustle of chill breeze.

Officer Colgon, who might have been listening in the next room, came in for more coffee, looked at Chris, then at Bradley.

Bradley was smiling again, stuffing papers in his top center drawer with a dismissive gesture. "Well, Chris," the old confidence back, "looks like you're free to go."

And Chris, nearly giddy with surprise and relief, got out of there too.

A small victory. But out here on the cold, slush-crusted aloneness of the Main Street sidewalk, a hollow one.

He hadn't won anything. Springer was only extending the game, privately girding for any future battles. He was enjoying this small challenge from a contemptuously insignificant but nevertheless handy opponent. Springer wasn't worried about defeat, only mildly concerned with how his own next assault would be more brutal. Springer never lost unless he wanted to.

Would Springer take revenge on Matty and the boy? It was Chris's one great fear.

Somehow he didn't think so, though. Not Springer's style. It would appear inelegant.

He would let Chris come one more time. Then kill him.

Chris turned into the stiff wind, eyes slit, started for the bed-and-breakfast, found himself looking at the red Lamborghini parked down the street before a restaurant.

Not conscious at all of his intentions, following his shoes, Chris let himself be led airlessly toward the restaurant's rustic brick facade. Construction noises—even this early—were already pounding at him from across the street, their attendant hot tar odors souring the clean mountain air. They were tearing down the real rustic and putting up new rustic. Like California's recent Santa Fe style fad, Chris thought. Not authentically southwestern, just mechanically distressed into something approaching it. Elder civilizations, it was being discovered, had actually favored bright, ornamental colors, even the ancient Greeks; contemporary artisans considered bright, undiluted palettes gauche, the theory being that nature's own earth tones tended more toward the monochromatic. Bullshit, thought Chris: What about the Toucan, the mandrill baboon? And he thought further: Is my mind in exhausted overdrive; is that why I'm conjuring unrelated thoughts?

He passed the parked sports car at the frozen curb and kept on going, right to the restaurant door.

He opened it without hesitation—without plan or forethought—stepped into food-smelling warmth, an enveloping blanket of it whose contact became only gradually pleasant.

Matty and Springer were seated across the large, oak paneled room near the corner, guarded overhead by the calm, sightless eyes of a mounted bighorn ram. Neither the ram nor they had seen him come in.

A smiling, middle-aged hostess approached Chris. Past her corsage-pinned shoulder, Chris saw Matty leave the table, thread, still not aware of him, through tables to the ladies' room.

Chris handed the waitress his coat. "Anywhere near the front. I'm going to use your rest room."

"Of course. It's just back there." She was obliviously pleasant and accommodating.

Eyes on Springer's back, Chris followed in Matty's wake, through tables, down a short darkish hall to the rest room doors side by side, one marked GALS, the other GUYS.

He watched Matty push through, turned himself to see if anyone was around, and pushed through after her.

She caught his reflection—her left hand raised in midmotion to brush away something—tears?—in the wide mirror above the old-fashioned porcelain sinks, turned to regard him as if not truly surprised, as if anticipating this sooner or later, perhaps even considering it clever. Clever, her face seemed to say, but hopeless. Foolish.

They stood on the white tile floor breathing strongly perfumed antiseptic from nearby toilets, stared at each other, the overwhelming *nowness* of it, such intimate proximity after so much alienation, too much to assimilate.

Almost like that first time on the little Thousand Oaks stage, Chris thought, something about her guarded anticipation making that distant moment seem as recent as yesterday, sharp and clear and etched with perfect detail, as though the rest of the white-tiled room could just vanish, and there'd be the two of them, standing in the black void like paper cutouts, waiting for the next scene to materialize around them.

"Well"—Chris had to clear a suddenly phlegm-clogged throat to complete it—"well, he isn't around now. How about some answers?" And added: "Wife."

Matty looked not away this time but just slightly past him, still avoiding his eyes, as though all the answers lay just there over his left shoulder. When she spoke, it was so good to hear her voice—a voice part hers, part his, shaped by all the minute details of their past closeness.

But everything she said, every word intoned, made her a stranger. "There's just nothing much to say, Chris." She gazed past him that way as if transfixed by the rest room's austerity. "I wish there was."

"Who is he?" Chris attempted.

Buttocks against the sink, she looked carefully at her hands, measuringly. "Who he says he is. Frank Springer. I could easily die for telling you this. He works for the government."

Chris nodded. "I suspected that."

"It's all I can say."

"Some kind of special agent or something? Is that why the local cops are in such awe of him?"

"It's all I can say."

Chris took a cleansing breath; they were talking at least. "All right. Let's talk about you. Were you—are you—married to him?"

"Yes. Legally."

And the pang, once arrowed through him, was finally over and therefore not so bad. "All right. Next question. Do you love him?"

Now, of course, she had to look at him, plain decorum dictating that. "I do, Chris. I'm sorry."

I'm going to stay composed, he thought; I'll be goddamned if I don't stay composed, no matter what the pain. "Why did you leave him, then?"

She shook her head—a movement that shook all of her a little—looked down at the tiled floor and up and down again. "There isn't time for this. I have to get back."

"There's goddamn *time* for it!" He trembled, anger so absolute he saw himself, in the blink of an instant, rushing back into the restaurant, plunging a steak knife into Springer's throat, rushing back here and doing the same to her.

His last words still rang against the tiled walls, begging a response from her that wouldn't come. To his further infuriation, it was she who seemed to be clinging successfully to composure. As though she'd had all these hours to rehearse for this, the way she'd rehearsed so carefully for his plays. As though this were a play, the actor's nightmare, in which she knew all her lines perfectly, was waiting with maddening patience while he groped clumsily, unprepared and enraged. Now that he'd let go, he couldn't seem to get himself back, his control slithering just out of reach.

Fighting the good fight anyway, he asked again, quietly, "Why did you leave him? I think you owe me that much."

Matty cast about the room absently. "I wanted to be an actress. Frank didn't want me to. Every time I tried, flew off to the New York stage, he squelched it. He's quite influential. Quite." She sighed. Remembering? "So, one day I decided if I couldn't do it that way, I'd do it another. I'd sell out to the movies. At least I'd be acting. Sort of."

"Except Hollywood—agents—would give you a high profile. Frank would find out."

She nodded. "The initial plan was to start in slow, keep to the outskirts in the beginning, do small summer stock parts in little community theater productions while I felt out the territory. Let some time go by. Eventually segue to shampoo commercials."

"He'd certainly find out then. Everyone would if you made it to TV."

"Yes, but by then maybe he'd take me seriously when he saw how determined I was."

"I see."

"I never said it was a well-conceived plan." Matty sighed. "Anyway, I kept to the fringes at first."

"Which is when you met me."

"Yes."

"And *married* me? I thought you *loved* the guy."

She seemed to be having difficulty breathing, arms pressed against her diaphragm as if to force the air out, replace it with a cleaner start. "I did love him. And I loved my career. And I thought—I stupidly thought—I could have both. That once he saw how good I was, he'd—"

"He'd what? Welcome you back with open arms? How magnanimous this guy is! Christ, Matty, am I hearing this right? Are you saying you spent the last three years *using* me? Just *using* me?"

And all she could do was stand there.

He stared at her impassive face, waiting for the laugh—the joke—that wouldn't come. Wanting very much to slap her hard. Wondering where the old Matty had gone, his Matty. Beginning to realize, like the utter fool he'd been played for, that the old Matty never really was. Which, in its way, canceled them both out, left him translucent as fine tissue.

He wouldn't accept it.

"You're lying," he tried.

She looked at him levelly.

"You're afraid of him, and you're lying."

She sighed again.

Goddamn her, she could have done *anything* but sighed.

"Yes," she nodded, "I am, in a way, afraid of him. He's a violent person. He has unimagined power, unlimited power. Contacts with people you'd never believe. I could die for telling you this. But I'm not lying. I'm not lying, Chris. I deceived you. I'm more ashamed of it than you can know, but the simple fact is, I deceived you. It was beyond selfish. Career-driven egoism, plain as that. I wanted, goddamn it, to have a career!"

She shrugged, twitched a sad smile. "And I wanted him too. So I tried to have both. And this is the ruin it brought us all."

He waited. So chilly, he felt, walking outside in the snow would be as nothing.

"I just was very, very stupid. So colossally stupid I can't even ask your forgiveness. I just got swept up in it and then it was too late to stop." She watched him, eyes dead, her expression chilling him deeper still. "I was *acting*, Chris. I'm an actress." She mouthed it as though the word were synonymous with decay. "I've been an actress, a faker, all my life. All my life."

I wish I were back in California, Chris's bifurcated mind drifted, I wish this part of my life had never happened, that I could cut it away like a tumor, be that other guy again.

There was only one thing left now, and he already knew the answer to that. "And Nicky? Is he mine?" His throat moving thickly.

That one made her cold, so the arms tightened under her breasts and she shuddered once, spastically, as in a fever. He imagined he could actually hear her teeth chatter lightly. "I don't know."

He stared at her.

Well. That was all there was to that.

For nearly a minute, until his chest hitched with the need to breathe, they were silent. "All right," he said softly.

The door opened behind them, Chris jerking around so swiftly it sent a lance of pain up his neck. A dark-haired woman came in—dark hair and eyes, an attractive woman, built well. She looked up with surprised shock at Chris. Something about her seemed familiar, and then he knew: the woman on the hotel elevator.

"We're cleaning in here," Chris said lamely, and the woman

looked at him a second longer, then at Matty, nodded, and backed out the door again quickly.

Chris needed out of there too. There was no air left in there. Perhaps none left anywhere for him. But he had to get in the final jab. "Rick was nearly killed."

Matty nodded, more resigned than alarmed. "I know."

Even that news couldn't reach her. Her inert impotency was infuriating beyond reason. He felt entirely capable of striking her dead.

Matty.

How?

Yet Sharon had seen it. Probably everyone had seen it, including Rick.

Everyone but Chris. Sluggardly old trusting Chris.

"Anything more you'd like to confess before I go?" he asked, not recognizing his voice.

And to his horror, he read in her face that there was more. She braced herself against the sink for it. "Nicky. That day he got lost, ran outside. When everyone was searching for him?"

"Yes?"

"That was a lie too."

He frowned. "What the hell are you talking about?"

Matty bit her lip. "I arranged that. Hid him under the bed. Knew where he was all the time."

Chris was dumb-struck. "*Why*, in God's name!"

Once rolling, she seemed to have to be done with it quickly. "I saw Frank one day in Ventura. He didn't see me—or I thought he didn't—but I knew he was looking. I had to get us out of there fast."

Chris groaned. "So you what? How'd you pull the rest off, if I may ask?"

She shrugged philosophically. "The rest sort of took care of itself. As soon as I heard of my uncle's death I knew it was my— our—chance. They offered the A-frame and I jumped at it."

"You hustled us out of Thousand Oaks on the pretext of being concerned for your child's health! Jesus, Matty, your own son!"

"Yes," her eyes, voice dead.

All said and done now.

His mind recalled the Robert E. Howard epigram: "All fled—all done, so lift me on the pyre: The Feast is over and the lamps expire."

"I have just one more question," he said. "How the hell does a person like you get to *be* a person like you?"

Not really expecting an answer, he didn't get one.

"I want blood tests," Chris heard himself blurt.

She looked up, not expecting it.

"To determine the father. I want blood tests. You can keep him for now, we'll worry about that part later, but you get me those goddamn test results and you get them within a month. Am I perfectly understood?"

"Perfectly," whispered at the floor.

And her tears, when they finally came, moved him not at all.

An actress. A fucking actress.

He turned curtly. "I'll be in touch."

Matty, abruptly alarmed, almost made a move toward him. "Chris! Don't go near the house again! Please. He'll kill you. He will."

He made himself pause at the rest room door. "Just have the goddamn tests ready. Do you think you can do that much?"

And he left her there against harsh, vapid tile, not waiting for an answer.

The baby, and the baby alone, was all that kept him from rushing at Frank Springer in the restaurant, crushing the smiling face with the back of a chair. Certainly Chris at this moment had the will for it.

But he might die in the process.

And he was not ready to die yet. Not until he knew about the child.

And the child's father.

CHAPTER 19

The phone was ringing when Chris entered his room at the bed-and-breakfast.

He snatched it on the third ring. "Yes?"

"Chris, it's Sharon."

"Sharon!" He swallowed. "Where are you? Are you still at the hospital?"

"Yes." No longer cool. Cold.

"How's Rick?"

"Healing. I imagine he'd like to see you."

"Listen, Sharon, I'm sorry about—"

"But I don't want him to. I don't want you around here, Chris, do you understand? I don't want you near the hospital."

"Sharon, please. I know you're upset—"

"I've been assaulted."

He couldn't breathe. "What . . ."

"In the parking lot, last night. Two men. Or maybe it was three. I had the feeling they were looking for you, found me instead."

"Jesus Christ! Sharon, are you all right?"

"No, I'm not. I'm not all right at all. I doubt I'll ever be completely all right again. Certainly Rick won't, will he." It was not a question.

Chris's throat was too dry for swallowing. "Did they hurt you?"

Silence a moment. "Yes. But not that way. They mostly scared me. They did a very good job of scaring me."

"Did you see who?"

"I didn't see anything, and I didn't hear anything. Is that perfectly clear? Saw and heard nothing. Like it never happened. Like it will never happen again. Right, Chris?"

"And Rick is okay?"

"For the moment. I don't—I pray—they won't bother us again. As long as you stay away. And you will stay away. Completely away. Don't even call. I don't know what you've got yourself into, Chris, but Rick and I cannot help you. This is our lives we're talking about. Do you understand me? You are not going to lose my husband for me, Chris. I will not allow it."

"What can I do, Sharon?"

"I already told you. Stay away. And keep that"—he would never know what she had almost said—"keep Matty away from here too. Don't call. Not here or back in L.A. Don't try to contact us. I want us out of this, completely."

"I understand, Sharon."

"Good-bye, Rick. And good luck." A moment. Then: "Tell Matty . . . well, tell her whatever you have to." And the line went dead.

Someone is in the room. . . .

Or just the old house settling? Chris didn't even remember drifting off.

The last thing he'd been thinking was that he should indeed have made a lunge for Springer there in the restaurant, slit his throat, bashed in his head, or at least attempted it. What difference did it make now whether he survived the attack or not? What difference did anything make? At his age, the idea of starting over seemed ludicrous. Starting anything, in fact, without Matty seemed silly. Strange, how in a few short hours, life could become so utterly meaningless.

He heard the sound again, felt his heart seize up. Someone was definitely in the room.

If he rolled over to look, they'd see.

Chris lay quietly on his stomach, faked slumbered breathing, blinking away sleep, ears straining, trying to get a location fix. By the bureau? Or had it come from the window? Yes, the window.

The Ruger was under the bed.

Very slowly, imperceptibly, he allowed his left arm to slide sideways under the covers to the edge of the mattress. His quickly formed plan, such as it was, was to dive suddenly over the edge, mask his body with the side of the bed, snatch up the gun, and blaze away at any movement in the shadowed room.

He was tensed to begin this when he heard a sharp, metallic click, and he knew instantly what it was and that he was too late, was not at all surprised by the pressure of sudden steel against his damp temple.

You're a dead man, Chris Nielson. *It will be your final thought.*

A not unfamiliar voice said, "If you're awake, please nod, Mr. Nielson."

Chris nodded obediently.

Another click, and the pressure left his skull. "Ah. Well, I did this rather well, don't you think?" Followed by soft movement and then the blinding flash of the bedside lamp going on in his face. Chris squinted up through seared pupils at Goldstein's smiling face.

"The question is, would they do it just as well? My guess is that they would, perhaps better. Were you very frightened?"

"Very. What's the idea?"

"The idea, Mr. Nielson, is to prove that one cannot be too careful these days. I have reason to believe someone is watching my shop." The attorney handed Chris the Ruger.

Chris took it, sitting up, rubbed at his eyes, thankful, despite a burning bladder, he hadn't soiled himself. "How'd you—? I locked the door."

Goldstein pulled up a chair. He was dressed all in black, even a black hat, like an ordained rabbi: black gloves, trousers, shoes. No part of him but his serene, smiling face showing pale. "I didn't use the door. I used the window. I did it rather well; would you agree?"

Chris nodded. "Very well. I shouldn't have been asleep."

"But you have to sleep sometime, yes? The question is, should you be doing it here any longer? I honestly did not think a man my age could climb a trellis in total darkness, pry open a window, and not be heard. Perhaps I have missed my calling. What would be your assessment?"

"How'd you know where the gun was?"

"It was where I would keep it."

"I could have shot you."

Goldstein smiled, clearly pleased with himself, with all the excitement. "A chance I took. I could not use the phone."

Chris stumbled toward the bathroom, fumbled himself out, urinated with grunting relief. "You're sure it's tapped?"

"Sure enough to be prudent. You've been away."

Chris flushed, splashed water on his face, came back into the room more awake. "A lot's happened. It's very good to see you, Mr. Goldstein. Don't be insulted, but I'd nearly forgotten about you."

"You've had a lot on your mind." The attorney hoisted a leather valise to his lap, unsnapped it. "You confronted our Mr. Springer, I take it?"

"Yes."

"And survived apparently. Your wife and child?"

Chris sat on the edge of the bed. "He still has them. I'm afraid I didn't prove very effective. He has help, Mr. Springer has. Powerful help. Government help."

Goldstein nodded, withdrawing papers. "Indeed. Here's something you might find of interest. . . ." He handed an eight-by-ten black-and-white photo to Chris, who rubbed at his eyes, peered at it.

Frank Springer and a sun-squinting entourage of cronies smiled at him from the Capitol steps. Chris recognized two of the suits near Springer as the men in the woods, the men at the dock that night. "Where'd you get this?"

"Faxed from a friend of mine in upper New York state. He in turn has a senator's ear in Washington. A senator that for now shall remain nameless. This much wasn't difficult to obtain. Other things, more enlightening things, will be more convoluted. And more dangerous." His delight was barely contained now. "It appears we're on the verge of something acutely clandestine."

Chris stared complacently at the photo a moment, handed it back. "You've been a busy attorney. Anything else?"

Goldstein replaced the photo carefully, like a prized jewel. "Much more. Truckloads more, if we're very, very lucky." Goldstein grinned ear to ear. "I'll give you the details when I'm sure. For now, I'm quite convinced your Mr. Springer all but owns our fair city of Greenborough."

"Owns it how?"

"I'm working on it. Actually, to be fair, Hershel is working on it. Hershel, my nephew. He's proving far more effective as a detective than as a potential attorney. Do you suppose it could run in the family, Mr. Nielson?"

Chris ran a hand through his rumpled hair. "Mr. Goldstein, you need to know something. . . ."

"That this is not a game. That people might—probably will—get hurt. That none of this is to be taken lightly. Yes, I'm well aware of that. Prepared for it."

"Are you prepared to have your tongue practically cut out?" He immediately regretted it, strangely embarrassed for Rick, who wasn't here to defend himself.

"Excuse me?"

"They nearly killed a friend of mine. There's no guarantee even now he'll ever walk again. Now they're threatening his wife. They'll do the same to anyone even vaguely connected with this thing. They're very powerful. Probably unbeatable. I can't ask you to be involved any longer."

Goldstein watched him for a moment, finally sat back in the chair. "I see." Then, after a reflective moment: "I wonder, did you have the opportunity to talk with Mrs. Nielson at all?"

Chris shot him a look, Goldstein presenting an incongruously comic figure in his black, cat burglar clothes and too large black hat. "This is a matter for the police now," Chris said tonelessly.

Goldstein watched him, seemed to melt back into the chair an inch.

Chris found himself rubbing his hands together absently, as if cleaning them, caught himself and stopped. He looked up at Goldstein. "I really think the police are the answer now. I have some friends in Los Angeles."

Goldstein said nothing.

Chris licked his lips. "I want to thank you, of course. And pay you. How much do I owe you?"

Goldstein shrugged. "Let me see . . . two days' work, the usual fee, shall we say two hundred dollars?"

"Fine. I'll get you a check." He started to get up, remembered. "Oh, my personal things. Well, I still have some funds in the Thousand Oaks account, but I don't have any checks. I don't suppose you take American Express?"

Goldstein watched him a moment, stood. "Tell you what, Mr. Nielson. You get in touch with your bank in California when you get time. Mail me a check when it's convenient. You have my address."

"Fine. That's very generous, thanks."

"Not at all. Well." Goldstein extended his hand.

Chris shook it.

Goldstein started for the window.

"Here," Chris insisted, "let me get the door for you. . . ."

"It's okay," from Goldstein, stepping to the window, pressing it open to a chill breeze. "This may be the last time I get to play James Bond. I'd like to make it last as long as possible. Good night, Mr. Nielson. And good luck to you and your family." And he stepped into the outer darkness.

Chris stood on the hooked rug staring at the empty window for five minutes without moving a muscle, contemplating thoughtfully, methodically, with what he suspected was the nearly hallucinatory state of his swirling brain, the precise meaning of the little attorney's last word.

Family.

Chris awoke, sprawled across the hotel bed, to the sound of the cleaning lady rapping lightly. Again, he hadn't remembered falling asleep.

He experienced a sublime nanosecond of prewaking innocence, pure and trouble-free, before the cobweb fled, jarring him back to the reality of Matty, the baby, the entire nightmare. Whatever respite he'd gained in oblivious sleep was immediately vanquished.

He felt bone-deep weariness again. Would he spend the rest of his life this way?

Now he knew why people committed suicide. Life *could*—as alien as the concept had always been to him—be unbearable. The mind could collapse, implode. He was close.

He called to the cleaning lady to come back, pushed off the bed, sat for a time with his head in his hands, fighting the dragging urge to fall back, reclaim the druglike doorway to sleep, to peace. Please, God, I just need a little peace. No man can withstand this much.

Instead, he struggled up, made himself shuffle thickly to the bathroom, stand under a stinging shower, the needling spray massaging crimped back muscles. He made himself towel, dress, finally remember to look at his watch. It was after ten in the morning. He'd lost nearly an entire day.

What day? Thursday? Or was it Friday?

What day had it been when he'd driven Rick to the hospital? He couldn't seem to remember, as though a puzzle piece had been removed. He didn't know why it seemed so important that he know the day of the week, only that it did.

Get a grip. Go downstairs and get some breakfast. You need to eat. Look in the morning paper to see if anyone found any bodies on the mountain yet. Cool off and let it sit for a while. Eventually you'll find a way, you'll make the bastard pay for this.

They threatened Sharon.

Chris thought about it, buttoning his shirt. He had heard anger in Sharon's voice before, maybe a couple of times in the years of their friendship. But he had never heard fear. Not genuine, soul-chilling fear. Not until now.

Don't think about it. Go down and order yourself something to eat, ham and eggs, coffee. Lots of coffee. You'll feel better. You're brain-dead, exhausted, burned out. But you're not beaten.

"No, goddamn it," he heard himself mutter, "I'm not beaten." Feeling a little better already.

He was shaving when a blast shook the bathroom mirror, made his reflection ripple as though seen through gelatin.

On the hotel stairs without quite realizing it—having not even considered the slow, wrought-iron elevator—Chris clambered down ancient wooden steps, shaving foam and a little blood flying, bare-chested, unbuckled, shoeless, hair wet and swept back. He knew again that same sixth sense of stolen reality experienced before, knowing and not quite knowing what to expect in the street below.

What he found, icy wind against his naked stomach, was black, greasy smoke billowing below a gathering crowd just off Main, just down a block or two, where he couldn't quite see. Just where Goldstein's law office squatted on the little side street.

Chris ran in his socks across freezing street, not feeling it, seeing only the black, curling smoke, pushing curtly past annoyed pedestrians, the brick corner coming at him, coming. Rounding it, the wall of heat hitting him, sirens blasting his ears now.

Someone was trying to pull him back, Chris yanking away savagely, running *no no no* into the heat, the reddish glow, plumes of flame billowing from the law office windows, nothing beyond it, beyond the ruined door but opaque, roiling blackness.

Fire trucks skidded sideways on the icy street, yellow-coated men leaping, tugging flat, serpentine canvas hose. Chris gripped himself against still unfelt cold, teeth chattering, the frigid wind shifting, pulling the smoke aside to reveal, briefly within, the charcoal husk of Goldstein still seated at his ruined desk, eye sockets empty, pink mouth open in surprise, black crown—hair burned away—trailing smoke like a cigarette. Until the wind shifted, sucked back the opaque curtain again.

And superimposed over it all, in Chris's mind, was the smiling photo of the men on the Capitol steps.

Someone jostled his shoulder, roughly sweeping by. Someone else shouted at him, finally wrapping a coat about him, trying to lead him away. Chris shrugged it off, fighting them, trying to make them understand that he was fine, that there was nothing wrong with him, that he had as much right to be here as anyone. As anyone. Anyone . . .

Chris sat in the noisy Greenborough bar all alone and as far from the crowd as possible in a knotty pine corner, drinking yet another drink. Thinking yet another time as he had now for the past hour: One more, one more drink and I'll get in the Volvo, drive up the mountain to Rick's rental car, pry the trunk up somehow to get to the artillery, drive on up the icy road to the A-frame, and blow that fucker's head off, get my wife and kid back. Or whoever's kid he is. Get them back and get the hell out of this god-awful town forever. But first I'll sit here in the warmth and noise and finish my drink because it's going to be a long, cold night.

And that necessitated another drink, and yet another, his courage never quite coming. Or not so much his courage—he was beyond anything like the conventional definition of courage—more the belief that all his actions, that *any* actions, could actually stop Springer.

Soon was too drunk to be very effective in any situation, much less a suicidal one, which was, he supposed, the intent all along. To prevent his getting himself killed tonight, like the others. To sit here in his aloneness, his utter, complete aloneness, sit here and just let the world move on past, forget him.

"Drink enough of that stuff and it will kill you."

It came from two booths away.

She was alone, tucked in her own corner, shrouded in smoky mist, shrouded in the drunken blur of his vision. Very dark hair, very dark eyes, almond eyes, and pretty. Very red mouth, contrasting, like the eyes and hair, against nearly iridescent skin. Maybe it was the light in here. It glinted dully off her own drink, lifted to the red smiling mouth.

"The pot calls the kettle black," Chris told her, and saluted with his amber glass.

She saluted back. "To overindulgence," she offered, and signaled the waitress for another.

Chris watched her with dreamy fascination, almost convinced he knew the voice, if not the dark eyes.

"Freezing cold in this place," she said after her waitress left, after another wincing swallow. "But it was the only saloon I could find," offering him another sad smile.

"People come here to ski," he told her, "people who enjoy being cold."

The dark head shook, shoulders shuddering. "I detest the cold. Really detest it."

Then why did you come here? he wondered.

And, swallowing—probably half plastered herself—she read his mind: "I turned thirty last Friday. Told myself if I was ever going to learn winter sports it had better be soon."

Chris nodded, poured another from his private bottle.

She watched him tip it back, watched him swallow, put the glass down again. The pretty woman shook her head. "No. I lied. I detest winter sports too."

Chris offered another salute. "To the detesting of winter sports." Drank, appraised her. "We've met. I'm sure. In the ladies' room?"

She smiled. "And in the hotel elevator. I was flirting then too."

Chris looked away a moment. "I had things on my mind."

She nodded. "I came up here to forget about 'things.' Friends, family, my job, which I also detest. And to find someone who detests the same things I do."

Chris looked at her. "Any luck so far?"

The dark eyes watched him again a moment, then signaled for the waitress. She paid with a twenty, picked up her purse. "Why don't we go over to my place and find out?" she asked Chris, rising.

In her apartment, or her hotel (Chris wasn't sure which, having half fallen asleep on the drive there), she snapped on the foyer light, swaggered out of her heavy fur coat, and tossed that at a chair, missing. She kicked off her heels and turned back to Chris, who was still guarding the doorway.

"Come in—Chris, is it?"

"Yes."

"Come in, Chris. I won't bite." She smoothed back an ebony lock. "Unless specifically instructed."

She wore a red dress the shade of her red mouth, and it showed everything and managed to be stylish at the same time, or stylish enough.

Chris came to her, embraced her, and kissed the red mouth as though it had been mutually rehearsed, as though both of them knew why they were here, decorum a thing behind them.

She returned his kiss with a firmer pressure than one who'd appeared tipsy, crossed her arms, and pulled at the straps of her dress. She took his hands, covered her breasts with them, still kissing him, deeply, holding tight as though fearful he'd melt, vanish like her whole vacation if she didn't cling tight.

When he'd tasted his fill of her tongue, he felt himself grow firm down there. (Thankfully: He'd been worried the liquor would ruin that.) He bent to kiss her throat, the small hollow there, then lower, to her breasts. She quickly reached out and snapped the light off again, plunging them into darkness, as though ashamed of what he was about to kiss there. Which was silly, Chris thought, because what she had was considerable and quite firm, quite lovely, and smelled wonderfully of perfume and herself, tasting just-right salty. When he found her nipple she arched and whispered, "Oh."

She pulled him down to the couch, which they missed, or he missed at least—she finding just the edge of it. She scooting down obligingly, pulling up the red dress for him, Chris kneeling between firm, muscular legs, warm thighs, finding no panties there.

And that's when it all slipped away. He found himself outside himself, watching the two of them, feeling very silly and strangely angry and detached.

She sensed it immediately, sighed deeply, resignedly. She sat back, cupped his cheek with her palm, smiling wanly down at him with the sad, dark eyes.

Chris shook his head. "I can't. I just can't. I'm sorry."

She shrugged round shoulders, sat back against the sofa with another sigh, low and long and drawn out, that ended in a little "whuff" of regret. She pulled down the bright red dress, smoothing it, making herself presentable, decorum rushing back on them. She pushed up, patting the top of his lowered head in passing, like mother to child. "I'll get the drinks. . . ."

Chris still kneeling in impotent darkness, foolish and stupid and more alone than ever, talked to the walls now: "I just can't."

Later, having poured them wonderful drinks, having made a wonderful fire, no resentment or apparent rejection in her movements, she joined him on the couch gracefully, as though no embarrassment had occurred, as though embarrassment was not a thing she wasted her time with. She sipped and smiled at him and asked, "Was she pretty?"

Chris nodded, sipped himself. "Is pretty."

"What's her name?"

He looked up at her. "Her name. My God," Chris whispered, "I don't even know your name."

"Janet."

"Janet. Well, I'm sorry, Janet."

"Don't say that, just forget about that, and quit looking restless. You don't have to perform for me, and you don't have to look for graceful ways of leaving because I don't want you to leave. Can't we just talk?"

It made him smile.

"Well, that's a start. Why the smile?"

Chris shook his head. "I really don't know. I guess because there's so much to talk about, and you wouldn't understand any of it."

"Try me."

He nearly started to. "Look, I really appreciate this, but the thing is, I don't really understand it myself."

Janet sat back patiently, nursing her drink. "She left you, this woman?"

"Matty."

"Were you married?"

That elicited another smile. "I'm sorry; I'm not trying to be deliberately coy. It's just so insane. Look—Janet—I really don't think talking is going to work. And I really don't think sex is going to work. So unless you have other suggestions, I think I really should leave. Thanks for the drink."

She rose before he could, took his glass. "Have another drink."

"Look, you don't have to—"

"I'm not. I'm not feeling sorry for either one of us. I'd just prefer it if you didn't leave right now; is that okay?"

Chris sighed, fingers laced.

She returned, handed him a fresh drink.

It was warmer than the first. And the room soon grew so warm and comfortable he began to feel his eyes droop. Janet, her knees cocked up there just so on the couch, her eyes on him, her smile, were the last things he remembered when the lazy warmth begged him to put down his glass a moment, close his eyes a moment. Just a moment . . .

She was asleep herself when he awoke sometime later, his bladder burning with need.

She was curled atop the sofa, legs drawn up now, chest rising evenly. She looked very young, very sweet. She is sweet, he thought, rising.

Padding, quietly as he could, he moved through the apartment in search of her bathroom. Standing there before the bowl, relieving himself in the strange bathroom, under the strange amber glow of the seashell night-light, Chris relived the sensation that at times like this, at this hour of the morning, life could be more like dreams. Dreams more like life.

He turned from the toilet, flushed—hoping not to wake her— padded back to the living room, hesitating a moment. He knew with sudden, utter certainty as he regarded the slim, oblivious length of her that even this was somehow wrong, even just being with her was somehow cheating on Matty. For all that she had put him through, he still found the idea of being unfaithful to Matty intolerable.

He reached for his jacket atop the chair back.

"Are you up?"

Shrugging into it, Chris turned to her. "It's okay. Go back to sleep, Janet."

But she was pushing up now, yawning at him quizzically. "You're leaving."

"Yes."

She stifled back another yawn, nodding at the kitchen. "I make a mean breakfast."

"I'm sure you do. I'll call you."

Even from there, in dimness, he could see the glow of her smile. "That's what they all say."

"I really have to go," he pleaded, feeling slightly trapped now that he was half there, out again into the friendly, cleansing cold and, by inference, closer to Matty again.

"Is she waiting? Matty?"

He tugged on his shirt. "No."

"Then you've no place to go but back to the hotel."

It was true. And the thought of four lonely walls tempted him, for a moment, to climb back in. Except that he was tired of lies, sick of lies. And in the end, really, this was just one more.

"I'll call you. We can have dinner."

"It's okay if you want to talk about her. I don't mind."

I mind. "No, it's all right, really."

"I'm a terrific listener."

Chris smiled. "You're terrific, period."

"It's very cold out there."

Colder than you know. "Please, you're very persuasive." He made himself hurry, come to her, kiss her forehead—which she allowed without movement, just sat there stolidly making the kiss feel perfunctory and disingenuous—patted her arm, and turned to go.

He reached for the front door, found that she had followed him into the hall, was leaning against the wall languidly, trying to look inviting, and succeeding.

"Sure you don't want to talk about it? I could put on coffee."

He left his hand on the knob. "It's really very complicated, Janet."

"Good. You can tell me in a hot bath. With bacon and eggs frying, fresh coffee."

He smiled. "You're going to make someone a great wife someday."

She didn't return the smile. "Thank you, I've been there. Come back inside."

"Really, no."

"Please? I can beg if you like, and not mind at all."

He studied her. "You're an amazing woman."

"Just very determined, when I know what I like."

"Thanks anyway," and opened the door.

"You really love her, huh?"

He didn't turn back. "I have to go, Janet."

"Sarah."

Now he did turn and found—her expression impassive—that the arm behind her was out in front now and clutching a silvery gun.

"The name is Sarah. Close the door quietly now, and come back in here."

CHAPTER 20

The woman named Sarah made coffee with her left hand, held the gun with her right, moving efficiently, confidently about the small yellow kitchen.

Chris watched from a yellow wicker chair at the glass-topped wicker table. Too much yellow, he was thinking absently, and everything too everything-in-its-place neat. It would get on his nerves eventually. Though, he supposed, that was hardly the point now, she being the one with the gun.

In the bright kitchen light, he could see that her figure, not only trim, was actually muscular, weight-trained, long legs hard, purposely delineated, the calves taut even without the dress heels, buttocks firm, round, almost boyish, apple-hard. Sarah was taut and lithe as a well-run machine. Some men would go apeshit for it. Chris preferred the lusher curves of his wife. Or did love have something to do with that?

And tanned. This woman Sarah was quite tanned, something he hadn't paid attention to before; she'd spent hours in the sun, in recreation or work. An athletic woman, dark woman—Italian?—the black patch between her legs visible as a shadow through the panties. A desirable woman, to any man who wasn't already smitten.

Sarah moved about the kitchen with quick, decisive gestures, finally putting the gun down on the counter when it got too much in the way, showing Chris she trusted both him and his curiosity not to betray her. He could have made a dash for the firearm, but Sarah didn't seem overly concerned.

She poured some Folgers into a paper strainer. "My purse is there on top of the fridge. Get it down, will you?"

He stood, reached for it, held it out.

Her back to him, no longer even close to the gun, she said, "Under the first inside flap, the wallet. Have a look."

Chris, sitting, opened the purse, found her picture on a green plastic card. Her hair was longer when it had been taken. "Sarah Jean Rawlings. CIA."

He looked up at her.

"Shall I make eggs now?"

"All right."

"I like them scrambled. Bacon?"

"Fine."

She clattered pans from the cupboard, ignoring the gun. When she turned to get something else—saw him—he had taken another, smaller revolver from the purse, was pointing it at her.

Unfazed, reaching into the fridge for eggs, she said, "The Colt's not loaded. Has a finicky trigger anyway." She swept up the Smith & Wesson on the counter and tossed it to him like a biscuit. "Try this."

Chris caught it, turned it over in his hand. Heavier than his Ruger. "What does the CIA want with me? Or should I ask: Why is the CIA bedding me?"

Sarah broke eggs into a sizzling pan. "Nearly bedding you anyway. And it's Sarah Rawlings, not the CIA. Because she wanted to. The CIA has been trying to screw you too, figuratively, but that could change. Depending on you. Toast?"

"Please."

"Look and see if I have any juice left, will you? There's a lot to talk about, and you're going to have questions. I'll start with Springer, if that's okay with you."

Chris set a carton of orange juice on the table. "Fine."

"Okay. Let's see. How up are you on current events?"

"Well, I'm more up on them when my wife and child aren't being abducted. I watch CNN."

"I'll shorthand, then. Basically it's this. The big threat of the post–cold war age is terrorism. To be specific, terrorism through illegal nuclear proliferation. It used to be all we had to worry about was the Soviets blowing us up. Now we have to worry about what the Russians are going to do with all that fissionable material lying around they decided not to blow us up with. In a nutshell, the end of the cold war was a mixed blessing. The Russians in Kazakhstan destroyed all these intermediate-range SS-23 missiles, chopped them up, and threw them away. But you can't do that with the nuclear core, the warhead. That you have to store somewhere. And what can be stored can be stolen. With me?"

"Yes."

Sarah handed him a cup of steaming coffee. "Tell me if that's not strong enough. Okay. We—the U.S., the CIA—we have people working on this all the time. Agents over there, agents over here. In Kaliningrad, a Russian enclave on the Baltic, we recently prevented the exchange of a one-hundred-thirty-pound case of gamma-emitting material between a middle-aged man from Saint Petersburg and a trading company executive. One of the largest recent hauls was the Lufthansa Flight 3369 from Moscow which landed in Munich with three hundred fifty grams of atomic fuel aboard. A Colombian and two Spaniards were pinched. That's just to name a few. It happens all the time. And even if some of these trades are successful, there probably would not—collectively—be enough to build an atomic bomb. That takes around eight kilos of pure plutonium even for a small one. The point is, enough of the stuff gets out, eventually you'll have what you need. Ka-boom."

Sarah lowered the flame on the stove, put in bread to toast, methodical and efficient. "What it comes down to is, the old threats are dead. The extreme leftists, Marxists and Palestinian allies, they no longer have much clout; their ideologies having crumbled. Who Washington loses sleep over today are the nameless Islamic extremists from Hezbollah, Hamas, and their sponsors. Iran in particular. Guys who think they're going to change the course of the Middle East and, eventually, the world. These are the buyers. And they're a problem, but not my problem. Bear with me now." She reached for the purse, withdrew a small manila folder, withdrew a series of eight-by-ten black-and-whites from that. "Christopher Nielson, meet Ivan Godunov."

Chris appraised the photos, three of them, grainy and blurred, of a bear-faced man with silvery hair, a massive, disarming smile, unpleasant eyes. "Looks like Yeltsin."

"Yes, a bit. Godunov is my problem. Perhaps the world's problem if he is successful at his latest vocation. Godunov is a seller."

Chris studied the cold, close-set eyes. Empty, compassionless eyes. "He sells nuclear material to terrorist groups?"

Sarah smiled, spooning scrambled eggs onto his plate. "Well, he probably did; everyone is who can. But that's not such a big threat."

Chris looked surprised. "No? How can it not be?"

Sarah sat across from him, folded a napkin in her lap, attacked her own eggs. "Hm, not bad. The price of plutonium is extremely high. It would cost millions to make a decent bomb, and no terrorist group—not even Hezbollah, which has state sponsoring—is going to get tens of millions of dollars for its own purchases, not when a country like Iran is trying to arm itself to become a world power. And Iran or Libya sure as hell aren't going to buy a bomb and hand it over to a bunch of ragtag extremists. You spend three hundred million or so on fireworks, you keep it for yourself. That's what we have to worry about, a large amount of plutonium being bought by a country trying to build a quick nuclear arsenal. The highest bidder in this game is going to be a state. That's where Godunov comes in. How's the bacon?"

"Good. You were going to talk about Springer."

Sarah chewed contemplatively, as if deciding the quickest way to get at all this. "Coming to that. Godunov first. Anyway, let's just say, to save time, that Mr. Godunov was in on the ground floor of the nuclear age. Way back during the Nixon administration we know that he held a position as one of the officials of the Russian Atomic Energy Ministry when it was under the sickle and hammer. We know that he personally knows Deputy Interior Minister Mikhail Yegorov, that he worked under Alexander Rumyantsev, director of the Kurchartov Institute, a leading nuclear laboratory in Moscow, and we know that—economic conditions being what they are in Russia—we know that the trickle of nuclear material flowing out of Russia into Germany and elsewhere today will be a torrent tomorrow. And if anyone can help direct that torrent, it's Godunov. He has the sources, the contacts, the intelligence, and—most importantly—the sociopathic nature to do it without blinking. As you may have surmised during this long-winded diatribe, the CIA would like him very dead."

Chris sipped hot, sweet coffee, feeling a little better with food in him. "Why don't you kill him?"

Sarah nodded, chewing. "Not so easy. Despite the progress between our countries, there is still much tension, still much delicately undecided between our nation and Russia. They—a lot of them, some important ones—think of Godunov as a very valuable man. Which he is, when he isn't threatening to sell off surplus plutonium. Something the Russian top officials deny, of course. But we have our sources. No, the guy has got to be terminated. It simply must be done discreetly. We don't want another Bay of Pigs. Not with all those McDonald's burgers waiting to be fried and served to those poor, undernourished Ruskies."

Sarah sipped coffee, shrugged in disappointment at the taste. "Which means we need the best. Someone who can get the job done, not only make it look like an accident but assure the Russians we had absolutely nothing to do with it. And more importantly, someone who can get close to Godunov in the first place. He's guarded like the pope, like Elvis. And more than that, he's smart as hell, maybe—probably—even smarter than we are. He's in this country right now, and we're not even absolutely sure of his location. He does that all the time, sometimes just to taunt us. His way of saying, If I can slip in and out so easily, then so can a nuclear bomb. Lot of insomniacs in my profession, Chris."

"I can imagine. So what do you do?"

"We hire the best, and we kill him. The best of the best. And that means just one man."

Chris hesitated in midbite. "Frank Springer."

Sarah raised a brow. "Very good. You get an A."

Chris sat back, coffee forgotten. "He's CIA?"

"Well, I'd give a qualified affirmative to that, yes."

Chris nodded, seeing a light. "And you're CIA. Who else in town is CIA?"

She couldn't repress a smile. "You'd be surprised. More toast?"

Chris stared into space. "The guys at the dock. The guys in the woods?"

Still chewing, she finished for him, "The guys in that picture on the Capitol steps that little Jewish attorney Goldstein gave you."

Chris felt a stab, found himself gazing at the silverware before him, the knife. "Your people killed Goldstein, didn't they?"

"Are you going to attack me with a butter knife, Chris?"

"Didn't they?"

Sarah chewed, sighed. "He wasn't supposed to be in the office, as I understand it. It was meant as a dissuasive measure."

Chris glared at her. "Well, he was certainly dissuaded, burning to death there at his desk. Excuse me, Sarah—if that is your name—but if you don't mind my saying so, I'm having a little trouble distinguishing your people from Iranian extremists."

She didn't find it funny. "Don't start, Chris. I'm telling you all this because I thought you were discerning enough to grasp the significance, to see the forest for the trees. Yes, we play dirty. All the time. As dirty as they do. Sometimes that necessitates—"

"Killing innocent civilians."

"—necessitates endangering the few for the sake of the many."

Chris rolled his eyes.

"Don't roll your eyes at me, goddamn it. And please spare me the sophomoric ends-justifies-the-means counterargument you defended in some seventies college sit-in. Mine is an unbelievably convoluted, almost always thankless job. Which sometimes—rarely—but sometimes requires doing things none of us—*none of us*—relish. So guys like you can sit in your big house in front of the fire and watch CNN."

Chris raised an ironic brow. "Guys like *me*? What house, what fire?"

"And for your sole information, my people didn't give the order on Goldstein's office. That was someone else's idea."

"Whose, the president's? You know, I'm beginning to think Iran has a point here."

Her face went to stone, lips a flat line. Then softened immediately. She commenced eating dispassionately again, in control. She resumed softly: "Chris, I can't give Goldstein back to you. I'm trying—I've been working very hard—to see if we can get Matty back to you. I put in a lot of man hours on Project Christopher Nielson, got a lot of argument from people brighter than both of us. But I punched it through. Now do you want to hear my ideas, or are we going to waste more time swapping personal ethos and definitions of patriotism while Matty sits up there fending off a sociopath?"

He watched her. Sat back. "I'm listening."

Sarah wiped her mouth with a napkin, had to get in a final shot: "You don't like me anymore—having groped me in the foyer—but you're listening now, that it?"

Chris said nothing.

"Never mind. All right. Forgive the irony, but we have to go back into my bedroom for the rest of it."

She got up, tossing down the napkin, led the way through the hall to the back of the apartment.

She opened the sliding closet beside the bureau and withdrew a leather case, hefted it atop the bed, and snapped it open. It was filled to brimming with neatly arranged manila folders, legal-size envelopes. Sarah opened a folder, began handing an astounded Chris Nielson picture after eight-by-ten glossy black-and-white picture of Matty, some from as early as her teen years.

Sarah sounded rote, almost rehearsed. "We have a file on her dating back to her kindergarten years. I can give you a list of every boy she necked with in the tenth grade, their current addresses, number of children, positions, and salaries. As well as your own. Give me a name, an hour, I can do the same with anyone currently living, most who no longer are."

Chris shuffled photos sourly. "What a unique talent."

She handed him a color Polaroid of a red-haired young man with crew cut and sideburns. "Recognize him?"

Chris studied the photo. "No."

"Nor are you supposed to. That's Springer. Age twenty-seven. His first year as an agent."

"You're kidding."

Sarah handed him an eight-by-ten of a dark-haired man with thick, Coke-bottle–lens glasses and a thin mustache. "Springer. Ten years ago. Nice nose, eh?"

"Makeup?"

Sarah chuckled. A deep, mirthless sound. "That's a Cold War face you're looking at, Chris. Naive as you may have thought the other side was, they knew a makeup job when they saw one. No, this is the real thing, plastic surgery. Done by the best." She handed him two more photos, neither of which looked remotely like the first two.

Chris gaped. "Springer?"

"I could go on and on."

"What's his real face look like?"

She took the photos from him—as though he'd already seen too much—placed them neatly in the case, and clicked it shut, sat beside it on the edge of the bed. "Who knows? It's in the file somewhere. I can tell you this. The face he has now is the face he had when he met your wife."

Chris turned away slowly, hands in pockets, leaned against the bedroom doorway. "She's not my wife."

Sarah watched him from the bed. "Sure, she is."

"The marriage is invalid. Springer showed me the certificate; I had it checked out."

"Just paper, Chris, just paper. Takes more than paper to make a marriage. Take my word for it." She let the cool facade slide a little, showed a lingering tenderness beneath. Was she defending Matty?

Then, all business again: "She met Springer in 1982. He was already a problem with the department, a wild card, always crossing over the line, having to be covered by the higher-ups or outright bailed out. He likes killing. It's that simple. He enjoys it. Which is his business as long as he gets the job done, right? That was the theory anyway. Cut the guy some slack because he's just so damn good at what he does."

"What are you saying?"

"I'm just trying to show you the whole picture. Few things in government—in world politics—are what they seem to an outsider. Clearly, Frank Springer is no saint, quite the opposite. He always had his detractors. One day he finally stepped too far over that line."

"What happened?"

Sarah looked out the window a moment as though the snowy walks enhanced old memories. "When you're that good, that influential, if you come from a chaotic background as Springer did, you eventually lose control of your demons. Springer had demons in spades.

"It was about this time your wife came into the picture. Two weeks after they were married, Frank—during what was supposed to be a routine operation—wiped out an entire family during the course of a two-week secret mission. A whole family including a teenager and two kids under the age of ten. That kind of unnecessary barbarism was bad enough. That it turned out to be the wrong family didn't help matters."

"Jesus."

Sarah nodded. "It gets worse. We always knew Springer was a little weird; the department just didn't grasp how far over the edge he'd gone. Springer apparently molested these children before killing them. Tortured them, really. People like Springer—icily brilliant minds like his—either embrace compassion, religion, the noble things in man, or they go the other way. Completely, irrevocably. There's a fine line between brilliance and madness. That Springer is mad, no one doubted. The department just couldn't bring itself to dump anyone so valuable." She looked up at Chris. "By that time, of course, he was already traumatizing Matty."

Chris felt himself tighten against the door frame.

"We don't have all the details, but it apparently began with mild perversion and declined rapidly into something fairly unspeakable. Matty tried to run away three times, was beaten senseless on the third attempt. She tried to commit suicide twice that we know of. Springer intervened. She tried to annul the marriage, with—unbeknownst to Springer—our help. Springer and his fleet of attorneys squelched it. In reprisal, he locked Matty in a closet for two weeks. No toilet privileges. She was at the Massachusetts State Mental Hospital for two months."

Chris felt a rush of burning hatred that seemed to shove all other emotion aside. "And still you did nothing!"

"Quit numbering me among them, Chris. I had, believe me, no say in any of this, try as I might. And I *did* try." She made an indifferent gesture. "In the end, Springer did it to himself anyway. They found this note in his effects, something he'd scribbled on an envelope, a plot to assassinate the vice president. Our vice president. That tipped the scales. They locked him away for two years."

"And Matty?"

"Matty was put under what amounted to a witness protection program, which included a new name, new address, new state, financial independence for the rest of her natural life. She wanted to be sequestered in Mexico somewhere. The department felt hiding in plain sight a better alternative, especially with someone of Springer's tracking abilities.

"We posed Matty as a divorced grade-school teacher in Montana, got her a job there, all legal and aboveboard. She spent every waking moment of his prison time orchestrating and finally being granted a divorce."

Chris felt his heart leap.

"Two days after it went into effect, the shit hit the fan."

Chris felt his joy turn to ice, pushed away from the door and came to sit across from Sarah on the bed. "What do you mean?"

Sarah stood, replaced the leather case carefully in the closet, shut the door slowly, as if she sometimes grew weary of its burdensome weight—as if shutting it away like that might keep it temporarily at bay. She turned back to him. "The department got hold of another piece of enlightening information. I could be—would be—shot for divulging the details. Suffice to say, it involves gamma rays and our friend Mr. Godunov. It was time to take off the gloves where the eminent Russian technician was concerned. Delicate political balance or not, we couldn't risk the wholesale slaughter of tens of thousands of our countrymen if what the information implied was true. Godunov had to die. And the only man capable of pulling it off was in prison."

Chris closed his eyes. "Jesus Christ, you let Springer out?"

"Provisionally. We promised a parole board review if he was successful in ridding the free world of Godunov. In point of fact, we lied."

"Lied?"

"Springer was a model prisoner. Which, with a man like that, could mean only one thing: He wanted out. With a vengeance. He wanted to kill not only Matty, but probably a whole retinue of former friends and acquaintances in Washington and elsewhere. He wanted his revenge for the humiliation of prison life. Clearly, Springer would have to die too."

Chris shook his head wryly. "But not before he did your dirty work."

Sarah appraised him. "Oh, are you defending Springer now, Chris? Does he fall under your heading of patriotic Americans who deserve to live?"

"Never mind the sarcasm; finish your story."

Sarah took the Colt from behind her, held it loosely in her hand. Chris had no idea how it got there, had not seen her with it since they left the kitchen. "Springer agreed to our offer. He'd track down and terminate the Russian in return for a fair hearing before the review board. Of course, everyone knew that Frank Springer—who is always two jumps ahead of everyone else—everyone knew that *he* knew we were lying, that as soon as his mission was over he was a dead man, or back in prison at the very least. And he also knew that *we* knew that he was already planning a means of escape once we sprung him."

"And did he?"

"Escape? Oh, no. That would have been the obvious tack, that would have been what we'd have anticipated. Frank would never do that. What he did instead was give us the slip long enough to go hunting for Matty."

"And?"

"He got to her in Montana before we could get there. Raped and beat her. We intervened, threatened to send him back to the slammer."

"Threatened but didn't."

"That's right, didn't. Matty, meanwhile, disappeared. Ran off to California, we found out later, even had some minor surgery done to her nose. Colored her hair, posed as an aspiring young actress out to make good. Of course, she never had any intention of getting anywhere near a camera or even a sizable audience. What she was really after was the suburbs, the mile upon mile of them in the Los Angeles area. She wanted to look and act so normal she'd be swallowed up in anonymity."

"Which is where I come into the picture."

"Yes. She did a good job of becoming invisible. We sure as hell couldn't find her."

"But Springer did."

"He found her general location anyway. Matty spotted him before he spotted her. She called us, terrified. Begged us to get her—you and the baby—out of California. To hide you somewhere else. We had this nice A-frame in Colorado we used once before in the protection program. Bulletproof windows and all."

Chris nodded hollowly. "And there never was any rich uncle, of course."

"Only rich Uncle Sam. The government financed the whole thing. The house, the move, the boat."

"Why the hell didn't your people stop him?"

"We did! We huffed and puffed and made our usual threats. And, naturally, having us over a barrel, Springer made a few threats of his own."

"Matty for Godunov, is that about it?"

Sarah nodded passively. "That's about it, Chris."

Chris couldn't seem to stop shaking his head in disbelief. "It's incredible. Incredible. Tell me, how'd you get the entire town of Greenborough to play along with you? Put a muzzle to each individual head?"

Sarah made a rueful face. "Hardly. We talked to the town fathers. Let them know we were moving in for a while, taking over temporarily, a kind of discreet martial law. The average joe citizen knew nothing, of course."

"Of course. And Sheriff Bradley and his crew, they were happy to go along? Or did they have to be coerced like Matty?"

Her expression remained stubbornly impassive. She was a professional now, a well-oiled machine, somewhere above him, doing her job and doing it well. "You don't coerce a community, Chris. You gather the leaders about you and offer them what they want. Money. In this case, new hotels, new restaurants, new ski areas."

"New sheriff's office."

"You teach them that being cooperative can be more rewarding than making waves. That not only will they prosper but serve their country in the interim. You don't push, you guide. Then, when it's done, you leave, as quietly as you came. We don't believe in interfering any more than absolutely necessary."

Chris kept nodding, shaking and nodding, shaking and nodding. "Yes, let's not upset the ecosystem. Who mutilated and nearly killed Rick Corman?"

"That was Springer. We had nothing to do with that."

"But it was your agents in the woods that night, on the boat dock that evening."

"Retired agents, most of them, renegades. Cronies of Springer's, not our people. Sooner or later, almost everyone in the department owes something to Springer. He has a lot of friends, many who hero-worship him, aspire to be like him. They were flattered to hang around, do his bidding, just to be in the company of a superstar. We had an eye on them. No one was supposed to get hurt."

Nodding, shaking, Chris paced. Turned to her suddenly. "So what's the upshot, Sarah? Did Springer kill the Russian or not? Why are you here?"

Sarah held the gun. "You're my assignment. I'm your guardian angel."

"Your assignment being to keep me away from the house. By fucking me, no less. That's some organization you belong to. Do they take American Express?"

"I think you certainly got a raw deal, anyone would, but that's not why I brought you up here."

"Why did you bring me up here?"

Sarah hesitated, as if having anticipated the moment. "There have been developments. A rethinking within the department. The upshot is that Springer isn't sticking to the rules."

"Why am I not surprised?"

"He's begun killing randomly again. Specifically three hikers up on Bolus Point not far from the house. There may be others. It appears he may be further gone than even we anticipated. His paranoia gone quite over the edge. He imagines the world is out to get him, sees conspirators in his morning coffee."

"You expected less from a madman? You people are amazing!"

Sarah cleared her throat, took a breath. "The department has voted to change tactics. Springer's dragging his feet, taking too long. Our fear is that Godunov will leave the country again before he makes his move. So, we're going to replace Springer. . . ."

"With who?"

Sarah stared at him.

Chris stared back, not getting it at all.

"With a complete outsider. With someone the Russians would never suspect, could never know. Someone skilled with a rifle, someone who's athletic, knows the area, has proven himself in combat. Someone who will learn quickly. Someone with a terrific memory for details."

Chris just stared at her.

And then he did get it.

"Are you crazy? *Me!* You're joking."

Sarah looked down at the gun in her hand. "It is, believe me, Chris, no laughing matter."

He just sat there. Reeling.

"Matty for Godunov, Chris. It's your chance to get her back. Your chance to get them both back."

"You're insane."

"Once the Russian is dead—the mission completed—the department no longer needs Springer. His reprieve ends the moment Godunov is reported dead. Frank Springer will be back in the slammer. Instantly."

Chris wasn't buying it. "I don't know a goddamn thing about this kind of stuff, this undercover stuff. You need a trained professional, for Christ's sake."

She shook her head. "No, that's the opposite of what we need. That's what the Russian would be expecting." And before he could interrupt again she pressed: "Chris, it was my suggestion to the department to use you. We needed a complete unknown, someone the Russian has never even heard of, much less seen, but someone close to the operation."

"Someone with a stake in the outcome," he added sardonically. "Anyone else would consider it suicidal."

Sarah nodded. "Dangerous, not suicidal." She leaned toward him, not bothering to hide the excitement in her eyes. "You were a hard sell, Chris. Very hard. The department distrusts outsiders. But I've done extensive research on your background, your capabilities. You're tailor-made for an assignment like this. And I'll be with you every step of the way." She watched him a moment. "I put my ass on the line for you, Chris, for your family."

"Yeah? Is that what you told Matty before you cut communications with her and let Springer take over?"

"I had nothing to do with that. Anyway, I told you: Springer is out. You're in. If you want it. Obviously I can't force you."

She turned the gun around in her hand, offered it to him, butt first. "If you decide no, you're going to need this. . . ."

"Is that a threat? And I already have a gun, thank you."

"I'm not threatening you, Chris. But I think you know Springer will eventually come after you anyway. Once he's through with Matty and Nicky."

He knew she'd said it deliberately to get to him (which she did) and he knew, also, she was right.

Chris paced.

He rubbed at his mouth, sighed. "What do you know about the baby?"

Sarah searched his face.

"Is the baby mine? Do you have that information in your files and computers?"

"I don't understand, Chris."

He looked at her. "What do you mean, you don't understand? Is the baby mine or not?"

Sarah gave him a disbelieving look. "You raised him for two years; you were there in the hospital when he was born. Yours is the face he saw in the delivery room."

"You know what I'm talking about. Is the biological father Springer, or me?"

There was a distance in her eyes he hadn't seen before. "Well, I suppose only a blood test would reveal that for sure. I'm sorry; I thought you were asking who the child's *daddy* is."

Chris gave her a sharp look.

He turned and reached for his jacket on the chair.

"Are you leaving? Is that your answer, Chris?"

He shrugged into the sleeves, not meeting her eyes. "I have your number."

"We don't have much time," she told him at the door. "Every second he's with her endangers Matty and the baby that much more."

He gave her a level look. "No one knows that better than I, I assure you."

And he was out of there, into the morning cold.

CHAPTER 21

Matty had not known real sleep for a day and a night now. Only interval snatches of restive repose, her beleaguered soul always brought jarringly back from the brink of real submission.

The baby had a cold. At least a cold. Maybe the flu, maybe worse, his wracking cough ebbing and flowing throughout the day where he sat lassitudinous and dreamy—drugged?—on the downstairs couch in front of clamoring Nickelodeon. Or in his own little car bed upstairs staring desultorily at Black Bear, the awful cough ebbing and flowing in daylight, a more harshly pronounced phlegm-cracked hacking at night.

Matty, exhausted with helpless terror, would lie there beside him, holding him, cooing to him, mind racing, coming close at times to gathering the tender form in her arms, grabbing a coat, and dashing off into the snow. Her chances out there in a freezing wind hardly encouraging but better, perhaps, than Nicky's chances here in this interminable redwood prison, shackled by their mad jailer.

Where, though, once out in the cruel elements, could she go?

The child was already desperately sick, and even if she could get to the car again, get it started, she was on her own completely. That was clear now. There would be no help from Stanford or

Kelly or the other agents. If help was coming from that direction, it would have been here long ago.

She was cut off, on her own, left to her own devices, her own ingenuity to set them free.

But why?

They'd had an agreement, she and the department, a contract, and they'd never let her down before, had gone out of their way to wrap an invisible envelope of protection around her, see that she and the baby—and now even Chris—were well cared for, looked after. She'd been over every page of the witness protection program, signed papers, then gone over it again and again during the long months of Frank's imprisonment. That and hiring an entire fleet of attorneys to finalize their divorce.

So how had the unthinkable happened? How had he gotten out? What could have gone wrong?

Why, after months, *years* of a solid, comforting relationship with the agency, why had she been deserted like this?

Surely they weren't afraid of him, not an entire governmental department. Surely not.

Meanwhile, Nicky was dying.

She didn't even attempt kidding herself anymore. You can't keep pumping sedatives into a child's bloodstream, feed him erratically (there was no food in the house, and all Frank offered in the way of sustenance was ordered-in pizza—always cold from the long drive from town in the snow), feed him chips and soda and other less nutritionally beneficial foods, deny him even cursory medical attention, even Tylenol to bring his fever down. You can't continue doing that, day after day, night after night, and expect a two-year-old to survive for long.

Yes, the child would eventually die. Unless Frank died first. And she must act quickly.

His mind was imploding.

One moment he was there, the next he'd floated off glassy-eyed somewhere. No thought of her, no thought at all of Nicky's failing health.

"He's sick, Frank. He must see a doctor. I'm begging you."

He'd sit there, staring into nothing, mouth agape, until she shook his shoulder. Shook until the smile came, that deranged, infuriating smile. "Kid's fine . . . youngsters always run a little hot. Your average Russian kid lives practically his whole childhood in bitter weather. You don't see them wimping out on their parents, do you?" Followed by the gradual, chilling focusing of his eyes. "I mean, he is my kid . . . right, kitten?"

Yes, she must act quickly. And there was only one way: the needle hidden beneath the mattress.

Which meant catching him—to the extent she could—off guard somehow.

Which meant having sex with him.

She turned from early morning sun, hair stringy and in her face, body limp with sleepless exhaustion, lidded eyes watching Nicky's shallow breathing there on his little bed. His sheets needed washing; she'd been too exhausted even for that.

And the bed was, realistically, too small for a full-grown adult. Yet she slept with him every night (Frank never bothered her—waiting for her to come to him), unable to leave Nicky's side while his temperature spiked so erratically, his chest spasming in cough after tortured cough. "Mommy . . . sick . . ."

And Matty would hold him, rock him, sing to him, try to hide her tears from him.

Sometime in the wee dark hours, sleep would find her for a few forgiving moments. That's when Frank would come with his needle and vials to drug the child and perhaps her. She was so bleary with exhaustion she couldn't really tell.

She drew a hot tub, lay back with a grateful groan.

Why had they deserted her?

Where had Stanford and the other agents gone? They had a deal, an understanding. How could they just vanish—cut off all communication—leave a two-year-old child this way in the hands of a maniac? How could they have let him escape in the first place?

She opened her eyes suddenly to billowing steam.

Unless they let him out on purpose!

No. She refused to believe it.

It went against everything they'd told her, all the long hours of work and planning it had taken to hide her, protect her. All the money spent, the man hours used—only to throw the two of them back together again?

But to what end?

She watched the lazy steam climb toward the redwood beams overhead.

Yet it was the only sensible answer.

The only reason they hadn't rescued him, intervened even in the slightest. Yes. They were in it together. Frank was an agent again, a temporary agent, anyway. It was the only thing that made sense.

But an agent for what? And for how long?

Until he accomplished some mission for them, of course. But how long was that? How much longer would it take? Until her baby was dead?

She closed her eyes again, settled deeper into hot suds, allowing herself, even in her fear and confusion, a small sigh of much needed pleasure.

It didn't matter what any of them were up to. The only thing that mattered was that Nicky be protected. And Chris too, if she could somehow accomplish that.

She had to kill Frank. Today if possible.

Come on, Matty, *think*! There must be a way. He's only a man, flesh and blood. And you're a woman. Seduce him. Think of a way. You're an attractive, desirable woman. He already wants you, he's always wanted you, can hardly take his eyes off you. Sticking you in that ridiculous translucent nightie every chance he gets, stenciling his mark of Russian pride on you like a goddamn rancher's brand.

He simply wants you to come to him, to initiate it, that's all. Maybe even beg, grovel. He wants—insists—on dominating.

All right. Let him dominate. Let him have it all, whatever he wants, however sick and degrading, just make it seem real. No hint of deviousness. He wants you to initiate it, but he's suspicious of your sincerity. And for good reason.

She cursed herself.

She should have thought of the syringe much earlier, been more on her toes. Been more submissive to him, less abrasive. Now it would be that much harder. Now she would have to be truly devious and he'd be anticipating that.

Think! There's always an answer. Even when dealing with the insane.

Try to remember him how he was. In the beginning. Way back in the distant foggy past when you actually thought you were in love with him. It wasn't all bad back then, not in the beginning. The first few nights in his strong, tanned arms had even been exciting, comforting. Before the beast emerged.

She sighed wearily in the soapy warmth, the faucet like a rushing falls behind her head.

A rushing falls . . .

Matty opened her eyes abruptly.

Niagara Falls, kitten . . . that's when we were perfect . . . the perfect couple.

Niagara Falls.

And in a moment she had her solution.

CHAPTER 22

Chris knocked at her door again almost exactly an hour later, the time it took to return to the bed-and-breakfast, change clothes, shower, and think about it.

To the extent he thought about it, which wasn't much, having known, even before he'd left her place, that he'd return. Known each of his steps away from her apartment, through slush-crusted streets, was just passing the time, to arrange the illusion of contemplation where no contemplation had, in fact, taken place.

He'd do anything that might bring Matty—their former life— back.

Probably, he guessed—standing there knocking, feeling slightly the fool—probably this woman Sarah had known it too.

She opened the door in fetching cashmere and tweed, brushed and groomed, glossy and unsurprised. "The coffee's still on," she said, turning, leaving him to come on in. Back to him, buttocks revolving nicely beneath the tweed, she came back into the living room, where she'd apparently been at something, a steaming cup of coffee set atop shaggy throw rug, between sofa and coffee table.

She resumed what Chris guessed was her recent position on the throw rug, stomach down, buttocks up, plump and signaling, eyes consulting mounds of creased paper—maps, it looked like to Chris. He tossed his jacket on a chair and bent to see better.

Sarah pointed a lacquered nail without looking up at him. "This is Greenborough, the sepia area. The green shows the national park around it, the forest. Where it gets gray-colored, that's mostly rock."

She pulled that map quickly aside to reveal another beneath, different colors, a tighter perspective. "Here's downtown. . . . Here's your house, approximately. Ivan Godunov is somewhere in this area. We think."

Chris was startled. "He's *here*? In Colorado?"

"Practically in our backyard."

Chris sat back on his rump with a confused grunt, arms atop his knees, studying the maps, then the woman named Sarah. "I don't follow. Godunov just happens—within the entire Western Hemisphere—to plop down here a few miles from where Springer found Matty?"

Sarah looked up at him, an expression of patience, as if waiting for Chris to catch up.

When he did, Chris knew renewed humiliation. "I see. You lied. You didn't 'hide' Matty and me in the house at all, did you?"

She waited for him to get through it.

"You already had the place set up as an operating base for Springer. You weren't sequestering Matty, you were handing her over to Springer. She and Nicky. And me," he added.

Sarah appraised him passively. "Like that coffee now?"

"Why'd you lie earlier? I thought you wanted my trust. This negates it."

She pushed up, an athlete's easy, liquid movement, moved confidently to the kitchen, poured him a cup. "It doesn't negate anything. I lied to you for the same reason I always have to lie in my work. To gain another foot. That's what my work mostly consists of, gaining ground. If I had told you the whole truth about the A-frame, you might not have come back this morning." She handed him the cup to see if he'd take it or storm out.

He took it.

She sat Indian-style beside him again. "Anyway, that's it for the lies."

"Is it?"

"There's nothing else to conceal from you. The rest is our plan for getting rid of the Russian, and I'm sure as hell not going to fib about that."

"Why should I believe that, Sarah?"

"Because, as I explained, I'm going along on the trip. Someone from the agency has to be there to confirm the kill."

Chris took a deep breath, cheeks puffing, took a sip of the hot, sweet coffee. "Assuming I do agree to this . . . this mission, when would we begin?"

"Now."

"Today?"

Sarah gestured at the map. "We have a slight hurdle to overcome."

"Which is?"

"We don't know exactly where Godunov is."

Chris put down his coffee slowly, eyes widening with disbelief. "Say again?"

Sarah folded the map into smaller sections, pointing again. "There's approximately ten or twelve ranch homes in this area, most of them vacation dwellings. The owners usually rent them out during peak ski season at an exorbitant price. We're eighty percent sure Godunov is in one of them."

Chris nodded wryly. "Eighty percent. Nice to know I'm in with such exacting professionals."

"It's the best info we've got, and we're lucky to get that. What we don't know for sure is exactly which house the target is staying in. The theory is that he keeps moving around. Godunov shares, believe me, all of Springer's paranoia about being knocked off, if not Springer's insanity. He's a cold, compassionless, extremely intelligent killer. Surrounded by a hand-picked entourage of extremely intelligent killers and bodyguards. Any man can be killed. But, it's always been assumed whoever kills Godunov will himself be killed."

"Is that supposed to be an inducement?"

"I'm just giving you the unvarnished facts, Chris. It's going to be dangerous. We've calculated the variables, considered the odds. It falls within the window of doability, but barely. We can't force you to do this."

"You've already forced me by forcing the situation. So, what you're saying is, Godunov rivals Springer in assassination expertise."

"He's certainly in the ballpark. He might not have Springer's relish for the kill, but he shares his sociopathic lack of remorse.

Yes, perhaps he's in Springer's class, the Russian equivalent. They share, apparently, a mutual admiration."

"They know each other?"

She shook her head emphatically. "Never met. May have spoken briefly on the phone; we're not sure. But we know for a fact Godunov and Springer have never met. Godunov, like most everyone else, isn't even exactly sure what Springer looks like. He may have seen pictures, but Frank keeps changing his appearance anyway. The 'Chameleon,' remember?"

"I remember."

"But they certainly know *of* one another. And their admiration runs deep. So do their individual egos. It's a love-hate thing. You like the movies?"

"Movies?"

"Alfred Hitchcock was asked once how he would like to die. His answer was, 'Being shot by a beautiful blonde, of course.' I suspect Godunov and Springer feel much the same way about each other. If you have to go, let it be at the hands of a superb foe. Bunch of macho crap. How easily can you obtain your usual lineman equipment without stirring up curiosity?"

Chris leaned back. "My lineman gear? Well, I've still got most of my old stuff in the car. Why?"

Sarah nodded approval. "We can get you anything you don't already have." She swept aside the map, pulled over a rolled sheet, slipped off a rubber band, unfurled the paper. "This is a schematic of the phone line system throughout Alpine County. Godunov is somewhere within it. If we can get you up a pole, say in this sector"—pointing—"have you tap into the line, we could trace it to the right house. That sound reasonable to you?"

"Surely the CIA or FBI has better-qualified people who can do that."

"Yes, and all of them have faces. I told you, Chris, Godunov's retinue knows every one of them. These are not uninformed people we're dealing with. These are extremely dangerous people used to tight places and how to navigate in them."

Chris thought about it. "Okay, let's assume I get up the pole, find the right line. How am I going to know Godunov's voice?"

Sarah was already holding up a patient finger, moving into the bedroom again. She returned with a palm-size cassette recorder, knelt beside Chris, pushed a button. A static-ridden but easily discernible voice crackled in Russian. Then, after a minute, in English.

"That's Godunov?"

"No. He never answers the phone. That's his aide, Slevenski. He *always* answers the phone. He and he alone. He has what they consider to be a pretty good midwestern accent. If you're midwestern, you may not agree, but it sure as hell doesn't sound Russian. What we do is, we have you record all your taps, then we transmit them back to the home office, where the lab runs tests. Finally, we wait for them to fax us back when we have a match."

Chris nodded. "I see. And from there you just get the phone company to trace the call to the right house."

"That easy."

"Okay, now we've got the house, now what?"

Sarah closed the map. "We get as close as possible without being detected. Set up our target, either through a window, or if he happens to give us a break, take a morning walk. Sight down on him and pull the trigger. Your weapon will retain maximum hitting velocity at a hundred yards."

"What weapon?"

"I'll show you in a moment."

"Fine. Now he's dead. What do we do?"

"Get back in our little lineman van and get the hell out of there."

"What about backup?"

Sarah shook her head. "No. We're on our own. The department cannot be involved outside the clandestine hiring of freelancers. It has to look like a hunting accident. Everyone will know what really happened, but it has to look like an accident."

"Will there be reprisals?"

"Oh, sure. But nothing you need be concerned about. The other side isn't interested in who pulled the trigger; we're just hirelings. They'll blow up one of our oil concerns in a third world country, something like that. Tit for tat. The main thing is, the world will be relatively nuclear clean for a few more years."

Chris sat thinking about it, then shook his head. "No, I'd better not think about it, I might say no. And you want to start today?"

"Tonight. It will be cold as hell, but we need to look as inconspicuous as we can. We'll provide you with an ALPS lineman's uniform and a logo-emblazoned truck, of course."

"And you?"

"I'll be in uniform too, in the back of the truck, with earphones and transmitter and a direct line to the home office. We'll get a match right there in the field if we're lucky."

Chris, throat unusually dry, took another sip of coffee, found to his amazement, the cup nearly empty already. "Okay, say we've got a match. Then what?"

She paused long enough to give him an intense look, rose, strode to the living room closet, rummaged within, drew back, turned holding a heavy-looking military-style rifle. She tossed it, from fifteen feet away, to Chris. Who caught it—to his eminent relief—one-handed.

Sarah came back to him, nodded at the weapon. "Heavy game .416 Rigby, built around a BBK 02 action. It has an English walnut stock. That's a Leopold scope in Warne rings, and that's where the rifle is special. No other scope on the planet can do what that one does. It's right out of the test lab."

Chris hefted it, brought it to his shoulder, sighted at a Chinese vase across the room. Saw nothing.

Sarah reached down, flicked a button, and the crosshairs lit, the vase blooming into perfect, automatic focus. "Jesus," Chris muttered, "that's neat."

Sarah hunkered beside him. "That's the least of it." She settled beside him, anxious to show off the new toy. "As you probably know, infrared is all the rage now. This rifle goes that one better. You sight down on your target, say a deer, with an infrared and you're reading the little red laser dot through the scope. Problem is, if your target is a man, he can read the little red dot too, duck out of its way. You lose your shot. Now look here. . . ."

She took the rifle from him, turned over the scope. "This is an advanced echo locator, something like modern radar. The infrared goes out like any maximum-velocity rifle, only it's invisible to anyone but you. The lens works off a polarized principle. In order to see the dot of light, you have to be looking through the polarized lens."

Chris made an impressed sound.

"Also—and here's the part I like—the echolocator sends a message back to the trigger. Once your target is lined up, a computer chip locks it in. Unless you're perfectly sighted on the *chosen* target, the trigger won't pull. It's foolproof."

"Christ, what will they think of next?"

Sarah smiled proudly. "You'd be surprised."

He looked up at her from the beautifully crafted stock. "You like your work, don't you, Sarah?"

She looked away, shrugged. "It's something I do well."

"Are they giving you a big raise for coming up with this brainstorm?"

She turned back to him coolly. "A raise and a better position, yes. Anything else?"

"Just curious," he shrugged, looking back down at the sleek design of the rifle.

She watched him. "So what do you think? Can you fire it?"

"Of course I can fire it. You knew that already."

She smiled. "You're dying to fire it. I knew that too."

He handed her back the rifle with a grunt. "Dying to target fire it, maybe. It's a beauty. Not dying to kill a man with it. I don't even like killing animals. I saw *Bambi* when I was a kid."

"Godunov's not a man, Chris."

Chris stood, made his way to the kitchen for more coffee. "Come on, Sarah, don't go poetic on me. He isn't a water buffalo. He thinks and breathes just like you and me."

"No, not like you and me. He sells plutonium waste to the highest bidder."

He came back into the living room. "How do I know Springer won't break out again, come after my family, especially once he learns who put him back inside?"

"He won't know. And he won't have time to get out. He'll be a dead man within a week."

"You guarantee that, do you?"

"I guarantee it. Once the Russian is dead, Springer is finished. You and your family can get back to a normal life."

Chris almost laughed. "Sure. You bet."

"Listen, Chris—"

But he waved her off. "Never mind, never mind. We're wasting time; let's just get on with it." He took the rifle from her, laying it back casually across his shoulder as he drank from the cup. "Before my knees start knocking again."

They sat in darkness within the van's cab, Chris at the wheel, lights off, all but a small penlight Sarah was using to read the map with.

They were no more than fifteen minutes out of Greenborough, but they might as well have been hours away. On all sides, for as far as the eye could see in the starlit night, were snow-capped peaks, the ghostly glow of the lower elevations.

"We have three possible locations for you to tap," Sarah was saying. "I'm just checking to see if we're on the right road."

She squinted, the penlight not offering enough illumination. Chris reached up impatiently and switched on the overhead.

"Hey!" She sounded the most genuinely alarmed since the first moment he'd met her. "That light will carry for miles out here. Turn it off!"

Chris turned to her patiently. "Look, we're trying to play it straight, right? I'm supposed to be a lineman out here with my assistant, checking on some corroded amplifiers. This is what linemen do. What would really look suspicious is if I sat here in the dark checking a map."

But he could tell from her expression this offered scant conciliation. She was scared.

He hadn't seen it before, but it was there now. She was fearful for her life. Sarah Jean Rawlings wanted that new commission very badly, badly enough to risk everything. But she was scared.

To comfort her, Chris almost switched off the light as instructed, but some inner anger kept him from it. "What happens if they don't buy it?" he asked her.

Sarah folded the map in her lap, leaned back in the seat. "They'll kill us."

"Kill two linemen in an Alpine County Phone District van?"

"There's a small chance they might recognize my picture. They have computers too."

"How small is small?"

"There's no point in worrying about it, Chris. They may already have spotted us. If they show themselves, it won't matter. It won't matter what we say or what we do. If they show themselves, it means they're going to kill us. Don't bother begging. They won't hear it. I'm not trying to scare you; I'm just telling you how it will be."

"Now that we're out here and there isn't time to turn back."

She tucked the map into a plastic folder. "The area checks. Are you ready?"

Chris pulled on his climbing boots, wondered vaguely if he wasn't out of his mind, and pushed open the door.

It was cold outside the cab.

Dark too, though that would decrease once he got his night

vision. He tugged up the zipper on his yellow, fur-lined ALPS lineman's jacket, stood beneath the redwood pole beside the truck, and looked up, making quick puffs of vapor.

Always the same: the wavery instance of vertigo at the poles' vanishing perspective, the ghosts of telephone cables latticed above, the fatter, higher high-tension lines above those on the uppermost cross beam. Chris dug in his spikes, climbed.

A good pole, fairly new, though weathered considerably more from the harsher climate than the California poles he was used to, fairly new and much freer of spike marks than the ones in Ventura County.

In his years of work, Chris had seen poles so severely scarred he'd refused to scale them, reporting them to the district manager for replacement—a costly operation management disliked.

Herby Deeter, a friendly though not close associate, had chosen to ignore the warnings five years ago, gotten himself halfway up a badly pockmarked pole in Moorpark, dug in to brace himself with his leather harness, only to find the pole cracking like a rifle report at his stomach, literally splitting in half under his weight. It happened too quickly for Herby to snap his safety catch. The startled lineman screaming and flailing, plummeting with the top half of the pole chasing him. The spar itself missed him, and Herby might have survived the fifty-foot drop to rough gravel had not the high tensions—dragged and snapped by the weight of the broken spar—descended like crackling serpents atop him. Frying Herby Deeter a scalp-sizzled black, leaving the medevac crew little more than charred chunks to trundle into their strobing, screaming wagon.

Chris climbed higher, placing each spike carefully, decisively. He had never, during a single moment of working for the county, ever been completely comfortable up here.

In the summer it was the heat, the wasp nests hidden beneath the amplifier cap. In the winter it was the rain and wind. And now, in Colorado, the snow and ice.

The latter he encountered higher up, a dozen feet under the lines. Sudden patches of it made his gloves slip, starting a thrill in his stomach that was assuaged by the deep, comforting bite of his boot spikes. There was an old rule in pole climbing: If you fall, let go. Don't try to grab the pole. You might break your back in the fall, but what those splinters would do to you on the way down would be worse. Tell that to the brain, though, Chris thought: Man's instinct when falling is to reach out.

Chris arrived at the first cross beam, dug in tight, looped the safety harness, and leaned back with a notch more confidence. Safety harnesses almost never broke.

He pulled the plastic dial-receiver from his utility belt, reached up with a cowhide-gloved hand, and tugged hard at the amplifier cap stuck fast with ice. He had to put the receiver away again and struggle with both hands before the cap came free in a fine shower of crystals.

Chris connected to the first hub—one of eight—dialed, listened to distant hums and clicks, a soft burring of far-off warmth and light, and finally the *tic* of someone lifting a receiver.

"Hello?" A woman's voice, aged. Their first dud.

"Phone company, ma'am, checking the lines."

"Oh? Is there trouble? It's all this snow."

"We've had some reports of downed lines. Yours seems to be fine. Sorry to inconvenience you."

"It's all this snow. Isn't it lovely, though? My favorite time of year."

Chris imagined gray hair, shawl, creased face lit by warm fire, black cat curled nearby. Loneliness.

"Sorry to inconvenience you." And Chris disconnected, not wanting to listen any longer to the loneliness and longing, feeling lonely enough himself up here in the wind and cold.

He connected to the second hub.

Nobody home. Sarah had warned him that might be a problem, that this could stretch into two, even three nights.

Chris connected to the next hub. A teenager.

The next, a frazzled woman barely heard above shrieking background noises: toddler wails, rattling pots and pans.

On the seventh attempt, a smooth, unhurried, slightly midwestern drawl.

"Yes?"

"Phone company, sir, checking the line."

"Oh?" Just bordering on suspicion.

This is it! Already!

Chris kept his voice monotone officious. "We've had some reports of downed lines tonight, sir. Has your household experienced any problems with your phone this evening?"

"I wouldn't know. You're the first to call. Phone company, did you say?"

"That's right."

"Where are you, phone company? You sound very cold."

"Well, your line appears to be fine, sir. Sorry for the inconvenience."

"Not at all. Glad to know Alpine County is on its toes. Where did you say you were calling from again?"

Chris hesitated, mind racing, debated, then decided on the truth. "I'm atop a pole in the south sector near Antelope Valley."

"I see. Sounds like terribly dangerous work."

"Sorry to inconvenience you, sir." Chris disconnected quickly, the sly, confident voice still in his ear, his heart thudding heavily, wondering if he'd somehow blown it.

He waited a moment, then punched at a red button on the receiver. Sarah came on the line.

"Well?" Chris asked.

"Sounds promising, I'm transmitting it to Virginia. Why the hell did you give away our location?"

"I don't know. I panicked. Lying seemed, I don't know . . ."

"It's going to take a few minutes to get a confirmation. Why don't you come down for some delicious thermos coffee? You must be freezing up there."

"I am, and will, thanks."

He put the receiver away, unbuckled, and headed down. He had to will himself to take it slow, dig in, though his nose was frozen and the ends of his fingers were becoming dangerously numb despite the gloves.

Inside the cab, phones over her ears, transmitters humming in the back of the van, Sarah handed him a steaming styrofoam cup. She was lit with winking transmission equipment, unsheathed from behind a sliding steel inner door that could be raised or lowered in case unfriendly eyes came around.

"Thanks. Seems like you're always placating me with coffee." He sipped, looked up to find her jotting notes, businesslike, worry etched in the pretty brow.

"I blew it with the location thing, huh?"

"Maybe not," she told him without conviction, tossed the pad and pen aside, and slid behind the van's wheels, grasping the shift. "Buckle up, we're on the move."

"There's still three terminals to go up there—," he started. He was interrupted by a distant growling sound that froze Sarah to the stick shift.

Chris looked out and up into blackness, the sound closer,

strobing knocks that became the insistent thumping of helicopter rotors.

He turned to Sarah, who was sitting quite still, hand atop the shift knob.

The chopping echo angled off in a moment, headed away. Face tight, Sarah started the engine quickly, checking the mirrors. "Never mind the other amplifiers; we can come back."

She wants the hell out of here, Chris thought. I did blow it. Shit.

He said nothing more, and she pulled out onto snow-crusted road, leaving the van's lights off for the first half mile.

Chris envisioned field glasses, telescopic sights, trained on them.

CHAPTER 23

They drove for twenty minutes or so, Sarah at the ALPS van's wheel, Chris tracing a finger over the map. Light snow had commenced falling, Christmas-cheery in the van's low beams. No other vehicles passed them out here. It was late, snowing, cold. Smart people were home in bed or dreamy-eyed before a flickering fire.

A light had flashed red on the van's receiver. Sarah had grabbed the headset, snapped a toggle, listened intently a moment, pulled off the phones, and hung them on a hook behind her. "Bingo."

Chris knew a wave of exhilaration, followed by stomach-pulling wariness. Now it was real—suddenly very real—the target had been found; his life was about to take a new turn.

Sarah, on the other hand, was elated. She drove as quickly as the icy roads would allow, face set, shoulders too, seeing, Chris suspected, promotions, accolades, a future bright with promise.

If they could pull it off.

They came round a pine-flanked bend, and she slowed immediately, nearly tromping the brake, breathed: "Oh, shit."

Chris immediately thought, We've been discovered! The chopper!

He jerked around within the cab, looking everywhere. "What?"

Sarah set the brake, took the map from him curtly, frowning. "Goddamn it to hell!"

He waited, in dim panel light, eyes jumping from her to the map. "What's going on?"

She tossed him the deeply creased pages, goosed the van, crested a rise, and killed the lights immediately, but not before Chris had glimpsed the yellow, striped sawhorses, the DEAD END— TURN BACK sign.

"Sarah, what gives? Where are we?"

She sat with the engine idling, a tight look on her face. "It's the Eastman place. I was afraid of this."

Chris started to say something, but she got out, shutting the cab door softly, making waffle-soled prints to the warning sign and past it.

Chris got out to follow, paused to look up into the inky night as the thumping echo returned somewhere up there, its precise location impossible to establish.

Sarah, not for the moment concerned with the sound, continued to another small rise, stopped, and stood still. Chris joined her, found himself gazing out over black, bottomless nothing. A chasm. "Wrong turn?"

She shook her head. "No."

She whirled, crunching snow, hurried back to the van, returned with the fancy new rifle. Chris watched her flick on the magic scope, sight down at the gloom beyond the cliff.

Sarah pulled the rifle down, nodding, handed it to Chris. "It's there. You can't see it without the scope, not at night."

Chris sighted, spotted the pillar of rock two hundred yards away. One of those strange freaks of nature, like the high, spindly solitary columns in Monument Valley, only this one was in Colorado. An island of granite festooned with sage and chaparral, amid which squatted a low-slung single-story ranch home, alone and preposterous as one of those TV commercials with the car atop an island in a sea of air.

"How the hell did they get over there to build it?" he marveled.

Sarah checked her watch. "The same way they get back and forth now. There's a chopper landing pad behind it, just off the east wing. You can't see it from this angle. Shit, I was afraid of this."

Chris scanned the rocky column, saw only the darkened facade of the house, no movement, no guards, but why would there be?

Who could get to them in this fortress? "You knew about this place?"

"I've heard of it. No one thought Godunov would use it because you need a private helicopter license to operate in this area. Apparently he got around that somehow." She sucked a tooth, nodding. "It's a smart move. That's a two-hundred-foot column he's perched on. He's virtually impregnable to anything but an aerial attack."

Chris squinted through the green crosshairs, disappointment crowding away fear now that the die was cast. "Or rock climbers."

Sarah shook her head. Apparently it had already been considered. "That's Chisum Point. All but one side is sheer rock: that's the northeast face, and it's a solid sheet of ice in winter. The greatest rock climber in the world would be hard pressed to get halfway." She shook her head. "We're screwed, Chris. At least this plan is."

Feeling Matty and the baby slipping away by degrees, Chris lowered the rifle, looked up at the inky sky again, as if searching for something to ferry them magically over. "It's a shame. I mean, they're probably so confident about their position, we could get right up to the window. If we could just get across. There are no foot bridges, of course."

"Of course not."

Chris nodded: stupid question. He was aware of how desperate he was beginning to sound.

Yet something was tingling inside. There *was* a way across, and for some reason he felt he—not Sarah and her group—held the answer. He just needed a moment to think about it. "Is this the only road in?"

"The only road." She didn't even have to check the map, icy vapor fluttering from pale lips. She was cold, wanted to get back into the van, this plan already red-lined in her mind.

Chris stepped to the edge of the chasm, looked down as his toe started a sift of silvery snow on its long journey down to dark and darker.

Sarah turned back to the van. "Come on. I'd better get you out of here."

Chris was back in the cab, pulling closed the door when it came to him. He stayed her hand at the ignition. "Wait a second. How wide is the perimeter—the distance around the pillar? Could we walk it?"

She started to say something, shrugged, and located the map, unfolding it. "Looks like under two miles. We could walk it if we had to. Why?"

Chris was nodding in the seat, then smiling. Yes. He turned to her. "I was thinking about some kind of rigged safety line, a grappling hook of some kind—"

"Chris—"

"I know, I know: It's too risky even if we could somehow project it that far. But there already is a line across the chasm, Sarah."

She frowned.

"How did we match up the house?"

Her frown deepened. "The phone line? Are you serious? Swing across on the phone line? Would it hold us?"

"No. But the power line above it would. If you can get your people to cut the power for a few minutes in this area."

She thought about it. "I can do that." She gave him a level look. "But how do we do it? Hand over hand? Is it possible?"

"I've done it before. Once."

"With a rifle?"

"I can sling the rifle. It'll be tricky, but probably the line is across the shortest distance anyway. Look, I'm not saying in this weather I can do it. But I think we should at least take a look. Call your people and find out where the lines come in. My guess is over there on the south end."

She watched him a moment, nearly smiled, picked up her headset. "Yes, it's me. I need you to check on something for me. . . ."

The lines were indeed near the south end, nearly hidden by brush and stands of Douglas fir, though whether this was by design or not, Chris couldn't guess.

He stood beneath the lone redwood pole and squinted out into the darkness past the cliff's lip. From here it appeared to be less than a hundred feet. But it was dark, snowing, and distances could be misleading. Still, he had a reasonably good feeling about it, assuming the cross beams up there in the dark weren't coated with a patina of ice.

Sarah stood nearby, also measuring the distance with her eyes, waiting for some comment from him, her posture less confident than his.

"I think it can be done," Chris finally offered.

She stood gazing out into the darkness a moment, the rear side of the house just visible at this distance on the column of rock in the gloom.

Chris thought for a moment she was going to suggest it was too risky, but Sarah turned instead and headed back to the cab. She was putting in a call when Chris slid in beside her.

Sarah handed him the headset. "You tell them what you need. You're the expert."

Chris accepted the phones. "You've got our sector?" There was an affirmative sound. "All right. What I need is a temporary outage for the entire area. For, say, an hour if you can give me that."

Chris could hear a shuffling of papers at the other end. "Well, we've got some problems. That line is connected to a hospital and an old folks' home. We'll have to see what kind of emergency backup they've got. Don't want anyone on a respirator turning blue on us. Give us a minute."

Chris handed the headset back to Sarah. "They're checking."

They sat in silence awhile.

"Is an hour enough?" Sarah asked him.

Chris shrugged. "I don't think they're going to give us any more."

Sarah looked askance as the distant thrumming of chopper rotors rose to greet them again. Her face tightened. She looked at the bank of transmitters, receivers, recording equipment. "If they find us before you get started," she told him flatly, "try to run. Look for an opening and haul ass. Try to hide in the brush. If they show their faces, that's it. There will be no reprieve."

Chris sat silently.

"They won't make it look that way," she continued solemnly. "They'll make you think they believe you when you tell them we're linemen for ALPS. They'll ask who you are. Then, the minute you tell them—no matter what you tell them—they'll shoot us. They won't take chances. So if you see them first, try to run."

She jerked reflexively as the red light on the receiver flashed, reached for the headset, pulled it snug. She nodded at the air. Looked at her watch, then to Chris, pulling off the phones. "We're set. The energy goes off at exactly twelve-fifteen, comes back on again at quarter to one. Will that do?"

How would I know? Chris was thinking. "I guess it will have to."

She spoke an affirmation into the headset, hung it on its hook.

She turned to Chris. "Okay, you're set."

He nodded, feeling a distant cold, ignored it, and set to strapping on his spikes.

"Hey . . ."

He looked up at Sarah, who was watching him with eyes tender as a doe's. "How about if I kiss you first? Would that be all right?"

Chris snapped on the left boot, straightened, looked back at her. "Why?"

She tossed her shoulders. "Just because. It's cold and I need to feel warm for a moment."

"All right."

She leaned toward him, and he turned his head to her lips, accepted their softness, the briefest caress of her warm tongue. Accepted another quick peck on his lips, another, then she was pulling back curtly, all business again, arranging her notes.

Chris climbed from the cab and headed for the pole. The outer cold he didn't feel at all. The cold was all from within now.

He shouldered the high-tech rifle, found the strap a click too loose, adjusted, grateful for the wasted time, reslung, and began to climb upward into darkness, the wood stock knocking his hip uncomfortably. He experienced a distant flash of National Guard training. Halfway up, he imagined he could see the fat high-tension lines above the phone company's thinner ones, though all was in fact cloaked in dark. He paused long enough to look at his watch. Still twenty minutes to go. Probably he shouldn't have started this early, but if upper-level ice was going to be a problem, he needed to know that in advance.

Just past the halfway mark he heard a quick toot from below. He turned, not terribly concerned for a second before realizing that Sarah would not do that unless there was trouble.

It came in a blinding glare of searchlight from below and from the forest behind the van. Chris felt all the courage seep out of him.

He watched breathlessly. Sarah, squinting in bright glare, was stepping from the van, hands raised. Chris felt his heart hitch heavily, thought for a mad second of trundling quickly up to the top, hiding there somewhere.

He could see men in white parkas, nearly military in their uniformity, with rifles proffered, long, silvery flashlights before them. They were ringing in Sarah's terrified form.

Chris started down slowly, already framing what he'd say, ignoring completely Sarah's admonishments until he'd leapt the last few feet and glimpsed the cold shock of terror in her eyes. She looked like one already dead.

Still, he refused to raise his hands. He faked a what's-going-on air, came to stand beside her.

One of the parkas was green—olive drab like a war uniform—the hood framing a lean hawk face with a nose like a red beak. The other parkas held machine pistols, Uzis; this man carried a Russian Luger.

He approached the couple in the ALPS uniforms calmly, raised the Luger, and motioned with it toward the van behind them. Three Uzi-carrying parkas dispersed—crisp, rehearsed—leapt to and inside the vehicle. Chris was wondering if Sarah had remembered to pull down the concealing metal screen, had the feeling it wouldn't matter anyway.

No one said anything for a time.

Silence but for the muffled sound of the three parkas investigating the van. The hawk face stared Chris straight in the eye. It was all Chris could do not to turn away. He held his ground, aware of his tightened gut, determined not to show it. Beside him, Sarah, visibly trembling, exuded fear in raw waves.

There was a clang and movement from the van behind them. One of the men called out something in Russian. They'd discovered the transmitter and phones.

The hawk-faced man straight-armed the Luger, pressed the cold end of the muzzle tightly into Chris's temple. For an instant Chris imagined with almost preternatural clarity that which every soul has pondered: the feel of a bullet through the brain, the flash, the pain, the rush of final darkness. . . .

"Who are you?" green parka demanded. Exactly as Sarah had predicted. It was Godunov's aide, Slevenski, the one Chris had spoken with on the phone.

Chris faced the impossible dread of knowing his next words, whatever they be, would be his last. He held his gaze on the man's black weaselly eyes. It became easier suddenly. Hopelessness exonerated him somehow. "Get that fucking thing out of my face," he spat, surprising himself.

The gun held firm. "What are you doing out here?"

Chris thought he heard Sarah's plaintive whimper, imagined her eyes closed, imagined her praying, felt an overwhelming sorrow for her; she wouldn't get that commission now, wouldn't get any kind of future now.

Then he thought of Matty. And the fact that he had nothing to lose gave him a curious bravery. The universe seemed, after all, a very silly place.

"One final time. Who are you?"

Chris glared at him balefully. "My name is Frank Springer, asshole, and I told you to get that fucking cap pistol out of my face. Now! Before I take it from you!" He couldn't believe he was actually saying this.

There was a momentary pause in which the Luger did not discharge and Chris did not die. Slevenski seemed somewhat at a loss for words. Chris could feel all the white parkas staring at their leader with anticipation. Slevenski licked thin lips. "You are Springer?"

"I'm not going to ask you again about the gun, Slevenski."

This time, at the mention of his name, the Russian's face did alter. Only an elite few could know his name. The gun stayed put, however. "What are you doing out here?"

Chris made an impatient face, put all his years of stage training behind it. "I'm stringing you a new phone line, dipshit. What the hell do you think I'm doing out here with a van full of ham operating equipment and a high-powered rifle? I'm assassinating your boss."

Just barely, finger still on the trigger, Slevenski offered a wan smile. "So?"

Chris nodded. "So pull the trigger, jerk-off. If you've got the nerve." He waited two beats until he could wait no more, then added, "Unless you think someone else would rather do the job."

The Russian hesitated, eyes darting askance to one of his men, who lifted a cellular phone to his ear with that same crisp, rehearsed motion.

Everyone waited a moment.

The man with the cellular called something in Russian to Slevenski.

Slevenski lowered the gun. Chris had to carefully conceal the desperate urge for a deep, long-needed breath. He thought he got away with not showing it.

Slevenski walked to the cellular, spoke into it. Nodded.

He came back to Chris and Sarah. "General Godunov invites you to join him in a late dinner."

Chris unslung the rifle, tossed it casually to one of the white parkas, feeling suddenly as if he was doing everything exactly right.

One of the parkas detached itself from the others, came quickly over, and patted Chris down. He found first the Ruger against Chris's back, took it, then—as Rick had predicted—the Nighthawk blade against his boot, took that too. That, but not the nail-file-thin prison shiv tucked and hidden in the lining.

Chris smiled to himself. "Tell the general we'd be delighted."

The chopper, small, black, compact as a wasp, and nearly as maneuverable, barely accommodated Chris, Sarah, and Slevenski, who flew the craft. It was waiting in a clearing not a hundred yards from the van. How it had managed to land so silently, Chris couldn't guess, though he knew something of the stealth of auto-rotation. At any rate, the jump across the chasm to the concrete pad before the bungalow took less than five minutes. Slevenski was an expert pilot despite possible updrafts from the canyon and the precariously small landing pad.

Chris used the landing to glance at his watch, Slevenski's attention fully occupied. It was just midnight by the luminous dials: The energy to the house was scheduled for blackout in approximately twenty minutes.

With the rotors still whining down, Slevenski stepped out, came courteously around, and opened the door for Chris and Sarah, a basso, metallic voice booming all around them abruptly. "Welcome! Welcome! I trust you had an enjoyable flight!" It came from a PA system, obviously, the speakers of which had apparently been hidden around the rock island, making the exact source location impossible to detect. The accompanying bark and baying of distant dogs didn't help.

But the voice probably came from the house. A nice house, one of those late sixties ranch homes with lots of additions, including a guest house in back, pool, new shake shingle roof, beautifully appointed garden, and attendant shrubbery, Malibu lights describing the flagstone path to generous, deeply stained double doors, lacquered thick as ancient amber.

It opened to a smiling Godunov.

He was a shorter man than Chris would have imagined, but compact, powerfully built, ruddy-cheeked as Yeltsin, with similar, though thinning, silvery hair. The face, in contrast to his subservient aide Slevenski's, was almost blockish, with what appeared to be a perpetual smile. The man exuded confidence and, apparently, geniality. The eyes were cold as death.

To Chris's shock, he was bear-hugged at the front door, Godunov beaming. "Ah, at last. May I say what an honor this is, my friend. I had begun to think it would never come to pass. Come in, come in!" And they did, which put the distant, eager barking noises behind them.

Chris and Sarah were ushered like royalty into the sunken living room, the rich smell of pine and furniture polish tainted by the greasy bite of fast-fried beef.

Open-armed, grinning, and expansive, Godunov directed them to the long burl-wood dining table, pushing aside two gigantic borzoi wolfhounds, whippet-thin, elongated muzzles, fur sleek and white as the outside snow, so friendly one of them thrust a cold nose into Chris's palm. Godunov swatted them lovingly aside, pulled out a plum-colored velvet-backed chair for Sarah, motioning her into it, gesturing to Chris for the one beside her. They were guests. At least for the moment.

Chris sat, glanced around at what could only be described as atrocious decor. Nothing matched. Old English here, a bit of Early American there, a few rattan couches straight out of fifties Miami, an art deco cabinet over by the wall, an Eames chair nearby: none of it inexpensive, none of it complementing the other. The only statement here was American, as though—despite his lack of taste—Godunov had gone to great lengths to avoid anything even vaguely European, certainly Russian.

Godunov, seated, seemed very proud of it, seemed bursting with pride, in fact, to have Chris—Springer—at his table, sharing his wine.

He poured liberally for his guests, smiling like a big, beatific bear. "I hope you like this. It's from your Napa Valley. You must forgive the McDonald's burgers. I have a terrible weakness for them, though I know you find them somewhat déclassé in this country. We've had them in Russia, of course, ever since glasnost, but it's not the same, even though they claim the beef is as they say, grade A." He shook his head, a grinning Santa. "Russian cattle are not raised on American grain, no matter what they tell you. I order the Big Mac with fries here every time I'm in the States. Can you forgive me?"

"Big Macs are fine," Chris assured him as a plate of them was put before him.

"And Coke or wine is it?"

"The wine is fine." Chris looked at Sarah, who nodded, too astonished at being alive to be outwardly fearful anymore.

Godunov assessed her. "And your lovely companion is—forgive me?"

Chris had thought about it. "My wife, Matty. Matty, Ivan Godunov, Russia's supreme assassin." He wondered if Sarah thought he was playing this as well as he thought he was.

Godunov smiled modestly, bit with relish into a dripping burger. "Please, you flatter me. Though some, I suppose, would say the *world's* supreme assassin."

Chris chewed his own burger leisurely, sipping wine. "You'll forgive me if I take exception to that."

Godunov chuckled with delight. "Oh, yes! It's the only thing that has saved you. I think you must know my men would have had done with you by now. You must tell me of your exploits. If only there were more time." He consulted his watch. "Unfortunately I am scheduled to depart for Munich within the hour. Pity. There's so much to talk about." He accepted the lab rifle from Slevenski as though the moment had been orchestrated.

Munching burger, nodding, Godunov hefted the piece, admiring the clean lines, polished stock. "Very nice, very nice. Good weight, smooth mechanism. You must explain this remarkable scope."

Chris reached for fries, not looking at Sarah. "It contains an echo-locator device for night firing. There's a guard on the trigger to prevent misfires. Take it with you; I'm sure your lab will find it fascinating." He used the movement of his arm reaching for the fries to glance at his watch: five after twelve.

Godunov handed the loaded rifle to his protégé, Slevenski, who retreated to the Eames chair, rocking back, rifle across his knees, no look of love for Chris. If Godunov radiated graciousness—however faux—Slevenski appeared barely able to conceal his contempt for the intruders, particularly Chris, and Godunov's apparent fascination with him. Jealousy? Chris wondered exactly what the relationship between these two was.

"You keep glancing at your watch, Mr. Springer. Why would that be?" Godunov wondered.

Chris sipped his wine without missing a beat. "Well, when one is scheduled to die, one sort of concentrates on the minutes, if you take my meaning."

Godunov, obviously delighted with this cool candor, patted fat, smiling lips with a crisp linen napkin. "Indeed. But at least there's this consolation. I guarantee, should it come to that, to be the one to pull the trigger myself. You will shuck this mortal coil at the hands of the best."

Chris made a corrective gesture. "Second best."

Godunov grinned, laughed. "Perhaps, perhaps. It's no secret I have long admired your style, sir, your form. Eh, Dimitri?"

Slevenski said nothing, held the rifle.

Godunov belched softly. "Yet another pity that we will not have time for some kind of contest, some kind of American fast-draw between the two best hunters on the planet, eh? You like the movies, Mr. Springer, the Westerns?"

Chris nodded. *"High Noon."*

Again that beatific look on the Russian's cherubic face. "Gary Cooper! Now, there was an actor!"

"Joel McCrea for my taste."

"Yes, yes! Did you ever see him in the Ernest Schoedsack version of *The Most Dangerous Game,* the marvelous Richard Connell short story? Wonderful film, a sort of dry run for the King Kong sets as I understand it. Now that, Mr. Springer, that is how I see us. Me as Count Zaroff, you and the lady as the hapless couple, fleeing my hounds. A game of skill and cunning between the two of us. What more could the most dangerous men of two continents possibly ask for? The most dangerous game, eh?"

"Sounds charming," Chris said.

Godunov was on a roll. "Just the two of us—or three of us, as it were—in the jungles of Milan or the desert wastes of Africa, some neutral territory where we have both excelled in the past. Just us, armed with perhaps only a single blade, each stalking the other. The final battle. The final decisive game that would prove to one and all who rightfully reigns at the peak of our rather peculiar profession. You really find the concept interesting, my friend, you are sincere?"

"Indubitably. As you said, a pity we won't have the time. Not that it's really necessary, of course. I think we both know who the finer huntsman is, General. A point I plan to prove before the evening is out."

Godunov fairly bubbled with joy. "By God, it's a genuine honor to be in your company, sir! How was it your somewhat loquacious Mr. Hemingway put it—'grace under fire'? It's admirable, sir, truly admirable. Dimitri! More wine for our guests!"

Slevenski reluctantly complied.

Godunov eyed Chris approvingly, cocked a thoughtful brow. "I wonder. No, I shouldn't even mention the idea. . . ."

Chris said nothing.

Godunov glanced to Slevenski. "I wonder if our Mr. Springer here could be trusted to defect to our side of the fence."

Slevenski looked away in disgust.

Chris put in a laugh of his own. "Fence? What fence? You work all the fences, Ivan, just like me."

This seemed to please the Russian even more. "Indeed, indeed!" He reached for a french fry, slyly toyed with it a moment. "You are of Russian ancestry, as I understand it?"

Chris felt a sudden chill. A test was in the offing.

Ivan Godunov was nothing if not cautious. He trusted no man, perhaps not even faithful Slevenski. He'd kept Chris and Sarah alive this long only because he needed absolute assurance the man before him was the real Frank Springer. Doubtless the Russian had photographs, faxes, but Springer changed his face more times than the Russian changed aliases.

"Of Russian ancestry," Chris answered confidently, "just as yourself."

Godunov nodded, biting a tip off the fry. If he knew Frank Springer as well as Sarah had said, then he must know Springer was a student of Russian history. That there would be some things only an expert like Springer was likely to know.

"Our motherland has always fascinated me," Godunov perused. "How, for instance, the entire country came of age in the eight centuries between Rurik, the founding Varangian in the seventh century, and Peter the Great, her first modern czar. Absolutely riveting, wouldn't you agree?"

The test upon him, Chris chewed his food leisurely, not looking up from it. "If you don't mind my asking, General, how exactly do you plan to rid yourself of Mrs. Springer and myself? I'm curious."

A wedge of pleasurable suspicion touched the Russian's lips, just enough to give him away. "All in good time. For now, let's enjoy our meal, and some good dinner conversation. You agree with me, then, about our fascinating nation's history?"

Yes, a test. And it was Chris's turn.

He shrugged amiably, mind galloping, things swimming into unbidden focus. He saw his own living room in the big A-frame, Frank Springer pacing before the coffee table with his glass of wine, expounding on the virtues of ancient Russia.

Chris chewed leisurely, aping boredom. "For the most part, yes. Though I think you've got your dates a bit confused there. Russia's legendary Rurik founded the nation's initial dynasty in the ninth century, as I recall, not the seventh. Of course," he smiled companionably, "I could be wrong."

Godunov flashed gleaming teeth, sipped daintily at his wine glass. "No, I believe you're right, it was the ninth. Dear me, the mighty huntsman grows older. Tell me, it was Yaroslav who pushed out from Novgorod and took Kiev in 778, wasn't it? Subjugated the nearby tribes and negotiated that arms treaty with the Byzantines?"

Chris took a moment to sip more of the sweet wine, gone abruptly sour in his mouth. Brain on overdrive, facts, numbers, nuances, and mental pictures flashed between synapses like cannon fire. He made a great show of not talking with his mouth full, secretly forcing himself calm.

It will come. Blank your mind and it will come.

It always came, unless he tried to force it.

Relax, don't concentrate. . . . It will come as a gift.

"Mr. Springer?"

Chris smiled nervously. "Please, Ivan, call me Frank."

"Thank you, I'd like that. It was Yaroslav, was it not?"

Chris, mind blank, pushed away his plate. "My dear Ivan, could it be that you've constructed some sort of test here? That you doubt my veracity?"

Godunov grinned like a Cheshire cat. If he'd had a tail it would be swishing. "Not at all, good sir. But certainly the real Frank Springer would be apprised of such mundane details about his mother Russia."

Chris folded his napkin solemnly, finally gave a patient sigh. "Well now, I'm afraid you've got me there."

Godunov's smile widened, all mirth drained from it. Across the room, Chris imagined Slevenski's hands tightening on the wonderful new rifle.

Chris looked to Sarah, who could offer him nothing but her beauty and terror.

It gave him—even under these dreadful circumstances—a strange sense of elation, her terror, a feeling of being somehow ahead of her at last, of being the one in control. The entire evening, the rest of their lives, hinged on him, on his next words.

He felt almost giddy with power. Strangely unafraid, bold, in fact, with sudden, newfound courage. Isn't that strange? he thought.

He sat back in the chair, folded his arms. Godunov was still waiting.

Chris cocked a brow, looked ceilingward. "No . . ."

Waited, for effect, feeling without seeing, the Russian leaning slightly forward in his own chair.

"No . . . as I recall, it went something like this. Russia's initial ruler was a man named Oleg. It was he who pushed out of Novgorod, not Yaroslav. And the year was 879, not 779, I believe. And let's see, yes, it was a trade treaty he negotiated with the Byzantines, not an arms treaty. A very lucrative trade treaty, as I recall."

Chris looked down at Godunov, who was no longer smiling, face impassive, impossible to read.

Chris continued: "It was Igor and Olga who extended Kiev's real power. Olga was the true champion here. When the tax-burdened subjects murdered her husband she retaliated brutally. As regent, however, she was a magnificent leader, later canonized as Russia's first truly influential convert to the Christian faith. As for Yaroslav the Wise, the great law giver, I believe he brought Kievan Russia to its true zenith, was a man of peace. Vladimir came next, didn't he, or do I have that mixed up?"

No one spoke at the table.

Godunov finally hinted at a sly smile.

Chris took another sip of wine, used the movement to glance at his watch: ten after twelve. If the power company was true to its word, the room would be black within five or six minutes.

"Very impressive, Mr. Springer."

Chris glanced askance at Sarah, found admiration in her weary face, a wedge of hope?

"What about you, Ivan? Your own lineage? 'Godunov.' A distant relative of the infamous Boris Godunov, by any chance?"

The Russian's mouth became a flat, mirthless line. "Infamous?"

Chris shrugged, into it now, maybe even overconfident, sensing he had nothing to lose. Another plan—assuming everyone stayed seated where they were—was forming elsewhere in his brain. If there was time. "You think the term inaccurate?" he asked, falling into the Russian's speech rhythms. "Forgive me, Ivan. I certainly didn't mean to offend such a gracious host."

"What makes you say infamous? Boris Godunov was one of the key players in the growth of Russian history."

Chris nodded, tossing a fry into his mouth. "He was certainly that. A very astute man. For a semiliterate."

Godunov frowned, and Sarah gave an involuntary gasp.

Chris, unabated, pursued more fries. "A Tartar, wasn't he? His sister was married to Fedor, then in rule. Godunov exploited the connection, made himself de facto ruler of Russia through it. There was a particularly interesting death in 1591, as I recall. An accident—or was it a murder. What do you think, Ivan?"

"I'm afraid I'm not familiar with the incident," the Russian replied evenly.

Chris felt Sarah's fingers needling his arms, shrugged them off. "No? It became the hub of a rather complex political era throughout Russia. It was a ten-year-old boy as I understand it—a mere child—found with his throat cut. Prince Dimitri." Chris looked across at Slevenski. "Say, that's your name, isn't it?"

Slevenski returned a look of hatred.

Chris demolished the remainder of the fries. "Of course, no evidence was ever uncovered to prove foul play, but it was certainly a political windfall for Godunov. He was elected czar shortly thereafter. After which, of course, there followed the country's infamous—that word again—Time of Troubles. Not a very good leader, I'm afraid."

Sarah shrank back in her chair. *What are you doing?*

Chris calmly chewed his fries, didn't even have to look at Godunov's face to feel the fury there.

That the Russian remained composed was perhaps the most amazing thing of all. "Excellent, Mr. Springer, which I think we can safely call you now. Your knowledge of Russian history is nothing short of astonishing. Almost . . . what is the word?"

He turned to Slevenski, Chris feeling a momentary slip of confidence.

" 'Eidetic,' " Slevenski supplied with a smirk.

Chris felt the slip turn to vertigo.

" 'Eidetic,' yes, that's it. An unusual quirk of the memory, gifted to one individual in a thousand, if my homework is correct. You wouldn't know of such an individual yourself, would you, Mr. Springer. It *is* Mr. Springer, is it not?"

Chris swallowed wine quickly to hide the other swallow. His watch read twelve-fifteen. The lights burned brightly.

"Afraid not," Chris answered, bravado fading, though not, he hoped, to anyone's notice.

Godunov stood, made his way to a teakwood end table, selected a fat tome from atop it, began leafing through it casually. Slevenski was grinning his weasel grin without restraint. Something was up.

"Of course," from Godunov, "your history of my descendants is hardly esoteric information. Not a few of your countrymen have read Pushkin. You recall Alexander Pushkin, Mr. Springer?"—giving *Springer* an added weight so it sounded phony—"and the wonderful Mussorgsky opera, of course, both works of which are named *Boris Godunov.* I believe each can be found in the average high school curriculum." His fingers riffled the pages of the book, found what he sought. Godunov smiled. "Here, however, is a less familiar bit of Russian iconography. You are a student of art history as well, Mr. Springer?"

Chris froze, abruptly out of his depth.

Godunov, beaming, held up the book, turned it about for the entire room to see, a brightly colored motif illustrated there. "This one, perhaps. A mythical siren. A creature with the body of a bird, the head of a beautiful woman. Said, since classical times, to have lured mariners to their deaths."

Even from here, Chris recognized the design, and his wonderful memory turned to his wife, her right breast specifically, the still-weeping tattoo embedded there, Frank Springer's rueful smile.

Heart thudding painfully, Chris glanced at his watch: twenty past.

Godunov smiled congenially, all composure, the perfect host. "Not that I have for a moment been in doubt of your veracity, sir, but as I'm sure you know, the real Frank Springer was quite entranced with these archaic markings. To the extent that he utilized them, in tattoo form, on the person of his wife. Not common knowledge, mind you, but like you, we have our sources."

Chris heard Sarah draw an uneven breath.

Godunov closed the book gently, replaced it carefully. "Indelicate as it may be, I think you'll agree the situation warrants, shall we say, unusual decorum. Mrs. Springer?"

Sarah jerked as if stabbed. "What?"

"Would you do us the honor, please?"

She gaped at the Russian, turned in horror to Chris. Back to the Russian. "What are you talking about?"

Godunov made an impatient sound, turned, and gestured to Slevenski, who was out of his chair in a greedy instant—setting down the rifle—around and behind Sarah, quick and graceful as a dancer. It was at that precise moment, Chris—hitherto not certain—was convinced the four of them were alone in the house, perhaps on the entire island of rock. It was a moment of acute revelation.

Holding her in place with his left hand, Slevenski used his right to urge Sarah from her chair, rip away her blouse in a single, smooth motion. She stood naked to the waist but for her bra.

Godunov regained his own chair confidently. "The right breast, I believe, Dimitri. . . ."

Chris's left hand dropped casually from the table to his knee, then his side. It hovered over his boot.

Slevenski gathered the material at Sarah's breast in his fist, made as if to rip it free.

"Dimitri, *please*! We are not uncivilized!"

Slevenski relaxed his grip, unhooked the bra in front patiently, pulled away the cups.

Godunov, glass to lips, actually choked on his wine.

Chris felt his own jaw start to drop—had to stop himself.

Slevenski's imperious demeanor, begun in triumph, faded when he saw his boss's expression, went white when he turned to behold the delicately tattooed design above Sarah's breast.

Chris could only stare.

Finally he looked into her eyes, read, at long last, the whole truth there. Her last deceit, her final surprise to all of them. Sarah Rawlings. Formerly Sarah Springer.

And Chris understood it all then: It hadn't been merely a company commission. Her hatred of Springer ran deeper even than the probing sting of the tattoo needle. It was probably why she had been granted the mission at all—a nearly suicidal task—because the department knew she alone possessed the blind passion to carry the thing off.

Godunov, always the obedient host, was the first to recover his composure, glaring vehemently at the befuddled Slevenski, who was still blankly ogling Sarah's naked breast. "Cover her, you fool!"

Sarah snatched up the remnants of her blouse, clutched it to her ignominiously.

For the first time since their meeting, Chris, himself still stunned to silence, actually heard Godunov stutter. "My apologies, sir! I hope—y-you must understand, distrust is a part of our business."

Chris found himself repressing the giddy urge to laugh. The fumbling acquiescence of this world-renowned assassin and child killer was almost endearingly sincere. The slaughtering of babies was inconsequential, but decorum was all. It was beyond ludicrous.

Godunov turned, slightly less nonplussed, to Sarah. "My sincere apologies, Mrs. Springer, for our boorish behavior. We are alone in the house, or I would have had one of the maids . . ." He turned in cold fury to Slevenski. "Will you get this young woman some decent *apparel*!"

Slevenski, bordering on panic, swept quickly across the living room rug toward the back of the house.

He was just past the Eames chair—the chair holding the rifle—approximately the same distance from the piece as Chris was, when the room went abruptly black.

CHAPTER 24

Naked, Matty sought the brightest bloodred lipstick from her jewelry box, popped the gold cap before the bedroom's tall bath mirror, and applied it expertly, deep red wax over paler red lips. She pursed those lips at the mirror, mashed them into a flat line, pursed again, stood back critically, and finally nodded. Yes.

She picked up the translucent novelty nightie from the sink, slid it up and over narrow shoulders, where it fell, then caught at impeding breasts. Matty reached up to nudge it down, pausing again on impulse, retrieving the gold lipstick tube, hesitating. Then, holding the filmy material away with one hand, she carefully applied the deep red lipstick to each of her coral nipples.

She stood back, nodded satisfaction once more, letting the gauzy nightie fall; it stopped just above the dark V of her crotch. She reached for the filmy panties, held them—eyes on her reflection—and hesitated again. Finally she tossed them on the sink again. Yes. Better without the panties. The silly things were invisible anyway.

She cupped her breasts a moment, lifted, head tilted speculatively, let them fall again, sag. But not much: heavy but firm, jutting, inviting. You could just see the dark tattoo through the nightie. He would like that, seeing his tattoo, his mark on her. She hoped.

She took her thickest-tined plastic brush, pulled it with measured strokes through coppery curls until they shone. Naturally curly, she'd never had much use for curling irons and plastic tubes. The hair needed cutting—past that point, really—but he'd never know. Men never did.

She put down the plastic brush, assessed herself in the harsh bathroom light (the bedroom would be kinder), thought: Okay, okay, that's enough, you're fine, get on with it. And left the bathroom to its glare.

Matty came back into the bedroom, rummaged through the stereo cabinet opposite the bed, found the *Niagara Falls Concerto* CD, positioned it, punched it in, and filled the room with soft thrumming. She turned, reflected a moment, turned back, nudged the stereo's graphic equalizers down to deep bass, transformed the room to a thunderous torrent.

She came to the bed, regarded its pastel sheets a moment, almost imploringly, drew them back, and lay her warmth across their crisp coolness. She lay there and tried to conjure images of sexy *Playboy* foldouts. She attempted a couple of inviting positions, curved her hip so, her arms back. Don't overdo it; this is probably obvious enough.

She lay there and waited for him. He would hear the CD's thunder eventually, and he would investigate.

Matty waited, a spider in her web.

Frank Springer said, "What are you doing?"

He said it from the bedroom doorway, having appeared there magically, soundlessly, making Matty jump a little inside but only there. On the outside, she was long and soft and patiently inviting atop the cool sheets.

"Just listening . . ."

Springer listened too for a moment. "What is it?"

"Don't you know?"

Springer listened. "Sounds different."

"I deepened the bass a bit, more like being there. Do you like it?"

He seemed to think about it from the doorway. "Little obvious, kitten, wouldn't you say?"

Matty lay with pounding heart.

No point in trying to bluff past it. The best way to combat suspicion with Frank Springer was to own up to it, use it against him. "It's supposed to be. Listen. It's beautiful."

"What are you up to, puss?"

In for a pound, Matty replied calmly, "Listening. Just listening and remembering."

"In your hot little nightie?"

She didn't answer for a moment. Then, dismissively: "Is it against the house rules? Sorry. I thought you liked it."

She heard his soft chuckle. "You're so sexy when you're curt. Why are you trying to seduce me?"

Ready for it, Matty rolled to her side, pale hip jutting into moonlight, nightie riding up just enough. "I think you know why."

He stayed in the doorway. She could not really see him, just his shadow. "No, I don't. Why don't you tell me?"

"Our son is sick. He needs attention."

"And you think I'll give him that if you let me fuck you?"

"No. This isn't about him. This is about me. Punishing me through him. You did it very effectively. But it's time to stop now and do something else."

"Is it now? And what is that, sweet kitten?"

"It's time to get on with it, Frank. I can't beat you; they can't beat you; no one can beat you. I'm tired of it. Tired and afraid for our son. I want you to stop this now, take us away from here, get on with our lives. Whatever they may be."

He lingered in the doorway, a vague lump. "Whatever they may be. . . ."

The room swelled with thundering water. You could almost feel the mist.

"Take us away where, kitten? Niagara Falls mayhaps?"

"Fine, anywhere. Only stop this, Frank. Anything is better than this."

Springer grunted from the doorway. "Is that supposed to be an inducement?"

"Why don't you shut up and come over here and lie next to me?"

The lump remained unmoving. "What have you got over there, a pistol under the pillow?"

"Come over and see."

And to her surprise, as though it was all going to be too easy, he did come over.

He stood in the wan light of the window, half of him dark, half ghostly silver. Matty looked up to find his pants front tented. And seeing this, she stretched languidly on the bed, like a fine young animal.

"Why the sudden change of heart, kitten?"

Head back, hair cascading across the pillow, Matty answered, "It's a trap. Chris is hiding in the closet, ready to pounce the moment you touch me."

Springer smiled. "Sweet little bitch." He went to his knees, seemed to inspect this bounty for a moment in the weak window light, put his face down there, kissed her softly, then deeper.

Matty made herself tangle her fingers in his hair, made herself gasp as with pleasure, body stiff with revulsion. Arched, then bowed, pushed his head deeper, gritting her teeth, thinking of Chris, then wiping that away, all of it away, making her mind just white, clean and white as the empty ceiling above. Don't think, not at all. . . .

To her unending gratitude, he stopped that after a time, stood, and got out of his clothes. His erection, a nodding spear, seemed to fill the room, made the room feel smaller.

Eyes closed, she felt the bed give as he knelt. She tensed just the slightest to accept him, to get this part of it done, concentrating on the syringe; when he's inside, when he's grunting and out of control, whip it back and plunge it into his buttocks or arm or—

All this was interrupted with white shock by a distant familiar buzzing in her ears, a forceful, insistent buzzing that became the doorbell downstairs, buzzing and buzzing with strident urgency, ruining completely whatever mood she'd conjured. Matty nearly cursed aloud. *Not now!*

She turned on the bed to find him pushing up, going to the window, erection and all, pulling back the curtained sheer an inch, and gazing down into luminous snow below. "You've got a visitor."

Matty—relieved, infuriated—joined him shakily at the bedside window, gazed down, and felt her anger dip to nearly laughable irony. "It's John Antler Horn."

"The Indian who left with his pie. He lives around here?"

Matty sighed, pushed back hair in disarray. "He's our nearest neighbor, three miles down the shore."

"Jesus, he must be freezing."

The old Indian wore only a T-shirt and opened checkered flannel, jeans, and sockless moccasins.

"He's brought something," Matty said.

"Yes, a book."

To her horror, Frank—still naked, still hard—began tapping at the frosty window. Tapping until the wind-creased, ancient face—just visible in porch light—looked up, regarded them quizzically with dark eyes.

Matty jerked back, but Springer held her firm, pushed her into cold window glass, her lushness aglow from reflective light of snow-mantled yard.

"Frank, *stop* it! He'll see me!"

Springer, grinning tightly, gripped her firmly, holding her to the window.

The old Indian was calling up to them, a muffled warble.

Matty stopped struggling, knowing that looked all the worse, finally lifted the window a notch so bitter air wafted greedily in, kissed and shrunk her pouting vulva. "Hello, John!"

She wasn't at all sure the old man could see clearly from this distance, though he craned upward in a seemingly pleasurable effort to do so. He held up the book. "I bring Chris Nielson wind sailer! I tow it across lake, tie it to dock? You understan'?"

Matty tried to wriggle free, felt Springer's grip turn to iron.

"I bring Chris Nielson new book on wind sailing. Better than first book. He go sailing with me now, very soon. Soar like hawk."

Springer, apparently greatly amused at this, barked a laugh, held Matty firm.

"That's fine, John," Matty said. "Thank you, but Chris isn't home just now."

A mistake, probably, because the old Indian's eyes shifted to the form behind her. If it wasn't Chris's dark form, then whose?

"Could you possibly bring the book back, Mr. Antler Horn?" What was Springer up to now, shifting around back there, giggling to himself. . . .

The old Indian called up something unintelligible.

Matty grimaced in reluctance, inched the window up another notch, freezing crotch and tummy now. "I'm sorry—what did you say?"

Goddamn it! She could feel Springer probing at her now with that big thing. She tried to reach back and swat him away, but he only gripped tighter, giggling.

"I come long way in cold! Bring fine new wind sailer! You come down and get book for Chris Nielson!"

Matty shook her head. "No, I'm not dressed, I'm—" She sucked in a breath, colored, snorted in surprise as Frank slipped past—hurting—then inside her . . . her legs wobbling . . . slid slow, quicker, very quickly up up up all the way to all there was.

Matty, legs flailing, gripped the windowsill, face like a stuck frog, made a deep, nearly musical sound.

Antler Horn regarded her curiously from the porch.

Stupid, Matty was thinking, being lifted now, airborne, her feet clearing the bedroom carpet, perched on Springer's rampant loins, his dark spear, his terrible strength rekindling awful memories. *Hoisted on his own petard*, Matty thought, and stupid, stupid, she should never have told Antler Horn Chris was gone, her whoring undeniable now.

The old man watched calmly as Springer hoisted higher, mashing her unmercifully against the cold pane until her breasts became squashed doughnuts whose holes were the darker areolas, her face flattened too against the frosty glass, nose and lips smushed. *"Frank, you son of a bitch!"*

That only elicited more breathy giggles from him, accompanied by excited grunts. "Come on in!" he shouted to the old Indian. "Bring the book upstairs!"

To Matty's horror, the old man started for the door, found it locked, of course.

He came back to below the window to stare at the antics of the two strange people above. "The door is locked!"

Springer shoved hard, slamming her into the pane so she was sure it must shatter, her breasts making squeegee sounds against it, nipples puckering resentfully against the cold.

"Mr. Antler Horn, please *go away!*"

The old man frowned indignantly, either unaware, uncomprehending, or unimpressed with what transpired above him. "I come long way with book for Chris Nielson. Teach him go wind sailing with John Antler Horn. Soar like hawk."

Matty cried out as Springer dug his nails into her buttocks, approaching the end. "Jesus!" he gasped pleasurably, "that cold breeze on my nuts!"

Antler Horn rang the buzzer indignantly.

"Please, just *go away*! Chris will pick up the book tomorrow!"

Then the breath was knocked out of her as Springer slammed her, uncaring, into the molding. He grunted, spasmed.

"I go! But not come back!" from below.

The old man scowled at them, turning to march off through the snow, shirt flapping, turning again to purse wide purple lips at them. "You fuck like prairie chicken!" Then trudging off again into cold and shadow and finally black.

Springer, spent, let her down by degrees. Matty's frozen breasts slipped past the painful molding, down, her toes, then heels brushing carpet again.

Frank slid under her, still holding her hips, slid under and out, taking what felt like part of her with him, leaving a pearl of empty aching.

Springer slid farther, to his knees, where he settled, resting, holding her up trembling with his powerful arms, holding her in place, hot face pressed to her thigh.

Matty closed her eyes, throbbing head cooled against cold glass, back burning up, front numb with chill, thinking. He came, he came already, and I didn't get the syringe, didn't even get close to it.

Somehow she'd have to get him back on the bed again.

She might have fallen asleep, couldn't quite remember, but she was awake for sure now and he was back, standing by the bed again, nude, gazing down at her.

Matty blinked, started to look away, but there was something in his eyes. Something new.

She looked up. "What is it?"

Springer didn't talk for a time, then came, finally, and sat close to her, something—she couldn't, in the dark, see just what—clutched in his hand.

"I'm sorry," he said, with apparent sincerity.

Matty pulled the sheet to her breasts.

He gestured as if about to touch her face, held himself in check. "That was really unforgivable. Disgusting. He seemed like a nice old man. I don't know what gets into me. I really don't. Will you accept my apology?"

Matty said nothing.

He looked down at his hands. "I don't blame you. Listen, I've been thinking. My problem is a thing of trust. In my profession you're taught not to trust anyone. At any time." He sighed, the movement shaking the bed slightly.

Springer shook his head. "This isn't going well. I'm not used to apology, wasn't trained for it." He shrugged naked muscular shoulders. "Anyway, my point is that without trust, you have, eventually—well, you have nothing at all. Sooner or later you have to trust something, someone. It's the basis, I suppose, of all religion."

He looked up at her. His eyes were glistening. Surely not tears. Matty held herself back from believing.

"I'm going to show you something. Something I'm not supposed to be showing you, something they gave me, would be very unhappy if you were to know about." He held up a small black case, the size of a cigarette pack. Turned it over in his hand, almost admiringly. "It's a homing device. An advanced—extremely advanced—kind of receiver. Watch. . . ."

Springer thumbed the object and a red flashing dot appeared on its surface. He smiled at her, his face flashing red . . . dark . . . red . . . dark . . . "That's you."

She looked up at him. "Me?"

"The flashing red dot. That tells me where you are." He stood, crossed the room, holding the device up. "See, the flash is slightly less powerful the farther I get from you. It will flash, however, within a three-mile radius."

He came back to the bed, handed her the plastic square.

Matty took it, thumbed the button until it stopped flashing. "What's this one for?"

"Push it."

She thumbed the second button below the first. A greenish dot began to flash.

Matty nodded. "Nicky."

"Yes."

She turned it off, handed it back to him. "No wonder you weren't unduly concerned about leaving the house."

He smiled.

"What's it transmitting off, that stuff you've been injecting us both with?"

"A mild, very mild radium solution."

"Radium!"

"No more toxic than that used in a common barium enema."

He looked down at the device. "Of course, with prolonged injections, a young child can grow ill . . ."

Matty gasped, pushed up and past him. Springer caught her. "Please! I'm trying to tell you. I'm not going to inject him anymore. I'm not going to inject either of you. I want us to trust each other, Matty. Do you think I'd be showing you this otherwise?"

She sat rigidly, enduring his pinning arms. "I think you'd do anything for a cruel joke."

"No joke this time. You have my word. I know you want out of this, Matty. So do I. Far out. Far away from them. You can trust me. The question is, can I trust you?"

She looked at him. "What do you want, Frank? You just humiliated me in front of my closest neighbor."

"I apologized for that. Look, it probably made the old geezer's day."

Matty looked away, unamused.

"I'm sorry. I've told you how sorry I am. But I've been doing a lot of thinking, kitten. A lot. And there's a way out of this. A chance for me, for both of us, all three of us, if you want it."

She stared into space. "What are you suggesting, Frank?"

"Come away with me."

She looked at him. "How?"

"It can be done. I have friends that can make sure it's done. Friends that will get us out of the country, for good. After one brief stopover."

She waited.

"I want to go back to the falls. I want to go back to our honeymoon lodge, to start over. To blank out the past. One brief evening with you at the falls. Then, into Canada and out of the country forever. Will you come? Will you think about it at least? Just say you'll consider it."

She sat quietly, his arms still around her. "How can I believe you?"

"Trust."

She shook her head. "I don't know. I'd have to sleep on it."

He seemed to relax. "Of course. I want you to."

Still gripping her gently, he laid her back down on the bed, pulled the sheet demurely over her breasts, bent, and kissed her tenderly on the forehead. Matty closed her eyes.

When she opened them he was still sitting there, smiling disarmingly. "Sleep tight."

He started to get up, turned as she touched his arm. "Frank?"

He bent down to hear.

"Kiss good night?"

He smiled, bent farther, and found her lips, started to pull back, and was stopped by her encircling arms, her probing tongue.

She maneuvered on the bed to make room for him, get him over and on top of her. He was more than ready, excited by her acquiescence?

Not pondering it, taking advantage of the moment, Matty reached down and guided him inside. Once there, his rocking movements gained a familiar rhythm. He seemed more relaxed this time, more patient. Perhaps he hadn't been lying. She pushed against him with a will, let him linger over her breasts, her right arm dangling with apparent abandon over the side, over the mattress, what lay beneath.

Into it now, jamming his mouth over hers, Frank increased his lunges, grinding down heavily, mashing her breasts. She had to yank away from his sucking mouth just to breathe. "Hey. That's hurting a little. . . ."

Which he ignored, past that now, grabbing her legs roughly, urgently under the knees, pulling high while shoving hard, her head slamming the headboard. "Please, that's really hurting!"

He didn't seem to hear, shoved, and banged her head in a rhythmic tempo that boomed louder than the thundering falls. He came up on his knees, a force of nature now, using her like a battering ram, heedless of her agony, oblivious to all but his own pleasure.

"Please!"

Slamming her, slamming. His face, when she looked up, locked in a cruel smile, eyes glinting. "It's not under there, kitten!"

Matty felt an explosion of icy adrenaline.

Frank slammed harder, laughing, head back. "I found the syringe yesterday!" And this seemed to put him over the edge. His features darkened, face flush with the rush of his orgasm.

Matty's fury welled up with a force almost apart from her, his gritted teeth, piggy grunts flooding her with abrupt, white-hot rage. Not even aware of it, her right fist swept back in preparation to strike that imperious face—swept back and hit the clock radio, the heavy bedside lamp. . . .

The lamp was in her hand before she knew it, the hand not really attached to the rest of her, possessing a life of its own. It gripped and swung the heavy lamp into the side of his hot, grinning face, bringing a bright burst of crimson, tearing him painfully free of her so they both cried out, the look of mixed pleasure and pain on his stupefied face almost funny.

Springer shunted sideways, slow-motion rag-doll limp, hips still mindlessly jerking, like a dog fucking air. He landed crumpled between bed and wall, eyes glazed, fighting for focus, knowing his life depended on it. Matty was on him in an instant, screaming, a high-pitched whine she did not recognize as herself, shrieking, slamming the heavy Santa Fe lamp into his face. Again, then again. Until the thick crockery cracked and Springer lay there void of comprehension, face vacuous, hair afire.

She squatted over him, breasts pendulous, chest heaving, raised the remains of the lamp with another hysterically triumphant shriek. Some part of her saw—as from a distance—the big limbering cock nod a gout of oblivious dribble, and she found she could not hit him again, did not have it in her to make the matted, crimson head black with his brains.

Instead, she kicked him once with her bare foot to see if he'd move, kicked again, and he slipped sideways down the wall, leaving a smear of blood, her own heel slipping in it. She tossed the lamp after him and ran, ran, ran, naked and blood-flecked, for the baby's room.

Nicky was waiting peacefully there, asleep and already dressed for this part of it, bundled warmly in his little parka, boiling hot because of this, but she could think of no other way and was glad now she'd prepared him. Matty grabbed him up, raced back to the bedroom for her own winter clothes hanging ready and pre-arranged in the closet. She shrugged into them, into boots and mittens, mind racing, eyes avoiding the bloody corner.

She grabbed Nicky again, murmuring, "Come on, baby, come on, baby, come on, baby," racing for the stairway, Frank leaping at her from the shadows, burying his knife in her back—

But not really. Only shadows. Matty ran down the stairs, two at a time, at the door now, hesitating one final time.

The knife.

Go into the kitchen and get the big carving knife from the top drawer. Take it up there in the darkness and put it into him, again and again until you're *sure* he's dead, really dead and would hurt no one anymore.

Hesitating but thinking too of John Antler Horn, of the vast, frozen lake, of the ice boats being her only hope and she not at all confident she could navigate one.

Out the door now, winter night stinging her eyes, legs churning, vapored breath billowing, Matty ignored the car, choosing the path John Antler Horn had taken, following the old Indian's footprints.

Hoping the old man hadn't yet left the dock.

Praying the sudden crunching behind her was some woodland animal in the snow, not Frank Springer, bloody and deranged, leaping down the mountain in pursuit.

CHAPTER 25

The moment the room went black, Chris was in motion.

He was out of his chair and diving, the ghost of the room's furniture lingering on his retina, headlong across the coffee table for the special rifle.

He might have made it. Might have grasped it perfectly even in blackness, had the emergency battery lights not flared an instant later, setting the room aglow against deep shadows.

The surprised but ever alert Slevenski spun, made his own dash. They reached the weapon at the same moment.

Chris, though, in his dive managed to capture only part of the wood stock with his right hand. The oily, slippery barrel he grasped in his left. Slevenski had the better grip, just in front of the trigger guard and under the butt. It would be a tug-of-war, the Russian clearly owning the advantage.

They locked, spun grimly, danced a comic two-step about the now dimmer room, synchronous as lovers: two figures as one—one grunt, one gasp—independent in their search for the better leverage, the precise angle that would spill the other free. Chris, teeth gritted, thought: This is all moot anyway—Ivan Godunov over there is going to reach calmly into his desk drawer, pull out a Russian pistol, put a bullet through the back of my head.

But as he and Slevenski danced around the spinning room—Sarah's tight face flashing by spectrally—Chris saw nothing of the master assassin. He'd either ducked low when Chris dived at the rifle or gotten out of there altogether. And now even Sarah seemed to have disappeared.

Slevenski, slim as a boy, proved weight-lifter strong, like those lithe Hong Kong street fighters, tenacious with speed. Jerking and pushing, using the weapon between them as a battering ram, the little weasel smashed Chris over the teak table with a musical clattering of broken things, knocked him into the unforgiving stone fireplace, nearly driving the wind from him. Chris held on, everything spinning now.

Slevenski pulled him out and around, Chris's hands melded to the rifle, mind on hold, aware only that his hands must not leave the rifle. The Russian yanked him into a wall, pulled back, and yanked him into the adjoining wall, Chris seeing flashing lights amid the dimming room. Finally, using the American's superior weight against him, Slevenski threw himself backward (a trick Chris should have seen coming), pulling the bigger man up and over to somersault and finally lose his hold on the weapon.

Chris, slammed hard on his back, ignored lancing pain through vertebrae and skull, scrambled around in deep shadow, not even trying for the gun again, going for the boot shiv while still on his knees.

Finding its smoothly wrapped hilt—seeing Rick Corman's grinning face—he withdrew the slim prison knife, coming up as the Russian shoved the bore of the rifle in Chris's chest and pulled the trigger. . . .

Whether the Russian had—in his haste—merely forgotten about the safety or whether this new weapon's design was simply foreign to him, the gun did not discharge. The Russian had an instant's respite to look down for the elusive safety before Chris sent the shiv in and deep at the other's solar plexus, nicked his lower sternum bone, and halted a moment before going deeper still. It produced a soundless, nearly grateful look of surprise across Slevenski's pale face, a silent rictus of yellowed teeth in need of dental care that froze, became his final response to this world.

He slipped back and off the blade, proffering in falling—almost handing—Chris the rifle. The Russian lay still, curled, as in sleep.

Chris flicked off the safety as Sarah had taught him, spun with the rifle, its muzzle scouring the dim room for Godunov's furtive form. Finding nothing.

Sudden movement to his right. Chris swung quickly, nearly pulling the trigger, halted by Sarah's alarmed "It's *me*!"

"Where's the Russian?"

"Not in the living room! I think he's taken a powder!" She bent over Slevenski's corpse, finding and withdrawing a Swiss automatic. "Come *on*!" She grabbed Chris's shirt front—taking some skin—pulling him toward the window as though this miracle turn of events was a gift not to be wasted. She yanked him to the sill, shoved it up with a grunt, leapt gracefully out and into freezing wind and snow. Chris vaulted after with the rifle, waiting but not receiving Godunov's ghostly slugs tearing into his back.

He landed on the run, pinwheeling, then finding his balance with the heavy rifle. Sarah was already far ahead calling back, "The chopper! We can't let him get to the chopper!"

Chris, not able to prevent himself from slowing for a paranoid moment, swiveled the dark rifle muzzle here and there in an erratic arc, so sure Godunov would descend on them from that shadowed hedge, this snow-capped outcropping, raining lead on them.

Where the hell was he?

"Chris, cover me!" Sarah called, already at the chopper door, bent low in case the Russian was hiding within. She reached out, jerked open the door, which showed an apparently empty cockpit.

Sarah leapt in, leaning into the console. "I'm taking the keys!"

Chris was flushed with sudden dread, didn't know why just yet. Except that the great Russian assassin was gone and it was too quiet, too easy. . . .

"Sarah! No!"

He ran after her—certain suddenly—arms thrown up and out, rifle dragging at him. *"Sarah!"*

His world went up in a dull orange plume. The shock wave hit first, knocking him flying, the chopper tank's fireball chasing close behind the roar of explosion, a heat so intense he must surely be incinerated.

But the snowbank he was thrown behind prevented that, if not the sunburn smear on nose and brow. When he scrambled up again to look, most of the heat and fire was already billowing skyward, borne by a black pall of greasy smoke, lighting the entire island of rock for a moment. There was little left of the helicopter but black, twisted skeletons. Chris mouthed "Sarah" silently.

Godunov's unearthly chuckle, echoing through the island's PA system, followed the concussion so quickly it seemed theatrically prearranged. "A pity. I do so detest the wasting of perfectly good pulchritude, especially when such exceptional breasts are involved. Wouldn't you agree, Mr. Nielson?" More basso chuckling, seeming to come from everywhere: the house, the lumps of snow-covered rock, the trees, everywhere, all around, making location impossible. It assured Chris—cringing stunned behind the snow-bank without the rifle—that he was doomed.

"Now, this is really much more what I had in mind. Count Zaroff against the most dangerous game, just the way it was in Mr. Connell's famous story. Delicious. And might I add, sir, a grand dry run for the more challengingly insane Mr. Springer. The *real* Mr. Springer. Who, I trust, will have better fortune than your-self." More speaker-tinny laughter just to keep in the spirit of things.

Chris, singed and tattered, near-deaf from the ringing concus-sion, ignored both pain and hidden speakers, pushed up and cast about for the rifle, his only hope. He knew full well what was coming next.

"Shall we start with the dogs, then? Just to keep true to the original scenario? Yes, I think so. . . ."

Chris sat perfectly still in the gathering dark, the chopper flames receding rapidly for lack of combustible material. He listened, head cocked, and heard the dogs before he saw them, the galloping impact of their paws, the light jingle of their collars. They weren't barking now. They were hunting. Silently, as if they'd done this sort of thing before.

He had no idea how many dogs there were or what kind (cer-tainly not the gentle borzois in the house) or if they—and Godunov—knew his exact location. He thought not, but that was just guessing.

Chris turned his head toward the growing rustle of their approach, guessed again at their direction (from the south end of the house where the pens must be kept), struggled up, and ran the opposite way, right over the fallen rifle, nearly tripping on it.

He snatched it up, knocking away snow clumps. The running sounds behind him were distinct now, clear as the icy night. He saw the lead Doberman lunging over a snowbank, black, graceful, and sleek with the breed's inimitable ghostly lope. He saw its ears prick at the sight of its quarry, saw the front incisors begin to show. Two more dogs quickly brought up the rear.

He lifted the CIA rifle, trembling, got off a clumsy round that kicked up snow far off target, not even breaking the lead dog's rhythm. He squeezed off a second round that exploded the lead dog's left ear and eye, tearing those away nearly bloodlessly so the creature snowplowed to its knees and stopped.

Chris sighted hastily and got off a third, then finally a fourth round that caught the next animal under the throat, ruining the main artery to the heart, which the dog ignored. It kept on coming, then collapsed—snapping—like a dropped marionette.

Chris sighted down again, or started to, before the third animal swept him up and high, teeth deep in his boot, through that and into flesh so Chris screamed once involuntarily, dropped the rifle, was shook, shunted sideways, released kicking, then bit again slightly higher through thinner cotton leggings. The dog, a grinning demon, was silent in its methodical destruction of him.

Chris felt himself slammed to the snow like a helpless hare. Terror-engulfed, he reached back and around, missed, scrabbling, then had the rifle, dragged it up, swung it muzzle first toward the flat, pointed head, the grinding teeth, placed it along spittle-flecked jawline, and blew the animal to hamburger.

"Dear me, now you've gone and given away your location." The basso voice, right next to Chris, made him spin, gasping, rifle before him. He found, nearly hidden behind a lump of rock, a short pole and snow-covered PA speaker. "Well! It's cozy like this, isn't it—just the two of us. I quite liked the nifty little phone company suits. And the power outage was marvelous. Sarah Rawlings was no surprise at all, however. You get so you can *smell* a CIA agent. Very distinct odor. The tattoo was a bit of a jolt, though, even for yourself, I think. Then again, commandeering a civilian is pretty inventive in itself, especially for a Western organization, usually so steeped in bureaucratic tradition. Rather artful, that. How on earth did they persuade you, Mr. Nielson? Not money alone, surely. Some sort of gold medal or citation, some once-in-a-lifetime tribute to Old Glory? Or something even closer to home? A wife perhaps? Something to do with our mutual friend, Mr. Springer?" Another metallic chuckle.

Chris peeked over the drift, saw the dark hulk of the house. Saw nothing else, no dogs, no Godunov.

"Oh, we're right in step, Mr. Nielson, with your best technology. An Apple computer by any other name, yes? We get all the latest transmissions. She's quite something, as I understand it, your Mrs. Nielson. Or is it Mrs. Springer? I do so confuse them. What's she up to at the moment, do you suppose? Fucking him, if my sources are correct. Fucking him rather smartly, as I understand it. I have some wonderful long-range pictures, by the way. Bit blurred, but I think you'll detect all the necessary details. Can I interest you in another glass of wine? We can have a slide show. Or shall we play the game out first? Yes, let's do that. First the hunt, then the naughty pictures." Much chuckling at this. "He has a rather large one, I'm told, our Mr. Springer. Do you think your wife . . . I mean, is she prepared to accommodate a man with Mr. Springer's attributes?"

Chris, hissing curses, blasted the speaker into a shriek of resentful metal, wasting yet another round.

It seemed to silence all the other speakers as well, for Godunov said nothing more.

Where was he?

Did he have more dogs? Were they coming for Chris right now? How many rounds did he have left?

What sort of weapon would the Russian use?

Chris crouched low in the snow, his breathing deep and shaky, a vague pain from possible broken ribs, not harsh enough to worry about. He longed for a lighter-colored jacket, thinking about reversing it so the paler wool lining would camouflage him somewhat. He found himself staring absently at his watch and remembered the power company.

Half an hour, they'd said, and the energy would be back on.

The watch told him he had just over eighteen minutes.

He dared to poke his head, try for another location fix. He could just barely make out the phone pole there to his right about two o'clock, already beginning to disappear behind a fresh curtain of falling snow.

What to do?

Chris considered it, getting his breath. Stay on the island and try to kill the Russian? Or go for the pole, try to swing across the canyon to the safety of the van? If the van was still there.

And what about Matty then? With the mission a failure, what of Matty and the boy?

He sighed, mind racing, looked down at the beautifully

designed weapon in his hand. He had a high-powered rifle, and he was sure he and the Russian were alone on the rock. It made the most sense to stay and fight.

But he had strong doubts about his chances against the greatest assassin in the world. And something kept tugging him toward the cliffside pole.

He crouched, trembling in the snow, repressing a burning urge to urinate.

Think . . . think!

A noise to his left—

Chris whirled, fired reflexively at nothing, hitting nothing, the round's echo knocking off across bitter, lonely canyons.

He heard Rick Corman's chuckling admonition. *He's gonna make you use up all your ammo, sport.*

Chris nodded at Corman's ghost, sat back, and removed his too-eager finger carefully from the trigger housing.

He looked up suddenly in revelation: use up his ammo . . .

Yes, but not so he could then shoot Chris. The Russian wouldn't play it that way—that crudely—using the gauche weapons of modern society. Like Springer, his kindred spirit, he'd · opt for the ancient Russian ways, close-in, hand-to-hand combat. Knives probably, law of the jungle and all that crap. Kill Chris the way Chris had Slevenski. Poetic justice. Guns were beneath a man of Godunov's standing. He'd want it close-up and personal, want to hear his victim's grunt, watch in triumph the light of life fade from the quarry's eyes.

He kept thinking about the phone pole.

With the chopper ruined, the power line was the only way off the island—at least for now—and for the Russian as well.

He thought about it. Assume for a moment Godunov was bluffing, knew nothing about tonight's plan, about the power company's time frame. If he saw Chris running for the pole, saw what he was up to—wouldn't he follow, probably without shooting, wouldn't he use the same escape route?

Or would he chance it, knowing that, if Chris made it across without mishap, he'd be waiting with the CIA rifle on the other side, Godunov an easy target?

But the Russian was the kind of man who loved challenges, cherished risks. That's what this *Most Dangerous Game* crap was all about. Godunov worshiped the chase.

Chris glanced at his watch again. He'd have to act now if he was going to act at all. In a matter of minutes the power would come surging back on. He wasn't even completely sure he could make it across now.

Yes. Get the Russian to the pole, get him to follow across the power line. He won't shoot. And he'll glory in the idea of Chris's running, fleeing in abject terror across the dizzy canyon on a slender line of hope, his fear of Godunov greater than that of falling.

He nodded to himself, could almost see Rick Corman nodding back; yes, the pole was the way.

Chris slung the rifle over his back, crouched low, and ran, loping, for the phone pole.

It was snowing heavily when he got there, visibility down to twenty yards or so. He adjusted the big rifle against his shoulder and, without the aid of the spikes now, began to shinny up the hard redwood pole.

He'd done it before, been caught and hauled away half a dozen times as a crackly voiced adolescent, climbed poles and trees and the sides of houses and anything he could find. Probably it was this passion for climbing that made him such a natural as a lineman. What was it Rick Corman always said? "You climb like a fucking monkey!"

He climbed now, clutching and inching, a methodical inch-worm, halfway, then beyond that. Knees pressed tight to cold red-wood, he still felt no accompanying vibration along the milled bark, the knocking thrum of another climber from below. Could it be this easy? Could he have outmaneuvered the master assassin with such ease?

Chris reached the phone lines, hesitated for breath—still feeling for vibrations from below—took the time to look down into swirling clouds of falling snow. Then he grunted upward once more, the heavy CIA weapon dragging, digging at his shoulder, threatening to topple him backward.

He craned up and saw the first set of crossbars, the dark length of the high tension lines. He paused again for breath, glanced at his watch through the swirl, and felt his breath catch.

The minute hand was not moving. The watch had stopped.

Chris gripped the pole one-handed, shook the watch, squinted again, found a hairline fracture, but deep, above the luminous 10 numeral, probably caused when the Doberman had slammed him to the earth.

How long had that been? Ten minutes? Eight?

He looked balefully out at the dark power lines trailing into darker night, doubtless coated with a lethal skin of ice. Even with a ten-minute loss of time, he should be able to swing across the short width of deep canyon within another ten.

Leaving him a good five minutes to spare.

If the power company was true to its word. If he wasn't slowed by icy lines, tricky canyon winds.

If he was really alone up here. But only if he began right now.

He undulated upward, came level with the closest high-tension wire, regarded it warily, began to reach a tentative finger toward it. He knew even the lightest touch—if the power was on—would fry him alive. Drawing deep breath, tensing, he stretched out, went for it with both hands.

He gripped tight, let go his legs to swing lazily into the air, a living pendulum, two hundred feet above rocky death. The weight of his body felt denser than he'd expected, back muscles cording, aching acutely already. He'd have to get this done quickly.

Hand beside hand then, gloves never leaving the wire, he began his journey across, not looking down, concentrating on the place-ment of his gloves, inching, sliding rather than swinging, in case he was met with unfriendly ice, the thick rubber insulation just fat enough for a decent grip. Any wider and he wouldn't get a decent purchase, any narrower and it would cut into his fingers. He could do this. . . . He could do this. . . .

Just past a quarter of the way, he felt a dragging desire to unburden himself of the heavy rifle. He hadn't counted on the additional weight being this cumbersome, unwieldy, the stock smacking at his back and butt, arms and fingers wrenching slowly from their sockets, a deep, knotting stitch starting across his shoul-ders that would only grow worse, perhaps even cramping up, locking his muscles, so he hung there, stiff and helpless. Before the plunge.

He wanted, grudgingly at first, then with growing desperation, to shift the rifle to the other shoulder, ease the terrible strain at his neck, but of course that was impossible, even if he could waste the time, which he could not.

A foreign pulsing, barely felt, traced the line. A vibration so feeble he thought it was caused by his own awkward movements. On impulse he twisted back, craned around.

The blood drained from his face: Godunov, a lithe spider, was swinging gracefully after him across the wire, hand over hand. He was grinning, moving as effortlessly as a circus performer, as though he'd done this all his life. His face, when clear of the powerful shoulders, beamed in triumph.

Chris heard himself whimper involuntarily, squinted across the gulf at the opposite pole. He knew he'd never make the thirty slippery feet to the safety of its cross beams before the Russian had him.

He tried anyway, continuing the sliding motion of his gloves at first, then—imitating Godunov and because it was faster—attempted the hand over hand.

He nearly lost his grip doing that, gasping in horror as the left glove let go completely, unimaginable pain and dread congealing in his right shoulder. He got himself a secure grasp again (although his fingers, stiff with cramping and cold, were nearing uselessness) started the sliding motion again, when the Russian was suddenly there. His heavy boots savagely kicked Chris's back, jarring his teeth, making his gloves slide but not quite slip along the narrow lifeline.

Another kick, to the kidneys this time. The Russian grunted happily with the effort, knowing exactly what he was doing. Another jolt to the base of the spine, Godunov chuckling delightedly, loving this.

Chris gasped in pain, hating to but having to give up the sliding technique, having—with great difficulty—to twist dangerously around and face his antagonist or be kicked off the wire. A wire that was drooping dangerously under their combined weight.

"Why didn't you wait on the cross beams?" Godunov asked, not even breathing heavily, wholly in his element up here. "You were safe on the cross beams. Why didn't you wait there and use the rifle as I came up?" He kicked out hard before Chris could respond, caught Chris in the ribs with the toe of his boot this time. Chris winced as the resulting pendulous movement cut into his fingers. One more of those and he'd have to let go. He couldn't hold on and he couldn't fight back.

The Russian, sensing it, kicked out again, both feet this time. But not into Chris's chest as expected. He kicked out and around, wrapping his legs about the American's stomach, tightened them like a lover, holding himself there, this further weight sending new spikes of agony up Chris's arms, across his exhausted shoulders, already paralyzed fingers.

Godunov chuckled merrily, began a swinging motion to end the game, laughing at the stupid American who had somehow had the balls to attempt this insanity. The Russian laughed and swung, a deranged ape, singing an old Russian song about boatmen and blond, buxom women. Sang and swung and waited. Until Chris's fingers—eyes and teeth jammed shut in mute agony—held no more elasticity, no more connection to the desperately commanding brain. And finally, nerveless and no longer really a part of his wrists, they let go of the wire. . . .

Chris fell.

But not far. Still gripped between the Russian's powerful thighs, Chris dangled there crazily, Godunov *still* laughing, singing, almost insanely pleasant, nearly soothing up there in the black friendless night. Chris knew he was close to passing out.

Still gripped between Godunov's seemingly tireless legs, Chris finally opened his eyes again. Beneath his snow-clumped boots he glimpsed a black, distant eternity into which flakes funneled, a lovely crystal maelstrom. With any luck he would not know the moment of impact, would not be aware.

"In the unlikely event you should survive a two-hundred-foot drop into solid granite, Mr. Nielson, please tell our friends at the CIA that I do not suffer impostors gladly. That it is Frank Springer I want. The real Frank Springer, the American covert genius. That I might, perhaps, in exchange for the pleasure of his company, have some very interesting information for them about a particular coming event in the midwestern portion of your great country. Can you remember that, sir? Or does your present situation make the whole thing quite moot?"

Chris grunted out of breath, ribs crushed between steel bands of flesh, thinking of the shiv in his boot. He might get to it even with his frozen fingers, might even thrust upward with a lucky shot, but then what if the Russian fell too—?

Godunov chuckled above him, a finality to the sound. "Very good, then. And a very good evening to you, sir. . . ."

And he let Chris drop.

It didn't seem to happen very fast at first. For the first few seconds, before the wind began to tear at his face, he felt almost afloat, as if he might actually survive such a hideous height ending in so much unforgiving hardness.

How many paratroopers—their gear fouled somehow—had suffered this? he wondered absently, his mind strangely lassitudinous, almost content now that the worst had happened. His brain—on weightless overdrive—raced ahead, past even the gory rocks below, past his own death to whatever—if anything—might be coming directly after that.

His last thought, before his chest was struck sharply, was of Matty. He was somehow quite grateful for that.

He was struck hard in the chest, but not by the rocks, by something elastic and giving that took the wind from him, jolted him back to now, back *up* a few feet. It was, of course, the narrow phone cable, stretched below the fatter power lines.

Chris's numbed fingers grabbed it instinctively, though they refused to work at all, much less grip a slender cable in a twelve-foot fall through cold and snow.

His fingers were useless, but not yet the arms. When the cable struck his chest, when the sharp line smacked his face, slapped him into focus, he wrapped his arms around himself determinedly, on the dim chance that even if he caught the narrow line in falling, it might actually hold him.

He did catch it, even managed to keep his arms locked stubbornly about his body. But the thin phone line, fragile in any situation, could hardly sustain (he knew this) the jolt of a two-hundred-pound man dropping upon it. It stretched resentfully, sang—an almost musical hum—then snapped with a rifle's crack at one end. Chris, falling again, was not at all sure which end.

Still gripping the thin wire, he saw that it was the end attached to the farthest pole, the far side of the canyon. He was sliding down it now, simultaneously sliding and swinging, arcing rapidly toward the *nearest* edge of the cliff. If he didn't run out of rapidly diminishing line—whipping, burning through his arms—he might actually make it to that nearest side as the line completed its arc, carrying him safely the rest of the way across the gulf. He might even live. If he didn't smash his brains out on the opposite pole . . .

But he ran out of line before that, the last of it slipping through his anxious arms, spilling him into empty space. Not, however, before he'd cleared the gulf—just cleared it—smashing not into the pole but into the wet snow beside it with a thump of finality. Deep enough to cushion, the snow, as much as the line, saved him.

Chris lay there facedown, half buried in the cold, soft embrace. Contemplating the miracle that he was not only no longer falling but actually alive.

In a moment, feeling the Russian's eyes on his back, he dug himself out, spitting snow, flopped over on his back, gasping like an exhausted salmon. He lay there, getting his breath, chest burning where the wire had cut him, gazing up listlessly at fat, descending flakes falling gently to kiss his bruised face. Godunov was now a tiny dangling doll high above.

Ignoring what might be broken, Chris pushed up and cast about for the rifle. Found it—incredulously—still attached to his back. He worked it off with unfeeling hands.

It was like lifting a yule log. Arm muscles, long ago stretched past their limit, would not respond. The rifle's muzzle wavered wildly, making true sighting impossible through the bright scope.

Trembling in exhaustion, he gave up on that, tore the scope free with unfeeling claws, shoved the bore skyward again and tried to make his finger—a distant, alien appendage—work on the trigger. He finally managed to pull it—knowing the shot wasn't even close, a wasted shot—the shock slamming his swollen shoulder into agony, the rifle flopping out of his feeble grasp.

Above, the gamboling figure of the Russian, smooth and tireless as a floating gibbon, closed the distance between himself and the pole, twenty feet away.

Chris cursed the night, fumbled to get the rifle upright again, could not stop, in his arm muscles' torpor, the muzzle from wavering ineffectually. He got off another round, which went wider than the first. He might have heard the basso chuckle from somewhere up there.

The Russian was twelve feet from the pole, eight feet.

Chris groaned commands, but his arms refused to obey. He dropped the rifle from nerveless fingers, not at all sure he could pick it up again.

Then, magically, there was no need.

Five feet from the pole, Godunov went suddenly rigid on the wire, arms and legs outstretched, stiff as a rigid corpse, which he was rapidly becoming. A low, sensuous hum issued from above. There were no expected sparks, but a faint blue corona further defined the body from darker night. A waft of ozone reached Chris, followed by something else. Then a high, strident chattering, which Chris finally realized were the Russian's teeth.

A ghastly pall of smoke rose from the powerful shoulders until, apparently burned through, the black fingers let go.

Ivan Godunov began his lazy descent. Slow but gathering rapidly, a hurtling ember, silent but for the wind-beaten coat flaps that would not become wings.

Chris dragged himself to the canyon lip, watched in dull exhaustion the falling trail of smoke. Until the distance and darkness below took that vicarious thrill from him.

The ALPS van, though rifled within by Godunov's goons, was nonetheless where Sarah had parked it, waiting at the side of the road, keys in place.

Chris threw himself into the seat, sat easing his exhaustion for a moment, then tried the ignition. He almost wept when the engine fired smoothly.

He locked all the van's doors against the possibility of white parka-clad figures, wheeled the vehicle around, and headed back down the snow-covered mountain road, not wholly cognizant of the miracle just achieved, that the mission—despite Sarah's death—had been accomplished. All his thoughts were directed toward the A-frame, toward Matty and the baby, toward Frank Springer, the final hurdle.

But the department can help with that. . . .

He grabbed a phone with one hand, expecting to find torn wires, punched in the numbers Sarah had given him and got a female voice.

"How can I help you?"

"This is Nielson! The Russian is dead! The mission was successful! Repeat: The mission was a success!"

Silence.

"Hello? Can you hear me? I said the mission is completed! Godunov is dead!"

"Please put agent Rawlings on the line."

"Agent Rawlings is dead. So is the Russian. I want you people to take care of Springer; do you hear me?"

Silence.

"This is Christopher Nielson, are you reading me?"

"One moment, please. . . ."

Chris cursed, twisting the wheel, sliding, nosing the van back into the proper lane—what he could see of the lane. God*damn* this snow! Goddamn these people! "Hello, hello! Is somebody there?"

A male voice now: "This is agent Stanford; can I help you?"

"Goddamn it, what is this, the fucking phone company? We killed the Russian, can you follow that? He's dead! I want some protection for my wife! Matty Nielson, remember her? I want someone sent to my house! I want Springer's ass, now!"

"Is this Mr. Nielson?"

"You're goddamn right this is Mr. Nielson!"

"Where is agent Rawlings?"

Christ! "Sarah Rawlings is dead! Dead! In the line of duty! Now, do I get some protection for my family or not?"

"Just a moment, Mr. Nielson. . . ."

Good Christ, they were putting him on hold again!

"Mr. Nielson?"

"Yes!"

"You say agent Rawlings was killed?"

"How many times do I have to say it?"

"And the Russian as well?"

"Yes, yes!"

"I see. All right. The thing is, we'll have to get confirmation on that. You understand."

"Get all the goddamn confirmation you want. Just get my wife and child the hell out of that house. That was part of the deal."

"What deal is that, Mr. Nielson?"

Chris felt an icy clutch. "Listen, you son of a bitch—"

"This is a big department, Mr. Nielson, with a lot of independent wings. I'm going to have to run this through channels. As soon as we get confirmation on the Russian, I'm sure someone will be in touch with you."

"My wife and child are in imminent danger, you bastard."

"I'm going to have to ask you to disconnect now, sir. This is private band and we need to adhere to strict procedure. Someone will be in touch with you. What is your present location?"

Chris stared at the road ahead.

Now that the spiky warmth of the cab was penetrating his extremities, he felt the return of a familiar chill.

"Sir? Mr. Nielson? I need your location."

Chris hung up the phone.

Drove recklessly on.

PART III

CHAPTER

The hour late, the mountain roads vacant, Chris made it to the A-frame with the van's big waffle treads in record time.

He set the brake, grabbed the CIA rifle, and leapt toward the front door, prepared to kick or shoot it in, aware of that floating sensation again, exhaustion just behind it, anxious to drag him down. But not yet. He felt near-reckless impatience, encased in a bubble of preternatural protection—impervious and omnipotent, ready to level fire at anyone or anything that stood between him and his family.

But kicking and shooting were unnecessary. The front door stood slightly ajar. Little comfort in that, particularly in light of Springer's bright sports car parked in the drive.

Something's wrong.

Chris nudged something with his toe, looked down. Against the weather stripping lay an open, snow-mantled trade paperback. He retrieved it, dusted the cover, held it to the foyer's inner light: *Techniques of Iceboating.* John Antler Horn had been here.

When? For how long? Had he gone inside?

Chris pushed into the billowing warmth of the big house, gun before him. He found the downstairs in darkness, a faint glow from upstairs lights.

He lingered a moment over the hall switch, punched it, flooding the foyer, living room, just a portion of the kitchen. All vacant. Matty's musky-sweet furniture polish reached him, making him ache for her.

He glanced around quickly, loped upstairs, rifle leveled before him. He poked quickly into each room in its turn, saving Nicky's for last, found that empty too.

He stood impotently in the familiar hallway . . . home but not home at all. His mind was blank.

With the Lamborghini here, where the hell could they be? Chris started back through the house.

Something caught him peripherally from the master bedroom, pulled him toward its glowing interior. He stood a moment assessing warily: the big hardwood bed frame, Ruth Orkin photo print on the wall, nightstand.

The overturned lamp, broken and scattered on the rug.

He came inside, heart hammering, found lamp pieces on the bed, attendant droplets of red, then a narrow, almost orderly trail of smaller droplets he'd somehow missed before, leading out toward the hall. He rushed that way, hit the bright hall light, followed the dark, erratic trickle to the stairs and down, heart actually hurting now. Down and into the foyer, toward the door. He was brought up short by the midwestern twang—deep and condescending—directly behind him:

"That's fine, just hold it right there! Now, drop that piece."

Chris turned, not dropping the rifle, found Sheriff Bradley emerging from the back of the house through dim kitchen fluorescence in a creaking, fur-collared leather police jacket, silvery .45 held before his considerable belly. "I said, drop the piece!"

"Where's Springer? Where's my wife?"

Bradley advanced, not pleasantly, cocking back the pistol's hammer, meaning business, pointing, jabbing an authoritative sheriff finger at Chris. "Don't play games with me, you L.A. asshole. Drop the fucking mare's leg!"

Chris held on to the rifle. "Go to hell! I want my wife and child—*now!*"

Bradley, not breaking stride, came on, straight-arming the .45 until the bore met with Chris's forehead, then on still, pressing hurtfully, grinning at the pain caused. "You're under arrest, city boy. Trespassing. Now, drop it!"

Ready to make a foolish move, Chris nonetheless let the rifle fall, clattering. He had to repress a violent urge to kick the sheriff's fat face as the big man bent to retrieve the weapon, toss it on the nearby sofa. "Pretty fancy. Where'd you score that? Your not too effectual friend Rick Corman?"

"Where are my wife and child?"

Bradley shoved hard with the pistol, vengefully, banging Chris's head back against the front door. "Whose blood is that on you, Mr. Ventura County? Or have you been deer huntin' again?"

Chris glanced down at his jacket front, surprised to find smears of dried brown there. His own, from the fall. "Listen to me, you tub of lard, I know you're on the take. I know the whole scheme, so don't play country gendarme with me. The Russian is dead. Do you know what I'm talking about? Godunov is a corpse. The deal is off! You can take that police special out of my face because the gravy-train ride is over. Now, what the hell have you bastards done with my wife and kid?"

Bradley glared at him, but there was telltale confusion there, enough to warn Chris the sheriff might not be in on all of it, might know nothing of the Russian connection at all. Which could prove problematic.

"You don't even know what the hell you're doing, do you?" Chris spat. Having emerged victorious from Godunov's embrace, he was overconfident, immune to this yokel's bumbling bravado.

Bradley hid behind authoritative fat, a comfortable facade. "I know this much. I got orders to shoot on sight anyone coming within fifteen yards of this house, and that makes you a prime candidate, junior. I got the paperwork sittin' in the right-hand desk drawer of my office, nice little restraining order 'twixt you and this property, all signed and legal by Mr. Springer."

"You ignorant ass! You have no idea what you're dealing with here. Springer's a homicidal maniac. And the people who put you up to protecting him don't give a shit about him anymore! Or you! You shoot me, and the only one who's going to step in and bother with your fat butt is the district attorney."

Bradley grinned in sarcasm, face tight with middle-age regrets, opportunities missed, the hatred behind his eyes palpable. "Big smart college boy from the West Coast. The genius play writer. Only you ain't writin' your way out of this one, hotshot. I got me a government guarantee here, high-profile stuff, lifelong and binding. A fat commission, a fatter house, on a fatter hunk of acreage up here on the mountain. Any goddamn place I choose."

He glanced around quickly at rafter and wall. "Might be I'll even take this place, if it suits me. I'm gonna fucking *own* this town when they leave, and nobody, fucking *nobody's* gonna cut me out of that deal!" He was so pumped by his own heated soliloquy he might have said more had a sudden distant scream not rung out somewhere beyond them.

Chris jumped, knowing Matty's voice. The boathouse!

He pushed from the wall, was shoved back by the sheriff's grinding pistol bore.

"Let me *go*, you son of a bitch!"

Bradley watched him, head cocked toward the scream, waiting and hearing a second one.

Beyond reckless now, Chris made a try for the barrel. Bradley lashed out before he could get there, slapping Chris sideways easily, knocking him to his knees, kicking him from there to kiss the foyer rug.

Sliding down the door, neck bent, room tilted, Chris perceived from this canted position a long, menacing shadow stretching amoeba-liquid across the dim kitchen's east wall. A man's shadow. Springer?

Chris grimaced bright pain back. Bradley, grunting, kicked him again, just beneath the buttocks into a muscle that would cause protracted agony and probably limping. Chris opened his eyes to find—beyond reddish pain—the shadow vanished.

He curled fetally, bracing for the next kick, hoping Bradley might eventually kick him toward the sofa and the rifle. He felt no kick. He turned dull-throbbing eyes to find the sheriff pointing the .45 at him with renewed intensity, a forgone expression on his tight, fat face telegraphing all that was coming. "No big-city asshole's gonna mess this up for me. I've waited too long, too fucking damn long."

When the shot crashed around the narrow confines, Chris actually thought the sheriff had missed, even at this close range.

He was prepared to receive the second shot when Bradley came tumbling toward him, eyes rolling white, scalp dangling in a fiery cone to his nose, face abruptly soft with childlike wonder— tumbled toward him and down with a flop like cement bags, black blood pooling instantly, copiously. The fat face, twisted away now in death, was hidden as if embarrassed by this excess of red.

Chris pushed up, feeling deeply the pain below his buttocks, saw the former shadow become Goldstein, the dead attorney, stepping toward him from the living room, the smoking World War II German Luger dangling from a pale left hand.

In this slow-motion state of recovery, it seemed to Chris more curious that the little lawyer was left-handed than that he was alive.

Goldstein reached out his right hand, pulled Chris wobbling up. He stood, smelling cordite and bile, staring incredulously at the bespectacled face, which wore an expression of philosophical peace. "You died in the fire," Chris whispered.

Goldstein stepped around to the sheriff's bloated corpus. "My nephew Hershel." He bent as if to double-check on the silent Bradley, nodded in satisfaction, stood, the Luger still trailing twin threads of smoke. "At the hands of this animal, I've no doubt." Goldstein shook his head. "Hershel was playacting attorney in my absence, trying out my swivel chair." He turned to Chris. "While I playacted at detective. He is young and dead, and I am old and breathing. God is unfathomable. This will be less cumbersome than the rifle." He handed Chris the Luger. "Go to your wife."

Chris, already in motion, accepted the antique gun with the cracked grip.

Chris caught Springer totally by surprise.

The killer was dragging Matty—kicking and struggling—and an unconscious Nicky up the narrow path of worn-away snow to the lake.

Chris, running, seeing his silent, dangling son, screamed, *"Freeze!"*

Everything seemed to happen in an instant and was over too quickly for Chris to analyze properly. He fired the Luger point-blank at the surprised Springer, aiming high not to hit Matty or the boy, then dove instantly sideways into snow-powdering hedge, anticipating the killer's legendary reaction time.

He lay there, breathing heavily, listening acutely for a moment.

A moment more.

Then cursed himself for not charging right in. Springer was not dead. Was not even hit.

Chris leapt up again with a cry of self-loathing, found the path in front of him empty, Springer and Chris's family magically vanished.

The maniac was either lying in wait somewhere ahead (probably not, Matty would make being quiet impossible) or had retreated back downhill toward the safety of the boathouse.

Casting all caution aside, gun before him, Chris launched himself down the slippery hill, inviting death.

He nearly lost the path in the darkness—eating up more precious time—found it again, and lunged suddenly from impenetrable, snow-flocked aspen to sharply contrasting open space. The wide, icy bank was highlighted in just-emerging moonlight, casting shore and motionless water in ethereal blue. Chris's heart stopped at the sight of the figure crumpled on the shadowed beach.

He sprinted up, gasping prayers, found the dark eyes of John Antler Horn glistening up at him peacefully from the lined, leather face.

"John!"

The old Indian clutched his thin chest, though Chris could detect no blood beneath the veined hand, and the narrow ribs moved rhythmically.

"Did you find the new book?" Antler Horn wanted to know.

"John. My wife and baby, did you see them?"

The old man scowled. "Your cousin is a thief and a wife fucker. He took my knife. He is a mighty warrior, but I kicked him in the balls."

"Did he stab you, John?"

"He stabbed John Antler Horn, yes. He took your family . . . my knife and my boat. A great warrior but a greater thief. I will not break bread with him."

Chris gazed across the wide lake, thought he saw in the ghostly moonlight something moving swiftly out there.

"John, let me help you to the boathouse. It's freezing out here."

The Indian shook his head. "An Iroquois does not freeze. I will rest here awhile. I brought you an Arrow. You owe me money."

"John, did Springer take Matty and the boy?"

"He has my Skeeter. It is very fast, but he steers like a woman. The Arrow is smaller but swifter. You can catch him easily. I will help after I rest."

Chris turned, scanned impatiently, saw the trim outline of the iceboat moored to the far end of the dock.

The old Indian grabbed his jacket with surprising strength. "Bring back my boat. We will sail together, Chris Nielson. Fly like the hawk."

"I'll bring it back, John." He left the old man there in the snow, raced down the dock to the dark hulk of the remaining yacht. He began, with no feeling of confidence or plan at all, to tear at the mooring line.

Under harshly gusting winds Chris guided the yacht across the ice-bound lake into more wind and darkness, gathering speed rapidly, aiming out toward what he perceived as a pale, retreating shadow. But it was Springer. He could feel it.

As a kid, he'd worked his father's Hatteras out of Sag Harbor, tacking around Montauk Point into the open sea past Long Island Sound, standing on the flying bridge beside his dad, legs braced against the big swells. But he knew nothing of ice sailing, save the little he had gleaned from cursory, late-night thumbings of John Antler Horn's book. Modern craft—he remembered from the book—can weigh over one thousand pounds, and when one falls on you, there's no cushioning water to offset the blow.

Chris tacked into a steadily rising wind, gusting more sharply now that they were away from shore. Eyes slit against the sting, he hoisted his jacket zipper a notch higher. He wished to hell he'd brought the heavy CIA rifle now: He'd be able to employ the night scope.

He grunted as the sails began to luff, grabbed the jib sheet, and powered her back into the wind with a movement that felt overcompensated and too easy.

It was. A rogue gust caught her hull, lifted them into a stomach-whooping bank, slamming Chris against the coaming with teeth-jarring shock, the yacht slewing, leaning dizzily, threatening to capsize. At this speed, already nearly seventy, the ice would feel like concrete in a spill.

Chris strained against the g-force, scrabbled for the wheel, runner shrieking beneath him, spewing shards of razored ice. He caught the wheel, hung on to the bank, 'hiking' across the lake on one runner, managed to keep from toppling, got the lines under control, played the wind to his favor, felt the runner drop.

He tacked again, searching the night, crisscrossing the lake, heading south, squinting over the bow into the searing wind for the other craft, maneuvering with growing, if guarded, confidence. There was no movement out there. Where had Springer gone?

The bullet's impact smacked his left hand, knocked him sideways, almost out of the boat.

Chris pulled the jib tight, took advantage of the next strong gust, ignored the blood, and stuck his throbbing hand under his armpit. Ducking low, he spotted Springer at three o'clock, tightened the jib, and powered after the larger craft. He gained rapidly on the other yacht, heedless, reckless in eager exhaustion. This was the closest he'd been to Matty in days.

He experienced a sudden nagging premonition that the shot that had crippled his hand had not been entirely off target. His attacker had meant to slow, impair, not kill. This was part of the game, the same kind of game Godunov would play. Quite possibly he was being deliberately lured out onto wider, more comfortable killing space, a place to parry and jab, delay the game. Something Godunov would also do.

Yes, but you beat Godunov. . . .

Not strictly true. He had *survived* Godunov.

He looked at his hand.

Blood streamed backward to his elbow in jagged scallops, whipped by the icy wind, but the cold was also cauterizing the wound, slowing, even stanching the flow. The fingers, though, stiff with pain when he tried to contract them, were slowly growing useless again, as useless as they had been dangling on the phone lines above the chasm.

The best he could do was hold the wheel with the heel of his hand, control the jib with the other, the little craft's twelve-foot runners rapidly closing the distance between yachts.

He needed a plan.

The wind took another coltish dip, jib luffing. Chris compensated with quicker reaction time, yanked evenly on the sheet, banking her back into the wind.

When he looked up again, the other yacht was moving rapidly away. It appeared to be heading—could it be possible?—toward the shoreline. Was Springer giving up? Already?

No, not the shoreline. Chris squinted into the gloom, perceived the narrow mouth of a frozen river nearly hidden amid snow-mantled scrubs, bowing fir. He perceived an opening, but not much of one, surely not something wide enough to accommodate a speeding iceboat. Springer wasn't that crazy.

Was he? He was still heading directly toward it.

Chris could see from their approach that entering the narrow mouth would be like surfing under a pier. Worse. There would scarcely be ten inches of room on either side of Springer's yacht, a little more on his own. Yet Springer held fast to his course. Into the game.

Chris took a deep breath, pointed the Arrow's bow toward the river's tiny mouth. In the end, he reasoned, it didn't matter if Matty and the child were aboard with Springer or not. Until the maniac was dead, they'd never be completely free.

Springer's yacht shot through the opening.

The narrow entrance rushed at Chris, a tiny mouth flanked with incisors of black stumps. He set the sheet, set his teeth, powered ahead, and was swallowed.

One moment he was surrounded by the wide, comforting lake. In the next, dark banks flashed past on either side, sickeningly close, a ribbon-thin runway festooned with jagged boulders, angled stumps. The Arrow was a toboggan now.

But it wasn't built for that purpose. It was built for the more forgiving latitudes of open space, demanding more maneuvering room.

Chris swallowed giddy fear, fought hard the desire to depress the brake. One minor miscalculation of wheel or sail now . . .

Ahead, the Skeeter appeared to pick up speed.

Chris plunged blindly into the gulf, like skiing down a culvert. Yet he was gaining on the Skeeter.

As was no doubt Springer's intention: Wait until the prey was neck and neck here in the narrow passage—until there was virtually no margin for error—then side-ram him, knock Chris into the shoreline—a half-sunken tree or rock—blow him to smithereens. And race on, laughing.

Chris eased back on the sheet, dodged the Arrow around a jagged outcropping in the ice, runners responding with the sound of nails on blackboard, moved in behind the bigger yacht's stern, searching for his family.

Now he could see the pale outline of Springer's back in the cockpit. The man wore only a T-shirt. *My God, he must be freezing!*

And there, shoved low—probably by Springer's foot—a tuft of russet hair. Matty.

Stomach clenched, Chris edged cautiously alongside the bigger yacht, eyes flicking from river to boat, river to boat, waiting for the next shot from Springer's pistol. . . .

He had one eye on an approaching rock when Springer yanked the big yacht into him, the hulls meeting with a hollow *crack*.

The smaller Arrow bounced away against heavier side panels, slewed dangerously sideways, and headed straight into the unforgiving shoreline.

Chris cursed, "No!" yanked reflexively at the sheet. Overcompensating, he threw the stern into a broach, fishtailed between bank and bigger boat. He glimpsed—at the height of this sluicing horror—Matty's pale face over the Skeeter's gunwale.

The Arrow spun recklessly, lazily, dropping back behind the big yacht.

Chris grunted as he struck a frozen sapling, bounced high—his stomach swooping with weightlessness—then slammed down with neck-snapping force, throwing a ten-foot geyser of shaved ice. The maneuver had knocked them, albeit inadvertently, back on course.

The Arrow gained on the other craft again, caromed giddily off an unseen rock, knocked to leeward, bow bucking, spinning out of control again, slamming hard into something—the Skeeter's transom?—slamming Chris forward, Fiberglas splintering skyward to be whipped back, tearing, past his startled eyes.

He looked up to see, with some satisfaction, Springer pitched over his own helm, the Arrow's rigging fouled in the broken shards of transom, sending both craft—locked now—into a steep broach.

For a heartbeat—their boats bound by an umbilical cord of wood—Chris and Springer locked eyes.

Then the bigger craft struck something. The left runner sang, bounced high, and tore Chris's boat free in a wriggly lash of rigging.

Springer, as if suddenly freed of all caution, leaned into the wheel, drove the reinforced hull into Chris's bow—again with sledgehammer force. The *Arrow* skittered away with a protesting screech of runners.

Chris saw movement behind Springer's straining back. Matty, the bundled baby under one arm, was reaching a white, clawed hand toward Chris's gunwale.

"Matty!"

Chris grabbed the jib, held it fast, reached for her, reached—

He caught her fingers as the two boats pulled apart, his back muscles tearing. He couldn't maintain a grip on her like this.

He braced his foot against the gunwale, pulled with the last of his strength, dragged her aboard. He caught the look of terror in her eyes, her head shaking violently, mouth screaming a protest the wind snatched away.

Nicky. Springer had maneuvered around, snatched the baby from her.

"Chris, don't—"

Too late. Inertia sent her crashing into him, throwing him off balance, his hands flying from the controls. Together—together at last—they flailed back and over the opposite gunwale, balanced a precarious moment, spilled onto flashing ice.

Chris hit first, taking the shock on his shoulders, Matty atop him, protected. The tearing ice ripped his jacket, his flesh. He clutching her tight, keeping her from it, not letting the river have her.

They were slowing now, sliding and spinning, a living sled.

Chris caught a final dizzy glimpse of Springer shooting away, working desperately at the Skeeter's controls. Then came shoulder-wrenching pain, a cold numbness down his spine. His left shoulder had collided with something—a frozen stump, probably—spinning them around. Matty dug in her toes instinctively to slow them further. Chris, breath knocked out of him, could only lie impotently, watch the canopy of spidery limbs flashing overhead.

Finally they struck shoreline, were dumped, still spinning, into a copse of half-submerged maples.

Everything that followed moved with dreamlike surrealness.

Matty—as if not hurt at all—was up on her feet and running down the frozen river after the retreating Skeeter, sliding, pinwheeling, shouting, screaming, *"Nicky!"*

Chris pushed up, disoriented, back afire. He slipped, found wobbly legs, and turned to chase after her drunkenly. "Matty! Wait! You can't!"

He caught her just as Springer's yacht rounded a distant bend, was plucked from their view. Chris pulled her close. "Honey, you can't catch him!"

She struggled against him, spitting like an animal. Wrenched away, ran on mindlessly. "You don't *understand*!"

She left Chris blinking in surprise, alone again, swept with nausea, fighting just to get a breath.

In a moment he was running after her again, calling, imploring, chasing her toward the river bend.

He came up short suddenly, nearly stumbling, rounding the bend. Matty was stopped dead, statue stiff, fists knotted at her sides as though just slapped.

She stared ahead at that singular point where the icy river suddenly ended. Vanished to black.

Chris stared himself. At the curled, white lip the water made in its torrential rush to the edge.

Frozen like a snapshot now, into the waterfall's silent plunge.

CHAPTER 27

They searched the immediate area around the base of the frozen falls. Husband and wife. Strangers.

They combed the area for nearly an hour, together and apart. Matty picked through every piece of broken hull, scattered debris. Chris, less methodical—perhaps less hopeful—made a general circumnavigation of the wider area, not only the icy river beyond but the banks opposite: trees, scrubs, all of it laid out before him in moonlit contrasts of dark bark and pale snow. Any foreign object would stand out in high chiaroscuro relief.

They found nothing beyond splintered wood, the flapping length of pinned Dacron sail. The scene was as desolate in the lonely, soughing wind as a TV Indian massacre.

Both parents were weary to the point of hallucination: bruised, bleeding, exhausted, nearly frozen through. Toward the end, they seemed to turn to each other at opposing ends of the river at the same time, exchange the same quixotic look.

Where—?

Then Matty did a strange thing. She stopped suddenly, looked up at the waterfall's illuminated lip. She sat down on the ice, sat down right in the middle of the hard, still river as though she had discovered something too personal to articulate.

Chris came to her, the pain in his legs and back dragging at him. "You're exhausted."

She didn't look at him. Neither had looked at the other, really, since they'd come back together. If this was togetherness.

"Matty, we need help," he offered ineffectually, "a search party." He didn't hint at what he knew she was thinking. That the child was gone for good this time. That the child was dead.

Matty gripped her knees on the ice, rocked a bit, looking both insulated from the world and frozen through. "And where would we get that?"

Chris made a floundering motion with his hands. "We'll call in help from Kingston, from neighboring townships. They can't have the whole goddamn state under their thumb."

She said nothing.

"Matty, you're freezing, exhausted. We both are. We need rest and food." Yet he was thinking: Nicky's not getting rest; Nicky's not getting food. "It won't do Nicky any good if we wear ourselves out. It will be light soon."

She looked up with her pretty brow cleft curiously, as though Chris were missing the obvious. "He isn't here, Chris. Did you think he was still here?"

He stared down at her, wondering if perhaps her mind had finally collapsed. "There are no breaks in the ice, Matty. It's too thick, even for a fall like that. At the speed they were traveling, their . . . bodies would have been projectiles. He might be way downriver somewhere, but he isn't *under* it. I'm sure. . . ." He trailed off because she was rising, shaking her head as she got to her feet. She looked up at the edge of the falls above them, a huge singular, dripping icicle, the outer edges translucent in moonlight, lovely as an old fairy-tale illustration. "He isn't dead, Chris. Not yet anyway. I'd know if he was dead."

Chris watched her.

She kept staring up at the lip of the falls, as though trying to relive the moment for Nicky, as if trying to share—take away—his terror for him. "Frank has him."

Chris, mind bordering a kind of dream state, was wondering absently how they would ever get all the way back to the house before collapsing. "Matty . . . it's a fifty-foot drop at least. I'm not saying—I mean, maybe if he hit a snowbank somewhere. But we've looked everywhere. We'll look again in the morning."

But she was shaking her head again, heading for the shore with a posture that bespoke calm certainty. "He's with Frank. I'll never see him again. He's with Frank." She walked away from Chris toward the dark woods.

Chris led them to Leaflock Road both because he remembered approximately where that was and because even if no car stopped to assist them, the narrow mountain road would eventually lead them back to the house. Though how they'd walk that far, half frozen, he had no idea.

They plodded along in painful silence, Chris—limping from Bradley's kick—trying simply to keep one frozen foot before the other, no sensation in his toes, his fingertips, wondering how long until Matty crumpled, until he had to somehow carry her. He wondered what she was thinking but was afraid to ask.

Car lights fell over them ten minutes into this, the vehicle slowing immediately, stopping. Its lights were left on, and Chris, squinting into them, tightened with uneasiness as two shadowed forms stepped out. One held a rifle, was coming toward them. Not that it mattered. Whoever it was, he and Matty were too exhausted and could not go any farther on foot.

Matty made an amazed sound as John Antler Horn stepped before the high beams, stood with his hands poked on his hips. "Did you bring back my boat, Chris Nielson?"

"I'm sorry, John. I'm afraid it's wrecked."

"Then I'll take yours."

"I'm afraid that's wrecked too."

The old Indian frowned in the moonlight. "You owe me money."

"Yes, I'll pay for them. Are you all right, John?"

"I packed the wound with coffee grounds and deer dung. Did you bring back my knife?"

"I'm sorry." Chris looked over to see the man with the rifle emerge into the headlights' corona, become the lawyer Goldstein, clutching the CIA weapon.

Moments later they were on the way back to the house, wrapped in the blessed warmth of Goldstein's Lexus. John Antler Horn fell asleep in the backseat, Matty on the other side, staring listlessly out at the glowing woods.

"How did you find us?" Chris asked quietly, head back, refusing any more to stay up, eyes closed against the toasty heat, the soothing hum of the big expensive car.

Goldstein nodded toward the backseat. "I found him, then he found you. Seemed to know where you'd be."

"How did he know that?"

"I haven't the slightest idea." Goldstein looked over at Chris. "Your son . . . ?"

Chris shook his head slowly.

Nothing else was broached until they reached the A-frame's glowing windows.

Inside, amid familiar warmth and light, Chris insisted Matty lie down upstairs or take a hot bath at least. She ignored him, explaining with almost eerie calm that she wasn't tired. She began busying herself in the kitchen, making them fresh coffee and hot rolls. She would probably have started to build a fire herself if Chris hadn't intervened.

John Antler Horn sat in the family room raptly engaged in a Mary Tyler Moore rerun. Goldstein, still clutching the rifle, moved restlessly from this window to that, peering out through the curtains at surrounding woods, black sky. Until, turning, he accepted a cup of coffee from Matty. "Thank you. I think we're all right, for tonight anyway. Probably for good." He turned to Chris. "For the record, I came here looking for you because you were my client. The back door was ajar. Bradley surprised me and I— thinking him a prowler—shot him accidentally."

"Where is he?" Chris asked, straightening from logs that had caught quickly, flamed high and reassuringly.

"In back. There's a little blood on your carpet, Mrs. Nielson. I have something at the office that will get it out."

"And you think they won't come for him?" Chris asked.

"Somebody might. But not them. I doubt we'll ever hear from them again."

Chris sat by the fire, reveling in its warmth, in the hot bite of his coffee. "Why do you think that?"

Goldstein sipped, still clutching the CIA rifle. "Because by now they doubtless know about the Russian. I'm quite sure they're already packing to leave town. They've no more use for us. No more interest in you. Certainly no further interest in Sheriff Bradley and his goons. Any kind of retaliation for his death now would mean they were somehow involved. And, of course, they weren't, right?" he said with sarcasm. "Still, to be safe, I suggest we spend the night together. You have an extra cot, perhaps?"

"We've plenty of room," Chris assured him, thinking of Nicky. He glanced up at Matty in the kitchen and wished his last comment hadn't come out quite that way. Plenty of room. Matty seemed not to hear it, or care. She seemed strangely at ease, yet expectant, as if waiting for something.

There was silence for a time.

Then, from the kitchen, pulling hot rolls from the oven, Matty told Goldstein, "I'm so terribly sorry to hear about your nephew. . . ."

Chris thought that a rather amazing, compassionate thing to say, considering his wife's present state of mind.

"Thank you," the little lawyer said. "It will help when we catch Springer, retrieve your child."

Chris looked up at the little man with the big rifle, who'd answered her with such conviction, as though catching Springer was not only inevitable but merely a matter of time. Is he merely being kind? Chris wondered. Is that why he put it like that?

Coming into the living room, silver serving tray loaded with steaming rolls, Matty was closest to the phone when it rang.

Chris started to suggest she perhaps consider before picking it up, but she was already there. "Yes?"

From the couch, before a blazing fire he thought he might never leave, Chris watched her on the kitchen phone. Her head nodded several times. He caught a soft yes and another, her head nodding again. Matty hung up.

She came into the living room, picked up one of the hot rolls, staring vacantly into the billowing fire, back to her husband. "It was Frank."

Chris, spilling coffee, got to his feet. Goldstein jerked from the library shelves near the den.

Matty took a bite out of the roll, chewed, and before Chris could speak, cut him off with, "He has Nicky. The baby's fine. Reasonably fine. He wants me to join them."

She swallowed the rest of the roll, then turned and headed for the staircase.

Chris was close behind. "Wait—*wait!*" Grabbing her arm. "Where—what the hell are you *doing*?"

She hesitated but did not give him the respect of her eyes. "I'm going to him, Chris. Please let go of my arm."

He spun her to him. "Going to him! Like hell!"

She wrenched away with such strength it left his inadvertent nail marks along her arm. "I have to pack some clothes, something warm. He wants me there by tomorrow night." She started away again, looking at him this time, coldly impatient. Chris got in front of her, cut her off from the stairs.

"Go where?"

"Chris, let me by. . . ."

"Go where, Matty? What are you doing?"

"What I have to do. I'm going to my son."

"And *him*! Where is he?"

As Matty pushed past him, Chris jerked her back and down off the first two steps, so that, in falling, she was able to whirl, use the fall's momentum, and slap him hard across the face. From the living room, Goldstein made a small sound.

The couple from California stood gaping incredulously at each other near the staircase, Matty apparently as surprised at her reaction as he.

But she'd meant it anyway. "Get out of my way, Chris! I mean it!" There was such animal intensity in her eyes he actually shrank back a foot.

"Matty, think what you're doing. I know you're exhausted—"

Out of patience, she pushed past him dismissively. Chris started for her, turned at the last moment, and headed across the room for the phone. Matty stopped halfway up, called to him demandingly, voice near cracking. "What are you doing?"

Not looking at her, taking command, Chris dialed stubbornly. "Calling the highway patrol."

"I wouldn't advise that, Mr. Nielson . . . ," Goldstein offered.

"Chris, put down the phone!" from a strangle-voiced Matty.

Chris ignored her. Then, his own patience gone, he whirled toward her. "Goddamn it, Matty, why didn't you keep him on the line? We could have traced the call or something!"

She screamed, "Put down the goddamn phone!"

He looked up at her blankly, easing the headset from his ear.

Matty swallowed, took deep breaths, fought for composure. "It has to be this way, Chris. If we interfere in any way, he'll kill the child. Think about it and you'll know I'm right. Frank is finished now. He knows that. He has nothing left on this earth, no power except the power to hurt me. He'll use Nicky to do that. Which at least means he's safe until I get there. Now, maybe I can figure some way to get Nicky away before they close in on Frank, and maybe I can't. Maybe he'll kill us all; I suspect he will. But he'll certainly harm the child if I don't do as he says now. I'm sorry I hit you, but you know I'm right."

When he found he had nothing to say to that, she turned and continued up to the next floor.

Chris replaced the receiver, followed her, but not with the reckless abandon of before.

She was in the bedroom, pacing between bureau and bed, tossing things into an open suitcase.

He stood in the doorway. On the way up he'd been sure he'd had something to tell her, couldn't quite articulate it now that he was there.

As if to fill in for him—face turned away, arms moving mechanically with the packing—Matty said to the suitcase, "We cannot involve the police in any way. The moment he sees a blue uniform, Nicky's life is forfeited. Do you understand?" She turned solemnly to him.

For the first time since he'd known his wife, she looked old. Not in years as much as in the acquisition of too much wisdom. "I understand," he said.

She went back to work. "I will not let my child be taken from me a second time."

"Third time." And when she turned to look at him, he added, "Ohh, that's right, the first time was a lie, wasn't it?"

She watched him a moment, turned away again, not buying into it.

"Wasn't it?"

Matty sighed, rifled a drawer for clothes she couldn't seem to find. "Chris, I told a lot of lies. I did what I thought I had to do. To protect Nicky, protect all of us. If I was wrong, I'm sorry. But I don't think I was wrong. Except involving you in the first place, perhaps."

"Well," he began, "all part of the script." This made her turn to him again, face like slate.

She started—coloring with anger—to say something, shook her head instead, and went back to her packing. "There isn't time. Believe what you like."

"What I'd like or what is the truth?"

She closed the suitcase, snapped the lid.

He blocked her at the door. "I want to know where you're meeting him."

"No."

"Matty, at least that. You owe me that."

Her look was one of incredulousness. "I owe you—?" But she let it go again, started past him.

"Tell me or I'll follow you." And he thought she might strike him again.

"You do that, Chris! You do that and Nicky will last just *that* long!" she said, snapping her fingers.

She pushed past him, leaving him off balance and impotent in the doorway.

Chris felt a white heat rising. He was sick of being directed by others, sick of the attendant feeling of impotence.

He caught her in the hall again. "You *do* owe me, goddamn it! I nearly got killed getting to you, getting to Nicky!"

Matty put down the suitcase. "And why, Chris, why did you do it? Why did you come after us?"

He searched her face. "What the hell are you talking about?"

"That day in the hotel, in the ladies' room. Did you ask yourself then, Chris?"

"Matty, you're out of your mind."

She nodded in irony. "The moment you found out he might not be yours, that's when everything changed, Chris. Not when I hid Nicky under the bed. Not when Frank first showed up at the house. Not even when you got locked out. Not when Rick got attacked. It started the moment I told you about your son. That he might not really be your son—your biological son—that's when it changed. That look in your eyes. That . . . *look*."

He stepped back, throwing up his hands. "How the hell did you expect me to react? Was I supposed to jump for joy from such wonderful news?"

"What news, Chris? That I didn't love you? That Nicky didn't love you? That one of us had cancer and was going to die? None of those things transpired! Nothing *changed*, Chris. He was still your child!"

"You said you loved Frank!"

"I was *lying*, goddamn it! Do you think that was easy for me? I was lying to keep you away, keep you from being killed. But you know something, Chris? It wasn't that hard after a few minutes. Because you believed me. You were so damned eager to believe me, think the worst of me, of us. It wouldn't have worked if you hadn't believed it."

Chris stumbled away, head spinning, made a little shuffling

circle, looked back at her, features etched with disbelief. "What the hell are you—you're trying to have it both ways! I'm damned if I do and dead if I don't!"

Matty hesitated, seemed to gather herself. "What can I say, Chris? How can I ever *begin* to apologize for what I've done to your life? I can't. Look at us. Neither of us trusts the other, never will again. Isn't it better just to leave it at that, let me go to him before we only make it worse? Isn't it?" She filed past him, down the staircase.

When he finally came downstairs, she was on the kitchen phone, calling for a cab. She hung up as he came to her. "At least let me drive you to your motel, or wherever it is you're going to phone the airport," Chris offered softly.

"No. Thank you."

From the family room came the sounds of John Antler Horn changing channels.

Chris stood stupidly watching the little bespectacled attorney flip through one of his books against the oak case near the foyer. When Goldstein became aware of Chris's eyes, he looked up. "Perhaps it would be better if I were to leave?"

Chris came into the living room, slouched in the green easy chair. "It doesn't matter. You're welcome to stay."

Abe Goldstein joined them in the living room, still carrying one of the books: *The Warren Commission's Report,* Chris noticed apathetically.

"Interesting book," Goldstein addressed the two of them. "Have you read it?"

Chris sighed. "Long time ago."

"And saw the Oliver Stone movie, did you?"

"Mr. Goldstein—"

"Interesting film. My guess is that we will never know the full truth behind who killed Kennedy. What a handsome young man he was, yes? What days those were! And Jackie. May I say, Mrs. Nielson, that in some ways—the hair aside—you remind me of the late Mrs. Onassis somewhat? Something in your style."

"Well, thank you, Mr. Goldstein. I'll take that as a compliment."

"Oh, certainly, it was intended to be." The little attorney leaned against the fireplace stones, thumbing through the book. "This place, the vicinity you're going to meet our Mr. Springer, it wouldn't be Dallas, I don't suppose?"

Matty said nothing.

"Mrs. Nielson?"

"No. It's not Dallas, Mr. Goldstein."

"I see. Somewhere far away though, yes? Somewhere near a border, I should think. Mexico or the like. Somewhere one could easily skip over into a neutral country. Let me think. . . . In North America that would mean only two places. Mexico or Canada, yes?"

Matty gazed at the fire.

"Purely conjecture on my part, of course, but if I were our Mr. Springer—if I were a desperate man with few resources, little time, and the added burden of a child, I think I might choose to rendezvous in some type of inconspicuous area. By inconspicuous I mean crowded. Hide in plain sight as it were. Say, a Disneyland or some such resort town. What would you say, Mr. Nielson, Mrs. Nielson?"

Matty and Chris said nothing.

"Someplace where one could amble about freely, as it were, and not look suspicious, because ambling about is what everyone else was doing. A place like, oh . . . Niagara Falls."

She could not help looking up this time, thus giving herself away. Goldstein smiled, almost apologetically, gestured toward the bookcase. "Several travel brochures describing the vicinity, there on your bookcase. They belong to Mr. Springer, do they?"

Chris looked at Matty quickly, up at the smiling attorney, back at Matty, who was gazing into the fire again. "Matty?"

She folded her arms, set her jaw. "He'll kill Nicky if anyone interferes, Chris."

"Not if he doesn't see me coming."

"No!" There was such plaintive desperation in her voice, both men genuflected.

Goldstein closed the book, placed it on the coffee table between his two hosts. "Forgive me, Mrs. Nielson, for that rather indelicate bit of sleuthing. I know you must be angry at me. It's just that I've been thinking about the marvelous Mr. Springer. This great international spy and assassin, this bigger-than-life figure who is, for all intents and purposes, merely a fugitive now, a hunted animal. If the CIA doesn't get to him today, then surely tomorrow, the next day."

"If they find him," Matty put in.

"Quite right. And I agree with you about the child, that Nicky is his hostage, really, his ace. The moment Mr. Nielson, or any figure of authority, shows his face, Springer can threaten with the child. I was thinking, though"—he began pacing before the fire—"I was thinking earlier about Dallas. And it seems to me we have a singular advantage, an ace of our own perhaps, something our Mr. Springer knows nothing about, would hardly be expecting." Goldstein paced to the sofa, where he'd left the CIA rifle. He held it up for both of them to see. He smiled.

Chris was out of his chair excitedly, taking the rifle from the little attorney. "Yes! Matty!" He came around in front of her. "He wouldn't have to see me. I wouldn't have to get anywhere *near* him. This thing shoots at night. Shoots with unerring accuracy. I've fired it!"

Matty eyed the weapon with trepidation. "It's too dangerous. He'll be with Nicky." But her tone had altered slightly.

Chris started to press when Goldstein stepped between. "I wonder. Now that the cat's out of the bag, could you possibly tell us exactly what it was you and Mr. Springer talked about?"

Matty hesitated, giving in to her exhaustion. She sighed in resignation. "He told me to meet him in New York, at the falls. It was where we honeymooned. He said he wanted to start over again, just the three of us. From there we'd go to Canada and from there somewhere overseas. He said he didn't blame me for the lamp, for hitting him, that he'd lied too but that all lying must stop now. He said that he loved me and wanted a fresh start. If I loved him, believed him, I'd come alone and go away with him. He never actually mentioned hurting the baby; it was more by implication. Of course he knew I'd say yes."

"Do you think he intends to keep his word, Mrs. Nielson?"

Matty glanced at Chris. "No. I think he intends to kill me. My life for Nicky's or something like that. It's his style. The last laugh. I betrayed him with Chris, and you don't betray Frank Springer. Afterward, he's off to Europe or Argentina to start over. Join the other side, maybe. Whoever the other side is these days."

Goldstein nodded, paced a short distance, turned back to her. "Where exactly are you to meet him? In a hotel, a parking lot?"

"The Rapids. It's a big hotel near the falls, with a restaurant on top. Big scenic windows with a view of Niagara. We've eaten there before."

"What time?"

"Nine o'clock tomorrow night."

Goldstein nodded, paced another moment. "Mr. Nielson, you have a fax machine perhaps?"

"Yes. I sometimes mail rewrite pages to New York."

Goldstein nodded rapidly, visibly excited. "Listen to me, please, both of you. I know you're frightened for the child, but I think we might have a shot at this if you're willing."

"What?" Chris asked hopefully.

"Niagara Falls is a popular tourist center. There are buildings and structures all around the falls now. Some of these will be closed at night. We could get Mr. Nielson into one of those buildings opposite to or adjacent to and level with this restaurant, even if it's several blocks away."

And Chris picked it up: "Get a bead on Springer through the infrared scope! Yes!"

Matty regarded the rifle dubiously. "Nicky will be right *there*, Chris. You'd have to be incredibly accurate."

"This thing *is* incredibly accurate!" He grabbed the rifle from Goldstein excitedly.

"It's a chance at least, Mrs. Nielson. And if it's a chance, perhaps we should consider it. For the child's sake." Everyone knew he'd added this last as inducement, Matty knowing it most of all.

She chewed her lip, daring to hope. "How can we possibly get set up, coordinated by tomorrow night? There isn't time."

Goldstein held up a finger. "I have friends in New York, people who have late-night access to the libraries there. Now what we need is some kind of aerial view of the vicinity, the falls and the structures surrounding them. I'll make some calls, get the information faxed to this number. We can plot out the whole thing right here before you leave."

Matty stood, began pacing herself. "What if Springer checks the airlines, is waiting there when Chris and I get off?"

"We'll have to take that chance," Chris told her. "One thing we can do is use separate airlines. That will cut the chances in half. Where's the phone book? I'll find out about flight schedules right now." He turned to Goldstein. "There's a separate line in my den; make your calls from there. The fax machine is on the desk. Matty, how about putting on some more coffee, lots of coffee?"

Both men moved quickly now, creating a new, heady energy in the house that Matty—trembling vaguely from both exhaustion and stress—allowed herself, finally, to be swept up by.

★   ★   ★

It was the fifth fax, the one from the Mid-Manhattan Library, that really turned everything around. It showed an artist's rendering of the general Niagara Falls area from a helicopter's vantage point.

Goldstein, delighted, pointed triumphantly at a circular structure beside the Luna Falls section, the legend below it. "There it is. The Rapids Hotel and Restaurant. 'World famous.' "

Matty nodded in confirmation. "That's the place. I recognize the area, that little park there to the left. Goat Island's over there. Here's a narrow walkway that leads past the falls. You need slickers and umbrellas to protect you from the mist."

Chris took the faxed illustration, moved it under the circular fluorescent magnifier on his desk. "Look here, this building here across the way. It's not in the legend, which may mean it's abandoned, not in use. This could be our 'school book depository.' "

Goldstein nodded. "There's another, smaller one just here. Not as close but it could give you a better shot at the restaurant."

Matty turned away from the light, shuddering. "Listen to us."

Goldstein looked up at her. "Mrs. Nielson—"

"I know, I know. It's just that there's something ghoulishly familiar about it." To Chris she said, "It's just a drawing, you know. An artist's representation. You're not allowing for trees, other obstructions the artist didn't bother with. Even the scale may not be exactly accurate."

Chris ignored her, but Goldstein straightened. "You have a point, Mrs. Nielson."

Chris looked up.

Goldstein started pacing again. "We need some kind of backup plan in case our first choice fails."

"How are we going to know that once we get there?" Matty demanded. "Chris and I won't be able to communicate!"

Goldstein glanced at his watch. "Three a.m. When does your flight leave, Chris?"

"Seven this morning."

The lawyer nodded. "Call the airline back; book passage for two."

Matty turned. "You're going with him?"

Goldstein picked up the illustration. "Precautionary measure. Springer doesn't know me, has never heard of me. My nephew Hershel has—had—a couple of those two-way amateur radios at my sister's house. I'll drop by and get them. Mr. Nielson and I can stay in discreet contact." He appraised Matty sympathetically. "I'll arrive at the restaurant before you, keep Chris apprised of what's going on after you arrive."

"I think that's a good idea," Chris agreed. "Matty, hopefully you'll get there before Springer. Be sure to choose a seat next to one of the big wraparound windows. The closer the better. I'd like a clear shot."

"What if Springer's already seated? What if he chooses a table somewhere in the middle or something?"

Chris sighed. "Try to get him to move closer to the outer edge. Make something up—the view, whatever—but don't make it look obvious. If he starts looking suspicious, let it go. I should be able to see you anywhere in the restaurant with this thing. I just want to make sure it's Springer that gets zapped, not another patron."

Matty swallowed thickly.

"Very good, then," Goldstein concluded. "I believe we're all set. I'll get those two-ways. Chris, you make that call to the airlines. Mrs. Nielson, I suggest you attempt a catnap. I suspect you'll need it."

They stood regarding each other quietly a moment.

Then turned in opposing directions. Setting the thing in motion.

CHAPTER 28

Chris pulled the rental car to the curb, shut down the engine, paused long enough to take a deep, even breath. A new city, a new day, a new beginning.

But what of the ending?

He reached over to the seat beside him, picked up the little palm-size two-way. Depressing a red button, he asked, "How're we doing?"

Goldstein's voice, tinny and far away, replied, "I'm in the restaurant parking lot. Looks good from here. Warm here in New York, yes? How about you, Mr. Nielson?"

Chris sat in the car watching an old man with a heavy shopping bag labor by, pink-cheeked, without looking up. "Not great. There's nothing vacant over here, nothing abandoned. Nothing high enough, anyway. I'm going for the harried businessman routine."

"I shall await your buzz."

Chris pocketed the radio, stepped out of the car into the unusually warm—nearly balmy—New York morning, turned to look across snow-dripping trees toward the rising plume of mighty Niagara in the distance, thinking, It looks farther than it did in the drawing.

He glanced down at his watch. He'd been bobbing his head toward the watch all morning, so often it had begun a small pain below the base of his skull. He turned and faced the opposite direction: an aged KFC stand, a pawnshop, several office buildings, and down the street, the dun facade of the structure he'd come to investigate, the one building that looked promising.

He came around to the trunk of the rental car, lifted it, withdrew a black businessman's briefcase. Within it, the CIA rifle was neatly dismantled, folded, and contained. The briefcase's outer leather hide perfectly complemented his businessman's charcoal gray suit, tie, and black Florsheims.

Chris opened the case in the trunk, looked both ways quickly at the small-town, unhurried streets, took out the night scope, and slid it into his outer coat pocket, shut the trunk.

He headed down the block casually, a businessman out strolling during lunch hour.

Half a mile away, Abe Goldstein, dressed as always in attorney blue, stepped from his own rental car, locked it, gazed upward at the twenty-three-story tubular facade of the Rapids Hotel and Restaurant, its huge doughnut-shaped glass-encased penthouse top reflecting the shimmering blue of both the sky and the thundering rush of the nearby cataract. There are a lot of people about, Goldstein thought upon entering the foyer, especially for the winter months. It must be the warm weather.

He stalled near the elevator, pretending to peruse a shelf of travel brochures extolling the virtues of wondrous Niagara.

Mr. Hackermeyer, slim and balding and officiously eager to please, showed Chris to the twenty-third floor, down the hall and to the suite of the Lange Building, which was currently available for lease. Mr. Hackermeyer seemed always to be in motion, seemed never at a loss for words: "One of the nicer offices on this floor. Of course, you know about our prices, substantially higher than what you'll find elsewhere in the area, but then we have the view; everyone wants a view of the falls. Some, of course, find it distracting, but I for one have enjoyed my office overlooking Niagara for nearly eight years now. Ah, here we are, two-thirteen." He produced a key, twisted it into a gold lock, sweeping back the door to an oak-paneled, vacant fifteen-by-twelve room. Moving quickly to adjust the thermostat for comfort, Mr. Hackermeyer noted officiously, "There's painting to do, of course, and it won't be ready for occupancy for another week. And I must tell you—Mr. Nielson, is it?"

"That's right," Chris confirmed.

"I must tell you there are two other gentlemen with applications ahead of you. Well, now. How about that view, then?"

Chris was already eyeing the postcard panorama of steaming falls and Canadian skyline speculatively from the two large glass picture windows. His right hand was thrust casually into his jacket pocket, jabbing away at the little red button.

Goldstein heard the muted beep in his pocket, turned immediately, and climbed aboard the hotel elevator, pushing the button to the top floor and the glass-enclosed restaurant with its 360-degree view of the area. He was, but for the little plastic radio in his pocket, alone on the elevator.

"I wonder if I might ask a small favor of you," Chris addressed the ever patient Mr. Hackermeyer. "I wonder if I could spend a couple of minutes in here alone, get the feel of the place. Would that be all right?"

"Well . . ."

"Just two minutes. It's a quirk of mine. I can't really get into a place until I know if I'm going to be able to live with myself in it."

Hackermeyer, looking Chris up and down, finally smiled. "I understand. I have some calls to make anyway. Enjoy."

When he'd left, Chris pulled out the night scope, withdrew the radio, squinted outward toward the tall, cake-topped structure across the way throwing shards of glare at him. He gave the red button on the radio two punches, no more.

The Rapids' assistant manager—early twenties and hired because he was dating the owner's daughter—turned from chewing out a Hispanic busboy twice his age to see who was rapping insistently at the Rapids' glass entrance doors.

The young assistant manager tried making motions with his hands, indicating the clearly placed sign on the door. When that failed to dissuade the smiling man rapping patiently, the young assistant manager was finally obliged to open up a crack, peer out with histrionic authority. He announced, "I'm sorry, sir. The restaurant doesn't open for another two hours."

"Oh, that's wonderful, that's just terrific luck! Very heavily booked tonight, are you?" Mr. Goldstein beamed.

"I'm afraid you'd need a reservation. We only accept those by phone."

"Here's the thing. I have this incredible favor to ask. My sister and her husband were married right here at Niagara Falls some years ago. They're coming in tonight to spend a second honeymoon, if you can believe such romance still exists in the world."

"Sir—"

"What I have in mind is a kind of surprise. At least for him. Sheila—that's my sister—Sheila's in on it, of course. What she'd like to do is have dinner with him tonight, same place, same table they shared ten years ago. Now I ask you, is romance dead in our troubled world? It's why I didn't call first, you see. I needed to be here to show you the exact table."

The young assistant manager started to say something, noticed the hundred-dollar bill issuing from the little man's wallet. "Not that we'd expect such a favor for nothing, not at all. Could I, do you think, take just a quick peek inside, show you exactly which table they sat at?" The bill slid through the crack. The young assistant manager gave the offering a disgusted look. Then he craned quickly over his shoulder, reached out, and made the bill disappear.

Inside, the young assistant led the little man officiously through the empty maze of crisp, linen-draped tables, Goldstein smiling convivially at the help setting up the silverware, the single rose vases.

They came to the wide, curving picture window that was the restaurant's outer wall, the view below breathtaking. "My goodness!" Goldstein exclaimed. "It really is quite something, isn't it? This would be the northeast area if I'm not mistaken?"

"Well, from the elevator, yes, but—"

"Ah, yes, this is definitely the way Sheila described it. I wonder, could you possibly indulge me with one more favor? I've been on the road all day. Could you spare a glass of water?"

"Water? Certainly. Just a moment." The young man turned on his heel.

Goldstein watched a moment, looked both ways quickly, drew the palmed radio to his lips and punched the little red button twice. "The eagle has landed."

"I've got you," came Chris from the tinny speaker, "but you're too far east. Move about two . . . three tables to your right."

Goldstein turned casually, radio palmed against his thigh, strolled before the spacious curve of window three tables down.

"That's perfect," from Chris. He squinted, focusing the CIA scope. "Put them right there and I've got a clear shot. And let's pray he lets Matty hold the baby."

"Your water, sir," the young assistant announced, handing a tepid glass to Goldstein, who took it, not drinking, not looking at the table at all but outward at some spot on the distant shoreline. "This is the very table they sat at; I'm sure of it. Oh, won't this be a nice surprise!"

"And that name, sir?" The young manager sighed, producing a pad, a pencil stub.

The attorney reached into his left shirt pocket, fishing. "The thing is, I'm not sure what name they'll use. It's this little game they play, pretending to be secret lovers, very naughty, very sweet. Here, here now. There's a snapshot of my sister. Lovely girl, yes? She'll be with a tall, blond gentleman, rugged-looking chap. Or she may come first, to surprise him. Just instruct the hostess, if you would."

"Well, it's a little unusual. . . ."

"You can't imagine what this will mean to them." Goldstein beamed, thumbing out another bill. "And of course we'll want to do a feature article on it. Did I mention I'm with the *News Chronicle*? I didn't?"

"And how are we doing?" smiled a patient Mr. Hackermeyer just seconds after Chris had replaced the scope in his pocket, put away the radio.

"Very well," Chris told him, "I think this just might be the ticket. I have one more location to check and then we'll see about that application. Would you have a card, Mr. . . . Hackenbush, is it?"

"Hackermeyer," came the cool reply, and he produced the requested card.

Chris took it, shook hands, and got out of there.

He smiled companionably at the security guard on his way out, noting the man's plastic name badge above the uniform pocket: NED POTTER.

Then he was back into sidewalk and warm sunshine.

Matty checked herself into the Armstrong, an unassuming budget motel six blocks from the Rapids. She locked the thin motel door, kicked off her shoes, slumped on the hard mattress. The weariness of the three-hour plane flight eased from her shoulders. She glanced for the millionth time that day at her watch: 5:33.

Her hands, she noticed, unbuttoning her blouse, were trembling slightly, uncontrollably. Whatever she touched, looked at, seemed preternaturally acute as an acid-induced college dream. What if Nicky wasn't with him? What if Frank didn't show at all, the whole thing just another of his cruel jokes? She had no guarantee of anything. Least of all that this wild plan would succeed. In the entire time she had known him, she had never once seen Frank Springer outsmarted, outmaneuvered.

A constant bubble of fear accompanied her everywhere.

She ran hot water in the little motel tub with the cracked tile floor, peeled out of her underthings, wishing the trembling, which had extended to her legs, would stop.

There were only two flights to Niagara: one in the early morning, and this one, which scheduled her arrival for late afternoon. She'd chosen the later one, chosen this small motel down the way because she didn't want any possible contact with Springer before the appointed dinner in the glass-walled restaurant. She didn't want to allow for the chance of anything going wrong, of Frank showing up early and whisking her away, destroying the plan.

She stepped into hot, rewarding steam and settled back with a groan, praying the bath would soothe her a little so she'd give nothing away tonight in the restaurant. You're an actress, she'd been telling herself all day. Here's your biggest part.

She glanced down to look yet again at her watch, forgetting she'd taken it off for the bath.

Goldstein arrived at the restaurant at exactly 8:30, having booked a single reservation that morning. He sat at a small table directly across from the designated window, directly in the line of fire. If the trigger was pulled this moment, he would receive the slug. His view, unobstructed, offered him a clear path to the other table. Which, hopefully, Mrs. Nielson would soon be occupying.

Goldstein ordered a big meal, one that would allow plenty of time both for preparation and consumption. He had brought along an evening paper behind which he could hide the little two-way radio, keep in constant contact with Nielson.

He sat back, paper before him, sipping from his water glass, watching the glass door for Mrs. Nielson's entrance. She would be early but not too early. And, just in case the hostess blew it, Goldstein would make sure she got properly seated. After which they would both sit praying, at opposite tables, that Springer showed. That he had the baby with him.

Chris arrived at the Lange Building promptly at 8:30, the night considerably cooler than the day as he stepped from the rental car, having parked around back in a nearly empty alley. Breath fluttered from his lips as he locked the car, briefcase in hand.

He moved quickly around to the front of the dimly lit building, pressed the silvery bar on the entrance door. He found it locked, as he knew it would be, peered inside for the guard seated behind the oak receiving desk. He rapped lightly on the glass. The guard, a large, squat ruddy-faced man (not the guard of this afternoon), came with mild annoyance to the door, produced a ring of keys, unlocked, opened a crack. He peered out. "Sir?"

"Ned Potter?" Chris inquired, ignoring the man's name badge.

"No, Ned works the afternoon shift. Can I help you?"

"Yes, I hope so. I'm supposed to meet a"—Chris produced the business card—"a Mr. Hackermeyer here tonight." He showed the card to the guard. "I'm a client, Chris Nielson."

The guard hesitated. "Well, no one's inside the building, sir, except me."

"Yes, Hackermeyer called to say he'd be late, that I should go on up. I'm leasing two-thirteen. 'Tell Ned to let you in,' he said."

"Well, Ned works afternoons. . . ."

"I see. Must have been a mixup." Chris consulted his watch impatiently with his best businessman's face. "Look, I have to catch a plane in an hour. If Hackermeyer's late and I don't get a chance to approve of that suite, there's going to be problems."

The beefy guard stepped back, opened the door, fumbling for his keys. "Come on in. I can open it for you."

Matty, checking herself briefly in the foyer mirror, came smartly to the restaurant entrance, smiled at the hostess. "Sheila Smith, table for two."

The hostess, a pretty teenager with terrific legs, began combing her reservation list, glanced up quickly at Matty, consulted the wallet-size photo hidden under the ledger, smiled, and picked up a menu. "This way, ma'am. We have a table for you right over here."

Goldstein, the first of many weights easing from his shoulders, breathed out gratefully, eyes on Matty crossing the room, exchanged a brief glance with her before settling once more behind his paper. He waited a conservative moment longer. Then, palming the little two-way, he depressed the button three times.

The fat guard turned at the beeping sound in the elevator. Chris frowned annoyance, muttered, "Damn pager. They never leave you alone."

The fat guard grinned, escorted Chris down the hall, opened 213 for him, accepted a five from Chris with a grateful salute.

"Thanks for your help. If you'll just inform Mr. Hackermeyer of my whereabouts, please."

"Will do, sir, and thank you."

Chris pretended to appraise the office, waiting until the door was shut and the night guard's footsteps had receded. He locked the door quickly, snapped off the lights, placed the briefcase below the window, thumbed the little red button. "Okay, I'm in. How goes it?"

Goldstein, paper before him, leaned into his palm casually, replied softly: "Mrs. Nielson's in place, red coat and all. Beep me when you've got a bead on her."

Chris snapped the rifle together expertly—he'd been practicing all morning—fitted the scope, checked the breech, and sighted through the darkened window. Matty's red coat and burnished hair bloomed between the crosshairs. Chris moved the scope just to the right, at the empty chair across from her, at Goldstein, hidden behind his paper, at the tables and wall beyond that.

Everything in place now, everything perfect.

All they needed to complete the picture was Springer.

And the baby.

Matty, shoulders tensing again, found herself applying lipstick absently. Not because she really needed it but to see if her hand was still trembling. Which, to her irritation, it was.

She snapped closed her compact, placed it in her purse, looked up, and saw her son, beaming, being led across the restaurant toward her by Frank Springer.

She had to choke back an overpowering urge to weep, so intense was her relief.

Frank, always smiling, bent at the table, kissed her cheek, lifted Nicky in his arms. "You're early, kitten."

Matty forced a smile, unable to take her eyes off her son. "Yes. The plane."

"I already had reservations over there." Springer nodded at a distant table.

Matty, stomach clenching beneath her loveliest black evening gown, forced an apologetic look. "Oh, I'm sorry. I already ordered an appetizer. They fed us *nuts* on the flight! Can you believe? I'm sorry, Frank, I was just starving."

Springer shook his head, waved her off, sitting down across from her with the child. "It doesn't matter. This is fine. My, you look lovely."

"Thank you, Frank."

"Have you got a bead?" Goldstein spoke into his palm softly.

He was shocked, seconds later, at the frantic reply from the tinny speaker. "What the hell?" Chris was shouting. "She's moved! That's the wrong table! I've got nothing but a white I-beam through this scope!"

Goldstein, abruptly perspiring, double checked the room around him. "They haven't moved, Chris. I've been watching Matty all evening. Are you sure . . ." He trailed off softly.

"Abe? What is it? Speak to me!"

"Oh, damn . . . oh, damn it to hell!"

"What? What is it?" Chris peered first through the scope, pulled away, squinted with his naked eye at the distant restaurant, *"What's the matter?"*

Goldstein fumbled, nearly upsetting his water glass, voice trembling now into his palm. "It's *revolving*! The goddamn restaurant's revolving! Jesus, they must have just turned it on for the evening crowd. Chris, can you hear me?"

"Is something wrong?" Springer asked Matty, lifting Nicky to place his napkin in his own lap.

She was glancing about curiously, brow cleft. "Are we . . . moving?"

Springer chuckled lightly. "You didn't notice? They've done some refurbishing since we dined here last. A three-hundred-sixty degree view of the falls. Pleasant, isn't it?"

Chris stood shakily, squinted through the scope, shouting into the radio: "I can't see a goddamn thing but two old ladies eating tiramisu! What the hell is going on, Abe?"

"The restaurant is *turning*! It must be a new addition. I've been sitting here all evening reading this vapid brochure, and it doesn't mention a thing about it. We're hardly moving. Can't you get some kind of bead on Springer?"

"I told you, he's hidden behind a spar. For Christ's sake, Abe, how the hell did this happen?"

"All right, all right, calm down. Let me think. There's a way around this, there's always a way around things."

Chris jerked down the rifle, tight with frustration, blood ringing in his ears. He spat into the radio. "Like hell there's a way! Once he comes out from behind that spar the shot will be realigned. It won't make any difference if you get up and leave your table or not. The round will strike another party."

"Oh, Christ," from a weakened Goldstein.

Matty, across the room, caught the attorney's expression, saw the city lights—nearly imperceptibly—moving now behind his head. It was true. Impossible but true. The entire restaurant was moving, turning, offering the garrulous patrons a spectacular view of the glorious Niagara on one side, the tumbling rapids on the other.

"Are you all right, kitten? You look pale."

Recovering quickly, Matty smiled. "It's just so good to see Nicky again is all. He looks well, Frank. Thank you."

Springer, leaning forward, supporting the baby in his left hand, covered hers with his right. "Everything's going to be fine from now on, kitten."

Goldstein, frantic, reached out to pull at the shirt of a passing waiter. "Excuse me. The restaurant, how long before it makes one complete rotation?"

"Just under an hour, sir."

"Chris! Chris, are you there?"

"I heard. We can't wait that long. What if Springer decides to skip dessert? Shit, Abe!"

"All right, all right. I'll just have to get them to switch tables somehow."

"No! Don't do that; Springer will never buy it. He probably set the whole thing up like this on purpose. Damn! If we'd only known sooner!" He lowered the scope, mind racing.

Then his eyes lit with inspiration. "Hold on, hold on a second, Abe."

"Chris? Chris? What are you doing?"

Rifle in tow, Chris raced through the hallway past the other darkened suites, counting doors, trying to calculate roughly. Stopping before 219, he hesitated, trying the knob, finding it locked, of course.

"Chris? Chris, are you there?"

"I've got a terrific idea," Frank Springer was telling Matty. "How about we just skip dinner altogether, get out of here, and get on our way? What do you say?"

Matty, perspiring heavily into the lovely gown, smiled falteringly. "Leave? But really, Frank, I'm famished. We just sat down."

"Kitten, you must know how dangerous this is for me. We'll be much safer—all of us—once we're under way. What do you say? I promise you a full-course meal at the best restaurant in Canada."

"Canada?"

Springer gripped her hand, smiling disarmingly with what appeared to be genuine sincerity. "Don't you see, kitten? I forgive you. I forgive you for him, for all of it. And you wouldn't have come here tonight if you hadn't forgiven me. Everything's going to be just fine now. Everything's going to be perfect."

Chris slammed his shoulder into the door. And again, pain rocketing up his arm, the metal door not budging. He adjusted the rifle in his hand, prepared to slam again.

"Freeze!"

It came from somewhere behind him. Chris turned, still gripping the CIA rifle, found the fat night guard, legs apart, bent at the waist, leveling his service revolver nervously.

Goldstein, beyond frantic, gripped the radio in sweat-slick fingers, calling, too loudly, "Chris, answer, please. Are you all right? Are you in some kind of trouble?"

Springer, holding both her hands now, looked deep into Matty's eyes, face devoid of anything but affection and trust. "Well, kitten? Will you come with me right now?"

Matty swallowed, plucked at her napkin. "All right. All right, just give me a moment in the ladies' room."

Springer smiled, kissed her hand. Then he tugged her back as she started from the table, kissed the hand again. "I'll be waiting right here."

"Just put the rifle on the floor!" the visibly trembling night guard ordered.

Chris faced him calmly, eyes on the big round key loop on the fat man's belt. "I need to get into this room. Will you open it, please? It's an emergency."

"I said, *put down the rifle!*"

Chris watched him. "All right." Bending slowly, he placed the rifle on the floor.

The radio beeped in his pocket. Straightening, Chris reached for the little plastic two-way, speaking into it. "Yes? Yes, he's right here. We're having a bit of trouble, I'm afraid. Your night guard doesn't seem to want to cooperate with the FBI."

Goldstein was thunderstruck on the other end. "Night guard?"

Chris nodded into the radio, walking deliberately toward the trembling, stiff-armed guard, holding the little radio out to him. "For you . . . It's Mr. Hackermeyer. He doesn't sound happy." He tossed the radio at the fat guard.

The guard, sweating and flat-footed, tried to aim and catch in the same movement, firing in inadvertent panic—too high—as Chris came leaping.

Matty, in the ladies' room, stared at her reflection in the mirror, saw dark and haunted eyes gazing back. "What can I do? What does Chris want me to do?"

Washing her hands quickly, drying, she flicked at her hair once, turned back to the door, mind blank, unable to come up with a single reason to keep Frank in that chair.

Chris hit the guard, and again with the rifle butt, grabbing the key ring without looking back. Jamming it into the lock, he pushed into the room, flicking on the night scope as he raced to the window. He squatted down, bracing the slim muzzle on the cement ledge, sighting through the scope in time to see Springer turning, a perfect target.

As Matty stepped in front of him, slim back directly in the crosshairs. Chris gasped, jerking up the muzzle reflexively—*that* close to having pulled the trigger.

Springer stood, hefting Nicky, turning with Matty to head through the crowded tables.

"They're leaving!" Goldstein howled. "Chris, goddamn it, where are you?"

"I see them! I can't get a shot; we're going to have to find another place! Stay with them, Abe!"

"Right, all right!"—dropping his napkin, knocking over his wine—"I'm right behind them!" He scooped bills from his pocket, threw them at the table, pushed past the waiter who was just arriving with his dessert. "Sir?"

★   ★   ★

Chris tossed the briefcase into the backseat, fired up the rental car, screeched from the alley, heading toward the Rapids Hotel, radio in hand. "Where are we, Abe? Keep me briefed."

"Just leaving the elevator. I stood practically *next* to the bastard. Matty was staring at me. I could have shot him, Chris, but the crowd, the baby!"

"It's okay," Chris said, dodging around nighttime traffic. "Just stay with them. I'll be there in a couple of minutes. Don't let Springer see you following. Is he still holding Nicky?"

"Yes, coming across the foyer now. Matty keeping her head up, her wits about her, brave girl. Through the restaurant door now. He's turning left on the concourse, heading along the railing beside the falls. Lot of mist here . . . darker. Hold it."

"What's the matter?" Chris honked at a lazy sedan. Cursing, he pulled dangerously into the opposing lane to lurch around a lumbering truck.

"They've stopped," Goldstein said. "Darker here, hard to see. She's telling him something . . . can't make it out unless I get closer."

"No, stay back. Don't let Springer see you. Keep your distance until I get there."

Matty touched Springer's arm as she spoke, felt the wonderful warmth of Nicky's little leg beside it. "Frank, listen to me. I'm prepared to go with you, be with you, do whatever you want. But I need your promise, you won't in any way hurt Nicky."

"Matty."

"Please, just tell me you won't hurt the baby, and I'll do anything you say, anything."

Springer smiled, bent with the baby to kiss her forehead, withdrew something from his pocket. "Remember this?"

Matty could just see it in the gloom. "The homing device?"

Springer turned, tossed the length of palm-size plastic into the brush. "Now do you trust me?"

Matty nodded. Forced a smile. Took his arm.

Goldstein squinted. "He's thrown something into the brush. A pack of cigarettes? Can't see very well. They're moving again. The baby is laughing. Matty doing well."

Chris pulled into the Rapids parking lot, waited behind the striped bar for his ticket, received it, scooted under the slowly rising bar toward the glowing lights of the hotel. "I'm here. Where are you, Abe?"

"Southeast side, near the rapids. Uh-oh . . ."

"What, *what?*"

"Damn it!"

"Talk to me, Abe!"

"He's got a car back here. I should have known it. Parked down here in the dark behind the restaurant. Where are you? Shall I try for him? I've got a clear shot."

"No, you might hit Nicky!" Chris screeched around a corner, slamming on his brakes to miss a gaggle of kids pouring from the path, squealing over the roar of the nearby rapids. "Abe, what's going on?"

Silence.

"Abe, did they get away? Answer me, Abe!"

Chris powered around the building, saw a small figure waiting below a lamplit sidewalk near a grassy slope, spectacles glowing as Chris roared up. He leaned across to throw the door open for the lawyer. "Get in!"

Goldstein regarded him idly, seemed to be using the lamppost for support.

"Abe, get in!"

The attorney crossed gingerly to the car, swayed drunkenly, caught the edge of the window. "Don't think . . . I can do that."

Chris felt his insides squeeze. "Abe! No!" He was out of the car and around the front bumper in time to catch Goldstein before he collapsed at the curb. A thin ribbon of red traced his chin.

The attorney's face was calm, but his pupils, dilated and milky, gave him away. "Son of a bitch put something into me. Never even saw the schmuck. . . ."

Breath hissing, Chris whipped off his jacket, rolled it, placed it gently beneath the pink, balding head. Goldstein's face was as unlined as a baby's, free from apparent pain. "I think that bastard's gone and killed me, Chris. . . ."

"Just lie still."

A woman in silver fur approached apprehensively with her dressed-for-dinner husband: an elderly couple on vacation and loath to spoil it.

"Get an ambulance!" Chris shouted at them.

The woman flinched, the man hesitated, then turned and ran up the green slope.

Goldstein's eyes were closed, his breath shallow. He was trying to pull something from beneath him, something he'd been carrying before. Chris helped him and retrieved a foldout map. "Go left . . ."

"What?" Chris bent low.

Goldstein's throat moved. "Go left. . . . Springer wouldn't trap himself on an island."

Chris glanced at the map, back to Goldstein, back to the map. He stuck it in his pocket and took the attorney's hand. "Abe."

"Get out of here."

"No."

There were people running down the slope toward them, several of them in white uniforms: waiters or paramedics. There had been no sound of sirens.

Goldstein opened his eyes, and Chris found anger in them. "Don't make a waste of this. Go to her!"

"I'll wait for the ambulance."

"Go to her, damn you!"

Chris squeezed the hand once. Rose, turned to look up the darkened street before him.

He sprinted to his car and leapt in.

He drove for three blocks, map opened beside him, before he came to the fork.

He sat idling in the rental car, biting his lip with indecision. Go left, Abe had said. Springer wouldn't trap himself on an island.

Chris dragged a hand across his mouth. According to the map, a left turn would head him off Luna Island, over a bridge and back to the highway. A right turn, and he'd end up on Goat Island, which divided the American and Canadian borders.

Chris turned the wheel, hesitated.

"No. You're wrong, Abe. The *average* guy would go left, get to the highway as quick as he could. Springer's never done an average thing in his life. We go right," and he yanked the wheel.

Ten minutes later, the white Goat Island sign post swam into his high beams.

Chris slowed, placed the map on the wheel before him, talking out loud as though he weren't alone in the car, as if Goldstein were still there. "Okay. According to this, the road we're now on simply loops around the entire island, past Horseshoe Falls on the Canadian side, eventually gets us right back to the main road, the revolving restaurant and American Falls. There's no other way off the island."

Chris grunted. "You think I turned the wrong way, don't you, Abe?"

The car was silent.

Something at the periphery of his vision dragged his eyes right. "Hold it, hold it—what's this?"

Chris slowed, eased to the curb behind a gray sedan with an Avis sticker in the back window. He left the motor running and leapt out, grabbing the night scope.

He bent to Springer's empty rental car. Straightened in a moment, cast about in all directions, lifting the scope, revolving this way, that, searching. Nothing.

He lowered the scope, exasperated. Then he cocked his head, listening acutely. "What's that sound?"

The familiar roar of rapids came back to him. And something else.

He turned, raced back, and shut off his engine, cocked his head again, swiveling it. "A boat."

He started running, down a dark, steep grassy knoll, the roar of rapids becoming louder, then thunderous.

Chris reached a clearing, stood panting at the edge of the shoreline, chest heaving, scope to his eyes. Through it he could see a fleeing stern, the back of Matty's russet head, Springer's broad shoulders behind the wheel as the powerboat knifed its way upriver against the current.

Chris nodded to the night. "Smart. He'll take the boat all the way upriver in the dark where no one can get to him. Probably has another car waiting somewhere up there."

He pulled the map free of his shirt, held it to the moonlight. Began talking out loud again, slowly, then faster. "The Niagara flows upstream past Navy Island, Grand Island . . . eventually all the way to Buffalo. It divides, becomes a fork here at Grand Island."

He consulted the scope again. "If Springer turns right there— follows the river around the island until it joins itself again below Lake Erie—we're pretty much sunk. However, if he elects to go left, hug the highway, he'll have to pass under Grand Island Bridge. There's no getting around it."

He shifted to the map again, hands trembling with a half-formed plan. "Okay. Now, he's bucking a pretty strong current. Even if he's got that boat at open throttle, I don't think he could outrace a car. If we can beat him to the bridge—"

Thought uncompleted, he lifted his naked eyes to the river again, shook his head dubiously. "We'd have a lot of backtracking to do, all the way across the falls and back to the highway. And Springer's got a head start on us. I should have turned left as you suggested, Abe."

But if you'd turned left, you wouldn't have seen his boat.

Chris stuck the map in his jacket pocket. "I'm wasting time."

CHAPTER 29

Matty, cold in the boat's spanking wind, was hardly listening to Springer's constant patter behind the wheel.

She was trying to secure Nicky's bright orange life jacket, shield his tender little body against the wind. Her palm constantly darted to his brow, reassuring herself that the long-endured fever had finally passed. The baby did, in fact, appear reasonably healthy, bright-eyed if clingy. It was so good just holding him there as they chopped against black current, she could almost convince herself it was enough, could almost forget that the plan had gone completely awry.

"So you really needn't worry," he was instructing her, "though it's true the current travels about eight kilometers an hour here upriver, we're a safe distance from the rapids back there near the island. Back there, near the lip of the falls, the water can hurtle up to forty-two miles per hour. We'd be hard pressed to buck that."

He winked at Matty as she rechecked Nicky's life jacket. "Back in July of 1960 a young man just a little older than Nicky went over the falls wearing that same style of life jacket."

Matty paused, not looking up, cinched the baby's straps tighter.

"Roger Woodward was his name. He and his sister Deanne were accompanying an older family friend on a motorboat ride here on the Niagara River. Distracted and playful, they didn't notice the boat had drifted into the rapids downriver. By the time they realized their fate, it was too late."

Matty plucked wind-matted strands from her face, turned to Springer finally. Keep him talking. Keep him distracted. Chris will come. "What happened?"

Springer sat back easily behind the wheel, calling loudly above the motor's wail. "All three kids had life jackets on, a good thing considering the boat spilled over after entering the rapids."

"Dear God."

"Deanne, the girl, tried to swim to Goat Island, a whole group of bedazzled tourists watching the poor child's efforts, not doing a thing to help her. About fifteen feet from the edge of the falls a man named John Hayes—a truck driver and auxiliary policeman from New Jersey—hung on to a guardrail by one foot and grabbed the girl's hand, pulled her to safe ground."

Matty held Nicky tight, shouting into the wind. "What happened to the little boy?"

"Roger?" Springer smiled. "There's a fleet of tour guide boats at the base of the falls called *Maid of the Mist*. The captain of one of them turned from his boatload of tourists to see an orange life jacket bobbing in the water near the base of the falls. Roger was plucked out of the swirling maelstrom with nary a scratch. Survived a trip over Niagara in only a little orange life jacket!"

Matty shivered in the wind. "What about the family friend? You said there were three of them."

Springer nodded. "Oh, yes. James Honeycutt. They found his body four days later." He turned to Matty, winked.

"There's the entrance to the bridge!" Chris addressed the empty car.

He consulted the map beside him to be sure. "Yes, the only bridge, according to this map, between the highway and Grand Island. It's a long one, though. It's going to be pure guesswork determining where Springer's boat will pass beneath. Just have to aim for somewhere near the center, keep a sharp lookout and pray." Chris grunted at himself. "Assuming, of course, Springer comes this way at all."

He turned onto the bridge, lit the Grand Island Bridge sign in his headlights, and headed out toward the structure's center. I'd have no chance at all without the night scope, he was thinking. The biggest problem will be traffic.

He nodded at himself. "What am I doing out here in the middle of the night in the middle of a bridge with a high-powered rifle? Suppose a tourist—or a cop . . . ?"

Worry about that when the time comes.

He could almost hear the little attorney say it.

Springer throttled down, the current less strong here, checked the gas gauge, other dials glowing on the panel. He swiveled to Matty. "What are you thinking about?"

She was turtled down behind the windshield, holding Nicky close to her breast, shivering slightly despite the heavy coat. "Of your story, I guess. I always think of barrels when I think of Niagara Falls."

Springer chuckled. "Many have tried. Few have succeeded. Actually, the first person to go over the big falls—the Horseshoe Falls on the Canadian side—was a woman."

"A woman?"

"Annie Edson Tailor. 1901. And she did it in a barrel. Solid oak, held together with iron hoops. Amazing thing about it was, little Annie couldn't swim."

"Good Lord."

Springer smiled into the wind. "They strapped her in with leather hoops, stuck cushions all around her, sealed her up on the American side and let her go. Only took ten seconds. She drifted over to the Canadian side, where rescuers pulled her ashore, popped open the lid. Old Annie looked up, blinked, and asked if she'd gone over yet. The falls had knocked her unconscious."

"Quite a feat."

"Yes, one she vowed never to repeat. Called herself the Queen of the Mist, went on tour to earn money from the stunt. Problem was, the public wanted to see the barrel, not poor Annie. She'd left the thing rotting in the river. She died in 1921, a pauper."

"Sad."

Springer adjusted the throttle to a smooth, level whine. "It's a sad world."

Chris nosed the rental car to the bridge guardrail, cut the engine. He flipped the emergency blinker on, leapt out, and came around to the rail. A ribbon of black water extended below and outward into misted night, invisible but for glistening winks of moonlight reflecting undulant current, swirling eddies. Chris reached through the window, extracted the scope, sighting down-river through it.

Darkness.

He lowered the scope, glanced from side to side along the narrow bridge. Little traffic this time of night. Still, the area was doubtless patrolled.

He returned his attention to the scope. Squinted as something caught the convex lens. Movement.

Chris held his breath, felt his heart hitch. There was a power-boat on the river. Coming this way . . .

He rested his elbows against the rail for support, resighted. Surely his timing couldn't be this lucky.

Yet it was. He could see Springer's grinning face, a pale blob against surrounding night, opaque waters. Matty was huddled against the opposite gunwale, hair fluttering, face indistinct, shoul-ders hunched against the night wind. Nicky was not to be found, possibly lying down in the seat between them, out of Chris's line of vision.

A swish of car tires. Chris turned to see a station wagon approach, light blazing. It slowed curiously, sped up again, and passed as he held the scope down against his leg.

The wagon disappeared, red fireflies in the night. Chris squinted through the night scope, felt a jolt of adrenaline.

The powerboat was slowing, practically stopping.

Chris cursed sibilantly. "Why the hell is he stopping in the middle of the river?"

"Why are we stopping?" Matty asked him.

Springer threw the powerboat into neutral, switched off the engine, turned evenly to her.

Something about his face made her draw back.

"Matty—"

"You promised!" she pleaded desperately, clutching the baby tightly.

Springer nodded patiently. "I know, I know. But just listen to me for a moment." He settled back into the plastic-cushioned driver's seat, a paternal professor to a confused undergraduate. "In our ancient Russia—the Russia that gave you and me birth—the initial state grew up around the great rivers that formed the main trade route between Scandinavia and Constantinople. Rivers not unlike the mighty Niagara. As you know, Kiev, on the Dnieper River route, became the country's capital in 882. . . ."

"Frank—"

"Because of its strategic location on the Dnieper, Kiev was the most important of all the towns of Russ. It was the southernmost fortified point of the forest region. In Vitichev, just below, flotillas of boats used to make the run south through the treacherous steppe to the Black Sea."

Her face was white with fear. "Frank, please! You promised!"

"The point is, Matty, the ruler of Kiev—a man who assumed this position because of the trading and military expeditions—also took on a political position of great importance. His name was Oleg and he was called Grand Prince. He was a fair ruler, but sometimes a stern one. When, as occasionally happened, a child was born from dubious union, both mother and father claiming it, Oleg was often prompted in those harsh days to do that which may seem less than civilized to you and me."

Matty pushed up, gripping the baby, cast about wildly at the cold, black waters, eyes wide as saucers. Springer threw her down hard again with a cry.

"If the couple in question could not agree upon the child's birthright, then he was simply cast into the—"

"Frank, *please!*" Tears stained her cheeks, the baby crushed to her face. "You said you wouldn't touch him! You *promised* me!"

Springer, sighing, patted her back gently. "Kitten, I only want what's best for all of us. I only want to assure us of a fresh start. How can we do that with this *thing* between us?"

"What's he doing now?" Chris addressed the night again. The figures in the boat didn't appear to be doing much of anything, just sitting and talking. Matty appeared somewhat agitated, or was that a trick of the light? Damn! He couldn't see that well from this distance even with the scope. He needed them closer for a good shot.

He squinted, bit his lip. Matty did look upset. Why was she holding the baby like that?

His breath caught suddenly. "Shit!"

Matty struggled up again, kicking at Springer as he tried to force her back. She lashed out, flailing, scratching with her left hand curled into a claw, the baby bundled against her, starting to cry. She kicked hard, getting in a lucky one, doubling Springer up.

Matty moved quickly, stepping awkwardly over the windshield

onto the rocking bow, thinking, If I jump, if I hold the baby and make for the shore, even in this awful dark I might make it. I'm a strong swimmer.

Springer recovered, lunged. Matty cried out, fell.

Springer grabbed her, patience gone, face like stone but terrifyingly calm. He pulled back, coming away with the child.

Matty shrieked, tripping, sprawling across the hobbyhorsing bow. *"Frank! No!"*

Springer steadied himself on the bow, legs apart, holding the baby above his head, commanding the heavens: "Thus we entrust this child to the dark waters. That God shall know his rightful place in—"

The first slug tore through his left shoulder, spraying blood and leather, spinning the baby from his hands.

Matty screamed, reaching out, missed as Nicky—an orange blur—whirled past, splashed.

She scrambled heedlessly after him, diving into black, shockingly cold water.

Springer spun like a strong dancer, clutching his dripping shoulder, face twisted with pain and amusement—amused at having been taken unawares. He turned drunkenly, squinting out across the waters to see who the clever person was. Through the mist, he beheld the ghostly ribbon of bridge upriver, a dim figure watching him from there, clutching something. Springer smiled.

The next slug slammed his chest—*whap*—dead center, the report chasing it a moment later. Springer was catapulted back and over the windshield, where, flailing and clawing, he might have caught the wheel. But he missed it, fingers trailing over the smooth plastic, missed the gunwale too, dropping heavily into the icy river, disappearing in a short, frothless splash.

Chris shouted over the railing, *"Matty!"*

He turned as strobing lights fell over the rail: a county sheriff's car swooping down on the rental.

Chris hesitated, let the rifle drop from his hands, sail downward and disappear. He retained the scope.

He began racing toward the police car, hands waving as the cop climbed out. "There's a woman in the water! Out there! A woman and a child!"

The cop—just drawing his service revolver—offered a confused look, glancing first to Chris then out at the dark river. "I can't see anything—"

Chris handed him the scope. "Out there!"

The officer squinted outward. "Christ."

Matty surfaced a moment later, gulped air hugely, porpoised high, and dove again. Again.

She emerged the third time, choking, coughing up water, hacking. Ignoring it, she dog-paddled a frantic circle, craning for the little orange life jacket *"Nicky!!"*

She hyperventilated, dived again, closer to shore, opening her eyes underwater to nightmare blackness, the greedy plucking of the current at her dress, her legs. She surfaced screaming his name. The black river gave her back nothing.

She paddled between the floundering motorboat and shore. Dismissing her exhaustion, she thought, Could he have somehow grabbed on to the boat?

She rejected it immediately.

She paddled, shivered once deep to her soul, the water making a little phosphorescent curve against her chest, the current deceptively strong, stronger than Springer had thought. Her teeth chattered reflexively.

No, Nicky hadn't grasped the boat, and he hadn't drifted to shore in this current. He'd been dragged downriver.

"Nicky! Nicky, talk to Mommy!" She swiveled in the water, outer limbs numbing quickly, toes and fingers already unfeeling. The sky seemed to explode suddenly, and she imaged herself drowning. She twisted to a blinding searchlight falling across her, its yellow beam turning the churning foam around her hands a rich, emerald green.

"Matty! Here! *Here!*"

She craned toward shore, saw Chris's anxious face, began stroking toward him. He was already wading out to her, the river dragging at his jeans, someone—a cop—behind him, restraining him. Which was okay, because she could make it all by herself. . . . Just give her a minute. She might drift a little downriver, but she could make it.

She soon felt the rocky bottom under her toes, put her legs down, and dragged herself, squinting into the bright glare. Why didn't they take that thing out of her face? It wasn't helping.

Chris's strong arms pulled her the rest of the way, and Matty collapsed into him, all breath gone. "The baby, the *baby!*" It was all she could manage.

* * *

In the backseat of the squad car, trembling uncontrollably, green army blanket around her, Matty kept reminding the officer behind the wheel through chattering teeth: "He was wearing a little orange life jacket. A little orange life jacket. You should be able to spot that *easily*!"

The officer, a seasoned veteran, drove professionally with one hand, nodding courteously at Mrs. Nielson, speaking softly, constantly into the car radio with the other hand, a mechanical, unhurried monotone, yielding crackling squawks from the dash, only parts of which Chris could comprehend: "Just over two years of age, blond-haired Caucasian, wearing a bright orange life jacket. Check. Check. Approximately ten hundred hours. Check. No, I did not. The mother is stable, on route to County General—"

"No!" Matty cried, grasping the back of the seat. "I don't need to go to a hospital! Get me to the falls! Get us to the falls!"

"Matty," Chris restrained her, "he's doing everything he can." His voice was drowned out by the sudden swooping beat of helicopter rotors vibrating the car's interior, a surge of hope in the black night. In a moment they beat away to the east, replaced by another swooping roar, and another, overhead searchlights lancing the river beside them.

"They'll find him, honey," Chris said, unable to look at her, using the excuse to comb the river in tandem with the searchlights. "He won't go under in that life jacket."

He glanced up to see the officer looking quickly away from the rearview, expression impassive, not hopeful.

Hunkered in a yellow Red Cross slicker before an electric-green Niagara Rescue and Recovery van, Chris desultorily sipped tasteless coffee. He watched the ongoing retrieval attempts here below the falls, the winking police boats scouring the dangerous white currents and tricky rapids beneath the deafening cataract. Brightly colored slickers and swinging, quickly turning lights lent an incongruous carny atmosphere to the scene.

It had been just under an hour, the mist-shrouded air thick with an encroaching sense of permanency and loss. Chris, unable to stop his heedless brain, had calculated and recalculated the distance between where the boat had overturned and here; when the police car picked up Matty; how fast the river was flowing; how far the falls were from that point; how long it would take the squad car to reach the falls as opposed to a floating two-year-old. Calculated these things over and over in mindless rote, brain on overdrive.

Here in freezing, billowing mist, mind further numbed by the continuous roar, not even his most optimistic guesses favored Nicky's survival. It was well past the time the tiny body would have made the plunge.

All rescue efforts were concentrated below now. But it was impossible to pinpoint exactly where—or even at which of the three concentric falls—the child may have tumbled over, though the team seemed to think the American side the most likely.

Perhaps in daylight, Chris kept thinking. But here in the dark amid stabbing, blinding searchlights it seemed more and more hopeless.

"The problem is," one of the Niagara Rescue Team volunteers told Chris—a tall, narrow-faced man who had taken it upon himself, probably not for the first time, to stay with the grieving parent, his posture having a sadly rehearsed air about it—"the problem is the plunge pool. Most people think that whatever goes over the falls just bobs to the surface again in a hurry, but sadly that's not the case. Many objects, including cows and horses, have been caught in the plunge pool, the basin directly below the falls."

Chris nodded absently, craned around to find Matty, still wearing the green army blanket, standing nearer the shore, dripping wet and freezing, staring at the rescue boats, unwilling to move from the spot until word came of her son.

"Ninety percent of Niagara's water goes over the Horseshoe Falls crest line, where the plunge pool is the deepest. A body can, theoretically, stay trapped down there in the whirlpools and swirling currents for hours. Now, luckily for us, your boy most likely went over here at the American side, which gets only about ten percent of the water and has a pretty shallow plunge pool. Also it's both winter and nighttime."

"What's that mean?" Chris wondered numbly.

A younger member of the squad had wandered up wearing a bright yellow slicker. "At night and during the winter months," the newcomer interjected, "we turn down the flow, so to speak, divert the water to the power plants. It's about half of what the tourists come to see in the peak summer daylight hours. Less volume, less velocity, better chances for your boy."

Chris nodded by way of thanks.

"Also," the young man continued, valiantly summoning any fact that held hope, "the cold water can actually work in our favor, slow the boy's metabolism, improve our chances of resuscitation."

"Thank you," from Chris, not looking up. Not looking at his watch any longer either, which had become an alien enemy clutching his wrist. His heart was no longer buying any of it.

After a few moments of staring at the jouncing rescue boats, darting helicopters, the two men moved discreetly away, leaving Chris alone against the shore. He found himself grateful for the solitude.

He kept thinking he should go to Matty. But unless it was his imagination, every time he'd approached her she'd seemed to drift away.

He walked over now anyway, put a tentative arm about her, steadying her against wind and involuntary shivers.

Matty didn't attempt to pull away. She said something and Chris had to lean close, ask her to repeat it. She did, not much louder, so he had to cock his head to get it. "He won."

Springer, she meant.

"He's at the bottom of the river, Matty. No life jacket."

She shook her head. "It doesn't matter. Life had no special appeal for Frank. Getting even, that was his thing. Winning. And he did. He took the one thing away from me that could truly kill me. He won."

Chris pulled her closer. "Don't think about Springer now."

She nearly allowed herself a cleansing sigh. Suddenly she turned to him so swiftly it sent a lance of fear through him, her eyes wide with sudden revelation. "Chris!"

She pushed out of his arms abruptly, ran sprinting along the shoreline toward one of the landing helicopters.

Chris, dumbfounded, thought, She's going to throw herself into the whirling blades!

He charged after her, shouting. Police and rescue workers turned in alarm, calling to them. Matty ran heedlessly, not altering her gait until she'd reached the chopper, grabbed hold of the pilot, began shouting into his startled face.

They were moving methodically, heads down through high, lazily waving weeds: Matty, Chris, and three men from the rescue unit, one of them the chopper pilot.

They were sweeping the area with flashlights and tungsten lamps.

"He threw it right over here somewhere!" Matty kept repeating anxiously.

Chris nodded in concurrence to the slicker in charge: "I heard Goldstein say he saw Springer throw something into the weeds. He couldn't see what in the dark."

An eerie, slow-motion dance ensued in the wind-swept meadow. Heads bent, bodies swaggering zombielike, the group slowly scoured the area beside the narrow restaurant walkway, no one speaking, normal-level talk impossible in the nearby cacophony of falls and rapids.

One of the rescue members straightened finally, turning to shout to the others, "Hey! Over here!"

Matty ran.

"This it, Mrs. Nielson?"

Chris, bringing up the rear, saw her accept the small plastic box the size of a soap dish.

She turned it over in trembling hands, searching. Finally thumbed a button, immediately producing an amber light, a small circular screen ringed with concentric circles. The object began emitting a piercing beep, easily heard even above the water's roar.

"That's me!" she told them eagerly, pushed that button off, and thumbed a second one. The screen relit, less intensely—dull green—the concentric circles pulsing feebly, the beeping nearly inaudible.

Matty held the device before her, swept it back and forth slowly, concentrating. The sound, the green light growing and fading with each swath.

"It's a homing device," someone said. "Christ, look at that."

Matty, arms outstretched, moved forward, head bowed, face lit from the thing in her hand. She made sharp, erratic movements—seemed to stray off course—then quicker strides as the pulsing sound grew louder.

Now she was trotting . . . now running, sprinting over clumps of brush and rock toward the mist-shrouded rapids, arm out straight as though pulled by an invisible leash, leaping like a young gazelle.

"Hey, lady!"

"Matty!"

Ignoring them, she ran on heedlessly, screaming, the device

before her, flashing bright, strobing her dripping face green. "He's *here*! He's here at the top somewhere! He didn't go over! He's somewhere right up here!"

Her darting form was flooded abruptly by the sharp glare of searchlights lancing from the big chopper's belly. The area around her became awash in harsh white light, Matty, a lithe, spotlit dancer in an angular Tharp ballet, mist sparkling like tiny diamonds around her, a pool of clear daylight highlighting her rushing form, pacing this wildly scrambling woman, searching with her, here . . . now over here . . .

And finally there. Nearly hidden by dead, brittle cattails, a swath of orange-colored canvas appeared in the lancing beam, pinned against a swirling dam of debris-trapped shoreline near the glistening, pearly lip of the great falls.

Matty shrieked. Chris came running up behind her, legs pumping, face a beet red mask of hope.

In a moment he was laughing—whooping—as another sound, just audible over the chopper's beat and the falls' thunderous cascade, drifted out of the night.

The plaintive song of a child's crying.

CHAPTER 30

Matty was having trouble with the motel's hot-water knob.

Unlike her old motel down the way, Chris's crisp Holiday Inn boasted all-new accoutrements: shiny shower head and stainless sinks, a single center knob for both cold and hot water. She was attempting a simple bath, and the fancy new knob would yield nothing but scalding hot water.

Matty grunted in frustration, grabbed a fluffy motel towel from a shiny rack, and walked into the single room to elicit help from Chris.

She found him hovering over the twin bed containing the sleeping baby, the bed nearest the heat vent, warmth blasting into the room from the overcranked thermostat, making Chris sweat lightly. He was gazing down at the little body curled peacefully beneath the covers tucked snugly around him. Chris glanced up as she came into the room. "Maybe we should have kept him at the hospital," he uttered for the fifth or sixth time within the hour.

"He's fine, Chris. The doctor said he was fine, very mild hypothermia. Just keep him warm and plenty of fluids in him."

Chris turned back to the blissfully sleeping child. As if it mattered, he thought, what the doctor or anyone else said. As if Matty would ever let the child out of her sight again.

He turned once more, shirt front clinging with sweat, found her staring at him. "What?"

Matty blinked, looked away. "Nothing."

Something had passed between them—or almost—Chris wishing he could get it back, uncertain how to try.

"Well," he announced after a moment, "I'm going down the hall for some ice. Can I get you anything from the Coke machine?"

"Thank you, no." Aware of his eyes on her cleavage, she put a hand there self-consciously, turning back toward the sanctity of the small bathroom. "Don't forget your key this time."

Matty heard him cross the narrow hall, shut the heavy security door behind him, realized she'd forgotten all about asking his help with the hot-water knob.

She bent to the tub again, twisting this way and that, getting nothing but hot water, the tub filling rapidly with it. Exasperated, she had reached up to switch it off when the light rapping came from the hallway.

Matty left the tub again, tucked the towel snugly into her bosom, went to get the door.

She hesitated a moment over the silvery knob, the words "who is it?" forming. Then discarded. She twisted, pulled back the heavy door, found a smiling, bespectacled Goldstein standing there. His right arm was swathed in a sling. "Greetings!"

She held the door for him, smiling warmly, gripping his good arm affectionately. "Abe!"

"Just stopped by to say my good-byes; can't stay. Is Chris around?"

"Just went down the hall for ice. Oh, Abe. How can we ever thank you? What could we ever do?"

The attorney smiled slyly. "All my life I've wanted to be hugged by a beautiful woman in a skimpy bath towel. . . ."

Matty, laughing, pulled him close, hugged hard, pulled away grinning, mouthing "thank you." Then on impulse, she pulled him close again, kissed him hard on the mouth. Eliciting, to her delight, deep color in the wan little cheeks.

"I can die a contented man now. Good-bye, Mrs. Nielson. God be with you."

"We'll see each other again, Abe, I know we will."

The attorney shrugged, smiled. "If the fates are kind. But under more pleasant circumstances, I should hope." And he left her there.

Matty came back down the hall to the bathroom, started in. She spied the gleaming length of the Ruger atop the motel bureau, hesitated.

She looked at Nicky's sleeping form a moment, then moved to the bureau, picked up the gun, studied its shiny barrel speculatively. Then she opened the top drawer quickly and placed the gun inside, shutting it snugly again. She turned once more to the tub, was just leaning to deal with the pesky hot-water knob again when a second rap came.

She pushed up with a grunt, tucking the towel, hurrying back to the door. And this time—not sure why—she found herself saying it: "Who is it?"

"Forgot my key!" Chris said.

Matty sighed, pulled back the door, turning to get back to the tub, already in the bathroom and barely catching his "Thank goodness for Kevlar."

She bent to the tub. Hesitated. Craned back, frowning. "What did you say?"

She grunted in surprise as Springer took her slim neck in both hands, slammed her hard against the bathroom door. Once, twice.

Matty, breath abruptly gone, sank dizzily, managed a croak for help. Springer picked her up, strangling her, lifted her as though she weighed nothing, carried her—a thrashing marionette—into the bedroom. Smiling, hardly grunting, he lifted her high, ignoring her kicks, her thrashing arms, enjoying the sight of her red face growing redder, then purple, eyes bulging. He enunciated very clearly so, over the rush of blood thundering in her eardrums, she wouldn't miss it, "Thank God for Kevlar!"

He tossed her high enough to scrape the ceiling.

She came crashing to the bed—not, thankfully, the one holding the baby—bounced awkwardly. Arms pinwheeling, she twisted in the air and caught him, upside down, grinning insanely, tearing his damp shirt away to reveal the heavy Kevlar vest, the center of it still dimpled from Chris's high-velocity slug.

Matty flopped painfully against the headboard, not feeling it, feeling only the sweet, searing rush of air down her throat, both hands clamped there as if to help force it in. Eyes bleary, she looked up in time to see Springer, shirt flaps open, pulling the big hunting knife from his belt, heading toward the baby.

Matty, with the shriek of the deranged, headed him off on legs of rubber, throwing herself in front of him, unthinkingly grabbing the steel blade. The edge bit greedily into tender fingers, sent a rinse of red across Springer's chin, the thick bulletproof vest.

She felt him wrest her away easily, shove her into a corner like so much dirty laundry.

He raised the knife over the child.

Matty was somehow up again, between him and the child, scrabbling for the blade, trying to get him to twist it, shove it into her, so deep he'd have a hard time getting it out, so the awful blade would never go near her child again.

Springer grinned, seeing what she was up to, obliged her by shoving the point under her chin, holding it there rigidly, drawing a pearl of blood. He started to say something—and was suddenly slammed forward with surprise into her face, the knife spinning away.

Matty fell backward, off balance, hearing but not comprehending the shattering sound of wood behind them. Her arms rose automatically to protect the baby. Her eyes jerked up to find Chris there with the broken remains of a chair in his hands.

Springer, flinging blood from the back of his head, was just twisting around, snatching up the fallen blade again, grinning at Chris.

Chris, eyes on the knife, stepped back, back. He craned right, swept a hand across the bureau top quickly, face confused.

Matty groaned, shouting, "In the top drawer!" Too late, Springer was already there, the knife descending, so all she could see was Springer's wide back and the knife coming down into Chris.

She cringed from Chris's wail of pain, her own scream joining his. The two men spilled apart, blood blossoming from Chris's shoulder, Springer laughing in triumph. Chris, face white, miraculously danced free of the next stroke, which whistled past his ear to stick soundly into the motel bureau and stay there.

It took Springer a second to dislodge it, and that was all Chris needed to spin, kick the big blond-headed man in the groin. Springer reeled backward with a grunt of pain.

Chris reached the drawer, came up with the Ruger. Springer just stood there grinning, grinning, even after the first slug smacked his chest, sent him powering back again, arms outstretched to grip the sides of the bathroom door. Chris watched in dismay as the slug dropped to the carpet, squashed and ineffectual.

He leveled the gun, fired again. Hit Springer dead center,

wrenched him—from such close range—violently back, through the door, arms flailing. The big man backpedaled across white bathroom tile, knees striking the lip of the tub, where he found his balance, grinned tauntingly.

Springer smiled. Charged.

Chris fired. The slug struck the Kevlar vest, slamming Springer back, over the tub this time, against the tile wall with a crack. Then Springer, grinning still, slid down the wall.

He hit the scalding water, where—still not shot—he began screaming like a gutted horse.

He screamed so loudly, the echo of it drove like a knife through Chris's head. Screamed and now thrashed, hands like claws on the slippery edge of the tub, roiling clouds of steam turning him into a ghostly marionette.

And, screaming still, Frank Springer shone bright pink from the frothing water. Pink, then lobster red, the burning claws finding purchase at last on the tub's lip, dragging him up with poached-egg eyes.

Until Chris stepped in smoothly, shot him again in the forehead, sending him back down into the vapor, under, thrashing, boiling alive.

Then, after a bit—lazily restful—boiling dead.

EPILOGUE

In the crowded little Florida clinic—not where he really wanted to be, a last-minute decision—Chris sat holding Nicky in his lap, trying to read *The Little Taxi That Hurried* amid crying babies, tripping toddlers, wearily complacent mothers.

Nicky, more distracted by this than Chris, kept craning over the top of the Little Golden Book at a pretty three-year-old across the room with Shirley Temple curls and bright red ribbon. She peered back coyly, her mother, probably Matty's age, reading a magazine, a look of contented resignation about her.

Every woman, Chris thought, when holding a child, shares that look. A unique bond men can appreciate from afar but never truly attain. The thought made him vaguely envious.

Matty had refused to come, hardly a surprise. In white shorts and halter, tanned and leggy, she'd stayed in the warm garden, fussing and smudging herself with a fresh load of gladioli from Home Depot. A bigger Home Depot than the one they'd used in California. The new house was bigger too. Bigger, newer but not yet a home. Perhaps never a home.

At first merely a place of refuge, the house was now truly theirs. Abe Goldstein had called one glorious morning to inform them that they were not to worry, that he had—for a very reasonable sum—sought out and dealt with the proper authorities. The Nielsons' new marriage certificate was even now in the mail, they would hear nothing further from any covert branch of the government, and he expected a settlement—also forthcoming—to be well into six figures. Chris could write an infinite number of plays on what the attorney was going to demand for them. Goldstein—as backup—had this cousin at the *New York Times*, you see, and the smiling attorney didn't see how any government here or there could threaten the entire staff of a major newspaper.

The marriage certificate had come, had been placed on the new white mantel above the fireplace, had remained there unopened, uninspected, gathering dust for two weeks. Like much about the relationship now, Chris ruminated, turning colorfully illustrated pages, gathering dust.

Nicky squirmed on his lap, perhaps seeking the fetching blonde across the way, perhaps just weary of the taxi story, the containing lap, anxious to explore the waiting room as he was anxious to explore everything these days. Chris could see an older, still curly head, bent earnestly over the designs of a new interstellar rocket mechanism, or scrubbing up before major brain surgery. He was aware that every father shared these dreams, sat selfishly enjoying the sensation too much to argue the odds.

A kind-looking woman in a crisp white nurse's uniform appeared suddenly over the brim of the book, smiling and tweaking Nicky's cheek. She informed Chris softly that the doctor was ready now, if they'd please come this way.

Chris, abruptly, not at all ready, sat holding his child tightly, staring up at the kind face with open-mouthed reticence. He had been wondering if he should tell Nicky about the needle, that it would hurt a little but not much, and afterward they'd go to McDonald's and play on the slides, after that home, and he could show Mommy his Band-Aid, tell her how brave he'd been.

He hadn't had a chance to tell his son that, though. And now it was too late, the kindly smiling nurse was here.

Chris, more terrified than a child, couldn't seem to get out of his chair.

Matty pushed up from the garden, bare knees stained green and mottled with fresh-smelling soil, bruised grass.

She dusted her hands, turned in afternoon glare to see her family coming toward her across the wide green yard, Chris's face,

Nicky's smaller one shadowed against cloudless, unyielding Florida sun. Their features thus darkened, they could have been any man and child but for their identifying gaits.

She stood there in winter weather warmer than California's, shading her eyes and watching the man the little envelope on the mantel proclaimed was her husband come toward her. Watched as he picked up the little boy in his arms. Wondering who he was. Wondering if some woman someday would ever feel that way about Nicky.

Skirting the inevitable, a trick she'd become adept at, Matty smiled a cursory smile and headed for the house with her clippers. "Would you like lunch?"

Chris stopped to let her by, watched a moment, then followed behind, followed the round, revolving bottom—enhanced by the frayed shorts—onto the patio, up the stoop. "Sure. Thanks."

Setting Nicky in his high chair, turning to see the white shorts now bent to the refrigerator, Chris let the moment have its way. Let her come to him for this one, maybe to see if she'd come at all, knowing, he guessed, she would, if not now then tomorrow.

And Matty, being Matty, made it now. "Well?" she asked coolly, as if it were merely polite conversation not a wedge that might determine their future. She arranged mayonnaise and lunchmeat, not meeting his eyes, another deftly learned trick.

Chris, with tricks of his own, didn't answer until she finally did look, not wanting to tell her this without benefit of response.

She waited, pouring milk.

He sat at the old kitchen table in the new house in old sunlight and told her that he didn't know, he hadn't gone through with it.

She looked away, swathed another piece of bread impassively as if it still wasn't particularly important, tilted her head. "Oh?"

Chris nodded. "I ran into this little problem at the clinic. Couldn't seem to get out of my chair."

She watched him, face softening.

"You were right, Matty. He's my son. No matter what. He's my son. Our son. Nothing can ever change that."

Relief, gratitude, brimmed unbidden in her soft eyes. She sat down, milk carton forgotten.

"Matty, I love you so. I've been thinking, how can I make it like it was before? How can I get us back there? But you know something, nothing is ever as it was before. Life doesn't do that. It just moves ahead. Maybe good, maybe bad. But forward, always forward. And it doesn't matter, Matty, it doesn't matter what happens if you're there to move forward with it."

She closed her eyes, swallowing, a single tear just forming, hesitant as if cognizant of her inner thoughts, indecisive because of them.

"I want to stay," he told her. "I want to stay with you and my son. If you'll have me. But no more secrets, Matty. That's the one stipulation. No more secrets."

She sat, stared at the table. In a moment she picked up and began absently pouring a cup of milk.

Later, Nicky asleep and safe in his own room, Matty came to Chris's door, leaned on her hip there in the frame. It was a way she had, an old signal.

When he looked up, Chris thought he'd never seen anything so lovely as this woman.

She turned when he smiled, and made her way to the bedroom.

Chris, rising to follow, paused to toss the slip of green clinic paper into his wastebasket, the paper with the names, the matching blood samples of Nicky's and Springer's.

He flipped it at the basket without looking back, went to join his wife on the cool sheets, holding the final secret within him.

The typeface used in this book is a version of Plantin, designed in 1913 by Frank Hinman Pierpoint (1860–1937). Although he was an American, Pierpoint spent most of his life working in England for the Monotype company, which he helped found. The font was named after Christophe Plantin (1514?–1589), a French bookbinder who turned to printing and by midcentury had established himself in Antwerp as the founder of a publishing dynasty—like Pierpoint, one who "made good" away from home. Plantin was not, however, a designer of type, nor was the modern font strictly speaking a revival (Pierpoint was unenthusiastic about Stanley Morison's revivals at Monotype in the 1920s). Plantin was based on what is now known to be Robert Granjon's Gros Cicero font, created for but never used by Plantin, which Pierpoint found in the Plantin-Moretus Museum. Later, its full-bodied but compact quality attracted Morison to Plantin as the model for Times Roman.